Toni

Hello to another
Madness Fan!
With very best wishes.
Evan Baldock

BANG BANG, YOU'RE DEAD

EVAN BALDOCK

Best wishes
Evan Baldock

RED DOG
UK

Published by RED DOG PRESS 2020

Paperback ISBN 978-1-913331-32-0

Ebook ISBN 978-1-913331-33-7

Hardback ISBN 978-1-913331-34-4

www.reddogpress.co.uk

This book is dedicated to the memory of Edwina McPherson. An extraordinary lady who I only had the privilege to know for 18 months between September 2000 and April 2002. We were thrown together as part of 'Project Lilac,' a multi-agency committee dealing with drug dealers in the West End of London. Edwina (Eddi) represented the Covent Garden Residents Association, and I was a Police Sergeant.

Meetings often took place in the vestry of St Giles-in-the-Fields Church, or an attractive little park called Phoenix Gardens. Afterwards, Eddi would invite people back to her nearby flat, which overlooked both locations, for coffee and to chew the cud. Occasionally, it was only me who went, and we would invariably discuss crime in the local area. We became quite good friends and she would express her views about local criminals quite frankly to me.

At the time I was writing a small comedy travelogue for myself and my friends, which Eddi was proof-reading.

She often used robust language about the perpetrators of crime in the streets around her flat, and one day expressed a wish for someone to write a book about a lady like her taking revenge. She looked at me and said, "I think you could write a novel like that."

So began my novel writing career. Sadly, when the project ended, Eddi and I slowly lost contact, and I shelved the book only half-finished.

In January 2019, I saw Eddi's obituary on the internet—she died the previous year in her early 80s. I felt terribly upset. In that moment, I decided to finish the novel in Eddi's memory.

I hope she's resting in peace and can forgive me for my tardiness in finishing the book that she inspired.

ONE
Thursday 12th November 1998

GLORIA JONES PEERED through the November drizzle at the couple loitering in the shadow of a doorway across the road, and recognition dawned. She knew them. Drug users, and violent ones at that. She immediately became uneasy—only too aware that, at nine o'clock on a dark night, she would be an easy target for them.

The couple were both white, in their early twenties and as thin as stray cats. The doorway was littered with crack cans, used syringes, discarded cling-film wraps that had once contained crack cocaine or heroin; there was the smell of human excrement and small pools of urine. Luckily, they were busy, and oblivious to Gloria's presence.

"Fucking hold on will you, I'll get a decent vein in a minute," the man shouted, his strong Scouse accent grating on Gloria.

His jeans and underpants were around his knees, while his girlfriend was yanking a tourniquet tight around his left thigh. In her left hand she was holding a syringe filled with light brown liquid.

"Here y'go," she said, handing him the syringe. And, as she did, Gloria noticed a large weeping ulcer on the back of the woman's wrist, which looked horribly infected. The man plunged the syringe into his groin, causing a thin spurt of blood to splash up the side wall. When he'd finished, he removed the syringe and handed it to his girlfriend, who injected the remainder of the contents into her left arm.

Gloria felt angry, physically sick and frightened. She'd witnessed similar things before, but none at such close quarters, and none so close to home. Unable to control herself, she exploded with fury.

"You disgusting animals! We have to live around here with your bloody mess!"

The girl span round to confront Gloria, her face contorted with anger, the veins standing out on her forehead. Her lank, greasy hair was dirty blonde, shoulder length, and parted in the middle. She held the syringe in her right hand like a dagger. A drip of blood from the end of the needle fell to the ground, and mixed with the rest of the mess.

"Piss off, you nosy old bitch! One more word and I'll stick this in your fucking face!"

She stepped out of the doorway, towards Gloria.

Terrified, Gloria backed quickly away and ran the twenty metres to the front door of Robinson Court, the block of flats where she lived on New Compton Street. Her trembling hands fumbled to get the key into the lock of the communal door. Once safely inside, she pressed the call button for the lift, which took her up to her third-floor flat where she slammed the door, and felt relief flood over her; she was safe.

Making her way into the lounge, she turned on the electric fire and collapsed onto her favourite comfy green armchair. Gloria loved her small, comfortable flat in the heart of the West End where she had lived since her daughter had married and moved out; it was her refuge as well as her home. She looked around her, at the faces of her family smiling at her from the photographs on her mantelpiece, and instantly felt comforted.

This wasn't Gloria's first brush with local low-life. Two weeks previously she had been attacked at a cashpoint in nearby Charing Cross Road, when a man had grabbed her by the throat until she handed over the fifty pounds she'd just drawn out. She'd only just regained her confidence after that attack and felt grateful that she had managed to get away from trouble this time. Her heart thumping hard in her chest, she began to weep.

It's not fair! she thought over and over. *People shouldn't have to live like this! I hate them! I really fucking hate them!*

One hour, two cigarettes and three cups of tea later, Gloria was still furious, but had calmed down enough to phone her daughter Sandra, who lived with her family on a smart, new estate in Newcastle. She liked to keep in touch with her daughter; she had lost her son, a heroin addict, ten years previously, and her alcoholic husband shortly afterwards to liver failure.

"I've had enough Sandra! I'm fed up with the drug dealers and robbers round here." Her voice shook. "I don't feel safe walking the streets anymore. One of them threatened me with a syringe on my way home tonight."

"Bloody hell, mum! Are you OK?"

"I was absolutely terrified! I hate them."

"Calm down, Mum. At least you're not hurt."

"I just wish the police would do something. It's getting worse and worse around here. Most people living on the streets are fine, but a few can be a nightmare. They don't give a shit about anyone except themselves, and they're getting more and more aggressive."

She went quiet for a few seconds, before adding quietly, "I wish they were all dead," her voice shaking with emotion.

"Come on, Mum. They're still human beings, you don't mean that."

"Oh yes, I do! They're not human beings, they're the scum of the earth! If they were to all die tomorrow, no one would shed a tear round here."

"That's a terrible thing to say!"

Gloria knew her daughter was right. She drew a deep breath.

"I know, and there was a time I'd have hated myself for saying it. It's funny, I never used to feel like this, but right now I mean every word."

After ten minutes of getting her feelings off her chest and offloading them onto poor Sandra, Gloria felt much better. She said goodbye and hung up. It was late, and after her traumatic experience, she was looking forward to bed. Lighting up a cigarette, she stood next to the open lounge window. Gloria always did this when she smoked, no matter what the weather was like, no matter how cold it was. She hated the smell of cigarette smoke in the flat, and made a silent promise to herself to give up before her 65th birthday, in a few weeks' time.

Leaning with one hand on the windowsill, she felt a small pool of condensation cooling her fingers, reminding her that the windows really needed replacing. Gloria's flat looked out over St Giles Churchyard. To her right, she could see through to St Giles High Street, and to her left

Phoenix Gardens, a small, pretty park. Gloria loved the view from her window. She knew how lucky she was to have trees and flowers to look out on, living in London's West End. In recent months, though, it was all too often ruined by the sight of drug users gathering in groups, waiting for a dealer to arrive.

The regular huddle of users, rough sleepers and beggars were in their usual spot, about eighty metres away from the window where Gloria stood. Leaning forward to stub out her cigarette in an ashtray, a small flash of light caught Gloria's eye to her right in the middle of the gathering, followed immediately by a loud crack that made her start. This had happened several times in the past couple of weeks with people setting off fireworks, especially bangers. *Christ, bonfire night was a week ago, and they're still mucking about.*

But when she heard a girl scream, and a man shouting, Gloria peered more intently through the rain streaked glass. She could see people gathered around someone lying on the pavement. This wasn't in itself unusual, because there were frequently heated arguments within the group, and scuffles often ended in violence. She'd seen it all many times before.

A shout went up: "Feds! Run!" A stocky black man wearing a dark baseball cap broke from the group and darted across the road toward an alleyway along the side of St Giles Church. As he entered it, the man temporarily disappeared from Gloria's view behind buildings. Within seconds, two uniformed police officers ran across the street pursuing him. Looking across towards Phoenix Gardens, Gloria watched with bated breath, her eyes fixed on the other end of the alleyway. She knew there were two right angle turns in the alley, the first to the right, the second to the left, meaning he would have been briefly out of the officers' view as he made those turns. Sure enough, the man hurtled out of the alleyway into Stacey Street, and Gloria thought she saw him lob something over a fence into an area of Phoenix Gardens that was closed off for repairs.

The police officers ran from the alleyway after him, and within seconds the chase had disappeared from her view, down towards Shaftesbury Avenue.

Gloria moved her nose slightly away from the window, as her breath was beginning to mist up the glass. Her mind was racing. Had she seen the man throw anything? If so, what could it have been? Drugs? A knife? Stolen property? She had no idea. It might have been nothing important at all. He could have just been throwing away something so that he could escape from the police faster: a bottle, a can of drink, anything. Thinking about it for a few minutes, she decided not to report what she'd seen to police that evening. She didn't want to appear stupid or waste their time if the item turned out to be something perfectly innocent.

Continuing to scan the area for a few more minutes in case anything else happened, Gloria was interested to see that the police attention in St Giles High Street had caused the gathering to miraculously disappear. A wave of tiredness washed over her, and she closed the curtains before heading off to bed.

TWO
Friday 13th November 1998

THE DAMP WEATHER of the previous evening had passed over, and been replaced by a cold, but wonderfully sunny morning. It was so bright that her deep red bedroom curtains seemed to have turned a light crimson colour, bathing her room in a warm glow.

Gloria awoke bright and early at seven, after a fitful sleep; she couldn't shake the images of the previous night's events from her mind, particularly seeing the man throwing something into the park. She'd decided to enter Phoenix Gardens as soon as it opened at nine, go to the spot where the object landed and recover it, whatever it was. Then, if it was anything important, she would contact the police.

Seated at the small breakfast table in her kitchen, Gloria sipped her early morning cup of tea and her mind started to wander. She remembered what a pleasant area it used to be, when everyone seemed to know everyone else. Sadly though, over the past few years, the drug culture had invaded the local streets. One of its first victims had been her son Darren, who died of septicaemia after sharing a needle. Her husband Graham, who'd struggled for many years with alcoholism and depression, drank even more heavily after his son's death, and became seriously ill. He was diagnosed as having cirrhosis of the liver only nine months after his son died. Within three weeks he too had died, leaving Gloria and her daughter, Sandra, to cope with their grief as best they could.

Gloria managed by throwing herself into her work at the local Department of Social Security office. She worked four days a week, with a long weekend every Friday to Sunday, but often volunteered to work extra hours and covered for colleagues who needed time off.

During her spare-time she worked once a week in local soup kitchens and drug treatment centres, trying in some small way to help others suffering from the same addictions that had claimed her son and husband. She was happy doing her bit helping out those who were less fortunate, and was a popular figure in the area with street beggars, drug users and the homeless. But she'd always detested the dealers, and those who resorted to crime or violence to fund their habits.

The sharp ring of her house phone brought Gloria back to the present, and she lifted the receiver. It was Police Sergeant Sean Aylen, from nearby Holborn Police Station—a good friend since they first met at one of the police and community meetings.

"Hi Glo. Sorry, but I won't be popping over for coffee this afternoon, something's come up at work. I'll call you next week."

"No problem, Sean. It's a shame though, because there's something I wanted to talk to you about."

"Ah, sorry Glo. Can't talk now. The boss wants to see me right away."

"Okay, love. It'll have to wait. See you next week."

Gloria was disappointed. She liked Sean's company on the occasions that he managed to visit, normally about once every ten days or so. She also liked using his influence at the police station, keeping up policing pressure on the drug dealing and crime in the streets near her home. He was an experienced officer in the drugs field, and she valued his advice. He might even have been able to tell her what the previous night's incident had all been about.

Shortly after hearing the St Giles Church Bell chime nine times, Gloria stood up and checked herself in the hall mirror. A habit instilled by her mother, and something she always did before going outside. She was pleased with what she saw: a woman of average height, trim figure, smartly dressed, an attractive face for her age, with short bobbed hair, nearer white than grey. She still retained an athletic build, thanks to forty years of badminton, which she'd once played at a high level. She only played occasionally now, but was still fit and strong for her age.

Pulling on her warm navy-blue overcoat, she stepped outside and walked the few dozen yards to the gates of Phoenix Gardens. The area was empty, apart from the full-time gardener, Terry, who waved to her from the large shed. Sixty seconds later, Gloria had reached the far end of the gardens, by the fenced off area. She glanced over her shoulder to check that Terry couldn't see her, and no members of the public were visible through the slatted metal fence in the adjoining alleyway. Gloria took her chance and clambered over the low fence into the sectioned off area.

Moving quickly to the place where she'd witnessed the man throw the object over the fence, she was dismayed to find thick stinging nettles blocking her way forward. Gloria started beating down the nettles with a stick, trying to locate whatever the object was. After three or four frustrating minutes she was about to give up, when one of her scything motions revealed something. Clearing the fallen foliage away, Gloria saw a black object on the ground: lying there, right in front of her, amid the shattered stalks of broken off nettles, was a black hand-gun.

She stared at it for a short while in stunned silence, thinking how much it reminded her of the gun James Bond carried in the film she'd seen at the cinema last week.

Shit! No wonder they were chasing him last night! He was carrying a fucking gun!

Should she call for help? Should she leave it where it was and phone the police? She didn't know what to do.

Regretting not bringing her mobile phone out with her, Gloria decided she couldn't just leave it lying there while she walked back home to telephone the police. After all, anyone might see it and climb in to pick it up, even a child, especially now that she'd flattened the nettles.

Aware that the square was overlooked from the surrounding apartment blocks, she knew even touching the gun would be a risk. She peered up at the windows, trying to see if she was being watched. Was that a twitching curtain, or was her imagination playing tricks on her. She knew a few people who lived in that block, too. What if someone recognised her?

After a moment, Gloria decided that she was probably just being paranoid, and finally took the plunge—after all, she was only doing her public duty, wasn't she? Taking the gun off the streets. She'd hand it in and explain it all to the police. Picking up the gun, she quickly placed it inside the empty, front zip-up section of her handbag.

Climbing back over the fence seemed for some reason to be much easier than the climb in. Feeling rather pleased with herself, she rushed out of the park gates into New Compton Street. She couldn't wait to telephone the police and tell them what she'd found. Moments later she was back at the communal door into Robinson Court and reached into her handbag for her key.

"Got anything good in there, Grandma?"

Gloria only had a second to hear the words before her face was smashed into the door. She was dazed and in serious pain, the arm holding her handbag falling limp at her side. Feeling the handbag being tugged at violently, she found the strength from somewhere to resist, pulling it back towards herself. Her attacker roughly swung her round, and she was horrified to be staring into the faces of the couple she'd seen shooting-up in the doorway the previous night.

The woman grabbed her throat, pressed her hard against the door, and moved her face to within an inch of Gloria's.

"Drop that fucking bag, you old bitch, or so help me I'll cut you." The vile words were almost whispered.

Gloria retched at the unwashed smell, and the woman's chronic halitosis. The whites of the young woman's eyes were more like pale yellow, with deep bags underneath. Without warning, the man punched Gloria hard in the side, causing her to cry out and double up in agony. Her grip on the handbag weakened and she could feel herself falling through the air. It wasn't until she hit the doormat with a painful thud that she realised one of the residents from her block had opened the communal door, causing Gloria to fall inside the hallway.

"What's going on?" shouted the young Thai woman who'd opened the door. "I'm calling the police!"

Looking up, Gloria recognised her saviour as one of the new residents who lived on the ground floor.

"Fuck it! Run!" shouted the man. The woman, who had released her hold on Gloria's throat as she'd doubled over in pain, gave one last pull at the bag, but Gloria's grip held firm.

The couple ran off along New Compton Street, turned left and disappeared from view. The slim young woman with long black hair introduced herself as Mano. She helped Gloria back to her feet, helped her into the lift, and walked with her along the corridor to her flat.

"Are you sure you'll be OK?" asked Mano. "Can I make you a cup of tea or something?"

"No, thanks, I'll be fine. Thank you so much for turning up like that; I don't know what they would have done to me."

"I do," replied Mano.

"What do you mean?"

Mano sighed. "I was mugged two weeks ago by three men. They took my purse and threw me to the ground; one kicked me in the stomach, and another spat on me before they ran off. They threatened to kill me."

"The bastards! Why would they do that? You poor thing, are you all right now?"

"Never mind me! What about you?"

"Oh, don't worry about me," said Gloria. "I'll be just fine."

After making Gloria promise to get her injuries checked and inform the police, Mano finally, reluctantly, agreed to leave her. She gave Gloria her mobile number before heading off.

THREE

CLOSING THE DOOR, Gloria sat down softly on one of the kitchen chairs. There were no tears this time, just a rage screaming within her that made her hands shake.

"They will never do that to me again. They will never do that to me again," she muttered repeatedly, like some kind of mantra.

As she stood up, she felt searing pains in her head and the side of her ribcage and a quick look in the mirror revealed why: a large area of reddening and an ugly welt mark on the left-hand side of her forehead explained the pain in her head. Taking her coat and jacket off, she lifted her blouse, revealing more reddening on the side of her ribcage, where she'd been punched.

Gloria picked up her handbag and checked inside the front zip section; she ran her hand across the cold black metal of the gun. *I'd better tell the police about this, and about what just happened,* she thought.

Having attended many talks by officers at the police and community meetings, she knew that her situation wouldn't be considered an emergency, so she picked up the phone and dialled the number for Holborn Police Station. After ten rings, she was greeted by an answerphone message: "This is the Camden Police Control Room. If your call is an emergency, please dial 999. All our operators are busy at the moment; you are in a queuing system and will be answered as soon as the next operator becomes available."

Fifteen minutes later, Gloria was still hanging on the line, frustration building inside her, so she replaced the receiver. The blazing pain in her side where she had been punched had become so intense that for a few moments she was struggling for breath, her ribcage complaining bitterly whenever she breathed in deeply.

Controlling her rising panic, and using shallow breathing to stop her ribs hurting, helped to make the pain manageable, but she was still in a great deal of discomfort. A quick visit to the local hospital A&E department would be a sensible idea.

GLORIA ARRIVED BACK home from the hospital just after half-past three, still aching, but feeling slightly better having been reassured that nothing was broken. Making herself a cup of tea, she took two of the painkillers she'd been given by the doctor.

Unable to get the gun out of her head, she decided to take another look at it. She slowly drew the gun from her bag; it felt cold and strange in her hand. She noticed it had a make imprinted on one side, GLOCK, made up of a huge G followed by a smaller LOCK. This meant nothing to her at all, so she started to inspect the weapon a little more closely. She found the number 17 just after the name, followed by 9X19 in brackets, followed by AUSTRIA. This meant even less, so Gloria logged onto the internet to find out a little more.

Within minutes she found that the GLOCK 17 hand-gun was a semi-automatic pistol, which meant it would fire each time you pulled the trigger, without needing to be 're-cocked,' making it relatively easy to use; the 9X19 meant 19 bullets of 9mm calibre in each magazine.

Further research showed that the GLOCK 17 had a 'safety trigger,' which meant it could not be fired accidentally, either by dropping it, or by unintentional sideways motion on the trigger. The only way to release the safety mechanism was to pull the trigger back half-way. To fire the gun, you simply needed to continue pulling the trigger all the way back.

At five o'clock, a second attempt at contacting Holborn police again proved unsuccessful. Furiously, she slammed the phone down; if she couldn't get anyone to listen to her, she would take the gun to Holborn Police Station herself, and hand it in at the front counter.

Her rumbling stomach reminded Gloria that she'd not eaten all day, so she prepared herself a meal before walking to the police station. A frozen Chilli-con-Carne was placed in the oven, and washed down thirty minutes later with a glass of red wine, followed by another glass, then another.

By the time she set off, it was just after six-forty and darkness had fallen. Still fuming about the beating she'd taken from the couple attempting to rob her, she walked determinedly, the red wine coursing through her veins giving her Dutch courage. The sky was filled with stars, and she could feel the bitter cold of evening nipping at her cheeks; autumn was rapidly turning into winter. The pavements were busy with office workers scurrying home, and theatre goers heading out for the night; the roads were heaving with stop-start traffic.

Gloria walked out of her road into St Giles High Street, crossed the traffic lights and continued along towards Holborn. She passed a few familiar street beggars and people sleeping rough, always greeting them with a smile and occasionally giving money to those she knew. Then, deciding to get off the main roads for a while, she cut through a couple of the quieter side streets. It was as if she had stepped into a different world, miles from the West End crowds.

A building site to her left was covered in scaffolding; labourers were still hard at work, shovelling liquid cement which poured from a lorry into a large hole in the ground, where pipe-work had been laid. On top of the loud roaring coming from the lorry's engine, the labourers were shouting various things to one another as they worked. Steel workers were hammering rivets into girders, deafening bangs that echoed around the nearby buildings. Gloria wasn't surprised, she knew that work at this particular building site sometimes continued until 8 p.m. or later.

Once she had walked a little further round the corner from the lorry, noise subsided, but the metallic banging sounds still reverberated loudly from the steel workers.

Forty metres ahead of her were two parked builders' lorries, blocking the road; on Bloomsbury Way itself were three lanes of noisy and slow-moving one-way traffic, creeping in short bursts towards Holborn. Gloria appeared to be the only person in the quiet back street, and the only vehicles were a dozen parked cars. She quietly congratulated herself on her decision to get off the main roads when she had.

Stepping from the pavement, intending to cross the road before turning right into Bloomsbury Way, she heard a shout from a dark and deeply recessed doorway to her right, covered in scaffolding and sheeting, only six metres from where she was standing.

"I don't fucking believe it. It's that old bitch!"

Gloria instantly recognised the voice as the woman who'd attacked her earlier. Frozen to the spot and trembling with fear, Gloria looked towards the doorway and watched as the woman slowly walked towards her, her sunken eyes not leaving Gloria's for an instant. The woman pointed at her.

"I fucking warned you I'd cut you, you sad old cow!" After glaring at Gloria for three or four seconds, she shouted, "Now, give me that fucking bag!"

Strangely, Gloria could feel the terror subsiding, replaced instead with rising outrage. Even so, aware that the girl was much younger and stronger than herself, she let her right hand slip slowly down to her handbag, reluctantly intending to hand it over. As her hand rested on the outside of the bag, she could feel the shape of the gun through the leather. Something in Gloria's mind snapped.

In that moment she decided that she wasn't going to be terrorised any more. She was sick and tired of being a victim; she would let this bloody woman have a taste of her own medicine; she would show her what it felt like to be scared. Opening the zip on the front of her handbag, Gloria reached in with her right hand, and took hold of the gun's handle. Standing her ground, she said, "You'll get nothing from me."

The woman's eyes widened. "Wrong answer bitch, wrong answer."

She took two steps forward, and Gloria watched in horror as a sharply pointed knife was pulled from her right-hand coat pocket. She looked enraged and pointed the blade straight towards Gloria's face from only four metres away. Standing her ground, Gloria calmly lifted the gun out of her handbag and pointed it at the woman's chest.

"Stay back and leave me alone," her voice trembling with a mixture of terror and anger.

The woman looked initially shocked, then her face contorted with fury and she moved quickly towards Gloria. She'd only taken a couple of steps forward, when Gloria's finger pulled on the trigger and with a tremendous bang the gun fired.

Time froze. She hadn't meant to shoot, she didn't know what had made her pull the trigger, she just did. It was as if the gun had a will of its own. She watched in horror as the result of her shot played out in slow motion before her eyes.

Gloria thought the gun had been pointing at the woman's chest, but a small hole appeared just below her left eye, stopping her instantly in her tracks. Although the street lighting wasn't great, Gloria could see blood splatter across the sheeting behind the woman as the bullet found its mark. The woman fell in a crumpled mess on the ground, her eyes still open, the knife still tightly clenched in her right hand. A slow trickle of blood oozing from the back of her head was pooling on the stone tiles of the doorway.

Gloria's heart was beating hard. She knew the significance of what had just happened and that her life had changed forever. She wanted to run, but curiosity got the better of her. Taking a step forward, so she could see a little more into the dimly lit doorway, she started in fear as she noticed the dead woman's partner running out of an alley by the side of the house, in response to the sound of the gun.

He was wearing the same grubby grey tracksuit as before, and for the first time she noticed that his scruffy brown hair was receding badly.

Seeing his girlfriend lying on the ground, he turned his gaze to Gloria. His eyes burned into her, his hatred and disbelief obvious.

"What have you done? You've fucking killed her! You bitch!"

Gloria's mind was now racing. She hated this man with a passion, and she was already thinking about the punishment she was facing for killing the woman. He knew where she lived, and he now knew that she'd killed someone! Gloria slowly lifted the gun and aimed at the man's face. She registered the terror in his eyes as he stopped in his tracks and squealed, "No, no, please, don't!"

She pulled the trigger.

The bullet hit him just below his hairline, and his head was thrown backwards by the force of the impact. As it passed through his brain and exited through the back of his head, blood sprayed against the cream coloured wall behind him. He collapsed against it, lying with the back of his head pushed forward, resting against the wall. He groaned slightly, twitched a couple of times, then lay still. One eye was open and one closed, but he was obviously dead.

Exhilaration, terror, relief, all competed for pole position in Gloria's mind. Her first thought was to continue to Holborn Police Station, hand in the gun, tell them what she'd done, and give herself up. Then something inside her said, *Why? You've done a good deed there. They were total scum. Don't throw your life away over them. You'll manage in time. That was just payback.*

Stepping away from their bodies, Gloria checked all around. The buildings nearby were all offices, unoccupied and in darkness. None of the builders had appeared, and she was certain they wouldn't have heard anything anyway, because of the cacophony of noise from the cement lorry and the banging of the steelworkers. No-one seemed to be paying any attention from the Bloomsbury Way direction either, where the traffic noise was intense. Could it be that no-one had seen, or heard, anything? That could mean there were no witnesses!

Gloria shook, a cold sweat prickling her skin. Slipping the gun back into her handbag with a trembling hand, she hurriedly walked the forty metres to Bloomsbury Way, but instead of turning right towards Holborn Police Station, she turned left, towards home.

FOUR

ALL THE WAY home, Gloria's mind was in turmoil, trying to comprehend what had just happened; the sheer immensity of it was threatening to overload her senses. She hurried along the busy footpaths into New Oxford Street, where every person she passed appeared to be staring at her, all seemingly aware of her guilty secret. One minute she felt sick, the next she felt positively giddy; the entire walk home passed in a kind of dream.

The feeling of safety as she closed the front door behind her enveloped her like a blanket of wonderfully soft cotton wool, protecting her from the evils of the outside world and making her feel secure. Looking up at the clock, she was amazed to see that it was only seven. Gloria had been out of the house for a mere twenty minutes, yet in that time her world had been turned upside down.

Sitting on the arm of the settee, without removing her overcoat or shoes, she stared straight ahead at a blank section of wall; she felt utterly numb, then began to cry. It all seemed impossible. How could a public-spirited action like handing a weapon in to the police result in her committing double murder?

Gloria eventually managed to pull herself together. As she tried to make sense of the evening's events, she felt herself beginning to experience perverse feelings of pleasure in the knowledge that she had taken revenge on her tormentors. Trying to justify the murders to herself, Gloria thought, *Why should I hand myself in?* Her words to Sandra the previous day came back to her: "No-one will shed a tear over those bastards."

Images of her victims' bodies kept flashing through her mind, especially the lifeless expressions on their faces. However, Gloria wasn't experiencing feelings of remorse or shame. Most of the time she felt nothing at all, but every now and then a sense of satisfaction, gentle waves of something close to pride washed over her. Pictures of the killings played on a loop in her head: the bullets hitting their targets and the gruesome results; the bodies crumpling to the ground; their unseeing eyes directed accusingly at her. She walked slowly into the kitchen and placed the Glock on the kitchen table. It seemed so incongruous there, alongside the fruit bowl and the tea caddy.

The loud buzz of the intercom made Gloria jump. Who could that be? Had she been seen? Slowly, she picked up the intercom handset. "Who is it?"

"It's the police."

Gloria froze: how had they managed to trace her so quickly? Maybe someone who knew her had witnessed it. Yes, of course, that's the only way they could have known it was her. Opening the door, her heart hammering in her chest, she was confronted by two officers in plain-clothes, holding up warrant cards.

"Good evening, madam," began the older officer, a tall man with a huge stomach, and a 1970s style moustache. "I'm Detective Constable Baldwin, and this is Detective Constable Lancaster." Lancaster was a slim, baby-faced officer who looked about 25 years old. "We want to talk to you about a recent shooting in the area."

"You'd better come in," said Gloria quietly, opening the door wide, and standing aside to let the officers pass.

"No, after you madam," replied DC Lancaster, holding out one hand with the palm opened.

"I won't run away, you know" Her smile felt forced and unconvincing.

DC Lancaster laughed. "I can't take that chance, madam."

Her conflicting feelings—fear of getting caught, not knowing what to do next to cover her tracks, and the weird sensation of numbness—all started to dissipate as she walked to her favourite armchair and sat down. The game was up. Strangely, Gloria now felt much calmer and was resigned to her fate: she had done the crime, now she must do the time. She indicated for the officers to take a seat and said, "I don't suppose there's any point in offering you a cup of tea?"

"That would be lovely, thanks," came the unexpected reply from DC Baldwin. "No sugar for me thanks."

"Two for me, please," said DC Lancaster. "I've got a sweet tooth."

Getting up, Gloria walked to the kitchen and put the kettle on. She shouted through from the kitchen, "I suppose this must have come as a bit of a surprise to you—the shooting."

"You're telling me," replied Baldwin. "Despite what people think, we don't get much gun crime around here."

"I'm afraid that's what people are capable of when they're desperate."

"I know. Still, knowing who did the shooting right from the start helps."

"Yes, I'm very impressed. Tell me, how did you figure it out so quickly?"

"He was recognised by two uniformed officers on foot patrol. They'd only been fifty yards from the shooting and gave chase; both of them could identify him by name. He managed to get away, and there was no trace of the weapon, so we think it's probably still in his possession. He's a big dealer though, so he won't stay away for long; we'll find him sooner or later."

At first, Gloria couldn't make sense of what she was hearing. Clearly the policemen were talking about the incident the previous evening, and it dawned on her just how stupid she'd been. The loud crack she'd heard wasn't a firework, it must have been the sound of the gun being fired, and the person on the pavement had just been shot!

Trying to control her breathing, and thankful that she hadn't already said enough to incriminate herself, she turned back to the kettle, and suddenly realised that the gun was lying right in front of her, next to the fruit bowl on the kitchen table. She checked that the officers would not have been able to see it from where they had sat down, then carefully picked the gun up, wrapped it in some kitchen roll, and hid it in the first place she could think of: a half full box of Cornflakes.

Gloria was aware of the men's voices speaking quietly in the other room and struggled to stop her hands from shaking. For the first time since the shooting, she was experiencing strong feelings of guilt and realised she needed to pull herself together, right now.

Taking a deep breath, her mind still processing the near-miss she'd just had, she poured out two cups of tea, placed them on a tray, walked back into the lounge and said cheerily, "Anyway officers, how can I help you?"

DC Baldwin informed her that they were conducting house-to-house enquiries regarding the previous night's shooting. A drug dealer from outside the area had encroached on a local dealer's patch. This led to a punishment shooting in the left kneecap of the interloper. Unfortunately for the local dealer, a man well known to police by the name Delroy Derby —AKA 'DD'— the shooting had been witnessed by two uniformed officers patrolling nearby.

"Did you see or hear anything?" enquired Lancaster?

"Yes. As a matter of fact, I heard a loud bang; I thought it was fireworks. They've been setting off bangers for a couple of weeks now. I looked out of the window and saw a black man in a dark baseball cap running towards Flitcroft Street."

"The alleyway by the side of the church?"

"Yes."

"Go on."

"Well, when I saw two police officers running after him, I looked over to Stacy Street, at the end of the alleyway, and saw the same black man emerge and run towards Shaftesbury Avenue; then I saw the police officers chasing after him. In no time at all they were out of sight."

"Now think carefully," asked the older man. "Did you see anything else at all?"

Gloria didn't like the sound of this question. Could it be that she was falling into a trap after all? She made a show of appearing to think carefully, as if searching her memory, then said, "No, nothing at all. Only what I've already told you."

DC Lancaster made notes in his pocket book, then closed it. Gloria was painfully aware that the most vital piece of evidence the two men were seeking was only feet from where they were sitting, and felt a chill every time their eyes strayed to the kitchen door. DC Baldwin looked down at the carpet for what seemed like an age, before lifting his head and saying, "Okay, that's it then. Thank you very much for your assistance. Someone may need to contact you at a later date if a statement is needed, but I doubt it."

The detectives stood up and Gloria showed them to the door.

"I do hope you catch him. We're all sick to the teeth of the drugs situation around here."

"Don't worry, madam. We know who he is and I can assure you he'll be in custody soon enough."

"Thanks for your efforts anyway, officers."

"No trouble at all. Goodbye then."

With that, Gloria closed the door, walked slowly over to her armchair and sat gently down. She didn't know whether to laugh, cry, scream, or whoop with joy.

She reminded herself that she wasn't out of the woods yet; there could be DNA or fingerprints linking her to the gun, so she resolved to wipe it clean thoroughly, hopefully removing any traces. Drawing the gun from its hiding place and using one of her stock of dusters, she proceeded to go over every inch of it.

Once this was done, she wrapped it in kitchen roll, used a small plastic food bag over her hand to pick it up, then pulled the bag inside out, so the gun was now encased in plastic. This should ensure no traces of her would be on the Glock when she eventually got rid of it. Gloria carefully placed the gun back inside the half-full box of Cornflakes. She must be patient; she must wait for just the right time to dispose of it.

FIVE

DELROY DERBY WAS not usually a nervous man. He was used to being in charge of his own destiny, in control of any given situation. Happily married, he lived in a pleasant mid-terraced house in Manor Park, East London, with his wife Alison and their two young girls. Delroy was physically impressive: six-foot-three, with a muscular build that made him an imposing figure for any adversary.

He worked very hard as a night delivery driver for a magazine company, enabling him to provide his family with a good lifestyle. Delroy worked twelve-hour shifts, from six o'clock in the evening to six next morning, Tuesday to Saturday. At least, that was the story Delroy told his wife, his family and his friends.

In reality, nothing could be further from the truth. Delroy Derby, known on the streets as DD, was the main drug dealer of cocaine, crack cocaine and heroin in the St Giles area of London. His 'job' as a delivery driver was a complete fabrication, a deception he'd maintained for six years.

He had first become involved in drug dealing after agreeing to keep lookout while a friend of his handed over a package. His friend always seemed to have plenty of money, expensive clothes and nice cars; Delroy had thought *I want some of that* and asked to be given a chance. When that chance came, Delroy was amazed to discover how easy it was, and he soon worked his way up the ladder, earning respect from other dealers. Being strong and stocky came in handy when he needed to intimidate people who tried to cross him.

After five years of street dealing, problem-free, DD was threatened one night with a hand-gun by a Soho dealer for encroaching onto his side of Charing Cross Road. DD had already lost two friends to turf war shootings and realised he needed to arm himself to stay safe.

A regular customer—who happened to be a convicted armed robber—offered to supply him with a hand-gun for five hundred pounds. They agreed to meet in Bloomsbury Square underground car park late one evening, and after brief instructions on how to operate the weapon, the deal was done. His customer told him that the magazine in the gun still contained fourteen bullets; not a man to take chances, DD released the magazine and counted out the fourteen bullets, making sure they were all there, before reloading it; he then checked the safety trigger. He was good to go.

One year later, DD hadn't needed to use the gun in anger; he hadn't even needed to threaten anyone with it and was wondering if he'd wasted his money. Then came the cold, wet Thursday night in November that changed his life forever.

He'd been doing well that Thursday evening. Arriving in the area at seven, he began walking his regular 'loop,' stopping at all his usual dealing locations. He'd already managed to shell out fifteen wraps of white (cocaine), £9 each, thirty rocks of crack cocaine, £9 each, and twenty-three wraps of brown (heroin), £10 each, and at 11 o'clock made his way to his stash, hidden inside a lamp-post in Bedford Square, where he re-stocked.

Returning to his patch, DD noticed a couple of his regulars smoking crack in a phone box. This was a surprise, as he hadn't sold them anything that night. Then, nearing his best dealing plot, he saw several of his regular customers, huddled around a slim man wearing a black woolly hat and grey puffer jacket. As he got closer, he saw the man deal from his mouth to three of his customers in quick succession. Exploding in rage, DD shoved the new dealer away from his regulars, moved right up in his face and spat the words, "What the fuck do think you're doing?"

"You charge nine for a rock, I charge eight, they're my people now." The man's reply was icy calm.

"You're fucking crazy! I've worked this street for years, now fuck off before you get hurt!"

"Diss me again," said the new dealer, confident and menacing, "and you're a dead man." With lightning speed, he produced a knife from his jacket pocket. He held it at waist level and took a single pace towards DD, who instinctively stepped back.

This was new ground for Delroy. He was scared, he was livid, and he knew that his regulars were watching, clearly keen to see whether he had the bottle to enforce ownership of his patch. He was being forced into a situation where he had no choice but to take drastic action.

For the first time, DD drew the gun from his inside coat pocket. He raised it shoulder height and pointed the barrel at the chest of the invader. The new dealer smiled, looked into DD's eyes and said, "Think you're a big guy with your piece? You don't fool me. You're scared. I can see it in your eyes."

This was a direct challenge. DD lowered the gun until it was pointing at the new dealer's left knee and, without saying another word, pulled the trigger. The new dealer shrieked in pain and fell to the ground; one of the female drug users screamed. Warning shouts of, "Feds!" rang out.

Through the crowd, DD got a very brief glimpse of two uniformed police officers running towards him. He swivelled and sprinted across the street as if his life depended on it, into an alleyway. Turning a corner at the end of the alleyway, DD threw the gun over some railings into a park. He couldn't remember exactly where he'd run, but he remembered hearing one of the pursuing officers shout, "Stop, DD!" After about five minutes, he realised that he was in the Covent Garden Market area, and he'd shaken off his pursuers.

Delroy had always given a friend's address in Tottenham whenever stopped by police, so he was confident they had no idea where his real family home was. He made his way back home to Manor Park, and resolved to lay low until the dust settled. He lied to his wife that he was exhausted, and that he'd taken two weeks' holiday at short notice.

Knowing the police had recognised him, and that they would be pulling out all the stops to find him, he was nervous every time the telephone rang, or someone knocked at the door. Delroy Derby no longer felt in control—he was a wanted man.

SIX
Friday 13th November 1998

GLORIA'S FRIDAY EVENING passed watching TV, although she wasn't taking in any of the programmes. She found herself reliving the killings and their aftermath over and over in her head. Why had she done it? Why hadn't she simply handed the bag over? These were questions she would never be able to answer now, a switch had flipped and she would forever have to live with the consequences.

She flicked from channel to channel, trying to catch the latest news bulletins, curious to see how they would report the shootings. She felt surprisingly calm, considering that she was now a double murderer. She wasn't overly worried about being caught, nor confident that she'd got away with it, she just felt oddly numb.

However, with no reports of the killings by the time News at Ten had finished, Gloria began to nod off; the day's events had taken their toll, and she was mentally and physically exhausted. She decided to turn in and watch the storm breaking on the morning news.

IT WAS SEVEN-TWENTY in the morning., and Gloria had slept for nearly nine hours solid. No nightmares, no fear and no sinking feeling in the pit of her stomach, just solid untroubled sleep. On waking though, the butterflies in her stomach returned, but Gloria realised that they were not the result of regret about what she'd done, but fear of the penalty awaiting her if caught.

The morning news reports did not let her down: the shootings were the top story on all channels. Grizzly pictures of the scene were paraded on screen, including a dark red stain in the doorway where blood had drained from one of the bodies. Strangely, it was not at all as Gloria remembered it. Watching reporter after reporter saying that the double shooting of a 'young couple, in the Bloomsbury area of London, had left police baffled', she felt more than a little relieved.

The broadcast made more of the fact that it had been not only a shooting, but a double shooting, in a public space, and less about the search for the killer. Questions of a rise in gun crime were raised, and it was soon clear that the police had no leads on the killer.

Realising that she needed to appear as natural as possible to everyone around her, Gloria stuck rigidly to her Saturday morning routine. She did her cleaning and vacuuming, then walked to get her newspaper. She always bought the Express or Mail, depending on which one carried the best lead story. On this occasion there was no contest: while the Express led with, 'Queen and Charles rift', the Mail opted for the more dramatic 'Two gunned down in London.'

On her way home, Gloria saw a familiar figure approaching. Paula Shortland was a 50-year-old cleaner at Holborn Police Station and had been Gloria's friend for over ten years. At first, Gloria thought Paula was going to pass her by, but then she caught her friend's eye and Paula greeted her, immediately pulling in for a conspiratorial gossip.

"Terrible about those murders, isn't it?" But nothing in her voice said she thought it was terrible.

"Yes, I don't know what the world's coming to. I expect it's extra busy at the station?"

"Yes, of course they've set up an incident room, so there'll be more mess for me to tidy up!"

Gloria liked Paula's attitude to life. She may have only been a cleaner, but she always dressed smartly, even when cleaning, and treated her family well, in recent years taking them away on nice holidays, paid for presumably by an inheritance of some kind.

"Better to be busy than bored, Paula."

"Yes, I suppose you're right. Anyway, see you later. And stay out of trouble." With that, Paula smiled and walked off, waving an arm in farewell.

As soon as she arrived home, Gloria began to scan the paper eagerly but found precious little information, except that the murdered couple were both believed to have been living in a squat. They were Kelly-Anne Watkins, 24, and David Border, 25. Kelly-Anne had lived in the area for four years, and David for six.

Once again, the butterflies were making an unwelcome return. Would her luck eventually run out? The gut-wrenching cramps in her stomach and uncontrollable shaking were becoming difficult to ignore. Then, a lunchtime news report brought Gloria a pleasant surprise.

BBC News had a breaking story that police investigating the deaths were anxious to trace two men, one black and one white, who were seen running away from the scene of the killings in Barter Street towards Bloomsbury Way at 7.15 p.m. This was only ten minutes before the bodies were found in the doorway by a builder leaving the nearby site. Police believed that tracing these two men as soon as possible was vitally important to their investigation.

Gloria could not believe her luck; it appeared that no-one had witnessed her leaving the scene, or if they had, they hadn't made a connection between a grey-haired lady and the double murder. Who would? Not only that, but police were now barking up entirely the wrong tree, making statements to the press indicating that they believed the two men seen running away from the scene were somehow involved.

Gloria sat down and began going over the earth-shattering events of the previous thirty-six hours: the threats and the physical assault she had suffered; her discovery of the gun that, however unintentionally, enabled her to take brutal revenge; and the likelihood that she may have escaped detection.

The phone ringing broke her thoughts. It was her friend, Sean.

"Hi Glo. Look love, I'm really sorry but I've been drafted onto this murder squad, so it'll be a while before I can pop over. I'll give you a call when things quieten down."

"No problem, I thought you might have got caught up in all the shenanigans. It's awful isn't it?"

"It is. Between you and me though, it looks like the couple who were shot might have been responsible for a number of robberies in the area. Keep that under your hat though, that's not for general release."

"Really, robberies? Well, who'd have thought it?"

"Do I detect a note of sarcasm, Glo?"

"Sorry love, I didn't mean anything by it. Look, you work hard to catch the killer, and we'll have a proper catch-up whenever you're ready."

"Okay. See you."

Gloria could have kicked herself. She'd let her feelings slip, and Sean had detected it in her voice. She must not let that happen again.

During the evening, friends phoned to speak about the killings; they were concerned for her safety, as they had happened so close to where Gloria lived, but some simply wanted to share in the dramatic events, getting a vicarious kick out of it. She noticed they all expressed common thoughts: something like this was inevitable; crime was getting out of control; the authorities should have seen it coming and taken action to prevent it. Listening to all their comments, Gloria was careful not to say too much, other than giving the kind of views they'd heard from her before.

At eight-thirty, she received her final phone call of the day, and this time it was hugely welcome. It was her friend Lily, from Bristol. They'd known each other since leaving school, and for the past forty-seven years, had remained firm friends, visiting each other about once a year.

"Lily! How wonderful to hear from you! How's things?"

"Good thanks, old and knackered like you, but otherwise I'm fine." They both laughed. Gloria loved talking to Lily and being with her—she made her feel young again. Every time they spoke, it was like they'd never been apart.

"Glo, I've heard about the murders in Bloomsbury, that's close to you isn't it? It must feel awful, being practically on your doorstep."

"Yes, it's dreadful, but it's been coming for some time. The crime and drug dealing around here is getting out of hand."

"Tell you what, Billy-Joe's going up to Yorkshire to visit his parents next weekend, why don't you come and stay? Get away from it all."

Gloria hadn't met Lily's new man, Billy-Joe, but she'd heard a lot about him. "Do you mean that Lily, really?"

"I wouldn't have offered if I didn't mean it. Come on, we'll have a laugh, it'll be like old times!"

"You're on. I can't come this weekend, but would next Friday be all right?"

"Sounds great."

After a few more minutes of conversation, they said goodbye. While talking, it began to dawn on Gloria what a great opportunity this would be to dispose of the gun, far away from where she lived. She was reluctant to get rid of it locally, fearing that if it was found nearby (and she knew that they would be looking hard) it would be easier for her to be linked in some way to the weapon.

Gloria couldn't wait for the following weekend to arrive. For a while at least, she could leave her troubles behind. An hour later she was tucked snugly under her duvet, listening to a strong wind hurling the rain against her bedroom window. She started obsessing about the shootings again, and whether she'd missed anything, but within minutes fell fast asleep.

SEVEN
Monday 16th November 1998

GLORIA RETURNED TO work on Monday, where dealing with the pressing problems of DSS claimants once again took all her attention. On her way there, she passed Paula again.

"Hi Paula, everything okay?"

Once again, Paula seemed a bit pre-occupied, but she greeted Gloria with a smile.

"Oh, hi Glo. Fine thanks. How was your weekend?"

"Oh, the usual; nothing special. I'm looking forward to visiting Lily in Bristol this weekend, though. What about you? I bet things are hotting up at the police station."

"Yes, they've set up an incident room; they're calling it Operation Chiddingstone and the bosses are in a real flap."

"Well, be sure to pass on any juicy information you overhear."

Paula laughed. "I'll certainly try. Sorry Glo, but I'm in a bit of a rush, I'm late already. See you soon."

With that, Paula walked quickly away. For some reason, she clearly didn't want to stay and talk.

TUESDAY MORNING DAWNED with a chill nip in the air; it was even cold inside her flat. Opening the curtains, Gloria was greeted by a thick fog, with visibility down to fifty metres. She never usually bothered with early morning television, but something made her turn on Good Morning Britain that day. The first item on the news was once again the shootings; there had been dramatic developments overnight.

"A black male, named by police as Delroy Derby, has been arrested in a house in Manor Park, East London, after a tip-off. Police want to speak to him in connection with the shooting on Thursday evening in St Giles High Street. The victim had been shot in the kneecap in what police believe to be a drugs-related punishment shooting. Derby has been taken to Holborn Police Station for questioning. A few moments ago, Detective Chief Inspector Simpson made this statement."

DCI Juliet Simpson's face appeared on screen.

"Ballistic tests carried out on the three bullets recovered from both the shooting of a black male in St Giles High Street on Thursday night, and the murders of Kelly-Anne Watkins and David Border on Friday evening, have revealed that all three bullets had been fired from the same gun. Delroy Derby, a thirty-two-year-old man from Manor Park, who had already been arrested for the shooting in St Giles High Street, has been further arrested for the murders of Kelly-Anne Watkins and David Border; we are not looking for anyone else in connection with these two incidents. Thank you."

DCI Simpson was deluged with questions from the assembled press, but ignoring them she turned around, and was ushered back inside by two colleagues.

Gloria stared blankly at the screen. The newscaster had moved onto a different news item, but she heard nothing, staggered at her good fortune. This meant that not only had she got off scot-free with killing her attackers, but the biggest drug dealer in the area had been arrested for the murders, with overwhelming forensic evidence stacked against him. What a wonderful result! *Talk about killing two birds with one stone!* Gloria was more than happy, she was ecstatic.

Hearing the plopping sound of something falling on her doormat, Gloria walked slowly down the hall to collect her post with a broad grin on her face, her mind still drinking in her luck. On the doormat was a brown envelope with nothing written on the outside.

She picked the envelope up and opened it, to find a plain sheet of white paper which had been folded in three. Unfolding the paper, she read the message written in block capitals: *I SAW WHAT YOU DID IN BARTER STREET, I'M WATCHING YOU.* In an instant, all her fear had returned, like an icy wave, drowning out the elation.

Desperate to discover who had posted the letter, Gloria opened her door, ran along the corridor, and checked the lift; it was unoccupied. She ran down the stairs and out into the street, her heart hammering against her ribcage. Who on earth could have sent a message like that? Who could have possibly seen what happened in Barter Street? And why hadn't they already gone to the police? Stepping outside the communal door, she looked up and down the street, but there was nobody in sight.

Back inside her flat, Gloria leaned against her front door and stared blankly into space. She was bewildered. Her whole body started quivering and her legs felt weak. Slowly she slid down the door until she was crouched on her haunches. Her hand holding the letter was trembling and she could feel a tightness in her chest; suddenly the simple act of breathing seemed difficult. The sudden plunge from her exhilaration after the news report, to her despair after reading the letter, was just too much to bear.

EIGHT

DELROY DERBY WAS not a happy man. He had been at home asleep in bed with his wife, when armed police forced open his front door and stormed into his bedroom. He was dragged roughly out of bed, laid face down on the floor, and placed in handcuffs. His wife was screaming and his children were terrified; they couldn't understand how their loving husband and father could be treated like this.

Suspecting they may have found the gun, and taken his DNA from it, Delroy was considering telling all, in an attempt to shorten his inevitably long prison sentence. But he would bide his time, and listen to exactly how much the police knew first, before coming clean.

The officer in charge of the arrest had been Detective Sergeant Palfrey and, after booking Delroy in at the police station, Palfrey was about to place him in a cell, when a woman that Delroy soon came to know as DCI Juliet Simpson, took the officer to one side and appeared to be passing on fresh information. Whatever it was she told Palfrey, it made him raise his eyebrows and glance over at the arrested man. He then walked back to Delroy.

"Delroy Derby. I am further arresting you for the murders of Kelly-Anne Watkins and David Border in Barter Street on Friday 13th November. You do not have to say anything, but it may harm your defence if you do not mention when questioned something which you later rely on in court. Anything you do say may be given in evidence."

Delroy was dumbstruck for a few seconds, then he said frantically, "Listen, I'll admit that I shot the guy on Thursday, he was working my patch, but I didn't kill the other two, I swear on my children's lives. I didn't kill anybody! You've got to believe me!"

He tried to pull away from the cell, but was forced inside by three officers. Banging on the cell door, he shouted, "Get me my brief. I want my fucking brief here now! It's a stitch up!"

NINE
Friday 20th November 1998

GLORIA HAD SUFFERED a miserable three days since receiving the letter, certain that whoever wrote it would pass on their information to the authorities. Every time the intercom buzzed or she heard footsteps outside her flat, Gloria prepared herself for the worst, expecting to open the door to a couple of stern-faced policemen. Sleeping had been practically impossible, and she was feeling shattered and jumpy. Nothing had happened though, and Gloria had not received any further letters. Getting away to visit Lily in Bristol couldn't come soon enough.

Friday finally arrived, and Gloria boarded the Bristol train at Paddington Station. Events surrounding the shootings had moved on over the past three days. Delroy Derby had been charged with the murders of Watkins and Border, but the charge of grievous bodily harm to the male shot in the kneecap had been dropped, because the injured man refused to press charges. The furore had died down, with most locals not surprised that the killings had been committed by a ruthless drug dealer like Delroy Derby.

Gloria had been looking forward to this journey for three reasons: it would reunite her with her good friend Lily; she could enjoy a weekend away from her troubles at home; but most importantly, she could dispose of the gun at some point on the journey.

She'd placed the Glock into the front section of her handbag, still wrapped in tissue and a small plastic food bag. Once the train was well away from London, as it passed through a dense area of woodland, or even better over a lake or river, she would find a suitable window, make certain that she wasn't being watched, and throw it from the train. The chances were that it would never be found.

Once on the train, Gloria searched several carriages looking for a window. Then came a serious blow to her plan: she hadn't realised the trains on this line were now fitted with electric doors, tiny vent windows and air conditioning. She walked to the buffet car, increasingly agitated, hoping to find an answer to her problem further down the train, but with no luck. After returning to her seat, Gloria saw the guard approaching down the aisle, studiously checking and clipping everyone's tickets as he went.

"Excuse me," she asked as he examined her ticket, "I feel a little travel sick; could you possibly direct me to a window where I could stand and get some fresh air?"

"I'm sorry madam, I can't do that."

"Why not?"

"Because all windows are sealed, apart from the air vents at the top of some of them."

"Isn't there a window anywhere that I can open to get some fresh air?"

"I'm sorry madam, they're phasing those trains out on this line, so none of the windows open. All carriages are fully air-conditioned though."

Turning down his offer of some water to drink, Gloria slumped back in her seat. This was seriously bad news; she was hoping to arrive in Bristol having successfully disposed of the Glock. Not only that, but the question of whoever wrote the letter had been playing on her mind since she boarded the train. Someone knew she'd committed the murders in Barter Street, but they might not know that she was still in possession of the gun. Without the police finding it, and linking it to her, it would simply be the letter writer's word against hers. She would dispose of it somewhere in Bristol, then her troubles would be over with once and for all.

Lily was waiting on the station concourse and dashed forward when she spotted her friend in the crowd.

"Glo! It's so lovely to see you! We're going to have such a great weekend! How are you? You look tired."

"It's okay, I'm really great! Lily, you look fantastic!" Gloria had always been jealous of Lily's looks. She had a naturally pretty face, olive coloured skin, an amazing figure, and the whole thing was topped by flowing locks of strawberry blonde hair. She looked more like fifty than sixty-five years old.

Linking arms, they slowly made their way out to the station car park, fully intending to enjoy their weekend together. As Lily reversed her car from the parking space and pulled out of the car park, they saw three drug users in a doorway. Gloria had seen this many times before where she lived. They were lifting tiny glass bottles to their mouths, sucking and blowing out clouds of white smoke. Gloria knew they were smoking crack cocaine.

"Why on earth doesn't anyone do something about it?" Lily said in disgust.

"That's what everyone where I live wants to know."

"There's been a spate of street robberies down here; nothing like the shootings you've had in London, but we've had old ladies attacked, and one man who'd handed his wallet over was still stabbed. I mean, why do that to someone?"

"They don't think normally Lily, they're just animals."

Lily drove them out to her neat, semi-detached house backing onto fields on the outskirts of the city. The friends settled down on comfy chairs in the heated conservatory with a glass of red wine each. Relaxing into her chair, Gloria smiled at her friend.

"Thanks for asking me here, Lily, this is just bliss, absolute heaven."

HOWEVER, THE SENSE of calm didn't last and Gloria felt increasingly uneasy during the weekend, the occasional image flashing into her mind of the horrific events which could potentially ruin her life forever. It hardly seemed possible that it had all happened just over a week ago. Her two major concerns now were disposal of the hand-gun and finding out who had written the letter. She simply had to get rid of the gun at some point over the weekend.

Lying in bed that night, Gloria kept thinking about the similarity between her own thoughts on the dealers and street robbers, and Lily's. She imagined the thousands and thousands of others thinking exactly the same, all over the country. The idea of an army of Gloria Joneses, waiting for their chance to strike back, briefly amused and comforted her. She couldn't stop thinking about the letter, though, and wondering if the person who wrote it would tell the police. She eventually drifted off into a fitful and broken sleep.

THE SOUND OF cattle lowing in the field backing on to Lily's garden roused a sleepy Gloria into a new day. She headed for the bathroom and turned on the shower. Powerful jets of hot water lashed her skin. As she soaped her body and washed her hair, she told herself this was now a situation she could do nothing about and at that moment, Gloria decided to enjoy whatever freedom she had left.

If the letter writer told the police, then she would deny it and fight her corner in court. If they didn't tell the police, she was home and free once she'd disposed of the gun. She dried herself, got dressed, and made her way into the conservatory.

"Morning Glo," said Lily, already seated at the table. "Did you sleep well?"

"Wonderfully, thank you," she lied.

After breakfast they headed into the city centre, for several hours of enjoyable shopping therapy. Much, much later, they arrived back home.

"Oh God, my feet are killing me! I haven't shopped like that in twenty years."

Lily smiled at Gloria's words, then dropped her shopping bags onto the lounge floor, before collapsing into the welcoming comfort of the settee.

"You're right, neither have I, but life's too short. It's no good having regrets when you're six feet under. Remember the old saying, 'Any day above ground is a good day.' Ask those two who were murdered up your way, that's what they'd tell you, if they could."

Lily had unwittingly reminded her friend of the killings. Gloria stared into space as she sat on the edge of an armchair; Lily's words had cut like a knife, and for the first time she thought about the parents and families of her victims. They must be suffering terribly, and it was all her fault. The couple she'd killed had probably been loved just as much as any other son, daughter, brother, sister, or friend. Their families and friends would hate the killer, and wouldn't rest until she was caught.

When bedtime came Gloria felt sad, knowing that in the morning it would be time to go home. Back to the old routine. Back to her flat, where on some evenings she felt like a prisoner because of the dangers outside. Back to the scene of her terrible crime, the memory of which Gloria was certain would return regularly to haunt her. And back to the unknown person who had tormented her with the letter.

TEN
Sunday 22nd November 1998

MORNING BROKE MISTY and overcast, which matched Gloria's mood. She hated the thought of having to go home and, to make matters worse, she realised she would struggle to find anywhere in a city like Bristol to get rid of the gun, especially when she was in Lily's company. Time was running out. Seeing her friend looking so down, Lily decided to take her to the local market.

The busy Sunday market in the centre of Bristol was in full swing. Lily and Gloria were wrapped up warmly against the cold, making the most of their last few hours together before Gloria's departure. She was booked on the 1.47 from Bristol Temple Meads, which would mean she'd arrive home by 4.30. Lily was planning to spend the rest of the day with her niece.

After enjoying a stand-up lunch of hot-dogs and cans of coke outside a burger stall, Lily and Gloria prepared to say goodbye.

"Are you sure you can manage that case on your own, Glo?"

"Lily, don't worry. It's just a short walk along the canal to the station and this case has got wheels and a pull-out handle. I'll be fine. You get off to see your niece; she'll be wondering where you are."

With a heavy heart, Gloria hauled her suitcase out of Lily's car, and the two friends turned to face each other.

"Thanks for a fabulous weekend, Lily, I've had such a good time."

"Me too. I'll come and visit you in London soon."

With one final hug and lots of goodbyes, they exchanged kisses on each cheek and Gloria walked off towards the canal.

The tow-path along the canal was practically deserted as Gloria pulled her suitcase along behind her, its tiny wheels making a 'clickety-click, clickety-click' sound on the uneven surface. A couple of small cabin cruisers and a brightly painted red and green narrowboat were the only craft on this section. All three were safely tied to their moorings against the tow-path bank.

Looking down into the murky depths of the canal water, she recalled seeing a true crime investigation on TV, where a body had been disposed of in a canal in New Jersey, USA. It had taken police divers three separate visits to the canal before they managed to locate the body of a young Hispanic boy, who'd been brutally murdered by his stepfather. Apparently the thick, deep, clinging mud at the bottom of the canal made things very difficult for the divers, as they searched by feel alone for the grizzly remains.

Stopping to blow her nose, Gloria opened her handbag and took out a small pack of tissues, inadvertently feeling the hard shape of the hand-gun as she did so. Whilst blowing her nose, Gloria stared again at the dark water. She looked up and down the tow-path; no-one was within a hundred metres. She could almost feel the canal water whispering to her; "In here! In here! No-one will ever find your secret in here!"

Gloria's hand felt the outline of the gun through the leather of her handbag. She really hadn't expected this opportunity to dispose of the gun, and her heart-rate quickened. Glancing once more all around, she walked to the water's edge, unzipped the front of her bag, and gently lifted the gun out.

"They're good, aren't they?" The shout made Gloria visibly start. "Sorry, didn't mean to make you jump."

Gloria looked around, trying to locate where the voice was coming from, but couldn't see anyone.

"Over here!"

A hand was waving from a small window on the narrowboat. Behind the grimy window Gloria could see a face, almost totally obscured by a thick grey beard. Trying to compose herself, Gloria managed to stutter, "Oh, hello there, didn't see you."

"Hang on, I'll come up on deck with my weapon."

Gloria's mind was spinning. Could she have been unlucky enough to have held her Glock up in front of some gun nut? Someone who could not only identify which gun it was, but could now identify her as well! She quickly replaced the gun in her handbag and fought to remain calm.

The man emerged through a small hatch at the rear of the boat. He looked about sixty-five, with shoulder length curly grey hair tied back in a pony tail, and a thick grey beard that grew down to his chest. His clothing had seen better days: a chunky orange polo-neck jumper, dirty grey tracksuit bottoms flecked with red and green paint, and a pair of lime-green socks inside open-toed sandals. He seemed to be hiding something behind his back in his right hand and was grinning widely.

"Dah-Dah!" cried the man theatrically, whipping his right arm quickly round to the front of his body, and displaying the hand-gun he was holding.

"Bloody hell!"

"I'll bet it's exactly the same model as yours," said the man excitedly, "and I bet I know where yours came from."

"I don't think so," stammered Gloria, trying hard to contain the rising panic inside her.

"I bet the same size flame comes from the end of mine when fired, as it does from yours. Look!"

Gloria was beginning to consider running; this man had wild eyes and was clearly completely insane. Raising his arm to the horizontal, he pointed the gun straight at her face. He was only a couple of metres away.

"No!"

As he pulled the trigger, in what seemed like slow-motion, Gloria watched a flame leap from the gun's nozzle. She winced, waiting for the impact of the bullet, then sort of half-laughed and half-sobbed, as she realised that the man's gun was actually a cigarette lighter.

"Best lighters going in my opinion," continued the man. "The Sunday morning market's been selling them for ages. I see yours even came wrapped in a cellophane bag, more than I got when I bought mine! Great little novelties, aren't they?"

Gloria was visibly shaking, and struggling to control her nerves, something that the man seemed oblivious to.

"Yes, they're really good." She was trying to think of a good reason for having it in her hand. "I bought one for my husband, I was just having a proper look at it."

"Great idea! He'll love it." The man lost his smile and seemed to be studying Gloria carefully. "I've not seen you around here before, do you live locally?"

"Yes," she lied. "Quite close to the market, actually." The man looked quizzically at the suitcase. Noticing his puzzlement, Gloria pre-empted his question. "I'm going to visit my son in Birmingham for a few days."

"Oh, right. Well, I'd better get on then, and let you catch your train. Good-day." The man dropped through the hatch and was gone as fast as he'd appeared.

Gloria could feel the sweat under her armpits and realised she was breathing hard. That was much too close for comfort. *From now on that gun stays where it is until exactly the right time to ditch it.*

Dragging her suitcase behind her, Gloria quickened her pace to the station.

"What a shit way to end a great weekend," she muttered to herself, as she turned off the tow-path and onto the underpass which led underneath Bristol Temple Meads station. She knew that if she'd dropped the gun into the canal, and been witnessed by that narrowboat nutter, he would have first torn her off a strip, then insisted that the river authorities got it back out! She was all too aware that one simple action could have cost her a life sentence.

The meeting with the man had delayed her, but she still had a bit of time before her train left. The light inside the underpass was dingy, and the air felt a little damp and chill. There were three large wheelie bins to her left, and one of them moved slightly as she walked past. Hearing a muffled cry of pain, Gloria froze, suddenly feeling vulnerable.

Looking around, there were no other pedestrians in the underpass. She'd already reached the mid-way point, so decided to walk quickly to the far end. The next few steps provided Gloria with an explanation for the cry. Two scrawny-looking white men were attacking an elderly woman. They were both about thirty years old, one with tight blue jeans, black donkey jacket and a skinhead, the other with a thick mop of blonde hair, and wearing a black hooded tracksuit. The man in the donkey jacket was pulling her head down by her hair, bending her almost double, while his mate yanked at her handbag, while kicking her in the side.

Gloria stopped in her tracks, shocked by what she was witnessing, then sickened, and then quickly filled with loathing for the attackers. She had to do something to help, but fear gripped her. Another vicious kick, this time to the woman's head, causing her to collapse on the ground, was the final straw.

"Leave her alone!" Gloria yelled at the top of her voice.

Both men looked round instantly. Gloria was only five metres away, and could see the wild look in their eyes. She feared she'd made a serious mistake.

"Fuck it, run!" shouted donkey jacket.

"Don't be a twat!" yelled back tracksuit man. "We'll do her as well!"

Gloria reacted without thinking. Within a couple of seconds she had pulled out the gun from her handbag, still inside the clear cellophane bag. She quickly removed the bag and pointed it towards the men. They stood stock still in horror at first, then the skinhead started smiling.

"That's a replica! I've seen them down the market; it's a fucking lighter!"

"Move, and I'll shoot!" Gloria said, firmly. She didn't hear the reply. At that moment, a train passing out of Temple Meads station trundled loudly on the tracks overhead, causing an almost deafening echo and rumble in the tunnel. Gloria saw the taller man mouth something to his mate, but his words were drowned out by the noise of the train passing overhead.

Both men moved quickly towards Gloria, tracksuit man directly in front of his companion. By the time he had taken three steps, Gloria had pulled the trigger. The bullet hit him in the middle of his chest, and a startled look came over his face. He was stopped in his tracks. His arms dropped by his sides, his legs buckled, and he collapsed where he stood, falling to the ground face down, slightly on his left side.

Gloria was surprised to see that the man in the donkey jacket was also on the ground; he was sitting up and writhing in agony, clutching his stomach with blood-soaked hands. She realised that the bullet must have passed straight through the first man, hitting the second man as well. Gloria was in shock. *This can't really be happening, can it? Not for a second time!*

There was no sign of anyone else entering the tunnel. The roaring noise of the train passing over the bridge began to subside, and Gloria became aware of the cries of pain from the man in the donkey jacket. The other man was lying on a small pile of rubbish, totally still and apparently dead. Gloria walked towards the second man, his pitiful cries of agony causing her mixed emotions; her instinct was to help a fellow human being who was obviously suffering agonising pain, but she also felt glad that he was getting the punishment he deserved.

Keeping a decent gap between herself and the injured man, she got her first close up view of his face. He looked like a thug with his cropped hair, squashed nose, and had what Gloria usually referred to as prison eyes—cold and hard.

"You fucking bitch," he gurgled as she stood over him, blood seeping from his mouth. "I'll fucking get you..." The end of his threat was partially drowned out, as yet another train passed overhead, causing a repetition of the deafening rumble and echo of steel on steel.

"No, I don't think so, son," replied Gloria calmly, pointing the gun straight at his face.

"No, no! I'm sorry!" he mouthed, whilst at the same time holding up his left arm, hand outstretched towards the gun, his palm facing Gloria. She couldn't have heard his pleas over the sound of the train, even if she'd wanted to. She took aim at his head and pulled the trigger. The bullet went straight into his forehead, and his arm dropped uselessly, followed quickly by his whole body flopping backwards. Both eyes remained opened, but there was nothing to see—the life in them had been extinguished. A pool of deep red blood was slowly growing around the back of his head.

Staring down at the carnage, blood now trickling across the tarmac from underneath two lifeless bodies, Gloria felt like the lead in a gruesome film; surely this couldn't be real, could it? She was about to turn towards the old woman, who was slowly coming back to consciousness, when she realised that she must not be seen or recognised. Overcome with fear and panic, Gloria looked carefully all around the underpass. She could see no-one, but knew that any second now someone could turn into the tunnel and see her. Quickly replacing the gun in the front section of her handbag, she turned away, telling herself that the first people to arrive would be sure to help the old lady.

Without even a backward glance at the two men whose lives she had just snuffed out, she grabbed the handle of her suitcase, walked swiftly out of the underpass, and into the main entrance of the station.

The sweat trickling into her eyes made Gloria wipe her forehead with her sleeve. Looking up at the departures board, she saw that the London Paddington train would leave from platform two. She glanced at the clock and was amazed to see that it was only eight minutes since she'd left the man on the narrowboat. How could so much have happened in such a short time?

Trying to remain as calm and inconspicuous as possible, Gloria walked slowly to the ticket barrier for platform two.

"Good afternoon, madam," greeted the guard, as Gloria fished for her ticket in her purse.

"Yes, good afternoon," she replied, with a slight crack in her voice.

"Are you all right, madam? You look a little flustered."

"I'm fine. Just had a bit of a rush for the train, that's all; thought I would probably miss it."

"No, no, you've still got five minutes." He clipped her ticket and returned it to her. "Safe travels."

Walking swiftly to platform two, she boarded the train.

Finding a seat at a table on her own, Gloria stowed her suitcase in the luggage rack. She listened intently for shouts, or the approaching scream of police sirens, but none came. The train pulled out from the station on time, and she removed her coat before sinking down into her seat, resting her head on her folded arms on the table-top.

A recent article she had read in a magazine came into Gloria's mind, where a Los Angeles detective was being interviewed about people who commit multiple murders.

"In the United States," he had said, "individuals who have killed four people or more over a period of time are classed as serial killers." Gloria wondered what the British definition was.

ELEVEN

GLORIA COULDN'T STOP her legs shaking, and she was certain the elderly couple on the opposite table were staring at her. Surprisingly, she didn't feel like crying, although she was an emotional wreck and her throat felt dry and sore. Surely this time she would be caught; someone must have seen something.

She took a book from her handbag and pretended to read it. A thought had crossed her mind that made her go cold: CCTV! All mainline train stations have CCTV! *What if they had it in the underpass?* Gloria's head started to throb as she battled once more to make sense of the past twenty minutes. She knew they would come looking for her, but they had to identify her first. She wasn't about to give herself up.

After two-and-a-half hours of mental torment, and for the second time in ten days, Gloria arrived home having just killed two human beings. If anything, this time she felt worse than before, knowing for certain that once any CCTV images were made public, she was likely to be identified.

She walked into the kitchen in a trance-like state, and made herself a cup of tea. The sudden ringing of the telephone made her catch her breath. Not feeling like talking to anybody, she sat and stared at the phone until long after the ringing stopped.

All she could see in her mind's eye was that poor old woman, being beaten senseless by two thugs. She prayed to God that someone had come along soon to help her. Then she took a huge breath and, just as she had done after the first shootings, she suddenly experienced another sensation: it was as if her chest was swelling with pride. Repeating over and over in her head was the same mantra: *Those bastards deserved it, they fucking deserved it.*

At five o'clock, Gloria decided to take a shower; she felt as if her whole body needed cleansing and hoped it might make her feel better. After that, she would make another cup of tea, and watch the six o'clock news. She was already fully aware of what was likely to be the headline story.

As she shed her clothes, Gloria could smell strong body odour on herself for the first time in many years. Even though no-one else was with her, she felt ashamed and, once in the shower, scrubbed herself until her skin burned, as if to erase the memory of the day's events.

Afterwards, she went into the kitchen and put the kettle on. Her handbag was on the kitchen table and she walked over to it, opened the front section and pulled out the gun, which was now back in its clear plastic bag. She laid it on the kitchen table.

"Well, finding you has caused me a few problems, hasn't it?" she asked aloud. "What am I supposed to do now, eh? I'm not the same any more, am I? How do I just carry on?"

Gloria stared at the gun for a moment, then made a decision. She knew that if they identified her, she was looking at a lifetime in prison; she also knew that if she tried ditching the weapon now and someone saw her, she'd effectively be giving herself up, with impossible questions to answer.

So she decided to keep the gun hidden in her flat, back inside the box of Cornflakes. It seemed a crazy thing to do, but she felt safer with the gun hidden in her home, than carrying it with her out onto the streets again.

"THIS IS SKY NEWS, live from the Sky News Centre, with Alan Elder and Lisa-Marie Smith." Gloria's attention was totally focussed on the television screen. As the opening credits cut away to the two newsreaders, the words *Breaking News* were set against a red background.

"Good evening, this is the six o'clock news," began Elder. His welcome was instantly followed by Lisa-Marie Smith announcing, "We have breaking news of a double shooting in Bristol. Over now to our Sky News correspondent, Andrew Boswell."

Gloria found herself watching a familiar scene and had to fight a sudden wave of nausea. The correspondent had just arrived at Bristol Temple Meads station and was standing close to one end of the underpass, which was cordoned off by tape and blocked by two police vehicles. He explained that police had confirmed two young men as dead, and an elderly woman as badly injured, but conscious and stable.

The two men had been shot at close range, one in the chest, the other in the chest and head. The elderly woman had apparently been badly beaten. Police hoped to find out more details from her, when she was fit enough to talk.

Gloria could feel her breathing becoming laboured, with the now familiar tightness pulling at her stomach. The one thing that made her feel slightly better was that the old woman was okay; Gloria would have never forgiven herself if she'd died from her injuries, because she hadn't stayed to help.

The correspondent enlarged on the story, saying that the two men were apparently well known by locals in the Bristol area. He then ventured the opinion that all three seemed to have been the victim of a violent attack by an armed maniac. The local police were keeping an open mind on the motive for the attack until they had more information. They would particularly like to speak to anyone who had used the underpass between twelve noon and one forty-five—the time the bodies were discovered. They were hopeful that the station's CCTV system might shed some light on what had occurred.

When the correspondent handed back to the newsreader, she announced that there would be a special report on Britain's seemingly "out-of-control gun culture". The report was to focus on two double murders by shooting in the past two weeks in separate parts of the country. A statistic apparently unprecedented in the UK.

"Our special report will look closely at what appears to be an alarming rise in gun crime; we will hear views from politicians of all parties on how best to tackle it. We will also be speaking live with Lieutenant Kent Warr, of the Brooklyn Homicide Department, to hear how the New York Police Department achieved a 50% reduction in shootings in only two years."

"Well, I seem to have created a bit of a stir," Gloria said quietly to herself.

Turning the volume down, Gloria flicked through the channels, hoping to find out more details on the investigation. All but one channel had moved on to other stories, so she turned the TV off then started unpacking her suitcase. She would keep herself as busy as possible and check the news bulletins at seven for any additional information. She tidied her clothes away and did her laundry.

Just as she sat down again, the phone rang and this time she answered it.

"Glo. Thank God you got home all right! Have you seen the news?" It was Lily.

"Yes, just seen it. I was about to call you. Bit close to you, that one!"

"You must have been within minutes of getting caught up in it! You must've walked through that underpass, didn't you?"

"Yes, but it was completely empty when I went through, unless they were hiding. Makes me shudder just thinking about it."

"Apparently they were found near some large bins. Perhaps they'd already been shot and were lying there when you walked past."

"Oh, don't say that Lily, it's too horrible. I'm shaken up enough as it is!"

"Sorry Glo... Oh, wait a minute, a policeman is saying something about the killings on South-West News at the moment." Lily went quiet at the other end of the phone as she listened to what was said.

"What's happening?" Gloria asked, after almost thirty seconds of silence, hoping her voice wasn't giving her away.

"Well that's absolutely typical. Another cock-up by the look of it," remarked Lily.

Gloria was intrigued. "What Lily? What's happened?" She tried to sound interested but not betray just *how* interested she really was.

"Some detective has just announced that Temple Meads Station was in the process of having a new CCTV system installed. Apparently, all the new cameras are in place, but the hard-drive for recording everything is still being worked on; it should have been up and running twenty-four hours ago. They've got absolutely nothing on CCTV."

Breathing heavily again, Gloria composed herself before replying, "So that means I'm not going to be shuffling past the screen on Crimewatch then?"

"Unbelievable isn't it?" said Lily. "What's the chances of the CCTV being down on the very day when it's needed most?"

"Pretty remote I'd think," replied Gloria, aware that she was now breathing a little easier, and thankful that fate, which had dealt her some pretty shit cards recently, had this time smiled on her.

Gloria could hear Lily's doorbell ring at the other end of the line.

"Bugger! Who the hell can that be? Glo, there's someone at the door. Look, I'll call you back later, I'm popping round to Susan's for pizza in a minute."

"No, I'll phone you. How about just after News at Ten?"

"Suits me, that way we'll be right up to date with the shootings. Speak later, bye sweetie."

AS PROMISED, GLORIA called Lily just after the News at Ten. Things had moved on since the six o'clock reports. Police had spoken briefly to the elderly lady, who'd apparently been on her way to a friend's house when two men attacked her. She'd been badly beaten, and woke to find herself lying on the ground with several people helping her. The two men who had attacked her were lying dead on the ground close by. She'd seen and heard nothing of the shootings, and police believed she must have been unconscious at the time. They were hoping she may be able to assist them further over the following days, as her memory slowly returned.

"Hi Lily. Did you watch the news just now?"

"Yes. It's really weird isn't it?"

"Weird? Why weird?"

"Well, it looks as though someone has stumbled across two robbers attacking an old lady, and shot them, before walking away without a soul seeing them. Surely somebody must have heard a gun being fired in Bristol, at Sunday lunchtime!"

"I see what you mean," Gloria was thinking hard for a different opinion to put forward. "Perhaps it wasn't about the old lady at all;

perhaps they owed money to some drug dealer... or maybe someone they'd hurt in the past was getting their revenge." Was she saying too much?

"Hadn't thought of that. Like a vigilante you mean?"

"Well, I wasn't exactly thinking of a vigilante, but now you mention it, I suppose so."

"Wouldn't that be great? Some kind of caped crusader going round knocking off the scumbags. They'd become a folk hero in no time. Well, they would round here, anyway."

"Really? Would you feel safe with some maniac going around Bristol shooting people?"

"Why not? If he's getting rid of the bastards who make life miserable for everyone else. I'm all for him!"

Gloria found herself smiling at Lily's certainty that the vigilante was a man.

"What makes you think it's a him?"

"Because people who kill with guns, in cold blood, are nearly always men. I saw a documentary about it. It's some sort of macho thing that gives them the urge to do it, something in their genes, and women apparently don't have that particular gene."

"Have they named the two men yet?"

"Don't think so. They'll announce that sort of thing tomorrow when everything gets into full swing; you know, press statements, door-to-door enquiries, that kind of stuff."

"What if the killer had jumped on a train heading out of the area?"

"Well, they'd be buggered then, wouldn't they? They'll never catch him."

"I suppose not."

Gloria and Lily chatted for another half hour, but conversation kept drifting back to the shootings in Bristol, instigated each time by Lily. Gloria began to realise that she'd better go with the flow and not keep trying to change the subject. Although nothing more of importance was said, Gloria was relieved when she finally managed to hang up.

Lily clearly had no inkling of what had really happened, but Gloria had felt uneasy several times during the conversation. And it made her sad;

the last thing she expected or wanted was to feel uncomfortable speaking to Lily.

Gloria's night was one of broken sleep and a vivid nightmare where she was being chased through a forest by an aggressive man threatening to "deal with her".

TWELVE
Monday 23rd November 1998

GLORIA WAS RELIEVED to be woken from her nightmare when her alarm went off. Monday morning was cloudy and grey, not too cold, with just a light breeze blowing.

She opened her eyes and a few seconds passed before her heart sank as she recalled with vivid clarity the events of yesterday. This was all too huge, too horrible, too life changing to be real. Not only that, but she still had no idea who had written the letter. Who was the person so certain that she was a killer? In all the drama of the past twenty-four hours, this was a question she had pushed to the back of her mind.

Realising she needed to get a grip, Gloria forced herself out of bed, throwing the covers off, and stretching before standing up straight. She made herself toast and marmalade with a pot of tea for breakfast, then got dressed and hurried out to work. On her way there, Gloria bumped into Suzie, a neighbour she saw regularly at meetings of both the Phoenix Gardens Committee and Residents Association.

"Hi Glo, how are things?" Suzie looked a little sheepish. "I heard about you getting attacked. I'm sorry I haven't called to see how you were, it's just, you know... busy."

"Don't give it another thought Suzie. I'm fine, really."

Suzie was clearly relieved, and smiled before saying, "I didn't think it could have been that bad—I saw you out the other morning. I was getting ready for work, and looked out into Phoenix Gardens. I saw you out there beating down nettles in the fenced off section. I was really surprised to see you there."

Gloria was horrified. She didn't know how to respond. "I... err... Well, you've got to do your bit, haven't you?" Gloria came out with the first remotely plausible excuse for her actions. "It's not like the council maintain it, is it?"

"What did you find there?" Suzie asked. "I thought I saw you pick something up."

Think Gloria, think.

"Oh... yes... Just a really old purse that had been there for months, I dropped it back on the ground; there was nothing valuable in it, and nothing to identify the owner."

"Oh. I thought you put it in your handbag."

Gloria shuffled her feet, unable to look Suzie in the eye; Suzie clearly knew more than she was letting on. Could she be the person who'd sent the letter? It had to be a possibility.

"Oh that? Yes, there was an old, black toy car," she lied. "When my son was little, he used to have one exactly the same."

Looking at Suzie's change of expression, Gloria could see that she'd successfully turned the tables. Suzie was fully aware of how her son had died, and it was now Suzie who was looking and feeling uncomfortable. Gloria moved in for the kill.

"It brought back happy memories when I saw it. I simply picked it up as a reminder of him, when he was small. I know it probably seems stupid to you, but for some reason I just wanted to keep it."

"Glo, I'm so sorry, I shouldn't have been so nosy."

"Don't worry Suzie, you weren't to know. I'm sorry, but I'd better be going, or I'll be late for work."

"Okay then. Let's meet up for coffee, I'll call you."

"That would be lovely. See you Suzie."

Walking quickly away, Gloria wondered whether she'd really convinced Suzie with her story, or was Suzie playing mind-games with her? Could it be that Suzie had seen the gun, and worked out that it was Gloria who had carried out the shootings in Barter Street? If that was the case, then surely it must be Suzie who'd sent the letter. Of course, at the moment it was all guesswork, but it did make sense. She would carefully watch Suzie's behaviour from now on; this was a potentially dangerous situation and had to be handled very carefully.

At work, Gloria made her way past reception.

"Ah, Gloria, can I have a word please?" The man addressing her was Harold, the office manager and a stickler for things being done right. "Two customers you dealt with last Thursday have complained about your manner. Are there any problems I should be aware of? If so, please tell me and we'll sit down and chat."

This apparent concern for her welfare was nothing more than a thinly masked rebuke, so she apologised to Harold, said no, she didn't have any problems, then walked to her desk and sat down.

Clearly, her behaviour had been unusual enough to upset some customers. It was hardly surprising, but she needed to try harder to remain in control. She turned to her overflowing in-tray, removed the top letter and began opening it. She unfolded the paper inside, and read: *TWO IN BRISTOL AS WELL, YOU'RE GOOD!*

Gloria's world tilted and she dropped the paper as if it had scorched her. The letter was on the same plain white paper, and once again folded into three. It was also in the same handwriting. Picking up the envelope in trembling hands, she inspected it. On the front was *GLORIA JONES, PRIVATE AND CONFIDENTIAL.* She tried to maintain her composure as she hurried to the post room where Steven worked, sorting all the office's mail.

"Steven, who handed this letter in?"

"No idea. It didn't come with the regular post; it was lying on the mat when I opened up this morning."

Gloria slowly returned to her desk, stunned and feeling physically sick. Could it have been Suzie? Had she been on her way back when Gloria bumped into her? The truth was, she just didn't know. It had to be someone who knew her well, someone who knew where she lived and worked. Interestingly, the letter seemed to suggest that the author was impressed by her actions. More importantly, whoever had sent the letters hadn't passed on their knowledge to the police. At least not yet. And that was something she could live with until she identified them.

56

THIRTEEN
Monday 23rd November 1998

"RIGHT, LISTEN IN everyone. Turn off all mobiles, pagers, and pay attention."

Detective Superintendent Gary Marshman's words brought almost immediate silence from the fifty or so police officers gathered in the stuffy briefing room at Bristol Police Station. It was the morning after the shootings. Only the awkward shuffling of those who hadn't turned their mobiles and pagers off broke the silence. All eyes were focussed on the balding, insignificant looking man addressing them.

"We all know why we're here: the murders of Edward Hewitt and Christopher Thompson. First, I'll give you a brief run-down of what we know so far. After that you'll be split into three teams, each under a DI, who will assign you to specific tasks. Remember, there is a lot of media interest in these shootings, so we will be under intense scrutiny throughout; I will therefore expect nothing short of total professionalism from each and every one of you in everything you do from this moment forward. Is that understood?"

"Yes sir," came the reply, spoken almost in unison.

Marshman may have been small of stature, but once he started speaking, he had huge presence, and commanded respect from everyone. Over his twenty-four years of police service, he'd built a reputation for being the best detective in the Avon and Somerset force area. A man who didn't suffer fools gladly, a man who worked really hard, a man who expected the same attributes from everyone under his command.

Twenty minutes later, after a short presentation during which Marshman had given full and graphic details of the crimes, including the fatal injuries received by the victims, and the fact that forensic examination of the scene had failed to provide anything of assistance, he split the assembled officers into three Action Teams.

Team one was made up of local Bristol detectives. Their tasks would be to find out everything there was to know about Hewitt and Thompson. Marshman wanted to know their friends, enemies, known associates, persons they had previously done time with, family ties, drug suppliers, and fellow users. Anyone and anything, in fact, that impacted, or may have impacted, in any way on their lives.

Team two was made up of detectives drafted in from outside the Bristol area to assist with the investigation. Their tasks would be to check all CCTV in the area surrounding Bristol Temple Meads Station; search for any potential witnesses who may have been in a position to see who entered, or left the underpass in the two hours before the shootings; trace as many people as possible who boarded any trains leaving the station between one and two. and search through all suspect details for gun-related crime in the force area throughout the past two years.

Finally, team three was made up of local community officers and officers taken from core relief duties to assist with the investigation. Their sole task was to carry out door-to-door enquiries at all homes and businesses in the area; this would include anyone living on the boats.

PC BOB CHALK was twenty-one years old, a fresh-faced young constable with only eighteen months service in the Avon and Somerset Constabulary, so he was thrilled at being one of the officers taken from normal relief duties to be part of team three, working on a double murder investigation. He was a conscientious, enthusiastic officer, and now had the chance to shine, a chance he intended to grab with both hands.

Detective Inspector Gary Langdown was the man in charge of team three, posting officers to residential and business locations, and Bob was hugely disappointed when Langdown gave him the task of enquiries with the residents of houseboats on the canal. He'd hoped for one of the rougher housing estates, where he thought someone with information about the murders was bound to be lurking. However, he was determined to do the very best he could with the task he'd been assigned.

Shortly after eleven, Bob walked out through the back yard of the police station, jumping back in alarm as an angry, impounded stray dog barked loudly, lunging at him as he walked past the kennels. Two female officers smoking cigarettes near the rear door of the station howled with laughter.

"Bet you wouldn't jump back like that if *my* mouth came towards your crotch Bob!" shouted one of them, causing more laughter from other officers nearby. Trying not to show his embarrassment, Bob hurried through the yard gates and out onto the street.

After several hours on his first ever murder case, Bob was getting fed up; this was not at all like the exciting murder enquiries he'd seen on the TV. This was little more than a paper round.

He'd tried really hard at the seven inhabited houseboats he'd visited so far, and had thoroughly checked over twenty or so other vessels for any signs of people squatting in them, but so far there was nothing of interest.

The next narrowboat looked much the same as the others, although perhaps in slightly better condition; it had obviously been recently repainted in red and green, and looked like it had new curtains.

Bob Chalk climbed aboard and gave a firm rap on the hatch. Within seconds it was opened by a man who Bob judged to be in his sixties, with a bushy grey beard and untidy curly hair down to his shoulders. He stepped out to reveal green socks, no shoes, and filthy grey tracksuit bottoms, topped off with an orange jumper with holes in the elbows. His smile was genuine, and he greeted Bob warmly.

"Good afternoon officer; how lovely to receive a visit from the local constabulary. How can I help you?"

"I'm making enquiries about the murders in Temple Meads Station underpass yesterday afternoon. Did you hear or see anything, anything at all, no matter how insignificant it might seem?"

"Sure," Narrowboat man smiled broadly, gesturing with an outstretched arm towards the open hatch. "I've got information alright. Why don't you come inside out of the cold?"

Bob Chalk could not believe his ears. Could this wild-looking old man really have useful information? If so, why hadn't he contacted the police earlier? Drawing on his interview technique training, Bob chose not to rush in with questions, but wait until he'd heard what this strange-looking man had to say.

The inside of the narrowboat smelt musty and was poorly lit, with an unwashed plate, knife, and fork lying on a small draining board next to a tiny basin. Obviously noticing Bob's glance, the man said, "Sorry about the mess, I've just finished breakfast, and haven't washed up yet."

"Don't worry sir, I see a lot worse, I can assure you."

"Please, call me Trevor. Trevor Hall to be precise, but Trevor will do."

"Okay, Trevor. I'm Bob."

"Bob the bobby. Gotcha. Tea?"

"Perfect. Now, about that information."

Over the next twenty-five minutes, Trevor Hall retold the events of his meeting with a grey-haired lady carrying a hand-gun, and how he'd observed her from his narrowboat window as she walked alongside the canal at Sunday lunchtime. He explained how he'd assumed that she'd bought the same lighter as him from the market.

Trevor then gave Bob a detailed description of the gun, before furnishing him with an even more detailed description of the woman. Finally, he informed Bob that he thought she may have been about to throw the gun into the canal, just before he approached her.

His excitement mounting, the young officer busily took notes of everything Trevor Hall said.

BOB HURRIED ALONG the tow-path back toward the city centre, and the police station. He did little more than a cursory check of the final three inhabited craft on the canal; he was in a hurry now—this information was too vital to hold back for long, it had to be passed on without delay.

Leaving the narrowboat had proved difficult, not just because it wobbled as he stepped ashore, but because Trevor Hall suggested, almost insisted, that Bob stayed for another cup of tea. In the end, after several polite refusals, Bob lost his patience and raised his voice to Trevor, pointing out the importance of the information, and how it urgently needed to be passed on to his senior officers.

Walking into the back yard of the police station, Bob's mind was working overtime. *Who would have thought? A grey-haired old lady!*

DI Gary Langdown was at the desk in his office. Hardly an office really, consisting of a square glass box about ten feet by eight, jutting out from a side wall of the CID office. Langdown was a plump man, with thin, receding, light brown hair that, with the passing of the years, was now turning grey. He was tilted so far back in his chair that Bob thought he might overbalance at any second. He was reading a report, his outstretched hand holding it far enough away for Bob to know that he needed reading glasses.

Bob knew that some DI's had fearsome reputations, not usually happy at being bothered by Woodentops, but he felt confident enough that the news he had would immediately place him in Langdown's good books. He rapped firmly on the glass door.

DI Langdown swivelled round on his chair, and smiled at Bob. "Come in, lad," he barked in a broad Yorkshire accent.

"Thank-you sir," replied Bob. He walked in smartly, and stood by the side of the DI's desk.

"Sit yourself down lad, sit yourself down; we don't stand on ceremony in here." DI Langdown waved a hand towards a pair of chairs against the office wall.

Bob pulled one of the chairs forward and sat down. He tugged his pocket-book out from the front pouch on his equipment belt, opened it and looked down at seven full pages of notes about the murder suspect. He studied these carefully, then looked up at DI Langdown.

"Right lad, what have you got for me?"

Bob drew a deep breath. "Well sir, I've got a full description of a suspect seen holding a gun on the canal tow-path at about the time of the killings. She was only 200 metres from the scene of the crime and looked as if she was about to ditch the weapon."

DI Langdown furrowed his brow. "She? Did you say she?"

"Yes sir, a grey-haired lady, about 60-70 years old."

"And you say she appeared to be about to ditch the weapon. Where? In the canal?"

"Yes sir."

A hint of a smile had appeared at the corners of DI Langdown's mouth. "You'd better tell me exactly what you've been told, and who told you, but I think I can guess."

Bob had only just started going over his conversation on the boat, when DI Langdown began to laugh. Bob stopped speaking, wondering what he could have said that was so funny.

"Are you okay, sir?"

Langdown brought his laughter under control. "I'm sorry lad, yes I'm fine. Listen, was this houseboat you visited red and green by any chance?"

Bob started to get a sinking feeling in his stomach. "Yes sir, it was."

"Did the gentleman who gave you this information happen to be called Trevor Hall?"

"Yes sir, but how could you possibly know that?"

"Wait here a minute, lad, I've got something to show you."

DI Langdown walked out into the main CID office, which was busy with officers working on the killings, and spoke with a chubby Detective Sergeant. A few seconds later both men howled with laughter, and the Detective Sergeant reached into the bottom drawer of a large filing cabinet and lifted out an inch-thick file which he dumped onto the desk. DI Langdown picked it up and returned to Bob in his office.

"This is how I know Mr Hall, lad." Langdown theatrically raised the file, before dropping it with a loud thud onto his desk. "Inside that file are over forty reports, false reports mind you, made by Mr Hall naming the perpetrators of various crimes near the canal, ranging from minor damage, to sex attacks, and the theft of a £150,000 cabin cruiser. In short lad, Trevor Hall is a Walter Mitty character, a fantasist, a liar, an attention seeker, and a WASTE OF MY FUCKING TIME!" Gary Langdown had stopped smiling, and was staring hard at Bob, apparently awaiting his reply.

Bob was gutted. It took a few seconds before he managed to compose himself before quietly replying, "I'm sorry sir, he was so convincing. I'd never heard of Mr Hall before."

Gary Langdown's expression softened, and he placed a fatherly hand on Bob's shoulder.

"It's not your fault lad; you thought you'd done well, and I'm sorry to piss on your strawberries. In future, check the information before running to a DI with it. We're busy people, and can do without our time being wasted. Now, accept this as a friendly bollocking, and get back to checking out the rest of the boats."

Bob turned to leave without replying, but at the door he looked back. "This won't happen again, sir, I'm sorry."

Langdown was reading his report again. Without looking up he said, "See that it doesn't lad, see that it doesn't."

As Bob walked through the main CID office, he could hear muffled laughter, and left with the words "Wanker" and "Met any nutters lately?" ringing in his ears.

He couldn't believe that something which had started so promisingly, could have left him feeling so embarrassed and humiliated.

FOURTEEN
Tuesday 24th November 1998

"I'LL BE AT yours in twenty minutes, so make sure the kettle's on or there'll be trouble!"

"You cheeky sod! I don't hear from you for nearly a fortnight, and that's all you have to say, is it?"

"I told you I'd be busy after those shootings, didn't I? Anyway, we'll talk more when I get there."

Gloria had always enjoyed Sean Aylen's cheeky humour—it was similar to her own, and one of the things that had drawn them together at the police and community meetings. Sean was an experienced copper, 45 years old, average height, stocky build, with a shock of red hair. He had twenty years' service in the police—twenty years that had left Sean with a healthy degree of cynicism.

Nothing more had happened since Gloria received the letter at work and, although still worried, she could feel the worst of her tension ebbing away slightly as each hour passed. News reports about the killings were as uninformed and wildly speculative as ever, with the police investigation in Bristol clearly struggling. So far, they were drawing a blank.

Gloria hadn't bothered to watch the evening news, then shortly after seven-thirty her intercom sounded. Lifting the receiver to her ear, she laughed out loud on hearing Sean's voice.

"Open the door for Christ's sake, I'll be frozen to the fucking spot in a minute."

Sean had no idea Gloria had been to Bristol, and he didn't know Lily, so was unlikely to ever hear about it. The only way he might find out would be if Gloria was clearly shown on CCTV somewhere near the area of the murders. She thought that was highly unlikely, given the failure of the CCTV system at the station, so she decided not to mention it. She also knew that she couldn't mention receiving the letters, although she felt uncomfortable having to be less than honest with her friend.

Gloria pressed the door release button and put her front door on the latch so that Sean could let himself in. She didn't feel too bad considering her current situation and was looking forward to having company during the evening. It was something she didn't have all that often, and it would help to take her mind off her problems.

Hearing the click of the latch as her front door closed, Gloria shouted to Sean from the kitchen, "Just making a hot drink; I take it you'll have your usual coffee?"

"Yes, please, but I'm trying to reduce the size of my belly, so just one sugar please."

Gloria brought the drinks through and handed Sean his cup of coffee.

"Thanks. Well, what on earth do you think's going on? Two killings here, followed a few days later by two in Bristol! Someone's going for it, aren't they?"

"What do you mean?" asked Gloria, genuinely perplexed. "They're totally unrelated, aren't they?"

"You're joking aren't you? I mean, one double shooting is rare enough, but two? Anyway, it was on the news. Haven't you heard?"

"Heard what?"

"The results of the ballistic tests. Fucking hell, Glo, have you not been paying attention? It's been on the news."

"Sean, what on earth are you on about?"

He sighed and shook his head in disbelief. "There's a national database which collates evidence for all shooting incidents in the UK. They compare marks on bullets to all other shootings in England and Wales in the past three years."

Gloria could feel the hairs standing up on the back of her neck. She tried to sound nonchalant.

"Really? And they found something?"

"They certainly did! The bullets in Bristol were fired from the same gun as the Bloomsbury murders, the same gun that shot that drug dealer in the leg in St Giles High Street."

"But how can that be? I thought the man who shot the couple in Bloomsbury had been charged. If what you're saying is correct, he can't have killed the two in Bristol?"

"Exactly! It looks like he didn't. According to him, he threw the gun into Phoenix Gardens when he was chased by police. We've given the gardens a thorough search and found all the nettles in that area beaten down. It looks like someone got there before us. Delroy Derby swears it wasn't him who removed it, but someone did."

Once again, Gloria felt a tightening across her shoulders; she was getting used to this. The pressure came on again as she thought back to her conversation with Suzie; if she had spoken to the police, Gloria knew she would have difficult questions to answer.

"So, who do they think did the shootings now?"

"That's what we're trying to find out. One thing's for certain, whoever carried out the killings up here killed the two in Bristol as well. It looks like we're dealing with a serial killer."

"A serial killer! But what's their motive?"

"No-one's got any idea. Could be a nutter; could be someone who's suffered at the hands of robbers; could be a dealer muscling in on territory. We don't have a clue."

"You say they announced the ballistic result on the news?"

"Christ Glo, are you living in your own little bubble or something? Everyone's been talking about it since they announced it a couple of hours ago. You must be the only person in the country who knows nothing about these shootings!"

The irony was not lost on Gloria.

"Yes, I think you're probably right. Never mind though, I'll soon catch up, we'll watch the late news together at ten o'clock."

FIFTEEN

GLORIA ARRIVED AT work early on Wednesday morning. It was 25th November, exactly six weeks and one day before she was due to retire. She'd led a relatively quiet life up until now, and yet somehow, she'd shot and killed four people in the past two weeks. *This isn't how I imagined approaching my retirement,* she thought.

Sky News the previous evening had not been easy viewing for Gloria. Sean was absolutely correct: ballistic checks had indeed shown that the bullets came from the same gun. An Assistant Commissioner from the Metropolitan Police had been put in overall charge, because the original murders were in London, and there was to be close co-operation between the forces. The press was going wild with speculation about where and when the serial killer would strike next, and experts had been dragged in to give wildly conflicting opinions about possible motives.

As usual, there were two people sitting on the doorstep of the Job Centre when Gloria arrived that morning. They were rarely the same ones, just whoever arrived first. Gloria recognised these two: they were both scruffy looking Mediterranean men, one with skin tight dark-blue jeans, a black leather jacket and black shoes, the other with light blue jeans, a black duffle-coat and light-blue trainers. She knew that they had been arrested a few weeks earlier for assaulting her friend Paula, who cleaned at the local police station. She had claimed they were trying to rob her, but the charge went nowhere due to lack of evidence.

Although wary of them, Gloria felt safe enough, because of the numbers of people passing by and the crowd congregating outside the Job Centre. Stepping over an outstretched leg, Gloria pushed the intercom button and smiled at the camera over the door. The man wearing the leather jacket shifted his position slightly, causing his right foot to scrape across Gloria's left ankle. She turned and gave the man a hard stare.

He responded aggressively, "Got a problem granny?"

The door buzzed, and Gloria pulled it half open. "I think it's you that's got the problem. Just look at the two of you. Have you no self-respect?"

"You try having self-respect when you're forced to sleep in shit accommodation every night and claim benefits."

"Don't bother with the sob story, I've heard it all before," replied Gloria, stepping towards the safety of the building.

"Miserable old bitch!" duffle-coat man called after her.

The door was slowly closing behind Gloria, when she first heard the sound of someone inhaling, then dragging phlegm up from the back of their throat. Gloria knew what was coming next and stepped quickly inside, just as she heard the spit. She wasn't quick enough; before the door closed, a huge lump of phlegm landed on the back of Gloria's right calf muscle, making her shudder with revulsion.

Gloria forced the door closed. The man in the duffle coat wiped his mouth clean and glared at her; his friend was laughing. Gloria could feel the spittle trickling down the back of her leg, and ran up the stairs to the first-floor toilets.

Once inside, she kicked off her shoes and removed her tights, which she held gingerly between forefinger and thumb, before dropping them into a waste bin. She hiked up her skirt, and managed to get her right foot up into a basin, where she scrubbed the back of her leg raw. The sight of the slimy mess on her tights in the bin made her gag. After washing her calf and ankle clean, she hopped across to a cubicle and sat on the toilet seat lid. Pulling off reams of toilet paper, she thoroughly dried her leg and foot, tears of frustration and fury pouring down her face.

Gloria eventually left the cubicle and went to wash her hands in a basin. She'd stopped crying and was leaning forward, braced on both arms, staring at her face in the mirror. Carefully studying the lines on her face, thoughts drifted to recent events in her life. Suddenly, her mind became clear. Looking hard at her reflection, she moved her face even closer to the mirror, and as she did so, the reflection nodded at her and smiled.

Something inside her had snapped. Taking the lift up to her third-floor office, Gloria knew that life had changed. Fear of getting caught for the murders, and the anxiety about who had written the letters had all but disappeared. She'd reached the stage where she didn't care anymore. Things had to change, and it looked like she would have to change them herself.

SIXTEEN

"RIGHT DELROY, SIGN there for your personal effects, sign there for your release, and sign there to say how much you've enjoyed your stay with us." The release officer at Brixton Prison grinned widely at Delroy Derby, as he cracked the joke.

"Think you're a funny man, don't you?" replied Delroy, unsmiling.

"Come on, Delroy, I'm just trying to inject a little humour into this."

"You might think it's funny, but I don't. How would you like to be accused of two murders you didn't commit?"

"Ah, but you did shoot that other bloke didn't you; I mean, you admitted it."

"Listen man, you're innocent until proven guilty. He won't give evidence, and I'm not about to admit anything, so in the eyes of the law I'm innocent. Now stop playing fucking games and let me out of this shithole you call a prison."

The prison officer's eyes narrowed as he looked into Delroy's face.

"You're all the same; think you're the big men, don't you? Well, listen to me son, you'll be back here soon enough, and when you do, I'll be here waiting for you."

Lifting the huge bunch of keys from his belt clip, he selected a large, black, heavy-looking key, and opened the door into the prison yard.

"Get this piece of shit out of here," he said to the young guards waiting to walk Delroy to the prison gate.

The youngest guard eyed Delroy up and down as they headed towards the exit.

"Ignore him; he always has to have a final pop at prisoners when they're being released."

Delroy didn't answer, didn't even acknowledge that the young officer had addressed him.

The young guard tried again.

"I bet you were grateful for those two murders in Bristol. They really got you off the hook, didn't they?"

Delroy stopped at the exit gate, while the officer who'd remained silent unlocked it. Delroy then turned to face the guard who had spoken to him.

"Fuck you!" he said, before turning and walking away.

There was one thought in Delroy's head: *I'm going to find whoever fitted me up. Someone out there will have seen something, or will know something. Someone knows who's got that gun, and I'm going to move heaven and fucking earth to find them.*

He walked away without a backward glance.

SEVENTEEN

THE INCIDENT AT the door had left Gloria in a strange, fiery mood. Back in her office, she dragooned two of the biggest men she could find into going downstairs with her, and forcibly removing the two men from the doorway.

Her male colleagues were surprised by her naked aggression towards the men. Neither of them had ever heard her swear before, and they were equally impressed that she showed no fear, while standing toe-to-toe with the guy in the duffle coat as they shouted at each other. Eventually, still hurling abuse at Gloria and her colleagues, the men slouched off into a nearby alleyway.

Gloria actually felt quite good about herself following the confrontation, but on arriving home with freezing cold, bare legs, she began to question these new feelings of bravado. There was a side to her character emerging that she had never been aware of, a coldness and fearlessness that shocked her, and she realized it could land her in big trouble.

Her concern over the author of the letters was subsiding, however, because whoever it was, appeared to have no interest in handing her in, for the moment at least. She would do all she could to find out their identity, but in the meantime, she was more worried about the police investigation.

Following a twenty-minute phone call to her daughter, Gloria did a little tidying before settling down with a coffee to watch the Channel 4 news. Not far into the broadcast came news of the ongoing investigation into the murders in London and Bristol. Apparently, the police had received nearly fifteen hundred calls offering information, all of which had been logged and would be looked at in due course. The man now overseeing the investigation, Assistant Commissioner Graeme Skelton said, "We have several promising leads, which will be followed up as soon as possible. We now have over two hundred officers from the Avon and Somerset Police, the Metropolitan Police, and colleagues from other forces, engaged on this investigation. We are certain that the perpetrator, or perpetrators of these terrible crimes, will be swiftly brought to justice."

The news item concluded with CCTV film taken on the day of the Bristol shootings: three separate fuzzy images of different white men, whom the police wished to eliminate from their enquiries. Gloria smiled as she blew the steam from the top of her coffee cup, and sat comfortably back in her armchair.

"Which means you've got absolutely no idea who you're looking for, have you?" she said quietly to herself.

The next news item quickly wiped the smile from Gloria's face. A two-year-old girl in the Balsall Heath area of Birmingham had been stabbed in the face with a syringe by a drug addict, after an argument with the baby's mother, Sharon Dibbs. Sharon had apparently clashed with the addict a few days before, over him using a large bush in her front garden to hide from view while he injected speedballs, a mixture of crack cocaine and heroin, into his thigh. She had called police several times, but nothing had been done. In the end she had become exasperated, and argued heatedly with him, but he still refused to leave.

Two days later, as Sharon wheeled her two-year-old daughter, Charlotte, down the garden path to the front gate, she had seen the man behind the bush, his trousers around his ankles, once again injecting into his thigh. She'd tried to forcibly eject him from her property, and in the altercation the man had pulled a syringe from his thigh and lashed out at Sharon. Unfortunately, although he missed Sharon with his lunge, he succeeded in sticking the syringe into her daughter's cheek.

Police were called, and they arrested the man, identified as Alan Bramhall, a short while later. He was charged with unlawful wounding, and remanded in custody to attend Birmingham Magistrates Court the following morning. However, his identification as the perpetrator of the crime was ruled unsafe on technical grounds and, because there were no independent witnesses, Bramhall walked free from court today.

Gloria stared open mouthed at the television screen as Alan Bramhall strutted, smiling, through the reporters, pushing one of them out of the way. He refused to say anything, other than shouting a torrent of abused which had to be bleeped out.

Sharon Dibbs could hardly speak for crying during her short interview with the press outside the court.

"How can this be justice?" she sobbed. "We're waiting for results to see if Charlotte has contracted HIV, hepatitis, or anything else from that animal. The past few weeks have been absolute hell for me, my family and friends. How can that man have walked free?" She then broke down for several seconds, before composing herself and speaking into the camera.

"We now have to go home, knowing that, at any time, we may meet this man in the street, or even that he will come back into my garden. The police don't seem interested, and we feel alone and scared. I really hope that one day soon this man gets what he deserves. I just want someone to take this seriously."

Sharon was ushered away by her friends and family, through a throng of cameras.

Gloria played back the image of Bramhall's defiant gesture in her head, then Sharon's agonised plea; it was as if she had been speaking directly to Gloria. She turned the television off, needing peace and quiet after what she'd just witnessed. She also needed to calm down and think clearly. In her heart, though, Gloria already knew what she intended to do.

EIGHTEEN

RUBBING HER PALMS up and down her tired face and massaging her weary eyes, DCI Juliet Simpson stared into the cracked mirror of the first-floor ladies toilet at Holborn Police Station. The reflection showed a tall, attractive woman heading towards forty, with long wavy brown hair, and striking green eyes—although here, the strain was beginning to show. She was well aware that the heat was now really on her.

The public may have been watching Assistant Commissioner Skelton, giving his press conferences on the state of the investigation each night; there may have been a Detective Superintendent from the Avon and Somerset force, and a Detective Chief Superintendent from the Met assigned as well; there may have been advisers giving opinions from all over the country; but the close control of the investigation—the daily handle on all matters regarding the murders of four human beings—had been given over entirely to her. She wouldn't be forgiven if she failed. Finding the killer was non-negotiable.

Juliet Simpson had been happily married for seventeen years to her husband David—a dog handler for the Met—and they had two teenage daughters, Jenny and Sam. Although she still loved her husband, she had once been unfaithful to him.

Eight years ago, as a Detective Sergeant, she had started seeing a charismatic Detective Chief Superintendent she'd met at a Christmas Party. He had attained the dizzy heights of DCS at only thirty-eight years of age; his career was everything to him, and although he loved the company of women, he'd never married. At one time, Juliet had considered leaving her husband for him, when her marriage was going through a sticky patch, but in the end, she'd decided to stay with David.

Two years into the affair, her lover was promoted to the rank of Commander on the National Crime Squad, a job which would frequently take him away from the area, and the relationship ended; Graeme Skelton's career still meant everything to him.

In the intervening six years, Juliet had often wondered whether she'd made the right decision staying with her husband. On the few occasions their paths had crossed since the split, the chemistry between herself and Skelton still fizzed. They exchanged glances, the occasional brush of hands when sitting together at a table, or standing a little too closely to each other in a lift.

Shortly after the incident room had been set up, it became clear to Juliet that he was considering assigning her to the job, which would be called Operation Chiddingstone. She'd argued with Graeme that day-to-day control should be assigned to someone more experienced, but he managed to persuade her that this was her big opportunity, and fought off opposition from several other senior officers to give Juliet overall control.

"It's my way of saying thank you for all the good times," he told her in a private moment in his office. He planted a gentle kiss on her cheek, a kiss that lingered just a little too long to be merely friendly.

"But I'm worried Graeme, I honestly don't know if I'm capable of handling an investigation of this size."

"Listen Jules, you're the best detective I've ever known, and I'm not just saying that because we fucked for a couple of years. If you can't solve this job, then none of those other wankers can either. Anyway, I'm the man in overall charge, and if anyone gets it in the neck for failing to catch this nutter, it'll be me, and I couldn't give a monkey's arse what they say!"

"CLOSE THE DOOR please, Bill."

Bill Jarvis was a Detective Inspector posted to Holborn Police Station, working for DCI Simpson on the murder investigations. He'd been the last of those summoned to the Conference Room at Holborn Police Station to arrive for the morning meeting, and dutifully complied with his DCI's request, closing the door quietly. The rest of the officers seated around the table were silent, making Bill feel a little conspicuous as he took his seat.

Nine other people were seated at the table, none lower than the rank of Detective Sergeant. All eyes were on the two people at the head of the table: AC Graeme Skelton, and DCI Juliet Simpson. Skelton was the first to speak.

"Thank you all for coming. I'll get straight to the point. I've just been given a ten-minute roasting by one of the Home Secretary's junior ministers. In short, he reminded me that it's been two weeks since the first murders, and four days since the nation was gripped by the notion of a serial killer being out there. I can tell you he made me feel most uncomfortable, when I had to inform him that we have made *no fucking progress at all*."

AC Skelton banged his fist hard on the large oval table, causing several people to jump and coffee to spill from two of the polystyrene cups.

"I want results," he continued, "which isn't likely to happen unless your officers start pulling their fucking fingers out! I need them out there getting their hands dirty, speaking to the street-life, the drug dealers and the local villains. Not sitting in offices shining their arses, pushing bits of paper around their desks, and talking on the fucking phone! I want some pressure applied to the most likely suspects; one of them will know who's done this, so let's start turning up the heat. If they won't talk voluntarily, then fucking well arrest them, and we'll speak to them on our terms. At least it will look to the public as though we're actually doing something!"

Juliet Simpson shifted uncomfortably in her seat; this tirade had taken her completely by surprise; she was more than aware that people's attention was not only focussed on Skelton's words, but also on her reaction to them. Ex-lover or not, Skelton clearly wasn't prepared to let the enquiry drift along. He'd decided to take matters into his own hands, by motivating his troops with his own personal style of bullying.

AC Skelton ended by reminding them all that although this type of case had the potential to be the making of their careers, it equally had the potential to be their undoing. As he sat down, Juliet knew that this would be her one and only chance to wrestle back some of the initiative, an opportunity to recover some pride and personal standing among her fellow officers. Rising to her feet, she launched straight into her own rant.

"You've heard what the guv'nor said. It might be my arse on the line with this job, but several of you will come down with me if we don't get a result. At the moment none of your teams have responded with anything of significance, and the public can't believe it—they think we're doing fuck all! Surely, I don't have to remind you that the first killings were a double shooting in the West End of London, during the early evening. Someone must have seen or heard something! It's our job to find them—and find them quickly!"

She carried on for several more minutes, before reinforcing exactly what she wanted from each individual team. Juliet closed the meeting with a few quietly spoken, but forceful words.

"If this nutter kills again, the pressure will really be on, and it's well within the bounds of possibility that he might. This isn't like other murder enquiries you may have worked on. This could end up being a protracted enquiry into an utterly ruthless and cold-blooded serial killer, the like of which we haven't seen in the UK before. We have to catch this person, and catch them soon. Are there any questions?"

The room fell silent, save for a few rustlings where people were tidying their papers.

"Right," concluded Simpson, "let's get to work then."

NINETEEN

GLORIA WAS NEXT in the queue at the newsagents, behind two old ladies. She'd been listening to their conversation about the murders and was pleasantly surprised to hear that they were firmly on the side of the killer. They both believed that someone was bound to take matters into their own hands sooner or later, because crime on the streets was getting out of control.

The headline on the Sun newspaper was, GUN! GUN! GONE!, this headline printed over the image of four coffins, and the shape of a male head in silhouette with a question mark on it. Most of the other newspapers carried the story on their front pages, all trying to cash in on the growing public interest, and general speculation about the identity of the killer.

"I wonder how long it'll take them to catch him?" said one of the women, choosing a magazine and paying the man behind the counter.

"I don't know," replied her friend. "They'll get him eventually. They always get killers like this, don't they?"

"That's true, but there were plenty of people at the pub last night who didn't want him to be caught."

"Really?"

"Oh yes. People reckon that the killer is someone who's fed up with all this street crime and decided to take matters into their own hands."

"Well, it wouldn't be a bad thing if a few more scumbags were taken off the streets!" The woman laughed out loud.

Gloria became aware of murmurs of agreement from people in the queue, all of whom had apparently been listening to the elderly friends' discussion with interest. She did not join in.

The rest of her Thursday morning walk to work was filled with thoughts of the story on the news last night, of poor Sharon Dibbs and her daughter, whose lives were being ruined by Bramhall, combined with images of people in the shop queue, and their evident approval of anyone prepared to take on the 'scumbags'.

FOR THE NEXT two weeks, as November slowly gave way to December, Gloria became more and more comfortable with who she'd become, and the way in which her life had transformed so unexpectedly. The police investigation was heading nowhere, and during Sean Aylen's last two visits, he gave her chapter and verse about just how little they had to go on. She'd noticed how television appeals for information and witnesses were becoming more and more infrequent, yet increasingly desperate.

Gloria had heard nothing more from the mysterious letter writer, and they'd obviously not passed their knowledge onto the police. Suzie still seemed the most likely suspect, but there was nothing to be gained by confronting her, for now.

Gradually, she ceased to feel so alone. She was beginning to realise that there were thousands, possibly tens of thousands of people out there who felt exactly the same as her. The only difference was that she had done something about it, albeit unintentionally, up to now. She also knew that, although all those people may not have been present when she committed the acts, they were with her in spirit, and that brought her comfort.

Even on her weekly visits to help out at the local soup kitchen, Gloria continued to be encouraged by what she heard. Many of those she spoke to simply refused to condemn the killer. Although most of them lived either on the street or in hostels, they didn't identify with or sympathise with the victims. One of her regulars, an elderly homeless man called Donald, spoke to her as he stood in the queue for food.

"Those four who've been killed were all nasty fuckers. Looks like someone's simply had enough and decided to take action. I've got no problem at all with the killer. Those two killed in Bloomsbury treated me like shit whenever I bumped into them. They're no great loss to the world."

The date on the digital clock in Gloria's office ticked over to four thirty-five. It was twenty-five minutes before she could start her three-day weekend. A weekend which Gloria had carefully chosen to mark a turning point in her life. A weekend during which she wanted to finally make a difference. A weekend during which she intended to carry out her first premeditated killing.

GLORIA HAD CHECKED maps of the area around Sutton Gardens where Sharon Dibbs lived; she'd read news reports about the incident involving Alan Bramhall on the internet, and interviews with local residents suggested that Bramhall spent most of his days hanging around the flats, or sitting in the old-fashioned brick bus-shelter. *No wonder poor Sharon feels trapped*, she thought.

Several incidents since she'd killed the two muggers in Bristol had conspired to lead Gloria down this path. The confrontation on the steps of her workplace, where she'd been spat on; the tears and desperate words of Sharon, whose baby had been stabbed with a blood-stained syringe; the sheer lack of remorse from Alan Bramhall; public support for the killer; and finally, strangely, her growing certainty that she would eventually be caught. Before that happened, she intended to make a difference.

At home time, Gloria packed her things away and wished her colleagues a good weekend.

"What are you doing for the weekend Glo?" one asked.

"I'm visiting the National Gallery, and the Portrait Gallery on Saturday; I could spend weeks in them, but one day will have to do."

"Sounds fun, enjoy!"

"Thanks. You too."

With that brief exchange, Gloria walked from the office, down the stairs and out of the door. In five minutes, she was home. She was particularly pleased how quickly she'd thought of the galleries answer, which dove-tailed beautifully as an alibi with her real plans for Saturday, a trip to Birmingham!

Gloria slept poorly on Thursday night; the seriousness of what she was contemplating was beginning to weigh heavily on her. Her victims all had families somewhere who would grieve for their son, daughter, brother or sister; even Alan Bramhall presumably had someone, somewhere, whose life would be turned upside down by his death. But then she remembered Sharon's face as she made her plea for help, and Gloria's determination returned; she, at least, was listening to Sharon and, what's more, she was willing to do something about it.

FRIDAY DAWNED BITTERLY cold, and Gloria awoke to feel an icy draught on her face; those windows really did need replacing. She covered her head with the duvet and must have drifted back off to sleep, because the next thing she heard was the bell of St Giles-in-the-Fields Church chiming. *Oh fuck! It can't be nine already!*

Yawning, she leaned over to look at her alarm clock and was horrified to find that it wasn't nine o'clock at all, it was eleven; she had overslept badly.

"Bugger!" she shouted, leaping from the bed, and quickly wrapping herself in her dressing gown.

Gloria was annoyed with herself because she'd promised to phone her daughter at ten. In her last call, Sandra had told Gloria that she needed advice about something; she didn't have time to explain what it was, but Gloria knew something was wrong. Sandra had said that she was only free until about eleven on Friday. So it was already too late.

Checking National Rail enquiries, Gloria researched train times to Birmingham New Street and found they were more than manageable. She found she was shaking with a mixture of fear and excitement at the thought of tomorrow's plans.

Memories kept invading her mind: being threatened by the woman holding the blood-stained syringe; the attack at her own front door; the old woman being beaten in the underpass. Finally, the incident which for some reason appalled her more than the others: being spat on as she tried to enter her place of work. And then, of course, there was Sharon from the news, and her poor daughter...

Having decided to cover her tracks for the trip to Birmingham, she walked to a local charity shop where she bought herself a three-quarter length purple woollen coat, a colour that everyone would know she hated; in another she bought a black woolly hat.

Back home, Gloria collected her post from her pigeon-hole just inside the communal front door. Once inside her flat, she placed her purchases into a large orange Sainsbury's carrier bag. She'd decided to travel in a pair of brown suede boots, black casual trousers (tucked into the boots) and her favourite quilted beige mac. She would change coat and hat on the underground, just before arriving at Euston Station.

Checking through her small pile of post, the sight of another plain brown envelope, once again with nothing written on the outside, stopped her dead. Shaking, she opened it. *YOU REALLY ARE A HIGHLY PROFESSIONAL KILLER.*

How had they gained entry through the communal door? It was the second time someone had managed to get through the secure door to leave her a letter. Who on earth could it be? The only person she could think of, who had access to the building was Mano, the Thai lady in number 7. She certainly knew that Gloria had been attacked shortly before the shootings in Barter Street. But what would she stand to gain from sending letters like this? And what on earth did the author mean by, 'highly professional killer'? That was the last thing she would describe herself as.

Gloria couldn't waste any more time worrying about the letters. Right now, everything was in place for her trip to Birmingham, and nothing was going to deflect her. She checked the Glock and decided there was no longer any point in placing it into a plastic bag. The goalposts had changed. She checked the number of bullets left in the magazine: there were nine.

That evening Gloria phoned Sandra, but got no reply. She would have to leave it until she reached Birmingham the following morning.

She stared, fascinated, at herself in the bathroom mirror, examining at close hand her neatly bobbed grey hair and lined face. Hardly the image of a professional killer! Her mind was almost blank, and a slight smile began to curl up one side of her mouth. She had a strange feeling of liberation, as she turned the bathroom light out and headed for bed. Nervous though she was, sleep came quickly to Gloria.

TWENTY
Saturday 12th December 1998

BY THE TIME the alarm sounded, Gloria was already up, showered and dressed, with the Glock in the front pouch of her handbag. She had been to the cash-point to draw out a hundred pounds, and was now waiting for two slices of bread to pop out of the toaster. She had woken up just before five with her heart thumping and her skin feeling cold and clammy, and decided there was no point trying to get back to sleep. She was terrified, but she would entertain no thoughts of backing out, or changing her mind.

After breakfast she watched a short report on police progress into the shootings which were now barely getting a mention on the news—it had been three weeks since the killings in Bristol, and with little progress, interest was waning. However, the report reiterated that the police—despite having arrested over thirty people and interviewed several hundred—were no nearer identifying the culprit than they had been on day one.

DCI Simpson made a brief statement to the assembled press on the steps outside Holborn Police Station. She looked tired and stressed.

"Someone out there must know who committed these terrible crimes. Perhaps you are the perpetrator and are ready to hand yourself in; perhaps you think you know who the killer is but are not quite sure; perhaps you think it's a member of your family and have divided loyalties. Whatever your situation, if you have any information, then please contact Operation Chiddingstone, or the Bristol Murder Room. Thank you." She turned abruptly and walked back inside before any questions could be asked.

Gloria realised with a start that it was almost time to go. A quick check confirmed that everything was in place, so she left the flat and walked out into the light drizzle.

A speedy five-minute walk to Tottenham Court Road tube station, and a quick change of coat while waiting on the platform. Gloria waited until she was on the underground train before she pulled on her black woolly hat. After the ten-minute tube journey to Euston, she found herself in a queue for tickets, feeling comfortable that she still had plenty of time to catch her train to Birmingham New Street. She was now wearing her purple coat and black woolly hat. She really didn't want to look like Gloria Jones on her arrival.

Boarding the train, she settled into a window seat with a newspaper she'd bought at the kiosk. She'd been anxiously scanning the crowds to see if she recognised anyone during her time at Euston, but she saw no one she knew. As the train pulled out of the station, she gave a deep sigh and settled down, avoiding eye contact with other passengers. She wanted to be left alone with her thoughts.

The journey passed without incident, and as the train neared Birmingham Gloria calmly moved about three carriages away to use the toilet. Once inside, she completed her transformation, swapping brown suede boots for a pair of black patent leather flats. She opened the carrier bag, and placed her suede boots inside. Along with her beige mac, she now had a complete change of clothes for the return journey to London.

The weather was overcast as the train pulled into Birmingham. Gloria left the toilet and joined the mass of people leaving the train.

ONCE OUTSIDE, SHE made sure she was far enough away from the station so that tannoy announcements couldn't be heard when she finally made that important call to Sandra.

"Hi darling, it's mum. Sorry I didn't call yesterday, I was whacked out and woke up much later than usual."

"Don't worry, Mum. It's just that I've got a bit of a problem developing here, and I need advice. You know our estate has always been safe for the kids to play outside—well, it's not safe now."

Gloria could feel herself stiffening with concern as she listened to her daughter. Sandra had always been the strong, practical sort, and the note of almost panic in her voice alarmed Gloria.

"Oh no! Why? What's the matter?"

"There's been a car turning up at all times of the day and night, a large black BMW. I've seen all sorts of undesirables gathering on the green; they swarm around this car as soon as it arrives. I'm sure they're selling drugs."

"The bastards! How horrible for you."

"Everyone's fed up to the back teeth with it. We've called the police repeatedly and they say they've stopped the vehicle twice, and it was clean both times. They seem to think we're paranoid, but it's obvious to anyone with a brain what's going on. My friend Laura is frantic with worry because her 14-year-old son's been hanging around waiting for the car. He's getting aggressive at home, constantly asking for money and skipping school. She's sure that he's being turned into an addict by these bastards. She's a single mum, so she's finding it fucking hard."

Sandra's voice was beginning to crack. Her use of the F-word was unusual for her and told Gloria all she needed to know. Gloria could feel the familiar anger flaming inside her, but she needed to be very careful with her reply; she couldn't afford to give anything away.

"Sandra, I'm so sorry. I don't know what to say."

"It's just that I daren't let Katie and James out alone at the moment. I know they're fourteen and twelve, but the horrible types hanging round the green really worry me. Hopefully the police will catch the dealers, and they'll get locked up for a while."

"Look Sandra, find out everything you can, and report anything of interest to the police. Call them every time the car appears; they'll soon get fed up and do something about it. I can't really think of anything else at the moment. Just make life as uncomfortable for them as you can."

"Thanks for calling mum. I just needed to get everything off my chest. Anyway, enough of my problems, what's happening with the investigation into your local murders? Looks like they're drawing a blank."

"Yes, I'm afraid they have so far. It's scary knowing there's some nutter with a gun wandering about the streets."

"It must be. Sorry, I feel awful bothering you with my problems—they seem small in comparison. Where are you at the moment? I can hear a lot of traffic noise in the background."

"I'm treating myself to a day at the National Gallery and the Portrait Gallery. I've been meaning to visit them for some time. I'm standing outside St Martin's in the Fields, opposite Trafalgar Square."

"Okay, have a lovely day. Thanks for the chat, and don't worry about things here, we'll sort it out. I suppose I just needed someone to sound off to. Bye mum. Love you."

"Love you too; I'll call you next week." Sandra hung up, leaving Gloria seething with anger. The call had reinforced her steely determination to complete her mission. She walked quickly to the taxi rank, climbed inside the first taxi in the queue and said, "Sutton Gardens in Balsall Heath please."

TWENTY-ONE

"SEVEN POUNDS please love."

Gloria handed the taxi driver a ten-pound note, smiled, and said, "Keep the change."

"Thanks very much," he said, placing the note into his wallet. He smiled back at her, before driving away.

Gloria had recognised Sharon's small terraced house, with the large bush in the front garden, as the taxi had turned into Sutton Gardens. She'd asked the driver to stop a little way past the house, near a brick bus shelter. Sutton Gardens was a very wide street, with two lanes of traffic in each direction, and a grass verge on either side.

Before deciding on a strategy, Gloria thought she needed to learn more about Alan Bramhall. Feeling hungry and thirsty, she decided to look for somewhere to eat; she knew it would be easy to make bad decisions on an empty stomach.

Crossing the junction, she reached the bus shelter and found an old couple sitting inside. It was one of those old-fashioned brick bus shelters, substantial and resembling a little house. She stepped inside.

"Excuse me, is there a café around here, I'm parched."

"Certainly love," answered the man. "If you walk to the end of Sutton Gardens and turn left, there's a café along there. It's about a five-minute walk, that's all."

"That's lovely, thanks for your help. Enjoy your day!"

"You too love," said the old lady.

Ten minutes later found Gloria with a steaming cup of tea and a huge toasted teacake inside the Welcome Café. She had chosen a small table facing out towards the pavement and was pondering how to broach the subject of Alan Bramhall with other customers without being too obvious. She knew that he was always around this area; she knew he had no remorse, and she knew he had no respect for Sharon Dibbs, her daughter, or anyone else for that matter.

Gloria took the time to enjoy every mouthful of her tea and toasted teacake thoroughly. When she'd finished, she stood up and walked to the counter to pay; she then intended to drop Bramhall's name into conversation with the man behind the counter.

She didn't hear the bell as the door opened behind her, but the man behind the counter shouted, "Go away. I've already told you you're not welcome in here. I'll call the police!"

"Why would you call the fucking pigs, you wanker? You all believe that bitch Dibbs, don't you? What about my side of the story?"

Gloria felt the hairs standing up on the back of her neck. She turned slowly to see the man she recognised from the TV as Alan Bramhall.

Another man behind the counter said, "Look Alan, we've all put up with your disgusting behaviour for years. No one likes you, you're a pain in the arse. Now get out!"

"Wankers!" shouted Bramhall at the top of his voice.

Gloria watched as Bramhall moved towards the door, and swung an arm across the table where two middle-aged ladies were sitting, knocking their salt, pepper, and vinegar onto the floor. He stormed out of the door, slamming it hard as he left, before turning and spitting onto the large café window, and walking off towards Sutton Gardens.

Gloria had been surprised at many things about Bramhall. How small he was, no more than 5'6" tall; that he absolutely reeked of body odour and feet (she could smell him from three metres away); how no-one other than the cafe staff stood up to him; and the clear contempt he felt for everyone, apart from himself.

With a look of grim determination on her face, Gloria picked up her bags, then walked out of the café toward Sutton Gardens. It was time for a chat with Mr Bramhall.

WHEN GLORIA REACHED the junction with Sutton Gardens, she spotted Bramhall fifty metres in front of her; he'd turned right into Sutton Gardens and was walking lazily down the right-hand pavement. She realised that in another hundred metres, he would be approaching Sharon Dibbs' house, and for a moment feared he might take revenge on poor Sharon for what had happened to him in the café. Gloria followed quickly, trying to close the distance between herself and Bramhall without being too obvious. She felt an overwhelming urge to be there for Sharon, if needed.

A young family was coming towards her, the woman pushing a pram and the man holding the hand of a small toddler. Within a few moments they were face-to-face with Bramhall, who refused to step aside, holding his line while walking slowly onwards and forcing the woman to move the pram into a gateway to avoid bumping into him.

Her partner shouted something at Bramhall, who simply carried on walking, only acknowledging the man's comments with a raised right hand—middle finger extended. *Bramhall, you really are a nasty little shit*, Gloria thought.

On reaching the traffic lights at the crossroads, Bramhall sauntered across diagonally and reached the bus shelter. He stopped for a few seconds, looked all around, then turned and walked inside.

Gloria followed exactly the same route, but walked deliberately past the front of the shelter, glancing casually in as she did so. She could clearly see into the right-hand recess and the rear benching, which was empty; she could also see that there was no one else in the shelter. Bramhall must be seated in the left-hand recess, almost totally hidden from the view of passing vehicles.

Walking on a little further, Gloria stopped to look around. Although the area wasn't busy with pedestrians, there were still one or two people around who might notice the sound of a gun being fired. It was also a residential area, although people were not likely to hear the retort from the inside of a brick bus shelter in their homes.

This was so frustrating! She had Bramhall exactly where she wanted him; there were no CCTV cameras that she could see; no-one knew her here and with her purple coat and black woolly hat no-one would be likely to recognise her. She might never get a better opportunity. But at the same time, she knew she needed more cover for the sound of the gun firing.

Gloria forced herself to think calmly and consider her options. Standing at the junction, she noticed that every time the lights changed to green in favour of the dual carriageway, the roar from the cars, trucks, and lorries increased significantly as they revved their engines to pull away. This lasted for roughly ten seconds, until the traffic was flowing freely. There was one major factor in her favour: Alan Bramhall was seated inside that substantial brick-built shelter, which would certainly contain most of the sound. If she timed it with the noise of traffic pulling away, it might just drown out the sound of the shot.

Gloria's mind was made up. She hadn't come this far to chicken out now. Striding purposefully towards the bus shelter, she stepped inside. She'd already unclipped the front pouch of her handbag and her right hand was gripping the gun's handle. Looking to her left, she saw Bramhall tightly tucked into the corner, his knees drawn up to his chest with his feet on the wooden bench, his arms wrapped around his knees. She could see that his brown hair was filthy and matted, but was surprised to see that his overcoat looked almost new, whereas his black tracksuit bottoms were clearly too big for him, and his white trainers were almost black with filth.

He glanced up at her, didn't say a word, but gobbed on the floor. Gloria was repulsed, recalling the sensation of spittle running down her leg at work. She stepped outside to check the pavements for pedestrians and was pleased to see that people had drifted away from the immediate area. In fact, apart from a group of six youngsters sitting on a wall at the far end of Sutton Gardens, and an old couple some distance away on the opposite side of the dual carriageway, no one was nearby.

Walking back inside the shelter, Gloria deliberately sat down slightly closer to Bramhall than he, or she, felt comfortable with.

"Fucking give me some breathing space, you old cow; what's wrong with the rest of the bench?"

"I don't like your attitude young man; in fact, I didn't like it when I saw you on the news the other night."

Bramhall was almost incandescent with rage.

"That fucking bitch Dibbs has ruined my life! I used to have respect round here, now I've got nothing! I've got HIV and Hepatitis B, and I hope her fucking baby gets them as well, that'll fucking teach her!"

Gloria had heard enough; she pulled the Glock from her handbag and pointed it at Bramhall's head. She was just over a metre away from him and was surprised how much she enjoyed seeing the terror in his eyes.

"What the fuck, lady? I didn't mean it. Don't shoot me, I don't want to die!"

He'd pulled his left hand up in front of his face, in a futile defensive gesture. His eyes had the same yellow tinge as the woman she'd killed in Bloomsbury, his teeth were rotten and his breath was rancid.

The traffic lights changed in favour of the dual carriageway, heralding the roar of engines which seemed to drown out most noise. Smiling at Bramhall's fear, Gloria quietly said, "Good riddance, you scumbag," and pulled the trigger.

Once again, everything seemed to happen in slow motion; the bullet passed through Bramhall's left hand and entered his right eye. She was surprised that there wasn't a splash of blood behind him on the wall. Presumably, this time the bullet had slowed down on its passage through his hand and had lodged in his skull.

Bramhall's head rocked back, and then forward, like a nodding dog on a car parcel shelf, finally coming to rest on his chest. She knew he was dead, but he would look to anyone who happened to be passing, like just another drunk having a kip in the bus shelter.

EVAN BALDOCK

TWENTY-TWO

HER HEART WAS hammering. Had she been heard? Had she been seen? Panic was beginning to set in, but over-riding the panic was another emotion – exhilaration. She certainly felt no shame at all for murdering a monster like Alan Bramhall.

Hurriedly putting the Glock back into her handbag, Gloria stepped out of the bus shelter, checking to see if any splashes of blood had got on her coat. Thankfully, there were none. There were no pedestrians in the vicinity and no-one appeared to be coming towards the bus shelter.

She began to relax a little. It seemed that nobody had heard the sound of the gun firing, or if they had, they hadn't realised what the noise was. Why would they recognise gunfire in a quiet suburb of Birmingham? Most people hearing a sound like that at a road junction where vehicles were pulling away would think it was a car backfiring.

Gloria walked to the junction and turned left. She had no idea where she was going—she didn't even register the name of the road she was walking along—but she understood the need to get far away from the scene as soon as possible. She didn't want to be anywhere near that bus shelter when Bramhall's body was discovered.

After half-a-mile Gloria turned left onto a busy road and saw a bus at a crowded stop. She joined the queue and paid £1.50 for her journey to the City Centre. Looking at her watch. It was just after twelve. She couldn't believe that she'd been in Birmingham for less than two hours, yet she had successfully completed the job.

The bus pulled into the City Centre at twelve-forty. Feeling the need to leave Birmingham as soon as possible, Gloria walked to Birmingham New Street Station, where the next train to London was due to leave shortly.

Showing her ticket at the barrier, she crossed to the correct platform. As soon as she had boarded, she went straight into a toilet and removed the purple coat, black shoes and black woolly hat, replacing them with her brown suede boots, beige mac, and neatly brushing her grey hair.

Ten minutes later, she was reclining in her seat as the train slowly pulled out from the station. Gloria stared long and hard out of the window, lost deep in thought about what was happening to her; she now looked like Gloria again, but she wondered exactly who she had become.

At Euston, Gloria joined the crush of passengers heading for the ticket barrier; she felt reasonably safe once more. Wandering into a side street, she found what she was looking for: three large wheelie bins close to the pavement edge.

Lifting up the lid of the middle bin, Gloria looked inside and saw that it was only two-thirds full. She reached in and dropped the orange Sainsbury's carrier bag into one of the back corners. It was completely inconspicuous among all the rubbish.

After closing the lid, Gloria breathed a sigh of relief, walked back to Euston Station and made her way down into the underground.

Less than twenty minutes later, she was walking through her front door and heading straight for the kettle. She took the Glock out of her handbag and placed it back in the box of Cornflakes, before collapsing full length onto the settee, grinning with satisfaction. She'd done it!

Gloria had only been out for eight hours, yet so much had happened. Realising she had the chance to be seen in one of the galleries, giving strength to her alibi, she swiftly drank her tea, and grabbed a sausage roll from the fridge. The Portrait Gallery was a ten-minute walk, and she was there by four o'clock, giving her two hours to learn about the latest exhibits.

Shortly after arriving at the Portrait Gallery, while browsing through Annie Smurkovic's photographic exhibition, Gloria felt a tap on her right shoulder. Turning around, she was delighted to see Sean Aylen.

"Hi Glo, didn't know you were a fan of photography."

"Hello! You know me, Sean, a real culture vulture! Anyway, what's a hard-nosed copper like you doing in the Portrait Gallery? Are you looking for someone?"

"I'm sure I've mentioned my passion for photography." He winked.

"Oh sure. You've gone on about it incessantly, since the day I met you!"

Sean laughed and nodded.

"Alright, well, I've met this wonderful Irish girl called Gail at the photography club, and I'm desperately trying to impress her. I thought that coming to the Smurkovic exhibition, then talking with her about it, without sounding ignorant, might do the trick. I know she's a big fan. What do you think; am I making myself look a complete tosser, or am I doing the right thing?"

Gloria chuckled. "Well, I'd be impressed if it was me!"

"Thanks, that means a lot. I've got to be heading off in a minute. There's another briefing this evening about lack of progress in the Chiddingstone investigation. We're expecting a serious bollocking from the boss, since we've still got precisely nowhere. Oh, there was one other thing. While follow-up enquiries were being carried out today you weren't in, and a foreign lady told the officer that she'd seen you being attacked near the front door. Why didn't you mention it?"

Gloria was instantly on her guard; she had no idea exactly how much Sean knew, and was feeling distinctly uncomfortable about the way this was going.

"Oh that." She needed to think quickly. "It was just a couple of junkies trying to get my bag. To be honest, it was nothing, and I'd forgotten all about it."

"Oh, it's just that this lady says you were pretty badly hurt, and she thought it might have been the same couple who were shot in Barter Street."

Gloria was struggling to keep her voice from wavering. Sean's tone sounded almost accusatory and suddenly Gloria was seeing Sean the policeman, rather than the man who was her friend. She needed to stick to her story.

"Really? No, I've seen their pictures on TV and it definitely wasn't the same couple. This pair were much younger; I've not seen them around before or since."

"You're sure? This is really important." Sean seemed to be watching her reaction closely.

Looking straight into his eyes, Gloria said, "Absolutely certain." She didn't like this; she felt terrible lying to him, but she had no intention of going to prison – not just yet.

Sean stared at her for a couple of seconds longer, then he suddenly seemed satisfied, his manner changing in an instant.

"Brilliant. That's good enough for me. I'll remove that action from our list and show it as completed. Got to go now mate, we'll speak soon. Bye."

"Bye Sean, hope it goes well with Gail."

Sean gave a broad smile, raised his eyebrows suggestively, and walked off down the stairs. Gloria found a nearby seat and sat down heavily, her heart thumping hard in her chest. That had been far too close for comfort.

She consoled herself with the knowledge that she now had a cast-iron alibi for the murder of Alan Bramhall. What could be better than having been observed, and interrogated, at an art gallery in London by a Police Sergeant?

TWENTY-THREE

JULIET SIMPSON KNOCKED firmly on the office door of Assistant Commissioner Graeme Skelton. She'd been working on intelligence files in her office, when a young DI had informed her that she was required in the AC's office immediately. She had no idea why she was being summoned like this, but sensed all was not well.

"Come in."

Opening the door, Juliet saw Graeme Skelton at his desk, flanked by Detective Chief Superintendent Hook, and a woman she knew to be the head of Human Resources—not a good sign. The atmosphere could have been cut with a blunt knife. Skelton briefly looked up.

"Hello Jules. Please sit down." He indicated the chair across the desk. His lips were pursed, and his eyes were now firmly fixed on his desk.

Juliet sat down, looked into the eyes of each one in turn, then directed her gaze at Skelton.

"You wanted to see me, sir?"

Graeme Skelton lifted his eyes to meet Juliet's gaze, breathed in heavily, exhaled and said: "I'll come straight to the point, Jules. I'm relieving you as OIC of Operation Chiddingstone. The new OIC will be DCS Hook," he nodded in the direction of Hook, sitting to his right. "And he takes command as of now."

She'd feared that something like this would happen, but she was still shocked. How could this man, that she had cared for so much, replace her, especially as he'd practically forced the job on her in the first place?

"I don't know what to say, sir. May I ask why?"

Skelton looked embarrassed and fidgeted in his chair.

"It was not my decision Jules, nor the decision of anyone here."

"So, whose decision was it?"

"The Management Board."

That was a serious blow. The Management Board comprises the Commissioner, Deputy Commissioner, four Assistant Commissioners, and two very high-ranking civilian officers—top brass. She said nothing, but shrugged her shoulders in resignation and nodded her head.

"I want you to know that I voted for you to remain, but the motion to replace you was passed by seven votes to one. There is immense pressure to make real progress on this, both from on high and the public."

Hearing that Skelton had supported her took a little of the sting out of the rejection; Juliet forced a smile.

"What will my role be now?"

Skelton again shifted uneasily.

"You're being taken off the case Jules, completely. A new role has been created for you, in charge of public reassurance."

She was genuinely startled and outraged.

"You mean all the hours I've put in, all the work I've done, and all the knowledge and experience I've gained leading this operation is being flushed down the toilet?"

"Sorry Jules, that's the Management Board's decision." Suddenly, his voice took on a steely edge, and he squared his shoulders. "Can you please clear your desk in the incident room? Then report to the duties office, where you will be taken to your new desk."

Juliet sat motionless for a few seconds, then slowly stood and walked out. Once outside AC Skelton's office, she clenched her fists and punched the wall, hard. So much for *if anyone gets it in the neck... it'll be me!*

"Fuck!"

"Are you okay ma'am?" A passing WPC looked in concern at Juliet.

Composing herself, Juliet smiled at the officer and said, "Yes, thank you. I've just had some bad news, I'll be fine in a minute."

She walked to the end of the corridor and entered the ladies' toilet. Relieved to see no-one else was about, she went into a cubicle, lowered the toilet lid, sat down, and howled in frustration. She knew how humiliating it would be once the officers under her command learned of her fall from grace.

After ten minutes, Juliet began to regain some command of herself. She left the cubicle, stood at the washbasin in front of the mirror, and wiped away the black mascara streaks around her eyes and down her cheeks. She spent a few minutes touching up her make-up, brushed her hair, pushed her shoulders back, and walked out of the room.

As she slowly cleared her desk, Juliet decided to make an announcement; she would be the one to tell the troops. She walked slowly from her office, stood in the centre of the main Operation Chiddingstone incident room and shouted, "Ladies and Gents, your attention please!" The thirty or forty officers present stopped what they were doing and turned to face her.

"I have just been relieved of command as OIC for Chiddingstone; the new OIC is DCS Hook. I would like to thank you all for the hard work and diligence you've shown in my time as boss. I'll miss you all, and I'm sure you'll continue working just as hard for DCS Hook. Thank you."

Juliet returned to her office, aware of the shocked murmuring behind her, and continued clearing her desk, saying "Thank you" to the stream of officers who popped their head inside the door to offer their commiserations, or to wish her well.

She thought back over her career, about how hard she'd worked to get where she was, especially as a woman on the force, and how it all appeared to have been for nothing. This type of snub stayed with you throughout what was left of your career.

In that moment, Juliet's whole mind-set changed; the Metropolitan Police would never again command her loyalty, it just wasn't worth it.

SEAN AYLEN HURRIED back to Holborn Police Station, and wrote off the outstanding action for Gloria Jones to be interviewed, marking it as completed. This meant that there were now no leads at all regarding the Bloomsbury Shootings, which in turn meant grief from the bosses at the evening briefing.

Forty officers crowded into the briefing room, and once again it was Assistant Commissioner Skelton who stood up to address the gathering.

"Right, I won't waffle on about the number of calls we've received, the number of people we've interviewed, or the number of arrests we've made. What I will say, is that there is still some nutcase out there who's killed four people, and we don't have a single lead to point us in his direction.

"Some of you may have seen the breaking news reports about the shooting of Alan Bramhall in Balsall Heath, Birmingham, around noon today. He had recently been the subject of news stories, and was alleged to have stabbed the baby of a local woman in the face with a used syringe. This bastard had HIV, and Hepatitis B, so maybe someone decided he had it coming. He was shot once in the head in a bus stop in broad daylight. Bramhall was clearly attempting to defend himself, because the bullet passed straight through his hand before entering his head through his right eye.

"The press are already comparing it to the murders in Bloomsbury and Bristol. I was on the blower half an hour ago to the DCI in charge at Birmingham and he's arranging for the bullet to be recovered and ballistic tests to be carried out.

"Suffice to say, it looks like we should prepare for a link to our own investigation when ballistic results come back in the morning. I can tell you here and now people, if this is the fifth killing by our man, then the junior Home Office Minister has told me there will be questions in the House. The pressure to find him will be ratcheted up, and make no mistake, there will be no hiding place for any of us.

"Now, I think we would all agree that this man was a Grade A scumbag, but his death is still a murder, and if this one comes our way, we're duty bound to investigate it just as thoroughly as we would for anyone else. We would all need to put our personal feelings to one side and act professionally.

"Sadly, I've had to replace DCI Simpson as OIC with a more senior officer. This was not my wish, but was forced on me from above. The new OIC is Detective Chief Superintendent Hook, and I know that you will all give him your full support. Mr Hook, the floor is yours."

The tall, powerfully built man in the smart blue suit who had been seated to Skelton's left stood up and surveyed the officers before him.

"Good afternoon, everyone. I'll come straight to the point. I've reviewed all the actions in this case and I feel we have missed opportunities in certain areas. I've highlighted several potential witnesses, and there are three suspects who need re-interviewing regarding these killings. In addition, I want you out interviewing all the street-life, dealers, and users who frequent locations in the area. In fact, anyone with that type of lifestyle within a half-a-mile radius from the murder scene."

This remark bought an audible groan from the assembled officers, sparking a furious response from DCS Hook.

"That's not the fucking reaction I wanted, people! So far, your troops have earned shed loads of overtime, and what have we got to show for it? Fuck All! You're spending far too much time in the nick checking through crime reports, trying to gather intelligence by sitting comfortably on your arses behind desks. It's been a total waste of fucking time so far, so it's time you all started working for a living! If I see anyone sitting at their desk in the coming days, I will be asking questions. Woe betide those who don't have a good excuse. I want you out there all day, every day, come rain, shine, sleet or fucking snow, until we've spoken to every single person who might know who's done this. Any questions?"

A stunned silence fell across the room.

"No? Good. Starting tomorrow there will be a daily scrum down for all officers of sergeant rank and above, in this room at five p.m. I'll expect to see many of you again then. Okay, let's get out there, let's get among them, and let's find this fucking killer!"

TWENTY-FOUR
Saturday 12th December 1998

DELROY DERBY HAD been going through tough times since his release. His wife was on the verge of leaving him, as it gradually dawned on her that he'd been lying to her for many years about what exactly he did for a living. Eventually there was a furious confrontation, and he confessed everything in a last desperate bid to hang on to his childhood sweetheart, his beautiful kids and his lovely home. Derby prayed that she would remain loyal to him, but doubted that she would.

Meanwhile, the police were on his back, watching and waiting for him to exact revenge on someone. Delroy was getting more and more desperate to hold on to his patch and his clients. At the same time he needed to figure out who'd found his gun in Phoenix Gardens, and whether that person had deliberately tried to fit him up for the killings in Bloomsbury, thereby, quite possibly, ruining his life forever.

On his release from prison, Delroy had quickly made contact with his many minions—the desperate users he employed to act as his runners, his lookouts and his snouts. He threatened every one of them with horribly painful consequences if they didn't bring him the information he so badly wanted.

However, there was a flaw in Delroy's plan. When people are in serious debt to dealers, they would say anything to get themselves off the hook.

ONE SUCH WAS John Heaven, and he had an idea. For him this was an opportunity to get both Delroy and one of the main Soho dealers, Wes Keers, off his back for good.

John came from a decent family, but like so many before him he'd sought the bright lights of London's West End, where he soon found himself taking crack cocaine and heroin—a lifestyle he was funding through shoplifting, street robbery, begging, and some evenings drug running for one of the Holborn dealers, Delroy Derby.

On other evenings, he'd be running for one of the Soho dealers, Wes Keers. Both Delroy and Wes were experienced in handling drug users as runners, and both had got John to the point where he owed them so much money for drugs they'd supplied him, that he was practically their personal slave. On the evenings he worked for them, they owned him. John had now reached the same tipping point with both dealers, a situation where he owed them so much, he could never manage to pay them off with cash, so he worked for nothing apart from the drugs to which he was now completely addicted.

Heaven was quaking with fear as he stood in a small alleyway called Denmark Place. It was nearing noon on Saturday and he'd phoned his boss, Delroy Derby, asking for a meet. He had lied to Delroy, saying he had some information about the shootings in Bloomsbury. John knew he was playing a seriously dangerous game, and that both these men he was about to stitch up were quite capable of killing him, or having him killed, if they chose.

John was leaning on the wall, facing towards St Giles High Street, the direction he was certain Delroy Derby would arrive from. He almost jumped out of his skin when he felt a strong hand on his right shoulder from behind, and heard Delroy's deep voice saying: "What's cooking John, got something to tell me?"

With a distinct break in his voice, John replied, "Oh, hi Delroy, you really made me jump man."

Delroy towered over him. "I *will* make you jump if you've wasted my fucking time, John. Now, I'm a busy man and I've got people to see, so tell me why you called me here and quit pissing me about."

John felt several stages beyond nervous, but he somehow managed to stammer, "I've heard from Wes Keers that one of his girls saw you throw the piece into Phoenix Gardens. The next day he went and picked it up and kept it for himself."

Delroy stared hard into John's eyes, trying to decide if he was lying.

"What about the bloke and the girl shot in the doorway? Was it him? Did that fucker Keers kill them?"

"I don't know, but Wes told me they owed him a lot of money. He was getting fed up with them always fobbing him off—said he was going to sort them out. He's a violent man Delroy, a real head case, I wouldn't put it past him."

Delroy nodded, and thought for a moment before replying, "Well done John, this is just what I've been looking for." He handed John five rocks of crack cocaine. "I'll reward you properly the next time I see you."

"I've hated seeing you in a state since you were banged up for those killings," John lied. "I just wanted to help."

"Look John," said Delroy. "Find Keers in Soho for me tonight, and give me a call with his whereabouts. I'll do the rest."

RUPERT STREET IN Soho was busy that evening, even for a Saturday. Perfect cover for Wes Keers to carry out his trade. He stood at his usual spot, inside an alleyway, giving him plenty of time to swallow any evidence, should he hear a warning whistle from his lookouts, indicating the Feds were nearby.

One of his usual runners, John Heaven, had turned up as usual at eight. He was working well, although Wes thought he seemed a little distracted. At nine, John told Wes he'd be back in five minutes, as he needed the toilet. Knowing that John often did this, Wes thought nothing of it. John walked hurriedly down Rupert Street to the phone boxes at the junction with Shaftesbury Avenue and, once inside, he made his call to Delroy.

"Hi Delroy, it's John. Keers is working his patch inside Tisbury Court."

"Good work, John, I'll be there soon."

"Okay, cool."

John's heart was pounding as he walked up Rupert Street. He knew Delroy wouldn't drop him in it with Wes, but he had no idea what direction Delroy's revenge would take.

"SOMETHING'S DEFINITELY GOING on here Sid, come and have a look."

Detective Constable Diane Canning's voice sounded concerned—alarmed even—and that bought DC Sid Wort's mind sharply back to work matters. He stopped texting his wife on his newly acquired mobile phone and joined his colleague.

DC's Wort and Canning were perfectly positioned in their observation point, a private flat above a shop in Rupert Street, giving them a clear view straight into Tisbury Court. This had been a pre-planned operation targeting Wes Keers and his dealing activities, but Canning's experience told her that something was not right.

"What've you got, mate?" asked Sid.

"Delroy Derby has turned up with two heavies. They've gone straight up to Wes Keers, and there's a serious row going on. We'd better get the TSG to move in now."

"But that'll blow our chances of tailing Keers and catching him at his stash. It'll fuck up the whole operation."

Diane Canning pulled the binoculars up to her eyes.

"Shit, Delroy's got a blade." She lifted the radio. "All units - there's a turf war exploding right in front of us! Go, go, go!"

DELROY WAS SHAKING with anger as he screamed at Wes Keers, "You found my piece, and then you killed those two in Bloomsbury, didn't you?! You fucking bastard. I've lost respect, I've lost my wife, my kids, my whole fucking life!"

Keers shouted back, "I don't know what you're talking about! I wouldn't do that, Delroy, man. Respect!"

It was too little, too late. As Wes finished speaking, Delroy plunged a long-bladed knife deep into his guts.

"You fucking shit!" he muttered.

He saw the shock and pain in Wes Keers' eyes as he folded up in agony, the knife in his belly. Delroy ripped the knife upwards, until the blade hit Wes's ribs, then watched as he dropped gurgling to his knees.

Suddenly, police officers, some with shields, moved in from all sides. Delroy was now boxed in, and a few seconds later he was smashed to the floor by three or four officers in full riot gear. Before he knew what was happening, he'd been rolled onto his front and handcuffed behind his back. Then he was hauled to his feet and thoroughly searched, before being roughly dragged out to a waiting police carrier, manhandled inside and the door slammed shut.

"Delroy Derby, I'm arresting you for the attempted murder of Wes Keers. You do not have to say anything, but it may harm your defence if you fail to mention when questioned, something that you later rely on in court. Anything you do say may be given in evidence," the arresting officer said.

Delroy knew that he'd been an idiot and, as he looked out at Wes Keers dying in the street, he knew he wouldn't be seeing the light of day again for many, many years.

While being booked in at Charing Cross Police Station, Delroy was further arrested for the murder of Wes Keers, who had been declared dead on arrival at St Thomas's Hospital.

"Look," said Delroy during his first interview on Sunday morning, "I killed him because he killed that couple in Bloomsbury last month. He tried fitting me up with it, and it's ruined my whole fucking life."

The interviewing officer laughed. "That's an interesting theory, Delroy, but it couldn't have been Wes Keers. You see, there was another murder yesterday in Birmingham, and the same gun was used as in the other four killings. Wes was stopped and searched by officers twice yesterday in Soho. We've got a crazy serial killer on our hands, but it's definitely not Wes Keers. Sorry, Delroy, you've made a big mistake."

TWENTY-FIVE
Sunday 13th December 1998

THERE HAD BEEN frenzied speculation in the media about whether the shooting in Birmingham was another of the serial killer's victims, but everyone would have to wait until the results of the post mortem and ballistic tests on the bullet.

Gloria had slept heavily, only just waking in time to catch the ten o'clock news. She was annoyed, because yet again she'd be late getting her papers, but she needed to watch the headlines.

"Good morning. It's ten a.m., I'm Hayley Crump, and these are the headlines. We've got breaking news about the shooting of Alan Bramhall in Balsall Heath, Birmingham yesterday lunchtime. Over to our chief crime correspondent, Marcel Hume-Rodriguez."

"Thank you, Hayley. Yes, I'm outside West Midlands Police Headquarters where, thirty minutes ago, a statement was issued regarding the murder of Alan Bramhall."

The face of a senior police officer appeared on screen, his expression grave.

"Good morning. I have a short statement to make regarding the murder of Alan Bramhall in Balsall Heath yesterday. I will not be taking questions at the end of the statement. At around twelve noon yesterday, Alan Bramhall, a 34-year-old unemployed man of no fixed abode, was killed by a single gun-shot wound to the head in a bus shelter in Sutton Gardens. The bullet penetrated his brain and would have been instantly fatal. I can now inform you that ballistic tests carried out on the bullet have shown that it was fired from the same weapon used to kill a male and female in Bloomsbury, London, on Friday the thirteenth of November, and two males in Bristol, on Sunday the twenty-second of November. I will be working closely with my colleagues from both the

108

Metropolitan Police, and the Avon and Somerset Constabulary, to bring the perpetrator of these crimes to justice. Thank you."

The storm was breaking, just as Gloria had anticipated. She was transfixed by the furore exploding on the screen in front of her. The newsreader promised further information as soon as they got it, and an interview with the Home Secretary was planned for one, followed immediately by one with the Metropolitan Police Commissioner. There would also be another programme about the killings directly after the interview. Gloria's telephone rang, dragging her back to the present.

"Hello?"

"Glo, it's Lily. Have you seen the news? There's been another shooting in Birmingham; it's by the same person who killed those two up your way, and the two here in Bristol!"

"Hi Lily. Yes, I've just been watching it. Whoever it is is getting around a bit, aren't they?"

"You're telling me! Looks like this bloke was targeted because he was on the news the other night. The bastard got away with stabbing some poor woman's baby in the face with a syringe. If you ask me, he had it coming."

"Yes, I saw that. Do you think the killer went there specifically to find him, and do him in?"

"I'm sure of it. There's a phone-in about the killings on Radio Five Live at three this afternoon. I'm going to try to get through, and some of my mates will be trying as well. I tell you what, I'm not prepared to condemn him. He's clearly the same as the rest of us—sick to the back teeth of all this crime and he's just snapped because nothing was getting done, so he's doing something about it himself. I think it's fucking great!"

"You're right. Let's hope he gets away with it." Gloria smiled to herself, as she echoed Lily's obvious conviction that the killer was a man.

"Sorry Glo, must fly. I've got tons to do. I just wanted to see if you'd heard the news about Birmingham. I'll call you again tonight, and we'll talk more."

After collecting her Sunday paper she bumped into Paula, and they chatted about the latest news reports. After that, Gloria popped round to see Mano, the young Thai woman from number seven who'd spoken to the police about the assault.

Over a cup of tea and custard cream biscuits, Gloria talked about the incident, reassuring Mano that she really hadn't been too badly hurt, merely shaken up, and that the couple who attacked her were definitely not the ones who'd been killed later that evening.

At first, Mano seemed doubtful but after further persuasion, and a second cup of tea, seemed satisfied that she'd been mistaken and accepted Gloria's version of events.

Thanking Mano once again for helping her after she was attacked, Gloria returned to her own flat, feeling confident that a potential problem had finally been laid to rest. She was still not totally free of the idea of Mano as the author of the letters, though. It was possible, but it seemed highly unlikely.

AT ONE, AS promised, there was an interview with the Home Secretary about the spate of gun killings. He was not at all convincing, delivering the usual stock answers of, "The government will give every support and assistance to the police in this enquiry" and, "We will not rest until the perpetrator of these violent crimes is brought to justice."

When pressed as to whether further government funding would be made available to the police to expand the enquiry, he replied, "Funding for police forces is set out at the start of the financial year. I have received no approach regarding additional funding." It was about as meaningful as an automated telephone reply.

My God, thought Gloria, as she tucked heartily into her Sunday lunch. *You boring, useless bastard. No wonder crime is out of control.*

The interview that followed with the Metropolitan Police Commissioner, Noah Fordree, was far more interesting.

"Commissioner, thank you for taking the time to speak to us this afternoon."

"It's a pleasure."

"Why haven't your officers made any headway in this investigation? The first killings were over a month ago. There are now five people dead in three separate cities, hundreds of miles apart. A serial killer is on the loose, a killer who could strike again anywhere in the country, and at any time. The public interest in this case is enormous. What are you doing to allay public fears?"

"Firstly, I'd like to say that I've just left a meeting with my senior detectives on this enquiry. They have informed me that the killer appears to have carefully chosen each location, to leave minimum clues for investigators. We are working closely in co-operation with officers from both the Avon and Somerset, and the West Midlands Constabularies."

"That's all well and good, but what actual progress are you making?"

"Well, CCTV from businesses, bus stations, train stations, shopping centres and residential properties in the areas close to the killings are being thoroughly checked by experts for three hours before, until three hours after the killings, searching for potential clues as to who the killer may be. We are confident that the killer will have been caught on CCTV somewhere."

"Why hasn't this been done already?"

"It has already been done in London and Bristol for two hours before until one hour after. This is now extended to three hours before and after. The Birmingham investigation is just starting, and it will have extended checks done from the start. We will then have far more data to compare."

"What type of lifestyle do you think this man is likely to be living at the moment?"

"Why are so sure it's a man?"

Gloria quickly grabbed the remote control and turned the sound up. All previous commentators had seemed to assume that the killer was a man. This was the first time she'd heard someone question that fact, and it was frankly unsettling.

"Are you suggesting that the killer is a woman?"

"I'm simply not prepared to rule out any possibility in this investigation. Obviously, previous history shows that serial killers are nearly always men, I'm fully aware of that. However, I don't want my officers to miss a potential clue, because they're fixated on looking for a male killer."

"Two final questions, Commissioner. What can you do, or say, to allay public fears about whether it is safe for people to continue going about their normal business?"

"I'm satisfied that this person has a personal grievance against people involved in street crime, and to a certain extent, people who are violently involved in the street drug scene. In particular, people who are aggressively anti-social or violent towards other members of the public. Therefore, I think that decent, law-abiding people should have no fear of attack by this killer."

"Let me get this right. Are you saying that the killer could actually be *targeting* people involved in street drug dealing or robberies?"

"Yes. More specifically though, it appears that all five victims were known to use violence or threats against members of the public."

Gloria finished her last mouthful of food without really tasting it, and took her plate out to the kitchen. As the interview had gone on, she had begun to feel increasingly uneasy; it was almost as if the Commissioner had profiled her. He had deduced that the killer was not necessarily a man; that the killer had a personal grievance against street robbers; that those killed were violently aggressive. And he had said that ordinary members of the public had no reason to fear or worry. Spot on.

The news reports which followed were exactly as Gloria had expected. Pictures of the victims looking their best were shown, together with scraped up friends and family, saying that they would be sadly missed, blaming society for having let them down in the first place. The main message from those contributing to the programme was that none of the victims deserved to die in that fashion.

Gloria turned the TV off, and switched on Radio Five Live in time for the phone-in.

"Good afternoon, this is Wol Spinks on Radio Five Live. For the next hour, we have a phone-in special about the so-called serial killer who has now claimed five innocent lives in London, Bristol and Birmingham. What do you think about the police efforts so far? Do you feel safe walking around your neighbourhood? Should we bring back the death penalty for serial killers? Did you know one of the victims or live where any of the killings took place, and if so, what is the feeling locally? Do you think the killer will strike again? We're ready for your calls right now. We'll go straight to the phones with our first caller, Samantha from Balsall Heath in Birmingham. Hello Samantha."

"Hi. I just wanted to say that I live around the corner from yesterday's shooting. I knew Alan and I know Sharon, the lady whose baby he stabbed in the face."

"And what's your feeling about all this, Samantha?"

"Well, years ago Alan was a nice bloke, but since he's been hooked on crack for the past four or five years, he's become aggressive and foul mouthed. He's broken into people's homes, robbed us, and threatened anyone who stood in his way. He was really vicious and, to be honest, most people round here will be glad to see the back of him."

"Strong words. Are you saying that most people who knew Alan might actually be happy that he's dead?"

"Yes, I am. Well, maybe not that he's dead, but glad that he's gone away for good."

"Okay. Can't say I go along with that, but you've made your point. Thanks Samantha. Let's go to Lily in Bristol."

"Hi Wol."

"Hi Lily, what do you want to say?"

A large grin spread across Gloria's face as she heard her friend's voice.

"I've had to put up with drug dealing, friends and neighbours being robbed, and aggressive behaviour from a small minority ruining the area where I live for years. I've been abused and threatened myself, just for looking at someone in the wrong way. All my friends and neighbours are sick to death of it. As far as I'm concerned, this person is not some cold-blooded killer, they're a vigilante. A hero. If they make life better for the decent members of communities by their actions, then I'm not prepared to condemn them."

"Hang on a minute, Lily, are you saying that you support the actions of a serial killer?"

Gloria winced at this question. *Don't go there Lily, don't go there.* But Lily did go there.

"If you're going to press me for a straight answer, then yes, I do support him. He's probably suffered at the hands of these scumbags

113

himself, and felt that nothing was being done. Don't get me wrong, I don't condone the killing of truly innocent people. I'd also like to point out that you were incorrect with your opening comments. You said that the serial killer had claimed five innocent lives; well, these people who have been killed were not innocent, they have been ruining decent people's lives over a long period of time, and now, finally, someone is standing up for the real victims."

"Okay Lily. Your comments are pretty extreme, but everyone is entitled to their opinion. Thanks for your call. What did you make of Lily's viewpoint? Do you agree with her or, like me, have serious reservations about this?"

The rest of the phone-in consisted of widely differing viewpoints. Some callers said the serial killer was a cold-blooded murderer, out to satisfy their blood lust, who was just as likely to kill a normal member of the public next time. This view was countered by several callers describing the vigilante as a hero, and a modern-day Robin Hood. At the end of the phone-in, Wol Spinks clearly seemed taken aback by the response.

"I'd like to thank those who took the time to phone in, and thanks also to everyone who tuned in. I am truly amazed at the response we've had, in fact I can't remember the phone lines ever being so busy. I've just been handed some figures by our producer, which are startling. It would seem that 64% of callers were either supportive, or not prepared to condemn the actions of the killer. Well, speaking personally, I think it's a sad day for Britain when the general public show that level of support for a murderer. If those victims deserved justice, did it necessarily have to be vigilante justice? What is the country coming to? I, for one, still believe in the rule of law. However, that's just my opinion, and I'm clearly in the minority. Thank you for listening. I'm Wol Spinks, now here's the four o'clock news."

Switching the radio off, Gloria paced slowly up and down her living room carpet. The level of support for her actions had given her a tremendous boost, reinforcing her belief that she was only doing what many other decent members of the community wanted to do. The difference was that she had taken action, whereas others either didn't have the nerve, or more importantly the opportunity.

Finding the Glock had provided her with that opportunity, and although she hadn't intended using it against her tormentors, fate had dictated otherwise. She had now killed five people in cold blood, and strangely enough, she knew that she was quite capable of doing it again.

Lily phoned shortly after six. They chatted for fifteen minutes about the phone-in, the surprising level of support for the killer, and where and when he might strike next.

Feeling tired early in the evening, Gloria had a relaxing bath, read the newspaper and went to bed early. She wanted to be as alert as possible at work on Monday morning.

TWENTY-SIX
Monday 14ᵗʰ December, 1998

HOWEVER, MONDAY MORNING didn't go exactly as Gloria had planned. It was still dark when she was woken up by an almost constant buzzing of the communal door intercom. She checked the clock. Six-thirty. *Who the hell?* She threw on her dressing gown and blearily stumbled out to answer it.

"Hello?"

"Gloria Jones?"

"Yes, who is it?"

"Can you let us in please Mrs Jones? It's Detective Sergeant Connors."

The voice was devoid of expression, but the words were like a punch to the stomach. In a daze, Gloria pressed the door release. Moments later, there was a sharp rapping at her front door.

Opening it, she was greeted by two detectives showing their warrant cards, and two uniform constables behind them. The shorter detective introduced himself as Detective Sergeant Connors. Gloria took in his unprepossessing appearance: his completely bald head, brown goatee beard and scruffy grey suit. Connors introduced his partner as Detective Constable Thayer, who was more smartly dressed than Connors, but painfully thin, clean shaven and with sharp features and lank, blond hair.

Connors immediately took hold of Gloria's right arm and said the words she had been dreading.

"Gloria Jones, I'm arresting you on suspicion of the murders of David Border and Kelly-Anne Watkins in Barter Street, London, WC2, on Friday the thirteenth of November. You do not have to say anything, but it may harm your defence if you fail to mention when questioned, something that you later rely on in court. Anything you do say may be given in evidence. Do you understand?"

Gloria remained silent. Her world had just collapsed around her.

"Mrs Jones, do you understand?"

"Er, sorry, yes." Gloria decided she had to play dumb for the moment; she had nothing to lose.

"Officer, I've nothing whatsoever to do with those killings. Why on earth are you arresting me? On what evidence?"

Connors noted down what Gloria had said, then replied, "That will be fully explained when you are interviewed at the police station. In the meantime, we need you to be present while we carry out a search of your flat under Section 32 of the Police and Criminal Evidence Act, 1984."

"But what are you searching for?"

"A hand-gun."

Shit. She knew that they would soon find the Glock, and that a lifetime in prison awaited her. Suddenly, thoughts of Sandra and her family swamped her mind. What on earth would they think? What had she done? Their lives were never going to be the same.

DC Thayer and the uniformed constables started the search in Gloria's bedroom. They were thorough, but replaced everything they touched and left the room tidy. After finding nothing in the bedroom, the bathroom, or the hallway, they concentrated on the lounge, but again found nothing of interest. Finally, they moved into the kitchen and Gloria started trembling; she was close to having a panic attack.

Thayer began searching the wall units, while the uniformed officers searched through the floor cupboards. Gloria swallowed repeatedly, but her mouth was still dry. DC Thayer removed items from each cupboard, meticulously checking through larger items, then replacing everything. DS Connors began to look irritated; he clearly thought the search was a waste of time and wanted to get moving.

The final cupboard to be searched was the one containing five different boxes of cereals. First, Thayer removed the Special K and Muesli, opening each and looking inside; this was followed by the Shredded Wheat and Rice Krispies. All that remained was the box of Cornflakes; Gloria was almost frozen with fear.

By now, DS Connors was pacing the floor.

"Are we done here?" he barked. "For fuck's sake, lad, this is pointless."

DC Thayer replied, "Sorry, sarge, I'll be done in a couple of seconds." He hastily shoved the boxes back inside the cupboard and slammed the door.

Hardly able to speak, Gloria croaked, "Can I have a glass of water please? This is terribly upsetting for me; I've never been in trouble with the police in my entire life!"

Connors nodded at one of the uniforms, who poured a glass of water and handed it to Gloria. She drank thirstily and handed the glass back with a polite, "Thank you very much," then said, "May I get changed please Sergeant? I don't really want to attend the police station in my dressing gown and nightie."

Connors directed a PC to take Gloria to her bedroom and wait outside while she got changed. Five minutes later Gloria opened her bedroom door, was handcuffed by DC Thayer, and escorted out of her flat down to a waiting police van.

To Gloria's immense relief, none of her neighbours seemed to be around to witness her humiliation.

ON ARRIVAL AT the custody suite at Holborn Police Station, DS Connors identified himself as the arresting officer.

"Time of arrest?"

"Six thirty-five a.m. Sarge."

"Any reply to caution?"

Connors checked his pocket book. "Officer, I've nothing whatsoever to do with those killings. Why on earth are you arresting me? On what evidence?"

After noting down the reply to caution, the Custody Officer said, "What are the circumstances of the arrest, please?"

"Sergeant, this is Gloria Jones. She has been identified by a female resident of Robinson Court, as a suspect in the murders of David Border and Kelly-Anne Watkins in Barter Street, WC2, on Friday the thirteenth of November. The female resident is Mano Theeravit, who lives in the same block of flats as Mrs Jones. She has provided a statement saying that Mrs Jones was attacked by a male and female outside Robinson Court, New Compton Street, WC2, only hours before the murders. As she helped Mrs Jones back to her flat after the attack, she witnessed her open the front pouch of her bag and check something inside. Although she only had a quick glance at the object—which she could see was black and metallic—Miss Theeravit thinks it may possibly have been a black hand-gun. She is also certain that the couple who attacked Mrs Jones were Border and Watkins.

"At six forty p.m., on the same evening, Miss Theeravit was standing near the window of her ground-floor flat, when she saw Mrs Jones leave the block, and head off in the direction of Holborn, which is also towards Barter Street. At seven p.m., Miss Theeravit was closing her curtains when she saw Mrs Jones walking quickly back towards the block, looking very flustered. This is around the time that the murders occurred. Sergeant, because of these facts, I believe that Mrs Jones had means, motive and opportunity to carry out these murders.

"Furthermore, yesterday, Mrs Jones visited Miss Theeravit and attempted to convince her that the couple who attacked her were not Border and Watkins. Miss Theeravit was certain Mrs Jones was lying, and was convinced she was attempting to deflect her from the truth.

"Arrest was necessary in order to secure and preserve evidence, and for the purpose of interview."

The Custody Sergeant looked over the top of his spectacles at Gloria, before saying, "I'm satisfied there is sufficient evidence to reasonably suspect you of an offence. Therefore, I'm authorising your detention to secure and preserve evidence and for the purposes of interview. Do you understand?"

Gloria nodded and replied quietly: "Yes. But I'm completely innocent. I've never committed a crime in my life. That wasn't a gun in my handbag, it was a black toy car." In her heart, she was beginning to think that her protestations of innocence were becoming fairly pointless.

Mano. It was her all along!

She had wondered whether Mano had written the letters and thought she had dealt with that threat. On the contrary, she had merely given her more cause to be suspicious. Why on earth had she opened the front pouch of her bag when Mano was helping her? She didn't remember doing it, but she must have. Anyway, it didn't really matter now, did it? The game was up.

The Custody Officer continued, "You are entitled to legal representation. You may have a solicitor of your own choosing, or the duty solicitor. Do you want to speak to a solicitor?"

"I don't know, I've never been in this situation before. Do you think I need a solicitor?"

"I'm not allowed to advise you. I would, however, consider the gravity of the crime you've been accused of."

Gloria shuffled uncomfortably. "I don't have a solicitor of my own. Could I see the Duty Solicitor please?"

"Certainly."

The Custody Officer instructed one of the gaolers to call for the Duty Solicitor.

"Do you want anybody informed that you've been arrested?"

"No, thank you, but can I call my work and let them know I won't be in today?"

The Custody Officer nodded, and Gloria was allowed to make her call.

The booking-in process continued. Gloria was thoroughly searched; all her loose possessions were taken and placed into a plastic property bag and after that, she was fingerprinted, photographed and had DNA swabs taken from the inside of both cheeks. The gaoler then placed her into cell number three.

As the cell door slammed shut, Gloria knew it was over for her. She sat down on the blue plastic mattress and burst into bitter tears.

TWENTY-SEVEN

GLORIA WAS GIVEN lunch, such as it was, in her cell. She had already been in custody for six hours. She wasn't in the slightest bit hungry, but eating at least broke the monotony, and the mind-numbing misery of the previous few hours. The events of the past month now played over and over again in her head. *Serial killers are nearly always caught.* She had heard those words spoken so many times, and now she was living proof.

The sound of a key turning in the lock made Gloria sit up. The cell door was opened by a young Asian civilian gaoler, who said, "Time for your consultation. Come with me, please."

Gloria dutifully followed him down the corridor. She was beginning to think maybe she should confess all and get this nightmare over with. The gaoler showed her into a room with the words 'Prisoner Consultation' on the door.

Waiting inside was an attractive blonde lady, no more than thirty years old, wearing a very smart royal blue skirt and jacket. Standing up and smoothing her skirt, the woman shook Gloria firmly by the hand and introduced herself: "Courtney Dill, Duty Solicitor, pleased to meet you." She indicated for Gloria to sit.

"Hello, thank you for coming."

"Now, it's Gloria Jones, isn't it? Do you mind if I call you Gloria?"

"No, that's fine."

The woman sighed deeply, as though summoning some enthusiasm. "Now then, I've been given the brief facts from the OIC."

She examined her immaculate fingernails. Gloria felt her anger rising; her whole future was on the line, and this woman acted like it was all too much bother, seemingly more interested in her manicure.

She continued briskly, "Now I need to hear your version. I need you to start at the very beginning; tell me everything that led to you being arrested. Don't leave anything out."

This was it. After everything that had happened, it was confession time.

"Well, it all started one Thursday in November. I was walking back home after Bridge Club when I saw a couple standing in a doorway. They were—" Gloria was interrupted by a loud rapping at the door, followed by the Custody Officer entering the room.

"What the hell are you doing?" asked Miss Dill. "I'm in consultation with a client!" She was clearly livid with the Custody Officer's interruption.

"I'm sorry Miss Dill, but James Williams-Glass is at the front counter; he's insisting that he be allowed to represent Miss Jones."

Gloria knew the name James Williams-Glass. Nearly everyone knew his name; he was the most eminent and highly ,paid defence solicitor in the country. He normally represented pop stars, footballers, members of parliament, and wealthy celebrities. Why the hell would he be interested in Gloria Jones?

"He can't," said Dill. "I've started the consultation."

Before she knew what she was doing, Gloria spoke up.

"I want Mr Williams-Glass to represent me." Turning to Dill she said, her voice rising with every word, "I'm sorry, but you really pissed me off just now with your attitude; you look like you'd rather be somewhere else. I know I'm just another client to you, but I'd rather be represented by someone who's at least reasonably fucking interested!"

She crossed her arms and glared at the young woman on the opposite side of the table.

The Custody Officer had a half-smile on his face as he said, "Am I to understand that you are dismissing Miss Dill as your legal representative?"

Returning the smile, Gloria said, "Yes please Sergeant."

Stiff with indignation, Dill rose, smoothed her skirt, hurriedly collected her things, and was shown out. A gaoler remained with Gloria in the Consultation Room, where she was joined after a few minutes by the man she recognised from the TV as James Williams-Glass.

He shook hands with Gloria as he introduced himself. The gaoler left the room, leaving the two of them alone.

Williams-Glass was shorter than he appeared on TV, though still around six foot, but she'd always imagined him to be taller. Sitting down, with Gloria sitting opposite him, Williams-Glass looked calm and assured. He was hard to put an age to, with well-cut, greying hair, immaculately dressed, carrying with him into the tiny room a scent of expensive after shave.

"We both know why you're here Gloria, and I'm here to help."

"There's nothing you can do, believe me, I know. Anyway, why would you represent me? I could never afford your fees."

Williams-Glass's face remained unchanged. "Never mind *why* I'm here to represent you. Just let me do my job."

Gloria was totally baffled by this turn of events.

"Okay, I'm listening."

"Do you know the Thistle Hotel in Bloomsbury?"

"Yes, of course."

"Right. On Friday the thirteenth of November, you attended the brasserie in the hotel at six forty-five p.m. While there, you booked a table for four for the following Saturday, the twenty-first of November, at which time you then had an enjoyable evening with three friends. After making the booking, you left the hotel shortly after six fifty, and arrived home again shortly before seven p.m. You simply wouldn't have had the time to visit Barter Street and carry out those murders. This provides you with an unbreakable alibi for the time you were away from your flat."

Gloria was baffled. "That's complete bollocks though, I've never visited that hotel; they're bound to check the CCTV. And anyway, why would you be prepared to do this for me?"

Williams-Glass smiled, not answering Gloria's question. He crossed one leg over the other and Gloria noted his expensive, glossy leather shoes.

"Three reputable witnesses will be completing the necessary statements within the next couple of hours. They will confirm that you attended the hotel, made the booking, and left at the times I have stated. The manager will also confirm that unfortunately, CCTV for the thirteenth of November has been recorded over, because they only keep CCTV for twenty-eight days. He will also confirm that on the twenty-first of November CCTV was down for maintenance from early evening through to the following morning. I just need you to stick to the story."

"I still don't understand why you are doing this." Gloria said.

Williams-Glass leaned forward almost imperceptibly and answered in a quiet voice, "Gloria, I'm the best friend you've got at the moment. I'm giving you a lifeline here! Do you want to be inside for the rest of your life, or do you want your freedom? It's your choice."

Gloria was no fool. She couldn't afford to look this particularly expensive gift horse in the mouth, so she nodded her consent. The next twenty minutes were taken up with thoroughly rehearsing the story. Williams-Glass then knocked on the consultation room door and told the gaoler he needed an hour to make further enquiries before interview. Gloria was placed back into her cell, while Williams-Glass left the station, ostensibly to speak with witnesses.

When Williams-Glass returned, Gloria was taken from her cell to find Connors and Thayer waiting in Interview Room Two. As discussed, she kept perfectly to the story, and Williams-Glass supplied the officers with contact phone numbers of three witnesses. These were hotel manager, Julia Cousins; the hotel receptionist, Amanda Garnham; and a guest at the hotel—Police Inspector William O'Neill, from the British Transport Police.

Once the interview had been completed, DS Connors said, "Thank you for providing your account of events on the evening concerned. Officers will be dispatched to obtain statements from the witnesses you've supplied. If they confirm your story, I'm sure you will be released without charge and no further action."

Still perplexed, Gloria said weakly, "Thank you."

Joined in her cell after the interview by James Williams-Glass, Gloria once again tackled him.

"Now, what the fuck is this all about? I'm eternally grateful, but how on earth did you persuade those people to provide me with an alibi? I mean, what's in it for them? Come to that, what's in it for you?"

Putting his papers neatly into his briefcase, Williams-Glass smiled at Gloria for the first time and said, "The less you know right now, the better. Let's just say you have powerful friends."

He held out his hand; Gloria hesitated, then shook it firmly. When the gaoler arrived, James Williams-Glass nodded at Gloria and walked out of the cell.

The statements duly confirmed what Gloria had said, and the Custody Officer was happy to release her with apologies for her time in custody and with no further action. However, she was advised not to take out any retribution on Mano Theeravit, who had been genuinely suspicious, and although she had been shown to be mistaken, had done the right thing in reporting her concerns to the police.

Gloria said, "Don't worry Sergeant, I don't hold any malice towards Mano, and looking back, I can see why she might have been suspicious."

She was released from custody exactly twelve hours after her arrest.

Arriving back at her flat, yet another plain brown envelope awaited her on the doormat. Opening up the letter inside, she read: *YOU'RE WELCOME!*

This was all too much. She had absolutely no idea who may have sent it, but it clearly wasn't Mano!

She poured herself a large glass of red wine and relaxed in her armchair. Considering the events of the day, she was feeling remarkably calm. On her walk home, she realised that this alibi meant not only that she couldn't have committed the Bloomsbury murders, she couldn't be responsible for the murders in Bristol or Birmingham either!

What did James Williams-Glass mean by 'powerful friends? Who the fuck did he mean? Why were they so desperate to provide her with an alibi that they had persuaded a hotel manager, a receptionist and a police officer—a fucking police officer—to provide statements?

TWENTY-EIGHT
Friday 18th December

DURING THE FOUR days since her arrest, Gloria had heard nothing more about why she'd been provided with an alibi by one of the top solicitors in the land. The morning broke with pouring rain and high winds and Gloria was up early; she braved the inclement weather to collect her newspaper, then bought her fortnightly food shop from Tesco. She was halfway through putting her shopping away, when the intercom buzzed.

"Hello."

"It's Sean, are you busy?"

"No, I'm just putting shopping away, come on up."

Sean walked in looking agitated. He paced the room for a few moments before slumping down on the settee. He shook his head and sighed deeply.

"Sean, what on earth's the matter? Anything you want to talk about?"

"I think that question should be coming from me, don't you? So, is there something *you* want to talk to me about?"

He stood and faced Gloria, hands on hips. She said nothing.

"Fucking hell Glo, why did they arrest you as a murder suspect?"

"Ah... I thought you might have heard about that."

"Heard about it? The whole fucking station's talking about nothing else! I'd been on three days' annual leave to visit my sister, and when I got back to work today, I copped this lot! Everyone knows we're friends, and I've been having the piss taken out of me ever since!"

Gloria leant forward and put her hand on Sean's.

"I'm sorry about that. It was all sorted in the end—just a misunderstanding. A neighbour put two and two together and got five."

She explained her arrest as it happened, then stuck to the story provided by James Williams-Glass.

Sean listened, amazed, then took a step back and whistled. He seemed satisfied apart from one thing.

"I'd heard who your solicitor was. How the fuck can you afford to have Williams-Glass representing you?"

Thinking quickly, Gloria explained, "He's a brother-in-law of an old friend down the road. Apparently, she saw me being carted off to the station, asked one of the officers what was going on, and decided I could do with some help. She knew I couldn't possibly be the killer, so she gave him a call and asked for a favour. Luckily, he had a quiet day and agreed to do the initial consultation. He turned up at the station, talked to me and, when he realised how daft the whole thing was, he quickly sorted it out."

"Fucking hell, James Williams-Glass. You lucky cow, he would have cost a fortune!"

"I know. Anyway, it was all a huge mistake, and I was released with lots of apologies. I must say, your colleagues were perfectly polite and professional. You can thank them from me."

Sean laughed, "Polite and professional? Are we talking about the same people!"

Gloria wanted to get away from the subject and sat down on the settee, patting it to indicate that Sean should sit down too.

"Enough about my notoriety, how are things going at Operation Chiddingstone? Other than arresting completely innocent old ladies, of course!"

"This new boss we've got is a complete nightmare. He's picking holes in everything we've done but, in reality, we're just going round in circles."

"Still no leads, eh? Surely something will turn up soon." She raised her hand to her mouth in a drinking motion. "Fancy a cup of tea or coffee?"

"Coffee please, Glo, and I'm back on two sugars again. No, no leads whatsoever. Hopefully something will turn up soon. I'm well in with Gail at the moment, but I can't get any time off to see her because of Operation fucking Chiddingstone. She'll soon start thinking I'm making excuses to avoid her."

"Haven't you explained the situation?"

"Of course I have, but she's a gorgeous-looking girl so I can't expect her to wait forever, can I?"

"Maybe you're right. Anyway, did you listen to Radio Five Live's phone-in last Sunday? Public support for your killer was pretty strong. In fact, he seems to have been re-branded as some sort of vigilante."

"I heard. They've had a poll in the Sun today that came up with sixty-one percent support for him! To be honest, the lads at the station have mixed feelings. They're mad that he's making us look like idiots, and we're getting bollockings on a daily basis because of it. On the other hand, he's doing a good job of eliminating the dross and some of them hope he gets away with it."

"What about you Sean, what do you think?" Gloria genuinely wanted to hear Sean's answer.

"I really don't know. One minute I despise him, the next I sympathise with him. I suppose if I'm honest, the answer is that I respect him in a funny sort of way."

Gloria was interested to hear Sean's admission, but she didn't press him to elaborate further. They chatted a while longer about everything and nothing, before Sean had to return to the station.

TWENTY-NINE
Thursday 24th December 1998

AS CHRISTMAS APPROACHED, Gloria had felt her stress levels rising, and not for the usual reasons. She knew someone out there was aware of her identity and was playing with her, and she needed to find out exactly who they were. There was no one else she could trust with her secret, so she would have to carry out any investigations herself.

Gloria started her Christmas break on Christmas Eve. She'd reserved a seat on the train from Kings Cross to Newcastle and was looking forward to seeing her family. What's more, concern about the drug dealing on their estate was troubling her greatly. She was confident that she knew how to eradicate the problem; more importantly, she had the means to carry it out. However, following her close call with the police, she didn't intend to take any more risks.

To make sure she didn't lose the plot, or do anything foolish during the Christmas holidays in Newcastle, Gloria left the hand-gun safely in her kitchen. In any case, she was loaded down with presents: two each for Sandra and Steve, and three each for Katie and James.

"Hi Mum, it's great to see you. How was your journey?" Gloria was practically squeezed to death by her daughter as she arrived in Newcastle.

"Wow! What a lovely welcome. I'm very well thanks, it's great to see you too. The journey was boring: I've done two crosswords and loads of Sudoku, but never mind, I'm here now!"

"Come on, let's get you home; we'll have a proper catch up over a cup of tea. Here, give me your suitcase, you can look after the presents."

They walked to Sandra's car and, fifteen minutes later, were parked outside her house, unloading the luggage. Once inside, Steve, Katie, and James gave Gloria a rapturous welcome, while Sandra put the kettle on.

It was Katie who raised the subject during the evening meal.

"I guess Mum's told you all about the drug dealers moving onto the estate, Gran?"

"Yes, she has. It must be cramping your style a bit, not being able to go outside while they're around."

"Yes, it's a pain. About twenty people appear from nowhere whenever their car is about to arrive. I've no idea how the word is spread, but they're pretty efficient."

"Sounds bad. What do you think, James?"

"I just wish they'd piss off!"

"All right, James," interrupted Steve. "We don't need that kind of language, thank you."

"Sorry Dad, sorry Gran. But we're not in some grotty council flat at the wrong end of town, so why should we have to suffer like this?"

"That's unfair James," said Sandra. "People in council flats don't deserve drug dealers any more than we do. It's our problem, on our estate, and we've got to deal with it."

"Have you heard any more from the police about this?" asked Gloria.

"Only that the information we've supplied has been passed on to the local neighbourhood constable, and he's 'looking into it'." Steve made a sarcastic quote gesture with his fingers. "Problem is though, whenever the car appears, and it looks like dealing is taking place, we phone the police. But by the time they've taken down the information, the crowd have moved off in all directions, presumably to find somewhere quiet to take their gear. The car roars off and fifteen minutes later the police arrive."

"No! How infuriating. Have you considered getting a deputation together, going out there when the car appears and confronting them? Make it clear they're not welcome."

"We've thought about it," said Sandra. "But everyone is too scared of repercussions, so I don't think we could get enough people together to confront them."

"Fair enough," Gloria said, and the conversation moved on to lighter things.

Katie and James were in bed by ten, partly because they wanted to spend time on their games consoles in their rooms, partly because they were getting bored with adult conversation, but mainly because, despite what they might say to the contrary, they were still basically children, and couldn't wait for Christmas morning to come.

The adults settled down to watch the ten o'clock news, which featured a report about the five murders, and the fact that the police were still no further forward in their investigation. They had an MP on, answering questions about phone-ins and polls showing surprising levels of support for the so-called vigilante killer. She was stumbling badly over her answers, but stuck to the party line that, "The law of this country applies to all, and this killer is a cold-blooded murderer who must, and will, be caught. The fact that certain members of the public choose to support this man does not change the fact that he will eventually be brought to justice." Gloria sat in silence, watching the screen, a small smile playing on her lips.

Sandra made everyone a cup of coffee during the adverts, and the second half started with the second of two reports from Norwich, about a spate of violent attacks on Lyne Heath, one of the city's parks.

"In our first report last month we identified three ringleaders of a vicious gang of Asian men, who have carried out attacks on elderly people on Lyne Heath, Norwich. Two of these victims are still hospitalised and others are too scared to go out, suffering from shock and trauma after the beatings they suffered while being robbed of cash and valuables.

"We can now confirm that, acting on our evidence, forwarded to Norwich Police four weeks ago, the youths identified by us were subsequently arrested and interviewed. They were then bailed to return to Norwich Police station, while the file was passed to the Crown Prosecution Service for a decision. However, although our film provides compelling evidence that these three individuals were involved with the gang, the CPS have decided there was insufficient evidence for a realistic chance of a successful prosecution. They have therefore directed that no further action be taken against them."

The reporter had visited the victims, still in hospital: a man named Ralph in his seventies and a woman named Elizabeth in her late sixties, whose small dog Timmy had been killed during the attack. Both had lost teeth and suffered terrible bruising. Gloria was transfixed by the report, in particular the anger felt towards the attackers by families of the victims, together with the victims' feelings of helplessness. Gloria could feel that familiar sensation building again.

When they repeated the original filmed evidence, she could see why the BBC thought they had sufficient material to enable the police and CPS to prosecute the three main suspects. There was film of brutal intimidation; of threats with weapons including knives and a cosh; finally, a terrifying, but slightly grainy film of an old man being stopped, punched in the face, then given a terrible beating with fists and boots while lying on the ground, and obviously incapable of offering resistance. You could clearly see distinctive clothing worn by the suspects, but this was still not enough for the CPS to form a prosecution.

"We now go to Norwich, where the youths identified in our report are talking to our East Anglia Crime Correspondent, Stuart Walledge."

"Thanks Eileen. I have here with me Yasser, Islam and Ahmed. They've asked to be allowed to give their version of events relating to attacks in the Lyne Heath area last month."

The first to speak was Islam. "Look, right, we've been fitted up by the press and convicted by the public, and that's not fair, right?"

Yasser interrupted, "This is a racist attack because we're Muslim. Nobody can stop us from hanging out in the Lyne; this is our territory."

The journalist, Walledge, broke in, "But there was pretty damning evidence against you. Surely you can understand the concerns of local residents?"

"That evidence is shit," snapped Ahmed, clearly losing his cool. "This is all a stitch up and we're not putting up with it. People should be careful what they say."

"That sounds remarkably like a threat."

At that point, Ahmed laughed and turned away from the camera, pulling the other two with him.

The reporter looked down the lens. "Well, there you have it. This is unlikely to alleviate the fears of local residents and users of Lyne Heath. This is Stuart Walledge for BBC News, Norwich."

"Bastards," whispered Steve. "Christ, we think we've got problems."

At first, Gloria didn't say a word, she just sat staring at the screen. The inability of the authorities to prosecute these men, who seemed clearly guilty, reminded her of the situation with Bramhall two weeks previously.

"Don't worry," she said quietly. "I'm sure if they keep behaving like that, someone will sort them out. Just you wait and see."

As she said it, Gloria was already starting to make plans.

THIRTY

CHRISTMAS DAY FESTIVITIES started early and finished late. Recent problems were hardly mentioned, which came as a blessed relief to everyone; they were all too busy eating, drinking and watching hour after hour of corny Christmas Specials on the TV.

Boxing day started much later, with the whole family sleeping in. After breakfast, Steve and James headed off to see Newcastle play Gloucester in the rugby, while the girls headed out to Eldon Square shopping centre for the sales.

By four Gloria, Sandra and Katie had spent far more than they'd intended, were carrying far too many shopping bags, and their feet were killing them. Gloria was busy loading her bags into the back seat of Sandra's car when she heard Katie's alarmed voice.

"That's them!"

Looking round, Gloria watched as a large black BMW with dark tinted side windows cruised through the car park toward them.

"That's the car that deals drugs on our estate, Gran," said Katie, anxiously.

Staring hard through the windscreen, Gloria could see two well-built black men staring back at her. She had no intention of looking away as they scowled back. The driver was grossly overweight, wore his hair in short, knotted dreadlocks, and was sporting a black puffer jacket with a white logo on the front.

The passenger was smaller, but still fat, with crewcut hair and stubble, holding a small black shoulder bag on his lap. As the car passed, it suddenly stopped and the driver's window wound down.

"What you staring at, grandma?" The driver had a deep, gravelly voice. He was not smiling. "See, I don't like people eyeballing me, it's not polite. You should show me some respect. You get me?"

"You deserve to be shown respect, do you? How much respect do you show the people of Newcastle? Decent people, who want to live their lives without open drug dealing on their street? I'll tell you how much respect you show them. None!"

"Gran, leave it, come on let's go home." Katie sounded scared and tugged at Gloria's arm, but Gloria wasn't budging. Other people in the car park stopped to watch the confrontation.

Without moving her eyes from the driver of the car, Gloria said, "Don't worry, darling. People like these two sometimes need to be told a few home truths."

The driver looked across at the passenger, who glowered at Gloria.

"Oooh, look," said Gloria. "Your friend with the handbag isn't very happy with me. You'd think intimidating a woman in her sixties like this would make him feel really tough!"

"That's enough, mum," Sandra pulled at her mother's arm, but once again Gloria was having none of it; she was enjoying this and wasn't about to back down.

"I could hurt you right now granny, you've just made a massive mistake dissing me like that. Next time I see your face, you'll regret what you just said." He started to wind the window up, but Gloria was on a roll.

"Sorry, did you say I've made a massive mistake 'dissing you'? What exactly does that mean for those of us that prefer to speak in the Queen's English, please?"

"Think you're funny? You'll live to regret the day you crossed me." Without waiting for another comment, the driver accelerated away with tyres screeching.

"Jesus Christ, Mum! What are you on? These people are thugs, and they don't make threats lightly."

"That's right, Gran," said Katie. "We have to live around here. You'll be going home in a couple of days. What if they spot Mum or me somewhere? We could be in trouble!"

Gloria suddenly realised that in her eagerness to confront the dealers, she may well have made matters worse for Sandra and Katie.

"I'm so sorry; it's just that I refuse to be intimidated any more. Listen, they hardly looked at you two—all their anger was directed towards me. Anyway, you tried to make me stop. I don't think they'll hold a grudge against you."

"Let's hope you're right," said Sandra. "Still, it was good to see their faces when you challenged them."

Katie started laughing.

"I don't believe you, Gran. Fancy taking on a pair of drug dealers in a shopping centre car park! My mates will never believe this when I tell them."

"Come on, let's go home," said Sandra, starting the car engine. "At least we'll have something more exciting to talk about than the boys will, no matter how good the rugby was."

During the evening meal, Steve and James were regaled with the story of Gloria's exploits, with both of them fully supporting her actions, while trying to reassure Sandra and Katie that no real harm had been done.

While the plates were being cleared away, Gloria stood at the sink looking out of the window across to the green, an area of grass and bushes about ten metres wide that separated the two sides of the road into a one-way system. She noticed there was a small group of people beginning to gather there.

"Sandra, I think our friends may be about to arrive."

The whole family gathered at the window.

"Turn the kitchen light off," said Steve. "That way they won't be able to see in."

Sure enough, within a few minutes the black BMW arrived, and the crowd swarmed around both the driver and passenger doors. Gloria was straining her eyes to see what was happening and she could see the driver passing items from his mouth in exchange for cash. She'd witnessed this behaviour many times before in London and knew it was probably crack or heroin.

"Look. The driver is mouth dealing the gear," she said.

"What does that mean?" asked James.

"It means he's holding the drugs in his mouth. He takes the cash from each punter in turn, spits the drugs out into the user's hand, then makes sure the user puts it into his own mouth, before he moves away. The user then sneaks away to somewhere quiet, so he can take the drugs."

"That's disgusting! Why do they keep it in their mouths?"

"So that if the police search them, they've got nothing on them. The drugs are wrapped in cling film, so if they get stopped and searched, they swallow them then wait for nature to take its course. Then they've got the messy job of trying to find them again."

"Oh my God, I think I'm going to be sick." Sandra had gone pale and gagged as she listened. "How on earth do you know all this?"

"I suppose I've just picked it up over time. I've had years of this where I live. I've seen it, been on committees trying to stamp it out, and heard many, many stories about it from my mate on the force, Sean."

In less than five minutes the crowd had whittled down to a couple of young teenagers, who didn't appear to have bought anything. The users had their gear, and were heading off to find somewhere to sniff, shoot up, smoke, or swallow their purchases in private. The car sped off before the driver had wound the window up. Gloria, Sandra, and Katie all recognised him from the car park.

THAT NIGHT, GLORIA hardly got any sleep at all. Although she had been told about the situation on Sandra's estate, seeing it actually happening and the effect on her family was another thing entirely. Although the car did not appear again during Gloria's last two evenings, she'd been shocked enough by the confrontation, and the brazen dealing on the estate, to know that she wanted to deal with the problem. However, she was too close to the situation, and realised she couldn't risk suspicion being directed towards her, not at the moment anyway.

Thank heavens I decided to leave the Glock behind. Tempting as it was to sort it out, this problem would have to wait for a while.

All too soon, Wednesday arrived and Gloria was back at Newcastle Station, bidding farewell to her family. She squeezed her daughter tight.

"Thanks darling, I've had a wonderful time. I'll come back up again shortly. After I've retired."

"It's been great mum. Hey, I bet you can't wait for your retirement, being able to lay around all day watching telly!"

Gloria chuckled.

"Oh dear. Hearing it described like that, I think I'll visit the agencies and search for another job straight away."

They laughed, hugged again, and said their final goodbyes. Sandra watched tearfully as her mum boarded the train, turned, smiled, and disappeared inside.

Several hours later Gloria was home. As soon as she was back inside her flat, she checked the Glock. Running her hands slowly over the smooth, cold blackness of the metal, she said quietly to herself: "You've got work to do, my friend. But will it be Norwich first, or Newcastle? That's the question."

She wrapped it, gently placed it back inside the Cornflakes box, and put the box back inside the cupboard.

THIRTY-ONE
Thursday, 31st December 1998

IT WAS NEW YEAR'S EVE, and Gloria had nowhere to go. Well, that wasn't strictly true; she'd received three invitations to parties, none of which had tempted her in the slightest. Instead, she'd decided to have a quiet night in, curled up in her chair with a nice bottle of wine in front of the television. There had been no more letters, and she'd heard nothing more about who had arranged the fake alibi; Gloria tried to put the whole affair out of her mind for one evening.

When the phone rang, Gloria assumed it was her daughter calling with best wishes for the New Year.

"Hello."

"Crikey! You sound miserable, what's the matter, love?"

"Lily! How lovely to hear your voice. Sorry, I was having a wine, and feeling sorry for myself. How are you?"

"Well, if you press the buzzer and let me in out of this freezing cold, I'll tell you in person."

"What! You mean you're downstairs? Here? Now?"

"Yes, and it's bloody bitter out here, so stop dithering, and let me in."

Gloria pressed the door release buzzer and heard the familiar click as someone pushed the door open. Stunned but delighted by the turn of events, she opened her front door and greeted Lily as she came along the corridor. The friends hugged. Then Gloria spotted that Lily had a suitcase behind her.

"Why didn't you tell me you were coming to stay? I'd have got some decent food in."

"No need. Tonight, we have a table for two booked for eight o'clock at Kettners in Soho. Anyway, I wanted to surprise you. I knew you wouldn't be going out anywhere. You never do on New Year's Eve. You're so predictable."

"Really Lily? Kettners? That's my absolute favourite. You really are the most wonderful friend anyone could wish for. Thank you so much." Gloria could feel herself about to cry.

Lily placed a comforting arm around Gloria's shoulder and kissed her forehead.

"Come on, you dozy cow, stop grizzling or you'll start me off. Let's get my stuff sorted, then we can get dolled up and hit the town."

LILY HAD BOOKED a table in the front room, where the grand piano was situated, clearly remembering that it was Gloria's favourite part of the restaurant. The pianist tonight was a very odd-looking middle-aged woman, wearing an outrageously flowery dress and a flamboyant lemon hat with a very wide brim.

"Thank you so much Lily, this is fabulous. How did you manage to arrange it? Kettners don't usually take bookings, it's normally first come, first served."

"You're forgetting, my sweet, it's New Year's Eve. You have to book everywhere."

"Well, however you did it, I'm just so, so grateful. Cheers Lily." Gloria raised her glass of champagne. "Anyway, how's life in Bristol?"

"It's great thanks, but I've got a slightly more important question for you." Lily leaned forward and looked directly into her friend's eyes.

Gloria nervously said, "Go on."

"Did you see the news this morning about the lady they're looking for in connection with the shooting in Birmingham?"

Gloria froze momentarily, before quickly regaining her composure. "No, what lady is that?"

"Apparently, before he was killed, that bloke was kicked out of a café, and this woman was in the queue in front of him. He abused the staff, left the café and walked off. The thing is, a few seconds after he left, the woman left too, walking off in the same direction. The police are urgently trying to identify her because they think she could have useful information."

Gloria's heart was hammering. She was fighting to stop her hands shaking as she sipped her champagne and asked, "Did they have a picture of her?"

"Only a very poor black and white video from a traffic camera; it shows Bramhall walking along the road where he was shot. Twenty seconds later, the woman walks into the road as well, so it's understandable why they want to speak to her."

"Yes. They must be desperate to find her; what did she look like?"

"I'd say she must have been between fifty and seventy, with absolutely no fashion sense at all!"

Gloria laughed.

"Oh dear, sounds like some of the women I work with. Come to that, it sounds a bit like me."

"Leaving aside the atrocious lack of style, darling, it could have been." Lily leaned back, grinning. "What with the first murders practically on your doorstep, and you being in Bristol when the second ones took place, is there anything you'd like to tell me?"

Gloria let out the breath she was unaware she had been holding; it was obvious from Lily's mischievous grin that her friend was teasing her, so Gloria decided it was time to turn the tables.

"Actually, Lily, it couldn't have been me. I've already been eliminated from their enquiries."

"Eliminated from their enquiries? What are you talking about?"

The expression on Lily's face was a picture. So much so that Gloria began to enjoy herself.

"Last Monday I was arrested on suspicion of the murders in Bloomsbury. They kept me in custody for 12 hours, removed all my possessions from me, fingerprinted me, photographed me and took my DNA. I was interviewed by two detectives in front of my solicitor, before they confirmed my story and released me with apologies." Gloria sat back, savouring the impact of her story, and taking another slurp of champagne.

Lily was dumbfounded. "Why didn't you tell me about this? You were arrested for murder, and you didn't phone me?"

"I was saving it as a surprise."

"Well that's certainly worked! Why the hell did they suspect you?"

Gloria realised she had to be careful what she said.

"Remember I told you about being attacked at the front door of our block? Well, a neighbour saw it happen. She was convinced that they were the same couple who were killed later that evening, but they definitely weren't. She then saw me leaving home in the evening and coming back twenty minutes later. Apparently, it was around the time the murders were committed."

"Where were you during those twenty minutes then? Did you have a good alibi?"

"At a brasserie, booking a table for myself and some women from the bridge club. Luckily three people who'd seen me made statements."

"Bloody hell! Just imagine. Gloria Jones, the 64-year-old serial killer! How on earth could they have suspected you? I mean, it's laughable!"

"That's what I told them. They even held me at home under arrest, while they searched my flat for the murder weapon!"

"No! That must have been awful! What are they playing at? Are they just arresting anyone to make it look like they're finally pulling their fingers out?"

Gloria decided it was time to change the subject, before she had to tell her friend any more lies.

"Anyway, enough about my non-existent criminal career. It's New Year's Eve—let's enjoy ourselves. What would you like to do after this?"

"I've always wanted to be in Trafalgar Square to welcome the New Year in with all the other revellers."

"Okay, if that's what you want, but most people are very disappointed, and it can be an absolute crush."

"Oh, please Glo!"

Gloria relented. "Okay then; as you arranged this wonderful surprise, your wish is my command!"

After enjoying a delicious meal, they walked arm-in-arm down Charing Cross Road to join the throng at the top end of Trafalgar Square. Forty minutes later they were welcoming in the New Year together.

"Happy New Year, Lily."

"Happy New Year. You were right about the celebrations. It was a bit of a let-down; you can't even hear Big Ben chiming."

"I did try to warn you. Everyone I know who's come here has been disappointed." Gloria hugged her friend, then said, "I still feel like celebrating, and I've got an expensive bottle of red in my cupboard crying out to be drunk. I know we've shared two bottles already, but how about one more glass?"

THIRTY-TWO
Friday 1st January, 1999

"OH MY GOD! My head is killing me. Why did you make me drink so much?"

Gloria looked up at a very green-looking Lily standing over her bed; she was reaching forward, offering a cup of tea.

"Thanks Lily, what time is it?"

"It's just gone half ten."

"Half ten! Then why do I feel so tired?"

"Because you kept me up drinking until nearly four in the morning! You older ladies simply don't have the stamina any more. I've been up for over an hour already!"

"All right, don't take the piss! Anyway, I'm only three months older than you! Tell you what, I'll make you a lovely breakfast."

Lily looked down at Gloria and shook her head.

"No, you won't, I had my breakfast watching this morning's ten o'clock news. One of the reports was horrible. An old couple on holiday in Norwich were walking in a park near the city centre yesterday evening, when they were attacked by a group of Asian men. It looks like the old lady will be paralysed for the rest of her life and they both took a terrible beating. Who on earth could do that to an old couple?

"Oh no. Not Lyne Heath?"

"Yes, it was. How on earth did you know that?"

"I saw a news report about attacks in that park a couple of days ago. Three men had been released because the CPS didn't have enough to charge them. Looks like they've carried on where they left off."

"They certainly have. The police are pulling their hair out. They seem to know who's committing these crimes, but can't get enough evidence to put the bastards away."

"I don't want to talk about it anymore. It's too depressing. Tell you what, how would you like a day out at the British Museum?"

"The British Museum? I've always wanted to go. Is it far from here?"

"About a ten-minute walk; is that close enough for an old lady to manage?"

LILY LEFT ON Sunday morning and headed to Paddington Station to catch her train to Bristol. They'd enjoyed their weekend together, with trips to the British Museum, the Royal Academy, and after queuing for tickets at the half-price ticket booth, an evening at the theatre watching Mamma Mia.

Feeling energised by her visit to Sandra, and the unexpected few days with Lily, Gloria returned to her office to complete the final week of her working life.

During her evenings, she made great efforts to contact friends and neighbours, many of whom she visited for a cup of tea and a chat, or to share a bottle of wine. One reason for these visits was to drop into conversation that she'd be away on Friday night, because she'd arranged to stay with a friend in Colchester for the weekend. They would have no idea that the friend was utterly fictitious, and that Gloria was simply laying the foundations of an alibi, should she need it.

One such friend she visited was Suzie. Without mentioning their contents, Gloria gently probed about whether Suzie had any knowledge of the strange letters that she'd been receiving. Suzie seemed genuinely perplexed. Either that, or she was an excellent actress. Gloria left Suzie's flat feeling satisfied with what she'd heard, and confident that Suzie wasn't the author either. So who was?

Each night, Gloria spent an hour carrying out research into the attacks on Lyne Heath. She concentrated in particular on the exact locations of the attacks and the usual haunts of the three main suspects featured in the news report.

She'd already booked her train ticket and, anticipating that being in the right place at the right time, with no witnesses would be tricky to say the least, Gloria resigned herself to staying in Norwich, at least for the

Friday night. If necessary, she would stay an extra night on Saturday to get the job done.

Good lord, I'm even beginning to think like a contract killer! She was struggling with the concept that these were indeed her own thoughts and plans, worried that she might actually be having fun, that she was enjoying planning the murders of three people.

THURSDAY THE SEVENTH of January finally arrived. Gloria was retiring and the staff at her work threw her a slap-up meal to celebrate both her birthday and retirement at the local pub. There were the usual gifts and embarrassing speeches. Drink flowed freely and she was nicely merry when two colleagues walked her the short distance home to her flat.

"It's very kind of you, but it's really not necessary." She had said to her gallant companions.

"There were two people killed not far from here a few weeks ago," one of her colleagues said.

"I know," said Gloria, smiling to herself. "But I'm quite capable of taking care of myself, honestly."

THIRTY-THREE
Friday 8th January 1999

GLORIA AWOKE, FEELING groggy, to a bitterly cold, crisp morning, with a touch of frost whitening the tips of the grass in the churchyard outside her lounge window. This was the first day of her retirement, and more importantly, the first day of her planned trip to Norwich.

She had risen at seven, showered and breakfasted by eight, then settled down with a cup of tea to watch the news, just in case there had been last-minute developments in either the serial killer investigations, or the Norwich attacks. Both were mentioned, but only briefly. Gloria turned the TV off, picked up her small suitcase, checked the gun was safely in the front pouch of her handbag, and walked out into the bracing morning air.

Her first port of call was Camden High Street, with its bustling shops and covered market next to the canal. There were plenty of charity shops from which to choose a change of clothing for the trip. The Oxfam Shop provided her with a thick grey overcoat and, once again, she chose a black woolly hat from a discount clothes warehouse.

There was widespread disgust in the press about the Norwich attacks, and the police had increased their presence on Lyne Heath to thwart further assaults. More importantly, one newspaper report had provided Gloria with a piece of information that could prove vital—the gang had moved into other areas of the heath, and were extending their activities into other local parks. Evidently, this was in reaction to the heightened police presence.

The train from London Liverpool Street to Norwich was crowded, but at least it departed and arrived on time. During the journey, Gloria began to have an odd feeling that people were watching her: the scruffy looking man across the aisle from her; the middle-aged businessman opposite. Another passenger, a tough-looking young man in jeans and a jacket, with what Gloria would call a boxer's nose, passed her seat twice during the journey and, each time, Gloria sensed him looking at her. *Get a grip. You're being paranoid.*

Norwich was cloudier than London and slightly chillier, with a biting easterly wind. Gloria was well wrapped up, having changed from her usual beige mac and neatly brushed bobbed hair, into the grey overcoat and black woolly hat. For this trip, she'd not bothered with boots, simply wearing her normal black shoes.

The hotel Gloria had chosen was very small and homely, and situated in the centre of a village on the north-east outskirts of Norwich, opposite a rather charming old pub, called The Walnut Tree. The taxi driver who'd picked her up at Norwich station agreed to wait while she checked in at the hotel and took her suitcase up to her room.

Having done so, she headed into the city centre. She was hungry, and an Italian Restaurant called Luigi's in a quiet, cobbled back street was the perfect antidote to her rumbling stomach. In fact, she left thinking that perhaps she'd eaten a tad too much. After settling her bill, she decided that a walk to Lyne Heath was required; she could walk off the pasta while seeing what she could discover about her targets.

Shortly after four, Gloria stepped onto Lyne Heath for the first time. The light was fading fast, and the temperature was dropping. There was no sign of any police, and the public seemed to be behaving quite casually. People out walking their dogs, couples strolling hand in hand. However, Gloria realised that she couldn't see anyone walking alone. She also noticed that no one was venturing into the heath's woodland, they were all keeping to paths close to the main roads that surrounded the heath. It looked like everyone was deliberately staying in sight.

Two middle-aged couples walking towards her with a pair of black Labrador dogs gave Gloria her first chance to engage the locals in conversation.

"Excuse me, I'm staying with a friend in the area and I wondered if it's safe to cross the heath after the recent problems? It said on the news there was an increased police presence, but I haven't seen any yet."

One of the men was first to speak. "There are plenty of police in the central area and the west side of the heath. That's where the majority of attacks have taken place. None of the attacks happened round here; those cowards aren't brave enough to attack defenceless old people too near the surrounding roads; someone might see them and fight back."

"It must have been terrible over the past few weeks, worrying whether it was safe to go for a walk, or when they would strike next?"

"It's been awful!" The shorter and older of the two ladies stepped forward. "Do you know, the bastards had the nerve to go on TV, and make threats against anyone prepared to stand up to them? It's an utter disgrace! The police should lock them up and throw away the key."

"Yes, I saw that interview." Gloria nodded in agreement. "It was absolutely disgusting."

Now the other lady chimed in. "People in our street are walking around together in groups for safety; that's why we're walking our dogs with Sally and Ian."

"How awful for you, having to think like that. Has the police operation improved things?"

"It has around here, and on the west side," the first man said, "but from what we're hearing, they've moved to the east side. I pity the poor sods living over there."

"Why do you think they've moved?"

The short lady answered swiftly, "Because it's quiet, and there's no CCTV like there is here. It was installed here after a spate of robberies three years ago."

"Well, I've heard enough. I'm too much of a coward to stay around here on my own with that type of threat. My friend will be home soon, so I think I'll go back to her house and spend a quiet night in."

"Don't let the bastards affect how you live your life!" The first man insisted. "You can join us, if that would make you feel safer."

"Thanks for the offer, but I do need to get to my friend's house or she might worry."

They said their goodbyes and Gloria watched as the four people moved defiantly off down the path. The encounter had given her some food for thought.

THIRTY-FOUR

IT WAS NOW almost dark, and Gloria needed to determine the exact lay of the land on the eastern side of the heath. This could prove vital in her decision making if, as she'd been informed, the gang had moved their operation over there. She needed to check out places where they might hide, places from where she could observe them, places where she could carry out her mission.

She arrived back in the city centre as night drew in. Darkness had fallen, and shops were busy with customers making their final purchases while they still could. She needed a local street map, one which included the Lyne Heath area. Finding one in a small kiosk, she settled down in a café with a cappuccino and studied the map long and hard.

Less than an hour later, Gloria set off again for Lyne Heath, but this time she made her way to the east side, which was bordered by a dual carriageway, with a wooded area that seemed to be some kind of nature reserve. There were several paths, and Gloria saw that, despite the recent assaults, people were still out jogging, walking dogs and strolling casually through the park. She could see a couple of police vehicles parked up on a main road skirting the heath. The officers from those vehicles must have been patrolling nearby.

Biting the bullet, Gloria walked onto the heath, and headed off along one of the footpaths, not knowing what to expect, or whether what she was doing was actually very wise. All she knew was that she'd come this far, so bottling out now wasn't an option. There were still quite a few people about, even though the paths were only dimly lit by intermittent street lamps. *Maybe it's still a little early for gangs of robbers to be active.*

The likelihood of there being a dangerous gang in the area seemed to be far from the minds of most people she saw. Gloria lost count of the number of times she had to reply to a polite "Good evening". Then, she noticed a small, wooden summer house that backed onto the edge of a coppiced area of woodland, overlooking a small pond. She could just about make out a group of youngsters enjoying a take-away meal inside it, visible through the single open side of the hexagonal structure.

Fifteen minutes later, Gloria walked back towards where she'd joined the path. It was now almost seven, and the number of people using the path had declined rapidly, although there was still the odd cyclist, and a few couples out for an evening walk. The temperature had dropped, and Gloria shivered, buttoning her coat up around her neck.

A female cyclist suddenly emerged from the gloom and appeared to be pedalling quickly; she braked suddenly on reaching Gloria. She was breathless, but managed to gasp, "I'd be careful if I were you." She was panting a little. "There's a group of six or seven lads coming this way; they're being rather rowdy and threatening. I'd stay close to others if you can."

"How far away are they?"

The cyclist turned round, looking in the direction she'd just come from, concern etched on her face. "They'll be here in a couple of minutes."

Gloria had felt completely calm and in control up to now, but now she could feel fear rising inside her.

"Thanks for warning me. Don't worry, I'll be careful, you get on your way."

The cyclist sped off, looking back over her shoulder and shouting, "Just be careful!"

Excitement and terror surged through Gloria's body in equal measure. Could this be the same gang that had caused such fear on Lyne Heath? Had the man who'd told her about their attentions being focussed on this side of the heath been right? She'd find out very shortly.

Her senses were heightened: she could hear the gentle crunching of her feet on the asphalt footpath, she could smell the scent of pine mixed with a distant bonfire. Gloria was confident they would not attack her, or anyone else, until there were fewer witnesses. She'd prepared her plan of action, which she hoped might just work.

Raised voices told her that the gang were indeed approaching. Steeling herself as they came into view, she quickly counted their number. One, two, three, four, five. In her panic, the cyclist had over-estimated. Within thirty seconds, they were ten metres in front of her, and she recognised three of the group as the suspects for the spate of violent assaults on Lyne Heath: Yasser, Islam, and Ahmed. Controlling her anger on seeing them, she took the initiative and stepped into role. Gloria smiled and addressed them.

"Evening lads, I'm from the Peterborough Herald, and we're currently running articles on miscarriages of justice. I was told you'd probably be here and wondered if I could grab you for an interview."

All five were plainly confused by this confident approach from an old lady on a dimly lit footpath. Yasser replied, "Let me guess, you want to destroy us in your paper, just like all the others?"

"No, no, not at all. Like I said, we're running articles on miscarriages of justice. Do you feel that you're being persecuted because of your faith? The police have released you with no charges and that should be an end of it, no? As you say, the press always indulges in character assassination, just to sell copies."

"Okay lady," Yasser said. "We hear you. We need to chat."

"No problem, go ahead, take your time." Gloria was desperately trying to stop shaking. She certainly didn't want them to see how scared she was.

The gang moved off the footpath and onto a grassy area ten metres away from Gloria. Two of them moved to one side, while Yasser, Islam, and Ahmed talked in hushed tones. Gloria strained to hear them, but couldn't make out a word they were saying.

Looking at the group closely, Gloria soon realised why the other two were not taking part in the discussions; they couldn't have been more than fourteen years old, whilst the other three looked around twenty-five, maybe even older.

The discussions ended and Islam became spokesman.

"We will speak to you now, in our office over there." He indicated the now empty summer house with an outstretched arm. "I'm afraid my two young friends will not be involved; they're going back to town."

He barked out orders to the boys, who turned and walked rapidly off towards the city centre. This sudden development had taken Gloria by surprise. Was this a ruse by them to attack her in the summer house? She blurted out an obviously flustered answer.

"Oh goodness, I hadn't planned for this. I don't have my notepad; I wasn't expecting to meet you until tomorrow, or the day after."

"No problem lady, chill, we'll have a brief chat then arrange to meet again tomorrow. That okay with you?"

Deciding she had no choice but to take the plunge, Gloria agreed to walk with them the short distance to the summer house. As she did so, she opened the clasp on the front of her handbag, and ensured that the gun's handle was in the correct position, should she have urgent need of it.

Gloria entered the summer house and immediately sat down to one side of the opening, thereby ensuring there was no possibility of having the men sitting on both sides of her. They seemed very confident and relaxed, their arrogance rising to the surface as soon as they were settled on the bench, legs spread out in front of them. Ahmed rose to his feet, smiled and said, "Sorry lady, but I'm desperate for a piss." He promptly opened his flies, turning only partly away from her and urinated through the open side. He was only one metre away from Gloria and in full view. When he'd finished, he shook his penis hard, spraying Gloria with drops and making Yasser and Islam laugh out loud.

Her loathing for the three men in front of her was in danger of making her explode. She fought hard to combat her instinct to draw the Glock and shoot then and there. But there were too many members of the public nearby, too many witnesses. She just about managed to control herself.

Ahmed sat down and Yasser suddenly became serious. "Why should we trust you to put our story over in the way we want?"

"Because I'm here, and I'm on your side. Remember, it was me who offered to help you, not you who approached me."

"Why would you want to help us though? I know you say you're doing stories on miscarriages of justice, but what's in it for you?"

Gloria had been waiting for this question and was ready with her answer.

"I'm not a great fan of the police, the government, or the tabloid press. Clearly I'm not a Muslim myself, but I have great sympathy with the causes of some of the more direct-action groups, if you know what I mean?" The words really stuck in Gloria's throat and were a complete shot in the dark. However, if they bought it, she knew they would open up.

The three men grinned at each other and Islam said, "Yeah, we know exactly what you mean. Nothing we like more than a white British sympathiser." He laughed. "What would you say in your article, if you knew that we'd committed the crimes they accused us of? You know, robbing them old people?"

Once again, she needed to conceal her real feelings and lie convincingly.

"Listen, I saw the reports, let's just say we all know the truth, we all know whether you're guilty or not. All I'm interested in, is that according to the law of this country you're innocent and that's good enough for me."

All three laughed again, childish giggles, then smacked hands together in high fives.

"Serious respect!" shouted Islam. "Serious respect, that's what you've just earned lady. What happened to those old folks, let's just say it was a redistribution of wealth from the old whites to the young Muslims, you get it?"

He's bragging about robbing and beating old people, I can't believe this! Gloria was appalled by this startling admission, but she couldn't react to it. Not yet. She needed to play the game.

"Yes, I understand. Look, my objective is to help you by writing a positive article, and you would be helping me by making me look good in front of my boss. Whatever has gone on before doesn't bother me. I'm not interested. So, do we have a deal?"

All three looked at each other and exchanged nods. "We'll be here tomorrow night at ten," said Yasser.

"Please, call me Ginny."

"Okay Ginny. I'm Yasser, he's Islam, and he's Ahmed. We're chuffed you're going to help us. Now, ten o'clock tomorrow night. That okay with you?"

"It's a little late; there won't be anyone else around at that time of night. Can't we just meet in a pub in town?" Gloria had asked the question in the full knowledge that anywhere in the public gaze would be unacceptable to them.

"When you're in our business, that's how we like it. No one listening to our discussions, and no witnesses to who we're meeting, or what we're doing."

Once again, they giggled and exchanged high-fives; they seemed, at times, like children, proud of their naughtiness.

"It's just that I'm not convinced how safe I'll feel, you three together, and me on my own."

"Look, if what you've just told us is true, you're our friend. If we'd wanted to do anything, you know, like rob you, we'd have done it tonight. This could be good for us. We like you, Ginny."

Yasser stood up swiftly, making Gloria jump. He motioned to the others, and they stood up too.

"See you tomorrow at ten; make sure you bring everything you need for the report."

Gloria's hand rested on the front pouch of her handbag. Caressing the shape of the gun inside, she said, "Don't worry Yasser, I'll bring everything I need to complete the job."

The three men swaggered off without another word, and without a backward glance. Gloria drew a deep breath, raised herself to her feet, and found that her legs were shaking so much, she had trouble standing. Looking out towards the footpath, she saw a young couple kissing; they were walking in roughly the direction she needed to go. On wobbly legs, she strode across the grass and onto the path in front of the startled lovers.

"Evening," said Gloria.

Not wishing to enter into conversation, she walked on ahead, while ensuring she remained in their line of sight.

Thirty minutes later Gloria was in a taxi returning to her hotel. Still shaky, she sat down for her evening meal, but slowly calmed down as the food and wine replenished her. Finishing her meal, she retired to her room.

Rivulets of hot water poured down her face, as Gloria washed away lingering remnants of the filth she'd met in the summer house. The images of their faces were etched into her memory, her hatred of them threatening to overwhelm her.

The shower wasn't great, but she enjoyed it anyway. Rubbing and scrubbing herself, she felt it was somehow cleansing her soul, and absolving her of any blame, before she set out on what she expected to be an extraordinary day.

The complete and utter disregard for decency displayed by the three young men, coupled with the brazen admission by Islam that they had been responsible for at least some of the attacks, reaffirmed her determination to do what she truly believed was the right thing. It was brutal, it was horrible, but it needed to be done.

THIRTY-FIVE
Saturday 9th January 1999

GLORIA HAD NOT slept well, her mind plagued by doubts about the task she had set herself. The fact that she'd made herself so vulnerable by agreeing to go to the summer house, coupled with the lies she'd told to bring them round to her side, were gambles that could have gone badly wrong. Another problem worrying her greatly was the two younger members of the gang who'd headed back into town. They had seen her face, and were now able to identify her. Finally, when it came to the deed, she would be outnumbered three to one, not a situation she had faced before.

Although not particularly hungry, Gloria went downstairs to breakfast at eight, where she smiled and exchanged casual pleasantries with other hotel guests. She deliberately chose a table in a corner, away from the others, who were all seated at tables with a view through the patio doors out onto the attractive gardens. She was deep in her own thoughts and wanted to remain locked inside her own world until the day was done.

Back in her room, Gloria prepared herself by standing in front of the mirror and giving herself a good talking to. This always made her feel better when she was facing a difficult day.

She decided to spend the morning carrying out a recce of the Lyne Heath area, in particular the area around the summer house. Holding her head high, Gloria opened her bedroom door and stepped confidently into the corridor.

At reception she ordered a taxi, and was soon in the centre of Norwich, from where she intended walking to Lyne Heath. Her hotel was actually only a thirty-minute walk from the heath, but she felt uncomfortable about approaching directly, aware that she needed to lay as many false trails as possible.

She felt remarkably calm—considering what she was planning—and unbelievably found herself looking forward to the evening. *What on earth is happening to me?*

Her earlier doubts were replaced by a sense of resolve, now that she was on the move. She headed past Norwich Castle, where she took the street map from her handbag – she would look just like any other tourist, trying to get their bearings. Keeping off the main routes would be her best bet. She knew that CCTV would be far more likely on major roads, so it would be safer in the back streets.

Stepping into a side street, Gloria saw two young boys walking towards her. As they came closer, she realised they were the young lads she'd seen in company with her three targets. One of the boys was thin, painfully thin, and was wearing a grey tracksuit. Looking at him more closely, Gloria could see that he was certainly no older than thirteen. The other lad, in jeans and a puffa jacket, was slightly chubby and also looked the same age. Realising this was too good an opportunity to miss, she approached them.

"Hi boys, how are you doing?"

Both boys initially looked startled at being addressed by an elderly woman, until the chubby one said, "You're the newspaper lady, aren't you? Yeah, we're okay thanks. Hey, you were mad speaking to those three nutters on your own; we were really worried that you were in for a beating."

"Nutters? That's an odd way to speak about your friends," replied Gloria. "Aren't you all in the same gang?"

The thinner lad said indignantly, "We're not in a gang. Those three are nothing to do with us! They saw us on the heath and made us go with them. They're total scum; if you hadn't turned up, we were terrified of what they were going to do to us."

This was all useful information, and Gloria realised she needed to use it to her advantage. She nodded and said, "They were very unpleasant once we were in the summer house. On the plus side, they talked to me about the story I wanted to write, and didn't hurt me in any way."

"You were lucky. They seem to like hurting people. Let's hope you'll never have to see them again, eh?"

In that moment, Gloria realised they had no idea of the appointment she had with them that evening. "Too right I won't see them again. I'm heading home to Peterborough soon, and they'll be just a distant memory."

"Good idea." The boys had begun to shuffle and look awkward, clearly keen to move on, so Gloria said goodbye and headed off toward the heath.

A BREEZE CHILLED the air, and Gloria was grateful for her charity-shop woolly hat and large grey coat. While crossing the heath, Gloria noticed two pairs of police officers on patrol; there were also people walking, cycling, and running. She also noticed, for the first time, just how remote from the nearest road the summer house was. This was ideal for her evening's mission, but at the same time could prove to be very dangerous should things not go according to plan.

She carefully checked each path leaving the summer house, registering where they all led to. There was no room for error; her life could depend on getting her research right.

Finally, she chose the path she would use if her mission was successful, and felt satisfied she had done all the preparation she could.

Gloria returned to Norwich city centre and settled down for a pub lunch, followed by an afternoon at the cinema, watching the latest Hollywood blockbuster, Titanic, as a distraction. Despite the constant churning in her stomach, she found herself enjoying her afternoon.

After the cinema, Gloria looked around the shops for a while, before returning to the hotel. She checked, double checked, then triple checked the Glock, before placing it in the front pocket of her handbag, ensuring the gun handle was perfectly positioned, should she need to grab it in a hurry. As soon as everything was ready, she went downstairs for her evening meal.

Once again, she returned to the city centre, where she visited the Red Lion pub for a large glass of wine. She needed something to calm her nerves, and alcohol seemed the best option, since cigarettes were now off the menu. Once she had downed the first glass, she was tempted to go for another, but knowing she would shortly need all her wits about her, decided against it. It was time to go.

Changing the route from the one taken that morning, she walked briskly to Lyne Heath, where she made her way to the east side of the park, the side furthest away from Norwich. It was noticeable that the area had become markedly quieter; she passed absolutely no-one on the heath. After walking for a few more minutes, she saw the summer house sitting in an open area of grassland, yet close to the edge of the woods. A slim crescent moon was reflected in the small pond. The temperature was dropping rapidly and Gloria could see her breath on the evening air.

Looking carefully all around and listening for sounds of activity, Gloria realised that it was absolutely silent except for the rumble of traffic on roads surrounding the heath. In the dim glow of the street lights, she could see that there was no-one else around. Gloria turned on her small torch and walked to the summer house.

Once inside, Gloria was relieved to find they weren't there yet. For the first time she realised just how hidden she would be. Although one section was open, it was a hexagonal structure, so it had only one sixth open to view from the outside world. The seating inside was around the edge of the walls and consisted of simple wooden benching. This made escape for her almost impossible if events took a turn for the worse. *My God, why didn't I notice this last night?*

For safety, she stood outside, turned off her torch, and waited, unsure whether the chattering of her teeth was the result of the cold night air, or her mounting nerves.

IT WAS NOW a quarter past ten, and Gloria had changed from being reasonably in control, to being on the verge of a panic attack. She was half-certain they wouldn't turn up—and a small part of her was probably hoping that they wouldn't. She was about to head back to Norwich when she heard a voice coming from the darkness.

"Hey Ginny, glad you made it!"

Gloria shone her torch in the direction of the voice and saw three men strolling towards her from the edge of the woods. She took a deep breath and replied, "Good to see you. I thought you weren't coming."

Ahmed said, "We weren't going to miss the chance of getting our side of the story out there. Let's go inside."

Gloria immediately felt vulnerable. "Can't we stay outside and talk? It's fine here, isn't it?"

"We like to keep our business private and out of public view. Besides, we've got a surprise for you," said Islam. He firmly took hold of Gloria's right arm and steered her inside.

Gloria's nerves were now at breaking point. She didn't like the way this was going at all, and she certainly didn't like being manhandled by the young man. However, once inside, Islam released his grip, and she sat down to the right of the opening, while her other targets sat spaced around the benching. The light from her torch allowed her to see them perfectly well.

"Right, I've bought my pen and notepad, and I've several questions I want to ask; are you ready to start?"

They all laughed and Yasser said, "Yes, we're ready, and we want to give you our story, but we've got a reputation to keep up, so firstly we want you to do something for us. Only fair." He looked at the others and smirked.

Gloria had a sinking feeling, but composed herself and said, "What's that?"

The three men stood up, and Gloria automatically pressed herself into the wall behind her. Without warning, they unzipped their flies, laughing as they did so.

"Three blow jobs, and we'll give you all the answers you want!" Ahmed was the spokesman this time.

Gloria couldn't believe her ears—or eyes—and fought the urge to gag. Thinking quickly, she said, "Okay. I'll give it a go, though I might be a bit rusty. Why don't you pull your trousers down a bit further? That way I can do a proper job."

They didn't need asking twice. In double quick time all three were reclining on the benches, wriggling their trousers down to their ankles.

They were clearly enjoying themselves, laughing, joking, and making lewd remarks and suggestions to Gloria. Once again, she thought how like adolescent children they were. With their dicks doing all the thinking. What they hadn't considered was the fact that, with their trousers at half mast, they were now practically immobilised.

Nonchalantly standing up with her handbag slung over one shoulder, Gloria removed her hat, as the tension was making her feel overly warm.

"Here we go then."

The men continued to laugh and were so caught up in their own excitement that they didn't notice Gloria pull the gun from her bag. Sitting nearest to her was Ahmed, then Yasser, then Islam. She calmly pointed the gun at Ahmed and said, "Bang Bang, you're dead."

Ahmed had a look of utter disbelief on his face, which soon turned to abject terror. He was about to say something when Gloria pulled the trigger. The bullet entered just below the edge of his hairline and the back of his head splattered over Yasser, who screamed in horror. Ahmed's body folded at the waist, then slid off the bench, head butting the floor on his way down; it twitched slightly, before lying still. Islam was silent, frozen with dread. Gloria saw that their erections were quickly disappearing and joked, "Not so hard now, are you?"

Islam started crying, pleading with her. "Please don't, I don't want to die."

"F-f-fucking hell," stammered Yasser. "It's you, isn't it? You're the one who's been killing all those people!"

"Correct," said Gloria, calmly shooting him straight between the eyes.

His head wobbled almost comically on his shoulders, then he fell forward, his bottom sliding off the bench before collapsing to the floor, his body contorted. Islam had staggered to his feet and was leaning forward, desperately struggling to pull his trousers up; he was facing the ground as Gloria calmly fired straight into the top of his head. He slumped, folding like a puppet whose strings had been cut, then twisted as he fell in a heap. Ahmed and Yasser were lying face down, but Islam was lying face up, his eyes open, but devoid of life.

Gloria slipped the gun back into her bag, replaced her woolly hat, and without wasting any more time, walked quickly onto her chosen footpath, which led to the edge of the heath farthest from town. She felt she didn't need to check the bodies; experience now told her that they were all dead.

She'd identified an inviting-looking pub in a leaflet from her hotel, and this would be her next port of call. She could hear shouts from the far side of the park where she'd seen the police; someone had obviously heard the gunshots. This made her speed up and in only a few minutes she'd left the heath, walked through a couple of residential streets and was safely seated in the Heath Tavern, sipping a white wine. As far as she was aware, she hadn't passed anyone en route.

Gloria let her hand rest on the familiar shape of the Glock through the front of her handbag; there was heat coming from the barrel. Adrenaline was pumping through her, and for the first time she looked around the pub at the other customers. There were only half a dozen: a group of four having a meal, and two single men drinking separately at the bar.

She started to feel herself calming down a little, finished her wine, then went to the bar and ordered another, just before the barmaid called last orders. After draining her second glass of wine, she left the pub and walked back to her hotel, arriving in her room at twenty to midnight. *Job done.*

THIRTY-SIX

GLORIA RAN HERSELF a bath and lay back, luxuriating in the hot, steaming water. Looking back, the whole sequence of events in Norwich now seemed surreal. She had placed herself in greater danger than ever before and had survived—no, triumphed! It was hard not to feel a sense of satisfaction, almost pride in her achievements. Three people had died, but Gloria would not mourn their passing. And neither would their victims.

She emerged from the lavender-scented water, once again feeling cleansed, then dried herself in front of the full-length mirror. The image looking back at her was confident, defiant.

That night, Gloria lay in bed staring into the darkness, the events of the evening replaying in her head. The next thing she knew was the sound of movement in the corridor outside, and her bedroom was bathed in the soft light of morning. It was time to go.

Hastily getting out of bed, Gloria hurriedly packed her things, then checked and re-checked that absolutely nothing was left in the room. At breakfast, she sat with the same people from the previous evening. Conversation was all about the murders on Lyne Heath; after listening for a short while, Gloria said, "Murders, what murders?"

"Haven't you seen the news this morning?"

"No, I slept in late; I haven't heard any news."

"It's awful," said one of the women. "They were shot dead in cold blood in the summer house on Lyne Heath, three young Asian men apparently. The police are suggesting there may have been a sexual motive, but they're not saying what."

"How on earth could there be a sexual motive for three shootings?" asked Gloria.

"No idea," replied the woman, "but that's what they're saying."

The conversation carried on in much the same vein for a few more minutes, and Gloria quietly finished her breakfast, while surreptitiously listening in for any more details. She said her goodbyes before collecting her luggage and checking out at the reception.

"How was your stay, madam?"

"Fine, thank you."

"Did you enjoy your time in Norwich?"

"It was lovely."

"That's one hundred and forty pounds please. By the way, the taxi you ordered is waiting outside."

"Thank you." Gloria paid in cash, once again ensuring she left no electronic trail.

"Where are you headed for now?" he asked.

"Back home to London. Ironically, I think I'll feel safer there after the events on Lyne Heath last night."

Laughing and nodding, the receptionist said, "You're probably right there!" Then he added, "Oh, I nearly forgot, a young man brought this in an hour ago; he asked me to guarantee I would give it to you in person."

He passed Gloria a plain brown envelope with nothing written on the outside.

Gloria took it and sat on a chair. With trembling fingers, she opened the envelope and removed a familiar white sheet of paper, folded into three. The message was written in a different hand than previous ones, but was still in block capitals: *EXCELLENT WORK LAST NIGHT! KEEP IT UP. I'LL BE TALKING TO YOU SOON.*

"Are you okay, madam?" asked the receptionist. "You look distressed."

The blood had drained from Gloria's face; she felt faint. Fighting to regain her composure, she replied. "No... er... sorry, I've just had some unexpected news. Did the man who left this give his name?"

"No, afraid not, he just handed it over, asked me to ensure you received it personally, then left."

"Did he have an accent? Can you describe him?"

"He was late-twenties, short brown hair... sounded Irish. And he was wearing a smart grey jacket."

Gloria thanked the man, walked from the hotel and climbed into the taxi. Fifteen minutes later, she was at Norwich station and on the train home.

Throughout the journey, she tried to get her head around what had just happened. How on earth could the author of those letters have known where she was? Had they followed her to Norwich? Had they seen what she'd done? And what did the last part of the message mean? 'I'll be talking to you soon'? Who the fuck could it be?

The journey home was uneventful, apart from Gloria persuading the workmen of a refuse lorry outside Liverpool Street Station to let her dispose of a carrier bag in their lorry. A carrier bag containing a grey coat, and a black woolly hat.

Twenty minutes later, Gloria was home. She had now killed eight people in four cities. She was mentally exhausted, and shortly after sitting down, she drifted off to sleep in her armchair.

THIRTY-SEVEN

GLORIA WOKE UP to hear her intercom buzzing. Her neck was stiff and, at first, she was disorientated. Then, remembering the previous night, she lifted herself out of the chair, picked up the receiver and said, "Just a moment," before grabbing the gun from her bag, wrapping it in tissue, and placing it back into the Cornflakes box.

"Hello."

"It's the police; can you let me in, please?"

"Of course, pull the door and come up."

Gloria's heart was pounding, but despite receiving the letters, and despite the traumatic events of the past 24 hours, she was certain that, whatever the police wanted, it wasn't about last night. She opened the door to an attractive, young, female PC, with dark brown hair in a ponytail.

Closing the door, she showed the officer through to the lounge, indicated the settee and said, "Please sit down. How can I help you, officer?"

Leaning forward with her forearms on her knees, the PC looked straight at Gloria and said, "Are you aware of the murders last night in Norfolk, madam?"

This wasn't a question that Gloria had expected.

"Yes, I heard about them on the radio, why do you ask?"

"It would appear that the murders last night were committed by the same person, or at least with the same gun, as those in London, Bristol and Birmingham. I'm afraid that every person we have interviewed so far has to be interviewed again, including you." Her tone and expression were apologetic.

Relief flooded over Gloria, and she happily recounted her story. She told the woman everything: about seeing the man being chased, and the assault she suffered in the doorway, ending with her being wrongly arrested on suspicion of the Bloomsbury murders. She was sure her story hadn't changed, and when Gloria had finished, made the officer a cup of coffee before she left.

TWO DAYS LATER, GLORIA was no closer to understanding why a young man would have followed her to Norwich and left the letter. Why not just leave it through her door like the others? She went back over her train journey and that strange feeling she'd had of being watched. In particular, she recalled the young man passing her seat who had caught her eye. Could he be the same young man who had delivered the letter to her hotel?

Originally, she had assumed it must be someone who knew her well, but now she knew that assumption to be completely false. The last letter had said 'I'll be talking to you soon' so Gloria decided that there was nothing to be gained by worrying herself sick about it. Instead, she would carry on as usual and await their contact. Whatever they wanted, it clearly wasn't to serve her up to the police.

Despite her resolve, however, there were occasions when the enormity of her actions nagged at her thoughts and Gloria would involuntarily shiver with fear. She tried to reassure herself that all would be well, while the world she had always known was falling to pieces around her. The killings, the police investigation, the letters, James Williams-Glass and his fake alibi, and now this mysterious young messenger. These were all things that two months previously she would have dismissed as unthinkable—the stuff of fiction.

Meanwhile, the whole country was in the grip of vigilante fever. There was only one topic in newspapers, there was only one topic on TV news reports, there was only one topic of conversation in pubs and clubs. Who could the killer be? Gloria joined in the speculation, making herself sound as puzzled as everyone else—something which she found surprisingly easy.

The eight killings, in four separate incidents, in four different cities across the country, had now spawned frenetic activity in the police operation. A total of forty-seven suspects had been arrested, hundreds more people had been interviewed, and thousands of members of the public had been spoken to during door-to-door enquiries and stops on the street. Yet, there had still been no new leads. That was until a young dog-walker walked into Norwich Police Station.

THE ROOKIE PC working the front counter was having a boring morning, mainly taking minor crime reports. However, things changed for PC Steve Hiles when a young man and his dog approached the front counter.

The man was slim, verging on skinny, with scruffy mousy hair, skin-tight jeans, and a dark blue hip-length coat. At his side was a brown and white Jack Russell, which looked better fed than its master.

"Good morning sir, how can I help you?"

"I think I might have information regarding the murders on Lyne Heath on Saturday night."

PC Hiles, who had been slowly worn down by boredom over the previous two-and-a-half hours, became instantly alert. "Right sir, can I take your name please?"

"Certainly, it's Andrew Turner."

PC Hiles carefully noted down full contact details for Mr Turner, fully aware of the bollocking he would receive if he failed to obtain them. Once the man's details were safely logged, PC Hiles looked up from his notebook and said, "What information do you have, sir?"

"Well, at about ten-thirty on Saturday I was giving my dog her final walk before bedtime. We were walking along Beech Climb Road, our usual route close to the edge of Lyne Heath, when I heard a loud bang like a gun being fired; it came from somewhere on the heath. I thought I'd heard similar bangs a few seconds before, but this time I was certain. I wasn't far from the edge of the heath and Quarry Hill Lane, so I was pretty scared. I stood still and listened for a few seconds, but it was all quiet apart from passing traffic."

"And then what, sir?"

"We carried on walking and went under the trees on the corner so my dog could do her business. That's when I saw a woman leave the park; she crossed at the junction of Beech Climb Road and Quarry Hill Lane."

"Could you describe her please?"

"Yeah. She was carrying a light brown handbag, had a dark woolly hat on her head, a long coat which looked light green or maybe grey, dark trousers and dark shoes."

"What about her physical appearance, was she fat, thin, tall, short, young, old?"

"I couldn't tell her age, but at a guess I would say oldish, perhaps sixty to seventy. She was slim, medium height."

"Was she walking quickly; did she look flustered?"

"No, she was acting quite normally. It's just that she came from roughly the same direction as the gunshots. The only thing that struck me as a little odd was that she was holding her handbag very tightly to her chest. I wondered if she was frightened, what with all the attacks on the heath lately. I didn't come before because it really doesn't seem likely that she's anything to do with it and I didn't want to waste your time."

"No, you were right to come forward, that's very useful information. Please come through sir, I'll take you up to the incident room, where I'll need you to complete a statement."

PC Hiles showed Turner into the incident room, which had been set up the morning after the shootings. Once Hiles had explained to a detective exactly what the young man had seen, he was taken into a side office by two officers.

"DECAF LATTE AND a blueberry muffin, please." Gloria placed her order in Starbucks, five minutes from her home.

"That's four pounds twenty, please." The young girl behind the counter gave Gloria a practised smile and handed her the order. Gloria paid, and the girl said, "Enjoy."

Starbucks had recently installed a TV system, which normally had the BBC News Channel on. The sound was turned down, with subtitles for viewers. Gloria chose a table with an excellent view of the TV, settled down and tucked eagerly into her Blueberry muffin. The latest reports about the serial killer were all over the news, and she was keen to see what was going on.

Finishing her latte, she was about to leave, when a breaking news report flashed onto the screen. Recognising Assistant Commissioner Skelton, she saw that he was standing outside Scotland Yard, making a statement. Gloria watched the text scrolling across the screen with mounting concern.

"Following information from a member of the public, we wish to speak with a female who was seen leaving Lyne Heath shortly after the murders occurred. She was seen to leave the heath at the junctions of Beech Climb Road and Quarry Hill Lane, then walked off east along Beech Climb Road. This woman is described as slim, aged between 60 and 70 years, 5'4" to 5'6" tall, wearing a dark woolly hat, a long overcoat, possibly light green or grey in colour, dark trousers and dark shoes. We urgently wish to speak with this woman, who we believe may have vital information regarding three murders on Lyne Heath. Anyone with information regarding the identity of this woman, please contact Operation Chiddingstone. I will be happy to take questions."

Gloria didn't bother watching to see what questions were asked. Stunned, she stared down into her empty cup, no longer taking in what was being said on the TV. The description he had given of her was thorough. Would there be CCTV images of her anywhere? Would anyone at the hotel have recognised her from the description? Would anyone inside that pub have recognised her? So many thoughts were in her head that she began to feel dizzy.

Standing up, she left the café, sucking in huge lungfuls of air once she was outside. *This is a disaster. How could I have not noticed that someone had seen me?* Calming herself down, she rushed back home and phoned Sean on his mobile.

"Hi Sean, it's Glo, remember me? You used to pop round sometimes."

"Sorry Glo, everyone has been put on twelve-hour days. It doesn't leave me much spare time to see Gail, let alone visit you. I promise we'll get together when we've identified this lunatic so-called vigilante."

"Don't worry Sean, I'm only joking. Come and visit me whenever you're free, no pressure. So, it's going into overdrive in the incident room, is it?"

"You won't believe it, but the bosses are desperate to identify a woman seen leaving Lyne Heath after the gunshots were heard; she was coming from the right direction. They're certain she must have valuable information at the very least."

"Blimey. Are they close to identifying her?" Gloria tried to keep the concern from her voice.

"They haven't found any CCTV of her yet, but a barmaid from a nearby pub has come forward saying that a woman similar to that description came in at around the right time, stayed for about half an hour and knocked back two glasses of wine, then left. Other than that, they're struggling. Look Glo, I'm really busy here, can we chat some other time?"

"Sorry, love. Of course, off you go. We'll catch up soon. Bye Sean."

Gloria opened the window. *Sod it!* she thought as she guiltily lit a cigarette, her first since her birthday, and stared out into Phoenix Gardens. The smoke drifted out into the chilly night air, but all she could see were images of the three dead men in the summer house.

THIRTY-EIGHT
Tuesday 12th January 1999

"RIGHT, LET'S GO through what we have so far." Assistant Commissioner Skelton addressed the senior officers' briefing. The room was uncomfortably full, due to the attendance of two officers from Bristol, Birmingham and Norwich. "We now have eight murders, in four separate incidents, in four cities. Ballistic reports have proved that the same gun was used in each incident. Whoever the assailant is, they have left nothing for forensics to work on at any of the scenes. No DNA, no clothes fibres, nothing. This is beginning to look very professional."

A DI from Bristol asked, "What about fibres on the benches in either the bus shelter, or the summer house, sir?"

"Good question," said AC Skelton. "Unfortunately, these are very public places; consequently, forensics found sixty-eight different fibres in the bus shelter, and fifty-four different fibres in the summer house. It's far too many to trace where they all originated from."

He looked around the room at the assembled officers and continued, "The victims were seven men, and one woman, all of them have been identified by members of their families. They are all described as being aggressive towards the public; they have also been identified as known drug users, or as suspected of involvement in street crime, often with violence. In the Balsall Heath and Lyne Heath incidents, the perpetrator may well have targeted them following their identities being revealed on TV news reports."

Skelton proceeded to show images of the eight victims on the screen behind him.

"So far we have only two leads. A woman was seen leaving the Welcome Café on Heath Road in Balsall Heath, shortly after Alan Bramhall caused a disturbance by having a particularly nasty verbal altercation with members of the staff. She was described as slim, average height, aged between sixty and seventy-five, wearing a long purple coat and a black woolly hat. She was carrying a tan handbag slung over her shoulder."

A Superintendent from Birmingham added, "We have made exhaustive enquiries in the area, but no-one in the local community has any idea who the woman is. However, another image from CCTV at Birmingham New Street Station appears to show her boarding a train to London at twelve fifty p.m."

"Exactly," said AC Skelton. "She boarded a train to London—the one o'clock to London Euston to be precise." Another image was shown on the power-point screen, of the same woman travelling on a bus from Balsall Heath towards Birmingham city centre around the time of the murder.

"I'm convinced that, if she lived anywhere near Balsall Heath, someone would have identified her by now, so she's probably an outsider. The question is, why was she there, and more importantly, who is she?

"Then we move on to our second lead. A woman was seen leaving Lyne Heath about two minutes after gunshots were heard; in fact, she was seen coming from the precise area of the gunshots. She was then identified by a barmaid at The Heath Tavern public house at around half-ten, where she stayed for thirty minutes and had two glasses of wine. Unfortunately, the glasses were washed, and the table where she was seated cleaned, so we have no prints or DNA. Sadly, The Heath Tavern doesn't have CCTV, so no images are available.

"Before visiting The Heath Tavern, she was seen leaving Lyne Heath by a man walking his dog, and he has given police a detailed description. She was slim, sixty to seventy years old, 5'4" to 5'6" tall, wearing a long woollen coat, light green or grey, a dark woolly hat, dark trousers and dark shoes. She was carrying a light brown handbag, which she held close to her chest. DI Joshi, please continue."

Skelton sat down and his place was taken by a young Detective Inspector, Dipak Joshi.

"In view of the striking similarities in the descriptions, we are now exploring the possibility that this is one and the same woman."

Detective Superintendent Marshman butted in, his voice scornful, "Are you suggesting that this old biddy is now our prime suspect for eight brutal murders in cold blood?"

This question was met with laughter throughout the room. AC Skelton was immediately back on his feet.

"What is so fucking funny?" The laughter stopped dead. "We have a woman of similar description in the immediate vicinity of two separate incidents, resulting in four murders, in two cities, over one hundred miles apart. To encounter one 'old biddy' as you describe her," he glowered at Superintendent Marshman, "close to a murder scene would be strange, to encounter two little old ladies of similar age, height, wearing the same hat and carrying the same handbag, would be a fucking miracle. Unless, of course, she had something to do with those murders. DI Joshi, please continue."

The room was silent apart from the uncomfortable shuffling of feet. DI Joshi rose to his feet again.

"AC Skelton would like you all to return to your teams, explain thoroughly what has been said here today, then direct all efforts towards identifying this woman."

There was a knock on the door and a young male Detective Constable entered the room.

"What do you think you're doing?" barked Joshi, "I didn't hear anyone say come in."

"Sorry sir, but I've got an important message from my Superintendent, from the British Transport Police."

"It's alright DI Joshi, this could be important," said AC Skelton. "What's the message, lad?"

"Sir, the BTP have reviewed the CCTV of everyone arriving at London Euston from the one p.m. train out of Birmingham New Street. The lady on the tape wasn't on the train."

"Shit," said Skelton. "Where else did the train stop?"

"Birmingham International, Coventry, and Milton Keynes sir. The Superintendent has already requested CCTV to be viewed from those stations; the woman apparently didn't leave at any of those stations either."

"What about the train, did that have on board cameras?"

"Yes sir, but the one p.m. from Birmingham to London had only just left the sidings at New Street, so the CCTV wasn't activated until about five minutes before departure. All footage from the train has been thoroughly reviewed; the woman was nowhere to be seen."

"How many people were there on the train?"

"The boss anticipated that question, sir; he estimates around six to seven hundred."

"So, that means that somewhere between fifty and sixty of them might be ladies of the appropriate age, maybe more?"

"I don't know, sir."

"Okay. Thanks for bringing that to us son; we really needed that information."

Turning to the packed briefing room, AC Skelton continued, "Well, who's laughing now? The woman was seen boarding the train at ten to one, but when CCTV was activated five minutes later, she's nowhere to be fucking seen! Clearly, she was trying to throw us off the scent. In my opinion, this woman should now be made a prime suspect, she could well be our killer."

Continuing to pace up and down in front of the power-point screen, AC Skelton seemed suddenly more energised.

"Right, ladies and gentlemen. Thank you for your attendance, you have your instructions, now let's get to work and trace this suspect. If she is the killer, she's certainly made us all look fucking stupid over the past few weeks. Now it's our turn to return the compliment. I'm confident we'll have her in the cells within a few days."

THIRTY-NINE

"ANABELLE CORBETT," called the Speaker of the House of Commons over the usual clamour of voices. It was Prime Minister's Question Time and Corbett rose to her feet.

"Mr Speaker, I represent the area of Camden and St Giles, so Bloomsbury lies within my constituency. The House will be aware of the murders of two people in Barter Street, Bloomsbury on Friday the thirteenth of November, followed by the murders of two men in Bristol on Sunday the twenty-second of November, and another murder of a well-known local man on Saturday the twelfth of December in Birmingham. Subsequently, this week, three young Asian men were gunned down on Saturday the ninth of January in an area of parkland in Norwich.

"All these terrible crimes appear to have been committed by the same perpetrator. Can the Prime Minister please inform the house of the latest news from the police investigation? Can the Right Honourable Gentleman reassure the public that every effort is being made to capture the killer? Does he realise that the whole country is in terror, because a serial killer is travelling unhindered around the UK? Finally, will he allow Commons time for a full debate on the matter?"

The Prime Minister rose to his feet.

"I can inform the House that I visited Operation Chiddingstone this morning, and was given a full update by Assistant Commissioner Skelton who advised me that a possible suspect has been seen near the locations of the murders in both Balsall Heath and Norwich. At my request, the Assistant Commissioner will be making a statement on the policing operation in about thirty minutes time, together with a further appeal for assistance from the public. I'm sure the House would not wish me to preempt what he has to say. I can confirm to the Honourable Lady that there will be Commons time made available for a full debate."

"John Jameson," called the Speaker.

"Thank you, Mr Speaker. Can the Prime Minister please pass on the thanks of this House to the officers involved in the investigation? I know the whole country is concerned that the killer has not yet been found, but this is not through lack of effort from these officers. We owe them our profound thanks."

"I fully agree with the honourable gentleman's comments. We have the finest police service in the world and they should be assured of our support."

"Sally Hayward."

"Thank you, Mr Speaker. I wish to disagree with the previous member's comments. Is the Prime Minister aware of the opinion poll in this morning's Daily Mail? It showed that over sixty percent of people polled had full, or some, sympathy with the killer, or the vigilante as they're now being described. Does the Prime Minister share this sympathy?"

"With all due respect to the Honourable Lady, I do not. I fully understand people's frustrations about crime, but people should report their concerns to the police and let them deal with it. Cold-blooded murder is not the way to solve problems."

"Peter Hermes."

"Thank you, Mr Speaker. Is the Prime Minister aware that violent crime is down thirty percent compared with two months ago; drug usage crimes are down twenty-five percent, and drug dealing crimes are down thirty-five percent? Would the Right Honourable Gentleman agree that the vigilante is clearly having some positive effect?"

"No, I would not. Murder, whatever its motivation or results, can never be regarded as positive. Assisting the police to do their job should be what we all strive for, not condoning a vicious killer."

IT WAS JUST after two in the afternoon, and the Press Briefing Room at New Scotland Yard was packed to the rafters with journalists, camera crews, TV news crews and three Members of Parliament. Assistant Commissioner Skelton was flanked by Detective Inspector Joshi to his right, and Detective Chief Superintendent Hook to his left. After a final check through his papers, and having received the all-important nod from the Scotland Yard Press Officer, AC Skelton spoke.

"Good afternoon ladies and gentlemen and thank you for coming. This morning I met with the Prime Minister at Holborn Police Station. We discussed the recent spate of killings and the certain knowledge that we were now hunting a serial killer."

AC Skelton then relayed the information received from witnesses at the Welcome Cafe in Balsall Heath, together with the information received from the dog walker, and the barmaid in Norwich. Finally, he disclosed evidence about the woman having boarded a train at Birmingham New Street, before either disappearing, or changing her appearance once on board the train, but that, whatever she did, it was unfortunately before any CCTV had been activated.

He concluded, "We now urgently wish to speak to a white woman, who was seen near the scenes of murders in both Balsall Heath, Birmingham, and Lyne Heath, Norwich. This woman is described as between sixty and seventy years old, slim build, five-foot-four to five-foot-six tall, and she regularly carries a light brown, or tan coloured handbag. At both locations she was wearing dark trousers, dark shoes and a dark woolly hat. At Balsall Heath she wore a long purple coat, and at Norwich she wore a long, light green or grey woollen coat. We are now treating this woman as a suspect in those murders. I am happy to answer any questions."

A forest of hands went up, as question after question was shouted at AC Skelton and his team. It took two minutes for the Scotland Yard Press Officer to bring matters under control; she then allowed one question at a time for fifteen minutes, before calling an end to proceedings.

GLORIA WAS TRANSFIXED by what she was watching on the news, finding it difficult to breathe normally, as the words of Assistant

Commissioner Skelton sank in. *Oh my God. They now genuinely believe it's a woman.*

She knew that this was a game-changing moment, and that managing to stay undetected had just become a whole lot more difficult. Not only that, but she realised that, without thinking, she had continued to use her favourite handbag, with the handy front pouch that perfectly fitted the Glock. However, that was now the item placing her at the location of murders in both Birmingham and Norwich.

Seeing herself on CCTV footage was bizarre; that scruffy looking woman surely couldn't have been her, could it? It didn't look like her; she didn't think anyone would recognise her from either the footage or descriptions.

Gloria stared out of her lounge window at the snow which had begun gently falling since early morning, transforming the view. Following fifteen minutes of unpleasant thoughts circling her mind, she began to settle down slowly and feel more rational. She realised that they clearly had no idea who they were looking for, and she told herself there was no point in worrying about something over which she had no control. She would do the same as she'd done so far and carry on leading her normal life. If she was caught, then so be it.

Gloria dressed in a warm coat with a thick furry hood, snow boots and chunky woollen gloves, then checked her face in the mirror. Despite the application of her usual foundation, dark circles were appearing under eyes—or was that just her imagination? She left her normal handbag at home, thinking that it would be wise to rest it for a while.

Leaving Robinson Court, she walked confidently towards the local shops. The snowfall had intensified, and it was now coming down in large chunky flakes as she walked into her local newsagents. Two minutes later she left, her black handbag slung casually over her shoulder, carrying her newspaper under her left arm. She stood in the doorway of an office block and leaned against one of the solid double doors, sheltering from the snow.

On the paper's front cover, she read the headline: WHERE WILL HE STRIKE NEXT? Gloria found herself smiling at this, knowing that the police were now looking for a woman. *Hmmm, maybe the headlines will be slightly more informed in tomorrow's papers.*

The *Fur Elise* ringtone of her mobile bought Gloria back to the present.

"Hello."

"Hi Glo, it's Sean, how's things?"

"Hi Sean. Pretty good thanks, how about you?"

"To be honest, I'm knackered. We're all working our bits off. Eight people now! Looks like we're dealing with a complete fruit-cake. Actually, that's what I wanted to talk to you about. Have you seen the CCTV footage from Birmingham?"

Gloria didn't like the sound of this. "Yes, I have, why?"

"Because if I didn't know better, I could easily have believed it was you walking down the platform and boarding that train. The way she walked and moved was exactly like you from a distance. Just as well we met in the Portrait Gallery, or I'd be putting your name up as prime suspect!" He laughed. "Didn't you notice the similarity?"

Gloria found herself briefly unable to reply.

"Glo, are you there?"

"Er, oh yes, sorry Sean. I just saw an old man slip over in the snow across the road. It distracted me." Desperately trying to remain in control, Gloria continued, "I can't say I saw any obvious similarity between that lady and me, but none of us know what we look like to others, do we?"

"Hadn't thought of it like that. Anyway, next time it's on have a good look. I'm telling you, it's you all over!"

"That's worrying. If someone else thinks it's me, they'll be coming around to arrest me again, won't they?"

"Like I said, good job we bumped into each other at the Portrait Gallery! You've got a cast-iron alibi!"

"So, I'm in the clear then?"

"For now, but just make sure you behave!"

They both started laughing, and Gloria felt much better for hearing Sean laugh it off. She would forever be grateful to his new girlfriend, because she was the reason he happened to be at The Portrait Gallery that afternoon. She had given Gloria practically the best alibi it was possible to have.

"Fancy meeting up for a coffee, Sean?"

"Sorry darling, I can't. I've been tasked with double-checking the area around the Bloomsbury murders. We've got to make sure no-one has been missed, you know, knocking on doors where no-one was in before. After that, Gail's coming round for a meal and to meet the family at my parent's house."

"Meeting the parents? That's moving quickly, isn't it?"

"It certainly is! Wasn't my idea, though. Gail's really keen to meet them for some reason. She's so pretty Glo, I think I'm falling for her."

"How about her family?"

"Haven't met them and Gail doesn't say much about them. Sounds like they might not be close."

"Well, good luck; she sounds lovely. Shame you're still caught up in this investigation. Surely all the enquiries have been completed already? Why are you going round again?"

"Of course they have. The boss is clutching at straws. I can't tell you how much they're relying on tracing this woman; they're desperate to identify her."

"What about you Sean? Do you really believe that the lady they're looking for is the killer?"

"If you'd asked me that question a week ago, I'd have laughed at the idea. Now though, I'm not so sure. She certainly has some difficult questions to answer. Anyhow, I've got to crack on now. I'll call you again soon. Take care."

"Bye Sean. Thanks for calling. See you soon, hopefully."

FORTY

JULIET SIMPSON WATCHED the briefing on the lunchtime news with her husband, feeling troubled. All her attention was focused on the TV. Seeing Skelton on screen created conflict in Juliet's mind; she still felt a lingering attraction towards the man, but also resented the fact that he hadn't kept her in the investigation. The burning disappointment of being relieved as OIC still rankled. She'd given it her all, working sixteen-hour days, but that hadn't been enough; the breakthrough hadn't happened and she'd been in the police long enough to know that the hierarchy wouldn't tolerate failure for very long.

Then something else caught her eye, and Juliet sat up and watched intently. It was the moment Skelton appealed for the identity of a woman seen boarding a train to London, shown clearly on Birmingham train station's CCTV images. Watching the clip, Juliet was convinced she knew who the woman might be. She looked just like someone who was part of the police and community committee in St Giles. It was very subtle, but it was definitely there.

Juliet had attended only occasional meetings, no more than two or three times, but she remembered that the woman had a very distinctive gait. She leaned slightly forward, and her right leg rolled out marginally with each step, just like the woman on the CCTV.

What made Juliet even more certain was that the woman she had just seen had a tan handbag with a long strap, just like the woman on the committee. She particularly remembered the handbag because she'd liked it so much that she'd considered asking the woman where she bought it. Juliet sat back and whistled. If she was right about this, and the two were one and the same woman, she realised that she could be vindicated in the eyes of her colleagues and that would mean a great deal, not only for her self-esteem, but also perhaps her career.

Juliet looked over at David and wanted to share her thoughts with him, however he'd drifted into a post-lunch snooze. She stared at him for a few seconds, before saying quietly to herself, "You're a lovely bloke, but my God, you're boring sometimes."

She was still fond of her husband, but in recent weeks had begun questioning many aspects of her life, including her relationship with David. Juliet realised that her theory would also give her a chance to see Graeme Skelton again, so she decided to pass her suspicions about the woman on the CCTV directly to him.

Firstly though, she needed to contact Sean Aylen, who attended most police and community meetings. He would know the woman's name—she was sure they had been friends.

Waking David, Juliet said, "Sorry love, something's come up at work. I've got to make a quick call, then I'll be leaving in about fifteen minutes. Can you make some supper and make sure the girls go to bed at a reasonable time? Might be late home tonight."

David replied with a groggy, "Yeah, okay love." He had been a detective's husband for seventeen years and was well used to last-minute changes of plan like this.

STEPPING OUT OF an office block in Bloomsbury, after another fruitless enquiry, Sean Aylen wondered whether the public realised how boring investigating a murder could be. Did they know what utter bollocks they watched on television? TV dramas about murder investigations were full of thrills, where it seemed to be exciting all the time. The truth was that most of a murder team's day was made up of routine and boredom, with only the occasional flash of excitement. He was truly grateful when his mobile rang, giving him something else to concentrate on, if only for a few seconds.

"Hello."

"Hi, it's DCI Simpson; can I pick your brain, please?"

"Certainly ma'am, what do you need to know?"

"Nothing earth shattering, I'm just thinking about speaking personally to all our community representatives. Can you remember the name of the lady who represents St Giles on the committee?"

"Sure, it's Gloria Jones. Why do you ask? I thought you'd been taken off the investigation."

"Yes, I have, but I've been given the job of trying to reassure people in the area, so speaking to anyone representing the public is a must. Do you have her address and contact number?"

"Yep. I'll text them over to you if you like?"

"That would be great. Thanks very much for your help, Sean. I'll see you soon."

"No problem ma'am. I'll text you in the next few minutes."

JULIET HUNG UP, then looked at herself in the mirror above her mantelpiece. Over her shoulder she could see David lying back on the settee, head lolled to one side, snoring loudly.

The text with Gloria's address and contact number arrived, but she was already beginning to doubt herself. Surely, it couldn't be Gloria Jones, that nice lady she'd seen at the meetings, could it? Before she approached Graeme with her suspicions, she needed to check her facts fully and be absolutely certain that the woman on the CCTV was Gloria Jones. Only then would she pass the information to him.

Juliet phoned the laboratory handling the Operation Chiddingstone CCTV enhancements. She'd made her urgent appointment less than an hour after seeing the news report. Two hours later, she was talking to a very helpful young lab assistant.

"I'd like to view CCTV images from Operation Chiddingstone."

"Certainly, ma'am, any particular piece of CCTV?"

"Yes, I'm interested in anything from the one p.m. train from Birmingham New Street to London, reference number DHC/32."

"Any others ma'am?"

"I'd like to see everything from when the train arrives at Euston, reference number DHC/33. That should do it, thanks."

"Follow me." The young assistant took her into a purpose-built viewing room. "Hang on here, I'll be back with your discs in five minutes. Help yourself to tea or coffee."

"Thank you."

The assistant left the room, and Juliet waited nervously, sipping slowly on a cup of coffee from the vending machine. She thought about her next step. She was only too aware that correct identification of this woman would look really good for her, nevertheless she was annoyed at the thought that the greater share of credit for her discovery, should she be proved correct, would probably go to Detective Chief Superintendent Hook, and AC Skelton, the two senior officers in overall control. It just didn't seem fair.

"Here you are ma'am," said the assistant, handing over two DVD's. "Are you happy working the equipment on your own?"

"Yes, thanks. I'll shout if I need help."

Juliet started with the train CCTV. She knew about the woman boarding, and that she was nowhere to be seen five minutes later once CCTV was turned on in the train. Starting with coach number one, Juliet studied all camera angles available, carefully scanning the faces of all women who looked a suitable age. Gloria Jones was nowhere to be seen. She moved on to coach two and carried out the same searches. After five minutes there was no trace of her, so she moved onto coach three, then four, then five. She was about to move onto coach six, and beginning to seriously doubt herself, when she noticed a woman entering coach five from coach six, holding a large carrier bag. *A bag of clothes, perhaps?*

The image only showed the woman from behind, as she walked down the aisle, but it was enough for Juliet to recognise the same distinctive walk. It was barely perceptible, but obvious once you were aware of it. The woman sat down, and Juliet quickly pressed the button to change camera, then changed again, then again. Finally, she could clearly see the woman settling down in a seat and checking her mobile phone. Zooming in fully on the woman's face, Juliet took a sharp breath. Without a doubt, it was Gloria Jones!

Juliet waved at the young assistant through the glass partitions. He re-entered the room. "Problem ma'am?" he asked.

"No, I'm done thanks. Could you burn me off a copy of this please?"

"Will do. Do you need a copy of the other disk too?"

"No, thanks, the one from the train will do."

"Give me ten minutes and you'll have it."

Juliet left the laboratory, happy in the knowledge that not only had she identified the woman they were searching for, but that she had probably also identified the killer.

Twenty-five minutes later she was walking out of the underground, heading for Holborn Police Station, with excitement building inside her, not just at the potential breakthrough she'd made, but—she had to admit—at the prospect of seeing Graeme Skelton again.

As Juliet crossed a busy road junction, she saw two men approaching a woman standing at a cashpoint; one of them suddenly pulled at the woman's handbag, and she was spun around by the force. Juliet instantly sprang into action, screaming at them and grabbing hold of the man's long hair. He shook her off, punched her hard in the stomach and she doubled up in pain.

Falling to the ground on her left side, she saw with horror the other young man pull a knife from his coat pocket. He bent over her and she prepared to roll, expecting to be stabbed but, at that moment, he saw his accomplice running off and jumped up, following him across the junction into a side street. Dragging herself painfully to her feet, Juliet walked over to the woman who'd been attacked.

"Are you okay?" Juliet asked.

The woman was about 40 years old and she was crying. "Yes, thank you so much for helping me, I was really scared."

"Did they get anything?"

"No, I managed to keep hold of my bag. Are you okay? It looked like he was about to stab you."

Her words chilled Juliet to the bone.

"I think so, but he did punch me pretty hard."

She touched her stomach gingerly and winced at the pain.

They were joined by three more women who had run out from a nearby restaurant. Looking towards the side street, there was no sign of the muggers.

One of the women placed an arm around Juliet's shoulders.

"Are you all right, love? We've called the police; they're on their way. We witnessed the whole thing from the restaurant. We couldn't believe it. Hopefully, they'll catch the bastards quickly."

Juliet forced a smile.

"Thanks, but I am police. I'm more concerned about that poor lady." She indicated the other woman. "Don't worry, I think we're both fine. I'll walk with her to the police station. It's only a hundred metres away."

Juliet thanked the ladies once more and made her way with the woman to the station. On arrival, she asked an officer to take a crime report from the woman. Then she went to the Chiddingstone Incident Room. The first person she saw there was DI Dipak Joshi.

"Hi Jules, what brings you back here?"

"Hi Dipak, I need to speak with AC Skelton, is he in?"

"No, he's at the yard in conference at the moment; should be back soon though. Anything I can help with?"

"No, it's fine thanks. I'll wait."

Juliet made her way to the station canteen, where she waited to be seen by the medical examiner to be checked over. Shaking with anger, Juliet found her mind wandering back to the attack. *What a shame it wasn't Gloria Jones who you'd attacked, you fucking cowards. She would have done the right thing and blown your brains out.*

Juliet brought herself up short. *What the hell am I thinking? Jones is almost certainly a cold-blooded killer—she needs to be turned in.* But the thought, once planted, would not entirely leave her mind.

The medical examiner had taken over an hour to arrive at the station, but on arrival gave Juliet a thorough check-over.

"Just a nasty bruise officer, nothing to worry about. Do you want to be signed off for a few days?"

"No, thanks, I'll be fine; thanks for coming down, doc."

"All part of the service. With any luck, they'll have images of them on the CCTV, so they should identify them soon enough."

This comment reminded Juliet of the reason she'd travelled to the police station on her day off. Speaking to Graeme Skelton and passing on the information was important, but the more time that passed since being attacked, the more anger she felt towards the thug who'd punched her. She knew only too well that she was fortunate not to have been stabbed, even killed.

FORTY-ONE

WHILE AWAITING GRAEME Skelton's return, Juliet's mind wandered. Firstly, should she make another play for him? She couldn't deny that there was still chemistry between them—a chemistry which seemed absent in her marriage. Secondly, seeing the woman being mugged, and then being violently assaulted herself, had reminded her of the distress her daughter Jenny had felt when she was threatened and abused by two men, high on drugs, six months earlier. Jenny had replied, "No chance," when they'd tried chatting her up from the doorway they were sitting in. After she said this one man shouted obscenities at her and the other spat at her. She remembered that Jenny had been upset for days afterwards and frightened of going out alone.

Her day-dreaming was interrupted by a voice she knew well.

"Hello Jules, what brings you here?" Turning, Juliet smiled, seeing Graeme Skelton. She looked around to make sure no-one was in earshot and said, "I think I might have information for you, Graeme, about the killings."

"Really? That's great. But why were you seen by the doc? The Duty Officer just told me you were punched."

"Oh, that. I saw a woman being robbed by two men on the way to the station. I grabbed one of them and the bastard knocked me to the ground; he pulled a knife, I thought he was going to stab me."

"Fucking hell, Jules!" He moved closer, a look of concern on his face. "Are you sure you're okay?"

She smiled at him. "I'm absolutely fine; apparently just bruising, no lasting damage. Now, do you want this information or not?"

"Okay then, as long as you promise you're all right?"

"I'm fine, really."

"Look Jules, it's nearly seven now, I've been working since first thing this morning and I'm knackered. My apartment's only ten-minutes away, so why don't you come around for coffee and a bite to eat and tell me all the details there?"

Juliet smiled, made sure nobody else in the canteen could hear her, and said, "Are you sure you don't want more than just coffee?"

Graeme Skelton anxiously looked around and put a finger to his lips. Leaning towards Juliet's face he whispered, "I can think of several things I want more. So, what do you think, do you want to give me the information here, or back at my place?"

"Well," Juliet replied, "having been to your previous apartment many, many times before, I've always been impressed with the service. So, yes, let's do this at your apartment." She smiled and stood up. "Give me the address, I'll be twenty minutes."

By seven thirty, Juliet Simpson and Graeme Skelton were locked in a passionate kiss in the kitchen of his smart apartment. His hands were all over her body and she pulled him close, feeling his excitement. Briefly separating their lips, he said, "Bollocks to food, let's eat later."

"That's a great idea," grinned Juliet.

With that, they practically raced toward the bedroom, tugging at clothes as they went. They collapsed on the bed, laughing, and then the laughing gradually stopped as they began to rediscover each other's bodies. It was as if the past six years had never happened and, over an hour later, they lay side by side, sweaty, breathless and exhausted.

Juliet sighed with pleasure; she had pushed her desire for Graeme to the back of her mind for so long, but the last sixty minutes had brought the sensations flooding back. She began to build a picture in her head of a future with him; the details were a bit hazy, but in the glow of the moment, she felt sure they could work something out—should work something out.

"God, that was good. Why did we ever break up, Graeme? We must have been mad."

He gently stroked her hair. "You went back to your husband, Jules; it was your choice, remember."

"I know and I've wondered if I made the right decision ever since." She rolled over, looked deeply into his eyes and whispered. "I love you Graeme; I think we're great together. Things are a bit different now; the kids are more independent and as for David and me—well—I just think we've reached the end of the road."

Graeme continued to stroke Juliet's hair, but his gaze was now over her shoulder.

"Wow, I wasn't expecting that! As you say, things *are* a bit different now. This was great, don't get me wrong, but you knew it was only a one-off, didn't you?"

Juliet felt a chill creep over her body and pulled the sheet up.

"What are you saying?"

"I care for you, always have, you know that, but there's no future for us. I'm seeing someone else, she's a barrister, and we're on the point of getting engaged. Sorry, Jules. I thought you knew."

Juliet felt as if she'd received another punch in the guts. She looked in disbelief at the man beside her, the man she had thought she knew, and her blood boiled.

"You shitty bastard! What was all that chat about at the station and asking me back here—just so we could have a quick fuck!"

"I didn't intend this to happen, Jules. I honestly misread the signals; I thought you just fancied some fun—and it was fun, wasn't it?" Graeme reached over to put a hand on Juliet's shoulder.

Juliet shrugged him off, pulled the sheet around her and swung her legs off the bed.

"Don't you fucking touch me," she yelled. "Just fuck off into the lounge so I can get dressed. Then I'm leaving."

"If that's what you want." Graeme grabbed his dressing gown, wrapped it round himself and left the room without another word. Five minutes later, Juliet walked out of the bedroom, fully dressed and furious.

"Jules, come on, be reasonable, I didn't know you still felt like that."

"You complete bastard. I'll be interested to see your girlfriend's reaction when I tell her what her adoring boyfriend gets up to behind her back."

Skelton sat on the sofa, calmly looking up at Juliet.

"I don't think you really want to do that, do you Jules? After all, what would David say if he knew where you'd been this evening and *exactly* what you'd been doing?"

Juliet felt as if all the air had been sucked out of her lungs. She looked at Skelton and it was as if she was seeing him for the first time. Silently reaching for her bag and coat, she turned to leave.

"Before you go," said Graeme. "What was it you wanted to tell me about the killings?"

She turned and looked into his cold eyes; the only expression there was curiosity.

"It's not that important. It was just an excuse to see you again. Stupid of me to waste your time."

She opened the front door and left without a backward glance. Graeme Skelton's apartment was in Covent Garden. Probably due to the freezing sleet falling, it was unusually quiet as she stepped out, with only about a dozen people visible. She turned left into James Street, then walked the short distance to Covent Garden underground station.

Stepping into the station, Juliet struggled to control her fury and disappointment. The triple effects of seeing that woman being attacked by the two men, being punched herself and feeling terror when threatened with a knife, then being used for sex and then dumped by Graeme Skelton. It had all ignited an almost uncontrollable rage in her.

"Spare any change, darling?" asked a beggar, sitting cross-legged on his sleeping bag, his back against a wall. He smiled at Juliet and held out a grimy hand.

"What did you fucking say?" snapped Juliet.

"Any spare change please?"

"You called me darling! Don't you ever call me darling; I'm not your darling! You'll get fuck all from me!"

"You can't talk to me like that!" yelled the beggar, at the top of his croaking voice. "What the fuck's the matter with you? Someone needs to give you a fucking slap!"

Juliet shouted, "Come on then, fucking try it!"

Several members of the public looked on, some in astonishment, others in amusement. A member of station staff moved in quickly and steered Juliet towards the lifts down to the platforms.

"Come on love, we don't want trouble, do we? Just make your way home. Forget about him."

Apologising to him, Juliet said: "You're absolutely right. Sorry about that, I don't know what came over me."

She could still hear the man shouting abuse as she entered the lift and felt even more fury—this is what Skelton had reduced her to.

Sitting on the underground train, Juliet had come to a decision. She would not be telling Graeme Skelton about Gloria Jones. She didn't want to give him the success it would bring. She wasn't even sure she would be telling anyone about Gloria Jones. In fact, if Gloria was the killer, then Juliet suddenly felt a wave of sympathy for a woman who'd obviously snapped when she couldn't take the crap any more. She'd almost reached that stage herself.

Then a voice in her head said, *If I can help you Gloria, then I will.* She knew that this would give her a measure of revenge, not only on the kind of thugs who had attacked her and countless others like her, but also on Graeme. She knew that he was under pressure about the failure of Chiddingstone and that the longer it took to identify the killer, the worse it would be for him. *If his reputation and career go down the tubes because of me, then good. Fuck him!*

FORTY-TWO

THE SECOND HALF of January passed without any breakthroughs in the case. AC Skelton and DCS Hook faced repeated questioning from the press, but they had no answers, no leads, and no break from the constant pressure.

TV News stations had continued with their coverage, but it was slowing as no new news came in. From time to time they would parade experts, psychologists, ex-police officers, criminologists, even current drug users, all giving their opinions. The tabloid newspapers tended to lead with stories about the huge reduction in street drug dealing, drug usage, begging, and robbery, and opinion polls continued to show support for the vigilante somewhere between fifty-five and sixty-five percent.

The broadsheets ran stories asking questions like, 'Why did the vigilante start killing?' or, 'Will there be copycat killers?' Some were even asking, 'Is this a permanent change in the public's attitude towards crime?' But with no fresh meat to feast on, the murders were inevitably slipping down the news agenda.

The rest of January was equally uneventful for Gloria until, arriving home from a trip to the supermarket one Thursday morning, she found another plain brown envelope on her doormat.

This time the message read: *DON'T WORRY GLORIA, I'M ON YOUR SIDE.*

Once again, this left her totally dumbfounded as to the motive or identity of the author. She knew for certain that the messenger was a young white man, and that he sounded Irish, but was he the writer as well? Hopefully she would soon find out.

Monday the first of February found Gloria still fast asleep at nine-thirty, despite the rain lashing her window. A thaw had wiped all the snow from the streets, leaving a mucky, slippery slush in its place. Her life had largely returned to normal. She would see her friends for drinks and meals once a week; she went to Bridge Club every Thursday, worked at the soup kitchen once a week, spoke with her daughter every two or three days, and was enjoying her favourite hobby of visiting museums and galleries.

One thing troubled her: Sean had seemed very distracted on the couple of occasions they'd met since her visit to Norwich. She'd probed him for reasons, teasing him about his relationship with Gail, but he fobbed her off and insisted he was fine. However, Gloria could see that he wasn't fine, he was very far from fine, he was deeply worried about something.

The buzzing of the intercom sounded, and it had buzzed again by the time she had grabbed her dressing gown.

"Okay, okay!" she shouted, as she walked down the hall tying her dressing gown cord. She lifted the receiver and said, "Hello?"

"Gloria, it's DCI Simpson here, can I come in please?"

Unsure what a DCI would want with her, Gloria said, "Of course, pull the door." Sixty seconds later, she heard a soft knock and, opening the door, she was surprised to see a woman she recognised from the police and community meetings.

"Hello," said Juliet. "Any chance we could have a chat?"

Simpson's voice seemed friendly, so hopefully she had nothing to be concerned about.

"Sure, come in." Gloria showed Juliet through into the lounge, offering her a seat on the sofa.

"I'll just get dressed, and I'll be back with you in a moment."

Less than five minutes later Gloria returned to the lounge and sat in her usual chair.

"How can I help, officer?"

Juliet smiled reassuringly at Gloria and said, "Well, you can start by not calling me officer; it's Jules, please."

"Okay then, in that case, call me Gloria. I recognise you now; you've been to a couple of the police and community meetings, haven't you?"

"Yes. Haven't been for a while though."

"Okay, how can I help you Jules? Oh, I'm sorry, where are my manners, would you like a cup of something?"

"Thought you'd never ask! I'm gasping for a tea; white, no sugar, thanks."

Gloria walked through to the kitchen, filled the kettle, then returned to the lounge.

"So, what brings you round, Jules?"

Juliet had a thoughtful expression on her face. "Let's get our drinks first Gloria, then we'll have a nice chat."

Gloria was a little taken aback by this, but said, "Okay, back in a bit."

Once the kettle had boiled, she poured out the drinks and brought them through.

"There you go, hope it's okay. Right then, fire away, I'm listening."

Juliet looked steadily into Gloria's eyes, weighing her up.

"I'll get straight to the point, Gloria. I believe I know exactly who you are and what you've done, but don't worry, I'm on your side."

She sat back, obviously watching closely for a reaction.

Gloria was in total shock; this was the last thing she was expecting to hear. Her confusion and panic must have shown on her face, because Juliet paused before continuing, "I recognised you on CCTV footage on a train from Birmingham to London, shortly after the murder of Alan Bramhall."

Gloria couldn't speak for a few moments, then said, almost too faintly to hear, "You... must be mistaken. It couldn't have been me. I was visiting the National Gallery and the Portrait Gallery all day. I even bumped into a police officer friend of mine in the Portrait Gallery."

"Gloria, I understand your concern, but you need to stop worrying. I told you, I'm on your side. You've been getting away with it so far, but I think you could do with my help."

Juliet could see the horror on Gloria's face and continued, in a gentle voice, "It was definitely you, I even noticed the coat you were wearing once you'd changed on the train. It's hanging on the coat hooks next to your front door. I saw it when you let me in just now. You boarded the train wearing the purple coat and black woolly hat. You must have gone to a toilet, changed clothes, then went to your seat. Am I right?"

Gloria just couldn't understand what was happening. Why wasn't she being arrested? Was Jules setting a trap? Was she wearing a microphone? Were there more officers outside waiting to burst in and arrest her? She felt queasy and uncertain what to do, but decided she would stick to her story.

"Look, like I said, I was visiting galleries all day."

Juliet leaned forward and placed a hand on Gloria's.

"No, you weren't Gloria. You were seen by witnesses near the scenes of shootings in both Birmingham and Norwich. Added to that, you live only a five-minute walk away from the first two shootings, and shortly before the Bloomsbury murders, you were attacked by two robbers in the doorway of this block. Was it revenge on those two Gloria? Was it payback?"

Gloria said nothing; she just stared numbly at Juliet.

"Now listen to me," Juliet continued. "I understand your fury. My daughter was abused and threatened by druggies, and I was punched and threatened with a knife recently; later the same night I had a run in with a beggar. I think you're a hero, or should I say, heroine. So does most of the population. Look, I know you've already been arrested and cleared as a suspect, and I really don't want to turn you in again. Please let me help you."

Gloria looked at the policewoman sitting in her lounge and realised she had to make a decision: whether or not to trust her.

"Okay, you're right," she said, reluctantly. Her head dropped, and she went on in a low voice, "I didn't mean to kill anyone at first. I was walking to Holborn Police Station to hand in the gun. I'd found it in Phoenix Gardens; it had been thrown there by that drug dealer. On my way to the station, a couple who'd attacked me outside this block threatened me again. I only meant to frighten them with the gun, make them go away, but the woman came at me with a syringe. I didn't mean to fire, I really didn't."

She started crying, sucking huge lungfuls of air in between sobs. She wasn't sure whether she was crying out of relief, or fear. Juliet knelt on the floor in front of her.

"Gloria, calm down, it's all right. Nothing's going to happen to you; I won't let anything happen to you. I know about you being arrested and cleared of any suspicion. You were released with no further action and given full apologies. Fuck knows how you managed it, but you're completely in the clear!"

Gloria gave a weak smile. "How did you know it was me?"

"You've got a distinctive walk. It's subtle, and I'm sure most people wouldn't even notice it, but as soon as I saw that woman walking down the platform, I thought it might be you." She smiled at Gloria, who managed to force a smile herself.

Juliet hadn't arrested her, hadn't called for back-up and, with every second that passed, Gloria began to feel more comfortable. She realised that one word from Juliet could see her incarcerated for the rest of her life, but decided there was nothing to do, except to take the initiative.

"So, what happens now?"

"Well, you can start by telling me how you ended up being a killer. I want to know the story, right from the very start, you'll find me an exceptionally good listener. Now, pour me another cup and tell me everything," said Juliet, resting back into the settee and handing her cup to Gloria.

Over the next half hour, Gloria did just that, starting from the incident following her walk home after bridge night, right up to her trip to Norwich and the elimination of three violent robbers. Apart from keeping quiet about the letters, and the alibi given to her by Williams-Glass with the fake witness statements, she left out nothing.

Apart from the letters. She'd not told Juliet about them because she feared it might alarm her, knowing that someone else was aware that she was the killer. It might even be enough to make Juliet hand her in. At the moment, she wasn't prepared to take that chance. The exercise proved to be surprisingly cathartic.

Sitting back, with a look of amazement on her face, Juliet shook her head slowly from side to side.

"Blimey, I've not heard anything like that in eighteen years as a detective."

"I'm not lying, Jules. That's the God's honest truth."

"I believe you, I believe every word you've told me. Look, you've told me your story, now I'll tell you mine." Juliet told her how her daughter had been abused and threatened; about being attacked and robbed herself; about the affair and final betrayal by Graeme Skelton in his apartment; about the beggar at the underground station; about how something in her mind snapped, just as it had in Gloria's.

Juliet looked directly into her eyes.

"Trust me Gloria, I'm right behind you on this; I won't betray you."

Gloria returned Juliet's gaze steadily.

"This is all a bit much to take in. I've been so scared about being found out since it started. Surely, if you handed me in, it would do wonders for your career, wouldn't it? You'd be the most famous police officer in the country."

"My career doesn't seem so important to me right now. In any case, that wanker Skelton will take all the glory if the vigilante is caught. No, I've made my decision and I'm sticking with it."

A look of concern came over Juliet's face.

"Are you okay? You're shaking."

"Wouldn't you be, in my position? For Christ's sake Jules, I'm a serial killer being hunted by hundreds of detectives throughout the country, and I've got one of them in my home sharing a cup of tea with me!"

"Well, put like that, you must be shitting yourself!"

They stared at each other for a moment, in silence before the corner of Juliet's mouth turned up slightly, bringing a ghost of a smile to Gloria's face. After a few more seconds, they were both laughing. Eventually their laughter subsided and Juliet said, "You've been inactive for over three weeks now. Do you have another target or have you 'retired'?"

Surprised by this direct question, Gloria answered truthfully, "I haven't got anyone in mind; in fact, I think my work is done. It's funny, on the last two occasions, I'd started to enjoy the killing just a little too much, especially those three arseholes in Norwich." She went quiet for a few seconds, looking thoughtfully down at the floor. Lifting her head again, she said, "I honestly don't know if I could do it again. Anyway, I'm obviously giving too many clues away; they've already sussed that it's a woman, so it can't be long before they catch me, can it?"

Juliet shook her head.

"Look, relax. I recognised you from your walk alone, but I already knew you. I took a punt, checked the train CCTV and there you were. Nobody else is likely to put two and two together like I did. They really haven't got all that much to go on."

Suddenly, Gloria remembered what Sean had said.

"Actually Jules, Sean Aylen phoned me a couple of weeks ago and said that the woman on the CCTV at Birmingham Train Station walked exactly like me. He said that if he hadn't seen me at the Portrait Gallery, I would be in trouble. He was joking, making fun like we always do with each other, but it's worrying all the same."

"Has he mentioned it since?"

"No. We've spoken on the phone, and he's popped round for coffee a couple of times since then, but he's not said anything. But what if he checked the same CCTV you did?"

"Don't worry. He didn't really think it might be you, he was just joking around; it's what we coppers do. There's no way he'll bother to check through the train CCTV; he's way too busy."

"Now look, I will help however I can. I'll pass you details about the enquiry whenever it's safe. You won't be getting much that won't already be in the public domain, but you'll get it earlier than the news crews. But, you have to understand, if it all goes tits up, you're on your own, okay?"

"Of course. That seems fair. Thank you so much, Jules."

"Nothing to thank me for. I haven't done anything."

"Yes, you have. Your silence means that I can get on with the rest of my life. I'm so, so grateful."

"Right then," said Juliet. "What are you doing for lunch today?"

"Nothing planned, why?"

"How about Nando's on Oxford Street. It's on me."

"That's really kind, shall I meet you there?"

"That would be great. I've got to show my face at the nick for a while, at least make it look like I'm working for a living. Meet you at one?"

"Great, see you then."

Gloria walked Juliet to the door, where they stood smiling at each other.

"Listen, call me Glo—all my friends do; and thanks again. I can't believe that a copper knowing I'm the vigilante could actually make me feel better."

Juliet placed a hand on Gloria's shoulder and said, "Don't be daft. You know what they say: 'A trouble shared is a trouble halved.' Make sure you're not fretting all through lunch!"

"I won't be. Bye Jules."

"Bye Glo. See you in a couple of hours."

FORTY-THREE
Thursday 11ᵗʰ February 1999

"THANKS AGAIN JULES, I had a really lovely evening. See you soon."

"Me too. Bye Glo."

Juliet had enjoyed spending time with Gloria over the past ten days, getting to know her better. The previous evening, they'd been to the cinema and enjoyed a meal afterwards. Her knowledge of who Gloria was and what she had done was no barrier to their friendship; they didn't mention it and she had no intention of doing anything with the knowledge which would endanger her friend.

At the same time, she was feeling much happier about the Graeme Skelton situation; she had come to realise that there had probably never been any future for them and that she was better off without him in her life. At home, now that she had consigned Skelton to the past, she found she could focus more on her relationship with David. Boring he might be, but she knew he was a good man and, now she had more time at home, things had certainly improved.

PUTTING DOWN THE receiver at her end of the conversation, Gloria smiled to herself and poured a cup of tea. Juliet was great company, and they enjoyed the same things. Deep down though, Gloria was still holding back a little; she still couldn't quite believe that Juliet didn't have an ulterior motive.

Sipping her tea while looking in the mirror, Gloria noticed that it was covered in smears. *I suppose I'll be spending the morning cleaning, then.*

An hour later, she had moved on to cleaning the sink and drainer when the phone rang. She picked it up in a rubber-gloved hand.

"Mum, it's me," said Sandra, before Gloria could even say hello. "Katie's been arrested."

"What? Why on earth has Katie been arrested?" Gloria got no reply; she could only hear Sandra crying at the other end of the line. "Right Sandra," she said calmly. "Try to take deep breaths. Pull yourself together and tell me exactly what's happened."

After a few seconds, Sandra finally managed to speak between sobs.

"Those bloody dealers sold some drugs to a kid called Jason; he's a friend of Katie's boyfriend, Ryan. Plain-clothes police stopped all three and searched them. They found nothing on them, but an officer spotted some of the drugs next to Katie's feet so they've all been arrested."

"Oh God, when did this happen?"

"About nine last night; we were at the station until two in the morning, when Katie was put into a detention room to sleep for the night. She's been given a duty solicitor and she'll be interviewed later this morning. Hopefully that idiot will admit the drugs were his, then Katie and Ryan can be released."

"Let's hope so, although I wouldn't bank on it; drug users like Jason aren't usually known for their honesty. What on earth is Katie's Ryan doing hanging around with a low-life like that?"

"Jason's not a good friend of Ryan's, they just know each other from school. Apparently, they'd met at the youth club, then walked back onto the estate together. The BMW turned up, and the users appeared from nowhere, that's when Jason broke away from Ryan and Katie, bought the crack through the driver's window of the car, then walked back to them. The BMW drove off, and shortly afterwards plain-clothes police moved in."

"What? The police let the dealer's car get away again?"

"No, that's not how it happened, mum. Apparently the plain-clothes officers were working on something completely separate. They were on their way back to their cars when they spotted known drugs users in the area; they'd also heard a car driving away at speed. Putting two-and-two together, they stopped and searched everyone."

Gloria needed time to think. "Where are you now?"

"I'm outside the police station with Steve. I have to be Katie's appropriate adult during the interview. Why?"

"You and Steve need to stay calm and supportive for Katie; try not to get angry. Let me know as soon as you're done with the interview. There's nothing we can do until then. Don't worry, Katie will be fine. I'll be waiting for your call. Love you."

"Love you too. Bye."

Gloria stood by the window in her lounge, shaking with fury. She lit herself a cigarette and drew heavily, sucking in a lungful of smoke, before exhaling slowly. Her feelings of love for her daughter and granddaughter were mixed with feelings of hatred of the drug dealers ruining their lives. These were emotions she knew well.

Slowly the shaking subsided; Gloria knew, in that moment, that the words she'd spoken to Juliet just a while ago had been untrue. Her work was not done; she would do anything in her power to protect her family, even if that meant killing again.

A couple of hours later, the phone rang again. It was Sandra.

"Hi Mum, all three of them are being released on bail for four weeks."

"You mean that little shit didn't admit they were his drugs?"

"No, no, that's not it. Jason admitted everything. Apparently, he was buying the crack for a mate; he doesn't do drugs himself. The problem is that he's refusing to give his mate's details to the police, and they're now looking at charging all three with conspiracy to pervert the course of justice!"

Gloria was incensed. "What a load of bollocks! I mean, I don't know much about the law, but surely, they're just trying to apply pressure, aren't they? Trying to get the name they need. Look, I've got friends in the police, I'll ask their advice."

Sandra started gently crying again, a sound that broke Gloria's heart.

"It's got worse since Christmas, Mum. The police have increased patrols, but the dealers always seem to outsmart them. They only turn up when there are no officers patrolling; it must all be arranged with their customers by mobile phone. I'm so scared for Katie and James. Just look what's happened in the past twenty-four hours. They shouldn't have to experience this when they're growing up, should they?"

"No, they shouldn't," said Gloria. "Listen. How about I pop up next week? It's half-term, so the kids should be ready for some for quality time with Grandma, shouldn't they?"

"Yes, definitely! You're welcome to stay as long as you'd like. When were you thinking of coming?"

"How about next Wednesday?"

"That would be fantastic! Shall we collect you from the station?"

"Yes please. I'll let you know my train time in the next couple of days. Now, how is Katie?"

"She's surprisingly well, considering. I'd be a complete mess if all this happened to me at her age. I think she's just glad to finally be coming home."

"That's good. Can you ask her to call me sometime, maybe tomorrow, once she's had a good sleep?"

"Of course, and thanks again for everything."

"Don't be silly, just look after my beautiful granddaughter until I can give her a huge hug."

"I will. See you next week. Bye mum."

"Bye sweetheart, and try not to worry."

THE FOLLOWING MORNING, Gloria's home phone rang again.

"Hi Gran," said Katie.

"Katie, how lovely to hear from you! Your mum tells me you've had a few problems," Gloria laughed, trying to make her granddaughter feel comfortable talking about the situation.

It clearly worked, because Katie laughed too. "You're telling me, Gran, it's been a nightmare. I was locked in a cell for the night."

"Yes, I heard. What happened exactly? Don't tell me if you don't want to." Gloria knew that by not insisting that Katie tell her everything, it would make her far more likely to actually do so.

"Well, I'd been out with Ryan at the youth club, and at the end of the evening we bumped into a friend of his called Jason. He seemed okay. We decided to walk back to the estate together. To be honest, up until then it was just a normal evening."

"How old are Ryan and Jason, Katie?"

"They're both sixteen, why?"

"No reason, just trying to get the full picture in my mind. You know I love detail. What happened next?"

"We'd crossed over the first road onto the green and the usual crowd was gathering in the bushes and trees. I thought nothing of it. When the black BMW turned up, they all swarmed around the car, same as usual. Then Jason said, 'Back in a minute,' and jogged over to the car himself. I was really surprised. Three or four minutes later, he came back, and the car drove off quite fast. He said that a mate had asked him to buy three rocks for him and given Jason a tenner for doing it. We told him he was mad, but he just laughed it off."

Katie went silent for a moment.

"Then what?" asked Gloria.

"All hell let loose. People were running in all directions, and I heard someone shout, 'Police, stay where you are!' Then two cops ran up to us and said they had reason to believe we were in possession of controlled drugs and intended to search us. So Ryan said, 'Fine, go ahead, we've got nothing to hide'.

"Then one of them started searching Jason, while the other searched Ryan. They found nothing on Ryan—or Jason, which surprised me— then a woman officer came over and searched me. Anyway, they found nothing, so they took our names. Then, just as they were about to let us go, one of them said, 'Hang on, what's that?' and pointed at the ground where I was standing. I looked down, and there were three small white lumps in the grass. The officer bent down and picked them up and showed them to us; the lumps were wrapped in clingfilm and I knew straight away what they were." Katie started to cry.

"It's okay Katie; remember, you've done nothing wrong, so there's nothing to worry about. Carry on telling me what happened."

"The cop who picked up the drugs asked which one of us dropped them; I said straight away it wasn't me, then Ryan said it wasn't him. We both looked at Jason, but he looked the guy straight in the eye, said he'd got no idea where they'd come from, and said they'd probably been thrown by one of the druggies. The officer smiled, shook his head, then told us we were all under arrest for suspected unlawful possession of controlled drugs. We were all handcuffed, and they radioed for a police van to take us to the station. You know the rest."

"Thanks for telling me everything; that couldn't have been easy."

"Actually, it was okay. You know I've always been able to talk to you."

"That's sweet of you. We'll have a special cuddle when I come up on Wednesday; I can't wait to see you all. I really need to go now, sweetheart. Please try not to worry. We'll get this sorted, okay?."

"Okay. Thanks for listening and for being so understanding. You're the best grandma in the whole world. I'll see you Wednesday. Bye gran."

"Bye Katie, love you."

As Gloria hung up the call, she felt a powerful wave of love for her granddaughter and, in that moment, she knew that she would have to deal with those scumbags.

At the same time, she knew that finding out who they were or what they were doing would be difficult, to say the least. She was determined, though, to make things right for her grandchildren.

FORTY-FOUR

FRIDAY DAWNED BRIGHT and sunny, but the briefing room at Holborn Police Station—where senior officers from Operation Chiddingstone had assembled—was not a happy place. Their number included a Detective Superintendent and Detective Inspector respectively from the Avon and Somerset Police, the West Midlands Police and the Norfolk Police. The officers from the Metropolitan Police—who had ownership of the investigation—were AC Skelton, DCS Hook, and DI Dipak Joshi. The room was packed and the atmosphere was tense.

Detective Chief Superintendent Hook opened proceedings.

"Good morning ladies and gentlemen and thank you for your attendance. I would like to update you on progress of the investigation. So far, between our four forces, we have arrested countless people, we have interviewed or taken statements from thousands more, we have reviewed over eighteen hundred hours of CCTV, and we have conducted around four thousand door-to-door enquiries. That is a huge amount of police work and resources which is costing a vast amount of money, and yet we have failed to make a significant breakthrough. To say our bosses are not impressed is an understatement and, needless to say, the general public are beginning to view us as an absolute joke."

Detective Superintendent Marshman from Avon and Somerset broke in sarcastically, "That's because we've asked the public to help with the identification of little old ladies at Birmingham train station and in the backstreets of Norwich! Dozens of criminologists have reviewed the evidence, and they all agree that the two women almost certainly aren't the same person! Yet, here we are weeks later, still chasing her identity. Nearly all previous serial killers worldwide, not just here in the UK, but worldwide, have been men. Aren't we barking up the wrong tree?"

A female DI from the Norfolk Constabulary agreed. "I think you're spot-on, sir. The woman seen on the street outside Lyne Heath and then inside the pub, showed no signs of hurrying or nervousness." She looked directly at DCS Hook. "Would that be the case if she'd just murdered three people in cold blood? I don't think so, do you?"

"I agree it's unlikely," said DCS Hook. "But at the moment, identifying that woman remains a priority for us. It matters not that it could be two separate women, they may still have vital evidence. In any case, if they are completely innocent of involvement, why have they not come forward in answer to all the public information requests?"

Skelton stood up. "Exactly. As DCS Hook says, why haven't they come forward? I honestly believe that the identification of this woman is pivotal to our investigation. She was seen leaving the Welcome Cafe in Balsall Heath shortly after Alan Bramhall had left; she was seen walking the same route as him just before he was killed; she was caught on CCTV boarding the train from Birmingham New Street to London Euston, and she completely changed her appearance after boarding that train. We have no idea which woman she is on the train's cameras, although thorough research and checking of the footage, including ruling out those that were too fat or too tall, showed she could be one of about sixty-four ladies reckoned to be between the ages of 50 and 75."

"Then why don't we release the images of all sixty-four as possible suspects?" asked a female DI.

AC Skelton cast her a withering look. "Because if we cast our net that wide, we may or may not identify this woman. On the other hand, we would almost certainly be served by the remaining women, with up to sixty-three lawsuits for defamation of character. Our solicitors are still looking through the legalities, but at the moment we've been advised that it's not an option. It is, of course, entirely possible that after getting changed, she remained in the toilet throughout the journey, or even got back off the train and disappeared into the crowds in New Street station. So, it's quite possible that we wouldn't identify her, anyway.

"I'm being ripped apart by MP's and journalists every day. To say I'm pissed off would be an understatement! Ladies and gents, we really need to pull our fingers out of our fucking arses and get moving on this!" His eyes slowly scanned each person in the room. "Now, has anybody got anything new?"

Over the next hour, a Detective Inspector from each force gave a thorough update on their individual operation. Nothing of note was forthcoming.

AC Skelton glanced at DI Joshi, nodding at him when it was his turn to take the floor. DI Joshi rose to his feet.

"Thank you all for your hard work. We now require a redoubling of those efforts..."

He was interrupted by a Detective Superintendent from the West Midlands force, who gruffly said, "It's easy to spout that. How are we supposed to redouble our efforts? My people are exhausted! Not only that, everything else that requires police attention in my area is suffering. Over one aggressive junkie?"

AC Skelton jumped to his feet, his face flushed with anger. "I want everyone here to understand, you will all squeeze more effort from your officers—until they fucking squeak if necessary. You will all approach your Chief Constables and request more officers and more money. The area covered by these killings is enormous, far bigger than the Yorkshire Ripper enquiry or the Moors Murders enquiry. This is now the largest scale murder investigation in the history of the United Kingdom."

The Detective Superintendent from the Norfolk Constabulary stood up, only one metre from Skelton.

"Haven't you been reading my emails? I've squeezed my officers already, they've nothing more to give! My Chief is already threatening to remove me as OIC from the Norfolk branch of Chiddingstone, because I've badgered him every week for more money and resources. And what if we did miraculously manage to receive the extra funding you've asked for? What enquiries could be completed that haven't already been done? Don't shout and swear at us like a petulant teenager. All officers involved on the investigation have worked their arses off. At some stage you need to understand that we are dealing with a very clever and very capable criminal here."

"Don't speak to the boss like that!" snapped DCS Hook.

"Why not?" asked Marshman. "I fully agree; he's behaving like some bloody slave-driver. We have been doing all that is humanly possible and we deserve more respect."

Other officers began to have their say and within moments the room was full of them, standing up, shouting and pointing fingers at each other. A few simply sat forlornly in their seats, shaking their heads.

"All right, all right, that's enough!" bellowed AC Skelton. "Can everyone please sit back down!"

Gradually, calm was restored, with those standing slowly re-taking their seats.

"I apologise if I went too far; I know you're all working hard. But, with intense pressure from the public and our paymasters, we need to make sure that everything is both done, and *seen* to be done. Can I please ask all DI's to review every piece of evidence and every statement?? It just might mean that we discover something that may unlock this case."

There were murmurs from the assembled officers, some of agreement, others of frustration.

FORTY-FIVE
Saturday 13th February 1999

SATURDAY PASSED IN the standard routine for Gloria. In the morning she had plenty to do: walking to the shop for her paper, doing her washing and ironing, then carrying out a thorough spring-clean of her flat. In the middle of it all, Sean had phoned saying he wanted to pop around for an afternoon coffee and chat.

It was one o'clock before Gloria started making her favourite lunch of beans on toast. While tidying up afterwards and loading the dishwasher, she leaned heavily on the work surface, the enormity of the transformation in her life hitting her again like a sledgehammer—as it so often did.

Not only was she a serial killer, but a DCI knew she was a serial killer; furthermore, someone else obviously knew she was a serial killer, and was tormenting her with letters.

She could feel her shoulders and chest constricting, and a rising sensation of nausea. This had happened to her many times in the previous three months; she knew the sensations she was currently experiencing would pass and that she would feel all right again soon enough.

When Sean arrived, he looked as if he'd got the weight of the world on his shoulders. Gloria made drinks, and they settled down in the lounge with a couple of steaming hot mugs.

"Sean, are you okay? You've been very distant lately; I'm beginning to get quite worried about you."

"I know. Sorry, it's not something I can really talk to you about."

Unusually, Sean wasn't able to look Gloria in the eye as he spoke, looking instead down into his lap, clasping and unclasping his hands.

"Okay then, but something's clearly troubling you. Remember that I'm your friend. If you ever need to unload, you know where I am." She squeezed his hand, but Sean withdrew his.

"Thanks, but it's not really something you can help me with; it's not something that anybody can help me with." His voice was faltering.

"It's not your girlfriend Gail, is it?"

Sean noticeably stiffened on hearing her name. Shaking his head, he said, "I'm not seeing Gail any more. Now can we please change the subject?"

Gloria realised she'd touched a nerve. She changed the subject.

"Anything happening with the investigation?"

"Apparently, there was a major bust-up at the senior officers' briefing yesterday." He winced as he sipped his hot coffee. "A lot of them aren't happy about concentrating on identifying this woman; they think we're wasting time. Some even think a woman couldn't have carried out those murders. I heard that the DS from Norfolk completely did his nut at Skelton, told him to stop swearing and called him petulant!" Sean almost smiled.

"Blimey! What brought that on?"

"Frustration, really. The investigation's going nowhere. Other than CCTV of this woman boarding the train in Birmingham, and possibly also being seen wandering about in Norwich, they have nothing substantial. They're even arguing about whether it's the same woman now." As he said this, he glanced swiftly at Gloria, and her unease increased.

"What are they going to do about it?"

"Same as ever. Go over every witness statement and every arrest interview to see if anything's been missed. We've already done it twice before, so it's a complete fucking waste of time."

Although Sean was talking to Gloria, his mind seemed somewhere else; he was visibly shivering. Once again, he stared at her with an odd expression on his face.

"So, someone will be coming around to speak with me again about my statement?"

"Almost certainly." His voice croaking. "By the way, did DCI Simpson ever come over to see you? I gave her your details a couple of weeks ago because she wanted to speak with you about something."

Gloria was beginning to seriously wonder where this was heading. She didn't know whether Sean had spoken with Jules already; she just couldn't read him right now.

"It was something and nothing really, just general reassurance of the public by using people like myself, you know, people on police and community committees, neighbourhood watches, that sort of thing."

"That's okay then. She's all right is Jules; did you get on okay with her?" Sean still couldn't look at Gloria for long.

"As a matter of fact, we've struck up a bit of a friendship. She's good company, and she's a good listener."

Sean sat up and looked suddenly interested.

"A good listener? What were you chewing her ear off about then?"

"Actually, I told her that I supported the vigilante, how much better living around here had become over the past few weeks."

Sean finally looked into Gloria's eyes; he stared at her long and hard.

"You mean since the killings started?"

"Exactly."

"And what did she say?"

"Nothing really. She seemed to have sympathy with my point of view though."

Conversation stopped abruptly as the intercom buzzer sounded. Sean suddenly stood up, tears welling in his eyes. He looked completely distraught.

"Sean, what on earth's the matter?"

He replied quietly, "Just open the door, Glo, and I'm so, so sorry. There was nothing I could do."

That's it, then, thought Gloria. *I'm about to be arrested.* She assumed that Sean had finally worked out that she was the vigilante and had informed his bosses. If he was handing her in though, she needed to hear it from his lips.

"Nothing you could do about what? Sean, I don't understand what you're saying."

The buzzer sounded three times in quick succession. Whoever it was, they were clearly getting impatient. Sean said urgently, "Glo, for fuck's sake don't keep them waiting, let them in!"

Gloria could tell from his voice that further questions were pointless. She lifted the intercom and said, "Hello, who is it?"

"A man with a strong Irish accent replied, "It's Mr Higgins, I've been sending you a few letters."

Gloria went cold. She looked at Sean and received a nod from him in confirmation. How the fuck could Sean possibly know that the letter writer would be visiting her? Pressing the door release button, Gloria said, "Come up, then. You know where I am."

Sean wrung his hands, rocking back and forth; tears lining his cheeks.

Opening her front door, she watched with interest as the lift doors opened. The first man out was a short, frail-looking man, somewhere between sixty-five and seventy-five years old. He walked stiffly with a slight stoop and had short grey hair that was thinning on top. He seemed to be in pain and clearly wasn't a well man.

He was followed closely by two other younger men, both not far under forty. One was over six-foot, well-built with crewcut black hair and a large scar on his right cheek. The other was a little shorter, but very powerfully built, with short brown hair. This man had a cast in his left eye, making it hard to gauge where he was looking.

The older man smiled at Gloria, bowed his head and in a very heavy Irish accent said, "Good evening, my name is Michael Higgins. These are my two sons, Declan," he indicated scar-face, "and Seamus." Gloria was surprised by how deep and powerful his voice was; it didn't match his pasty, lined face and frail body.

He looked at Sean and said, "Hello again, Mr Aylen." Looking back to Gloria, he said, "Shall we go inside?"

It wasn't a question. Gloria moved aside to let them in. The three men seemed to fill her narrow hallway. She showed them into her lounge, where they sat down – Higgins on an armchair, the two younger men on the settee. She threw Sean a worried glance, but he couldn't meet her gaze.

"So. Can I offer you gentlemen a drink?"

"A cup of tea with one sugar would be wonderful, thank you," said Higgins.

"And what about your lads?"

"What would you like boys?"

"Coffee. Two sugars."

"Nothing for me."

"Okay, I'll be back in a minute." Gloria walked through into the kitchen, closely followed by Sean. Once they were alone, she hissed at him while putting the kettle on, "What the fuck's going on? Who are these people?"

"Listen to me," Sean grabbed hold of Gloria's left arm. His eyes were full of tears, and he spoke in a strained whisper. "The old man, Michael, is the head of the Higgins clan. One of the most notorious organised crime families in Britain. They run protection rackets, brothels, carry out large scale robberies, and they're major drug suppliers. This is a man you really don't want to cross!"

"But how do they know you?"

Sean looked down at his hands as if willing them to stop fidgeting. He didn't speak for a few moments, then said, "Michael is also Gail's father."

"You mean your Gail? The photographer?"

"Yes! She wasn't interested in me at all—she was working for him. Once I'd taken her to see my family, she came clean about who she is, and more importantly who her father is!"

"Shit. So that's why you've sounded so worried recently; you should have told me! What the fuck does he want with me though?"

"Glo, they've got me in their pocket. Gail passed all the details of my family to her father, and he's used that knowledge to blackmail me. He's threatening to harm my family, unless I agree to pass information to him."

He looked deeply into Gloria's eyes, before saying, "Glo, I know that you're the killer; they've told me everything, including the letters. What the fuck were you doing?"

Gloria was unable to speak.

Sean continued, "They insisted that I was here today when they arrived. I was told not to say anything until they got here; for some reason they wanted me here when they spoke to you."

Gloria was in a state of shock. No wonder he had been so distant; he knew she was the killer!

"Sean, I can explain. I never wanted to kill anyone. The first shooting happened by accident, I didn't mean to kill them. I was taking the gun to Holborn to hand it in. That's the truth, I swear. Then things just... got out of hand."

Sean looked at her with misery in his eyes.

"When they first told me about it, I really struggled to believe it could have been you, but trust me, that is now the least of your problems. These people see you as a potential recruit. That's the reason they've targeted you with the letters."

Michael Higgins shouted from the lounge, "That's enough chit-chat! Man could die of thirst in here."

Gloria poured out two cups of tea and two coffees, her hand shaking so much she could barely fill the cups. Returning to the lounge, she handed the cups to Higgins and Declan. After Sean's revelation, there was no point in pretence or denial, so she'd nothing to lose by being direct. She tried to keep her voice from shaking.

"Right. Sean's explained who you are, and why you're here. Would you like to tell my why you've been sending me letters, Mr Higgins?"

Michael Higgins smiled, regarding Gloria over the rim of his teacup, before gently placing it down onto a coaster. His smile faded, and he waved a hand at Gloria's armchair. Once she'd sat down, Sean sat on the arm of her chair next to her.

"Forgive my unorthodox methods, but I needed to ensure that you were the right person to join us. Obtaining top-quality people who can carry out operations undetected is vital for someone in my position."

"What are you suggesting?" asked Gloria. "That I join your organisation? No fucking way! I'd rather admit my crimes and go to prison."

Michael sighed, shook his head, then picked up his cup and took another sip of tea. He nodded at Seamus, who removed a plain brown envelope from his jacket pocket and handed it to Gloria. Sean moved to stand next to her as she opened it. She removed about a dozen colour photos and gasped in horror as she looked at photographs of Sandra and her family in different locations: Katie and James at school; the family outside their house and in the garden; Sandra in the supermarket; Steve driving his car and at work.

Higgins leaned forward and fixed Gloria with an icy stare.

"Mrs Jones, you really have no choice. If you refuse, then not only will I pass on information to the police about your recent activities, which will result in you being imprisoned for the rest of your life, but members of your family will almost certainly be involved in terrible accidents."

Incandescent with rage, Gloria stood up and looked desperately at Sean. He simply shook his head slowly and gestured for her to sit back down. Michael grinned and nodded his head.

"Mrs Jones, you are probably aware that Mr Aylen recently dated my beautiful daughter Gail. He foolishly believed her advances and played straight into my hands." He glared at Sean with his dark green eyes before continuing, "Luckily for me, Mr Aylen was stupid enough to introduce Gail to his family, and the information she passed to me has proved very useful. After I showed Mr Aylen similar photos to those of your family, he wisely agreed to join us. So, he'll be doing exactly what I tell him."

"Okay," said Gloria, her brain spinning with the speed of events. "I can understand you wanting me, because I'm useful to you, but please leave Sean and his family alone."

"How sweet," said Higgins. "There is a very good reason I want Mr Aylen in my organisation." He turned to look again at Sean.

"You will deflect the vigilante investigation away from Mrs Jones, and you will pass me information about any other investigations into my operations." He breathed out heavily. "I want you both working for me. If either of you refuse, those you love will suffer. Your granddaughter Katie is a beautiful girl, Mrs Jones; you wouldn't want her to lose those lovely looks, would you? The same goes for Mr Aylen's niece."

Gloria screamed, "You vicious bastard! I'll fucking kill you!"

She leapt to her feet, but had only taken a couple of steps towards him, when a blow to the back of her head sent her sprawling onto the floor. Dazed, and with her vision blurring slightly, she was hauled to her feet by Declan and dragged back into her armchair. She looked up and saw Sean being held at gunpoint by Seamus. Michael Higgins remained impassive, sitting there calmly sipping his tea.

"Excellent! You've displayed how much you love your family, so we have something in common!" His expression changed—angry now.

"Be assured that if anything should happen to me at your hand Mrs Jones, my sons here," he waved a hand towards Declan and Seamus, "will be far, far more depraved than me when punishing members of your family."

FORTY-SIX

TRYING TO CONTROL the sickening pain in her head, Gloria said, "All right, all right. I understand. I won't try anything again. But you didn't finish explaining about the letters; why didn't you just contact me after the first time? You could have approached me to join your organisation there and then. Why send all those cryptic messages? I don't get it."

Michael leaned back on the sofa, crossing his legs with a grimace of pain.

"The first killings were seen by chance, by a cleaning lady I recruited some years ago. She sometimes works at Holborn Police Station, and sometimes in the National Crime Squad offices, where she has proved very useful."

"Jesus Christ! Paula! You mean Paula, don't you?"

Higgins was clearly enjoying this.

"Yes, your friend Paula. Let me tell you about Paula, Mrs Jones. Like you, she was terrified when I first recruited her and very reluctant to cooperate. Now, look at her. After being with me for four years, she carries out her work as normal, she leads a normal life, but she's now also a fairly wealthy woman. Work for me, and you'll both be wealthy too, especially you Mrs Jones."

"And she informed you about me?"

"Yes. She'd just arrived at some offices she cleaned regularly in Barter Street when she heard shouting. She stayed hidden in a doorway and watched everything. Later, she described the shootings to me in great detail. I always enjoy hearing about a professional job and wanted to send an anonymous message that I was impressed. I admired what you did, but at that moment, I really had no intention of contacting you again. Then came the killings in Bristol, and I began to take more of an interest."

"I still don't understand; why not make your move then, why bother tormenting me with letters?"

"I needed to see whether you could still operate if you were under pressure. The additional uncertainty of who was watching you and sending the messages reflects the scrutiny that I and my employees have to work under. I only truly started to consider you as a potential recruit once you'd carried out the Birmingham job. That's why that message said what it did."

Realisation dawned on Gloria's face.

"Ah, now I understand. But how on earth did a letter arrive at my hotel?"

Higgins grinned, "After Birmingham, I realised you wouldn't be stopping anytime soon, so I had your flat watched. Every time you left you were followed, on that occasion all the way to Norwich!"

"But how did they know I'd be staying in that hotel?"

"He didn't. He followed your taxi in another taxi. You'll need to keep your guard up better than that when you're working for me." Suddenly, Higgin's demeanour changed—he looked impatient. "I need your answer Mrs Jones; take a few moments to discuss this with Mr Aylen, then give me your decision."

Gloria nodded and followed Sean into the kitchen. Sean spoke first, urgently.

"Right, shut up and listen to me. I've dealt with some of the victims of the Higgins family, and believe me you don't want them attacking you or your family; they're fucking psychos. I suggest you accept his offer for now, then we'll consider our exit strategy from a position of safety. One thing we can't do is go to the police; Paula is already on their payroll, and we have no idea if anyone else has been recruited. They'll kill us at the first inkling that we might be deceiving them, and if they can't get to us, it'll be one of our family members. This conversation can't go outside these walls; you must promise me you won't tell anyone. Agreed?"

Gloria nodded.

"Sean, I don't know whether I can handle this. I'm beginning to break up here; I've been a wanted woman for three months now, and three people other than you have already identified me as the killer!"

"Three people, what the fuck are you talking about?"

"Paula obviously witnessed the first two killings; the Higgins mob knows everything and then there's Juliet Simpson."

"My God, Jules knows?"

"She recognised me on footage from the train back from Birmingham and confronted me. I don't think she wants to hand me in, though."

It was now Sean's turn to be shocked.

"That could be a complication, but we'll have to play it by ear."

Gloria forced a smile.

"We've got no choice. Let's go and accept his offer. Like you say, we'll work out our exit strategy later."

She took Sean's hand, and they walked back into the lounge. Gloria stood in front of Michael Higgins and said, "We accept your offer, but I have two conditions."

Higgins growled, "What the fuck do you mean, conditions? I don't normally accept conditions."

"Firstly, none of our family members are approached, or made aware in any way about our agreements. That goes for both my family and Sean's."

"I admire your guts," said Higgins, smiling. "Agreed. And your second condition?"

"I have one piece of outstanding business, and I intend to conclude that business."

"What business?" asked Higgins, exasperated.

"My family's life is being ruined by drug dealers in Newcastle. I intend to eliminate them."

At that, Sean looked horrified, but Higgins smiled broadly and said, "Mrs Jones, you are wonderful. I agree. But after that, you join my organisation."

"In that case, I accept."

"Excellent!" Higgins stood up, facing Gloria.

"Once we shake hands, you become one of my staff. That means you obey orders and carry out my instructions without question, understood?"

Reluctantly, Gloria nodded, and they shook hands.

Higgins smiled broadly and said, "Welcome to the family. You'll be very well looked after, extremely well paid, and you'll receive the might of my legal team supporting you with any problems." He fixed Gloria with his gaze and said softly, "Of course, you've already been acquainted with my legal team, haven't you Mrs Jones?"

Realisation dawned. "It was you who arranged James Williams-Glass and the false witness statements?"

Higgins grinned at her, "You see? You are already a part of my team. How else do you think you got off? And you're welcome, by the way! Like I told you—we look after our own."

He took a step closer to Gloria.

"Now for my conditions. When I require your skills, you will not be using your own weapon; my staff will provide you with everything you need."

Looking at his sons, he cocked his head to one side indicating that it was time for them to leave.

"You'll hear from me whenever I need you. It could be tomorrow, next week, or in six months' time. It depends on what needs doing. Fail me at any time, or betray me, and you and your family will regret it."

Gloria suddenly looked furious again. She was about to say something in response, when Sean quickly grabbed her, saying, "Forget it Glo, don't say anything."

Higgins glowered at her and said, "Mrs Jones, listen to Mr Aylen, he speaks wisely." He looked from Gloria's face to Sean's, then back to Gloria's.

"Remember Mrs Jones, I own you. I own both of you."

With that, Higgins and his sons left the flat. The room suddenly felt empty without their menacing presence. Gloria and Sean stood there a moment, before Gloria slumped into her armchair.

"Right," she said. "Start talking. I want to know your side of the story; you already know mine."

Over the following ten minutes Sean explained exactly how Gail had deceived him. She had encouraged his advances on the instructions of her father, who was not only aware of his position in the police, but was also aware of his friendship with Gloria. The visit to his parents' house provided all the details they needed, and it was on the car journey home that Gail dropped her mask—and a huge bombshell.

She had told him that Gloria was the vigilante, explaining everything they knew about her, including how she had been sent several letters, and how one of their staff had followed her to Norwich. She warned him that if he involved his colleagues in the police, his family would suffer. At first Sean was incredulous; this couldn't be the Gloria he had known for so long. But as she revealed more and more details, he began to believe the impossible and he knew they were in deep, deep trouble.

Two days later, Gail took him to a rendezvous in Holborn, where he was introduced to Michael Higgins in the back seat of his Bentley. Higgins handed him a plain brown envelope containing several photographs. Sean saw with horror that they were all of his family: pictures of his parents leaving their house and inside their car, and pictures of his sister and his twelve-year-old niece Bluebelle, including pictures of her at school. By the time Sean had reached this part of his story, he was crying and Gloria put a comforting hand on his knee.

Higgins had then explained that his main enforcer and hit-man had been sentenced to life in November, leaving him with a vacancy that needed filling. He explained how, having identified Gloria as a formidable killer, he had come up with the seemingly crazy idea of employing her. It was perfect –not only was she a woman, but an older woman, making it much easier for her to get closer to any potential target without arousing their suspicion. Finally, he told Sean to arrange a meeting with Gloria at her flat, where Higgins would turn up, and tell her she was joining his organisation.

"Jesus Christ, Sean. What the fuck are we going to do?"

Sean placed a hand on top of Gloria's.

"We have no choice. Understanding that Higgins and his family are complete psychos is vital to our chances of staying alive. We know that he won't hesitate to either torture, enslave, or even kill members of our families if we fail to carry out his wishes so, whatever he demands in the foreseeable future, we comply with fully. There must be a way out of this, and we will discover what that is in due course. In the meantime, we play the dutiful foot-soldiers he wants us to be."

He squeezed Gloria's hand.

"So we just carry on as though nothing's happened? We just carry on living our lives exactly the same as before? I'm not sure I can do that. I'm Britain's most wanted right now, and now I'll be killing more people, for the fucking Higgins family!"

"To answer your question, yes, we carry on as though nothing's happened; we've simply got no options, we've got nowhere to go. Stay calm, and eventually we'll escape this nightmare." Sean's demeanour suddenly changed; he looked angry.

"Anyway, what the fuck was that about Newcastle? You can't seriously be intending to kill again. And making conditions like that with someone like Higgins, are you fucking mad?"

"Sorry Sean, this one's non-negotiable. My family's lives are being ruined by those two scumbags – my granddaughter was arrested for God's sake! I'm going to sort it. I have to. After that, I'll be available for Higgins as often as he wants."

Sean looked at the floor and sighed heavily. Standing up, he gestured for Gloria to stand too. She lifted herself to her feet, and they held hands.

"Glo, I've got to go now. You take good care, and we'll speak again very soon."

He kissed her on the forehead. Gloria didn't reply. She held Sean's hand tightly and walked with him to the front door. He left without another word.

FORTY-SEVEN

ONCE THE DOOR was closed, Gloria leaned against it with her eyes shut for a few moments before heading to the kitchen. She reached up and opened the cupboard where she kept her cereals, lifting down the Cornflakes box, and placing some kitchen towel on the table. She lifted the Glock out of its hiding place and held it in her left hand, stroking it gently with her right.

"Sorry, but you've got one more job before I'm done with you, then you can retire," she said, before wrapping it in the paper towel, and returning it to the Cornflakes box.

Gloria spent much of the evening in a state of restless anxiety, sick with worry. She'd already killed eight people and thought she had got away with it; how naïve she had been. At least four other people knew she was the killer: Paula, Higgins, Sean and Jules, not to mention Higgins' children. On top of that, she now had the additional worry of being forced to become part of the very criminal world she so despised, where she could be required to kill or maim on demand. Was it really worth taking the chance on killing two more?

She picked up a photo-frame containing a picture of her husband and son, sitting on a pedalo together on holiday in the south of Spain; both beaming. Happier times. Too long ago.

She spent the rest of the day and evening agonising over her options; she had so much to consider, and so many decisions to make. By half-nine, mentally exhausted, Gloria went to bed, but sleep did not come easily; her thoughts were all over the place. Her situation had suddenly gotten so much worse. No longer was her main concern being arrested for the vigilante killings, she was now consumed with worry about having to do whatever the Higgins family ordered her to.

Gloria tossed and turned restlessly, eventually drifting off to sleep sometime between two and three in the morning.

FORTY-EIGHT
Monday 15th February 1999

AFTER A BRIEF and fitful sleep, Gloria awoke early at around seven. She turned over and tried relaxing, but was unable to get back to sleep. At some time during the night, Gloria had come to a decision: she was going to take care of things for her family.

The idea of travelling up early had entered her head; this would present difficulties—like avoiding all contact with her family until Wednesday—but also opportunities, like having extra time to find out more about the dealers and their operating methods. During the morning she cancelled appointments with a couple of friends, using the almost truthful excuse that she'd decided to travel up to see her daughter earlier.

Gloria left home and, once on the street, frequently glanced over her shoulder, checking there wasn't anyone behind her. *Would Higgins still be having me followed?* Every person she saw apparently paying the slightest attention to her started her heart racing. She had taken her old-fashioned black handbag, knowing that her favourite tan bag had become far too easily identifiable.

Gloria took the tube to Kings Cross, where she knew there were plenty of charity shops. Wheeling a large suitcase would be very handy once she'd obtained a few changes of clothing. In the Salvation Army shop, she purchased a light blue, three-quarter length mac; in the Sue Ryder shop, a white, sixties-style woolly cap; and in the Red Cross shop, a patterned, royal blue scarf.

She would change into them at the Premier Inn in Newcastle, where she'd booked a room that morning by telephone. It was close to the city centre, and well away from the north-eastern suburbs, where her family lived.

"Weekly return to Newcastle please," said Gloria, handing over cash to pay for her ticket. She had twenty-five minutes to spare before the train would be leaving. She could relax. It was Monday, but her family weren't expecting her until Wednesday. She had no intention of surprising them by arriving early, but she fully intended to surprise two drug dealers in a black BMW.

The train was busy but not full, and she chose a seat with a table. A young woman sat diagonally opposite her, but Gloria didn't strike up a conversation, which seemed to suit the young lady just fine. Settling down with the Daily Mail crossword, Gloria heaved a sigh of relief. She was on her way. Her concerns about the Higgins family would have to take a back-seat for a few days. Helping her family came first.

Arriving in Newcastle, Gloria quickly found a kiosk, where she purchased a cheap street map of the city. The Premier Inn Quayside was easy to locate and five minutes later she'd checked in. Gloria had formulated a plan: one she hoped would make her task easier, but one that that could also put her in considerable danger.

By seven in the evening, she'd showered, changed into the charity shop disguise and enjoyed a Big Mac with fries at the nearest McDonald's.

Walking out into the night, clutching a paper bag, she headed back towards the train station, knowing from previous experience that streets around stations attracted drug users; therefore, she figured, they would also attract drug dealers.

An hour later, Gloria had carried out a thorough reconnaissance of the area around the station. Just as she thought, there were about a dozen people hanging around, all of whom also looked like users, although she couldn't be certain. Taking the plunge, she approached two men sitting on large sheets of cardboard in an underpass; they had dirty black sleeping bags wrapped around their shoulders. Both looked to be in their mid-twenties, both had short brown hair and both looked thin and gaunt. One was wearing navy jeans, the other had grey tracksuit bottoms on.

"Here you go boys, something to warm you up." Gloria handed them the paper McDonald's carrier bag, containing two cups of coffee, plenty of sugar sachets and two large vanilla milkshakes.

"Thanks," mumbled the man in jeans.

"It's a pleasure. I believe people in your situation need all the help you can get, especially at this time of year."

He looked up for the first time. "Most people don't give us a second look, like we're something they've just trodden in."

"Well, I don't think that. I always like to help others if I can. Can I ask you guys a personal question?"

"Depends." This time it was the man in tracksuit bottoms, who so far had seemed less appreciative of Gloria's donations. "We don't like nosy parkers, do we, Luke?"

"Come on, Josh, this lady's been kind enough to buy us coffee."

"S'pose so." He looked Gloria up and down before replying. "All right then. What do you want to know?"

"I've recently moved into the area and would really like to get involved in drug treatment work; it's something I've done in the past. Before I apply for a position though, I want to do some research into the drug scene around here, you know, where the dealers operate, how big the problem is, the number of people dependent on drugs in Newcastle, things like that. Could you help me?"

Both men looked at each other, but said nothing. Gloria had been ready for this and adjusted her strategy.

"Look, I'm sorry, you're clearly not happy with this. I don't want either of you to feel uncomfortable, so I'll go and bother someone else."

As she turned to walk away, Luke called her back, "Hey, chill, I trust you." He looked at his friend. "What about you Josh, she seems okay, yeah?"

Josh shrugged but said, "Okay, fine by me."

The two men stood up and approached Gloria. Her plan was working.

"What's your name?" said Luke. "You know both our names after all."

"I'm sorry, it's Holly. I should have introduced myself."

"Okay Holly," said Josh, who seemed to be the dominant one. "We'll tell you what you need to know, but we've got to be careful. By the way, you obviously know we're both addicts—well, we both use speedballs. You okay with that?"

"That's a combination of two drugs, isn't it?"

"You do know your stuff," said Josh.

"As I said, I've done some work like this before."

Josh replied, "Okay Holly, here's the thing, you are currently standing less than a hundred metres from where the main dealers in Newcastle will be operating in about three quarters of an hour. We can show you where it all happens, but when the dealing starts, you keep out of the way, right?"

"Fine by me. Where do they deal from? Do they have a car? And they must have a stash somewhere?"

This time Luke spoke, "Yeah, they have a car, and we reckon we know where the stash is."

Gloria felt a pulse of excitement; she hadn't anticipated this.

"Really? How could you possibly know where a dealer's stash is? I'm not being rude, but they're normally so secretive about things like that aren't they?"

Luke answered again. "It was just luck that we discovered it. Last November, we were walking down an alleyway when we saw their car going down into an underground garage. We could see Chunks getting out of the driver's door and using a swipe card to get in. The stash might not be in there, but we're guessing that's probably where it is."

"Sounds like you might be right." She tried to keep the eagerness out of her voice. "Where is this car park then?"

"At the rear of a small block of empty offices, just off Barrack Road, near the football ground."

Luke interrupted, "The main man and his sidekick drive round in a black BMW; they never leave the car. Anyone wanting to buy has to approach one of the car windows."

This was interesting information. It sounded like the same car, but Gloria wanted to make sure.

"A black BMW, eh? How typical! Small man syndrome; I bet they're both weedy little men."

"No," said Josh. "The driver is an enormous guy called Chunks; the passenger's pretty big too."

"What's his name?"

"Calls himself Boon. You'll see them for yourself in half an hour."

Gloria stayed chatting with them for about twenty minutes, mainly about their lives on the street, and how they became hooked on drugs. She began to feel genuinely sorry for them; they seemed like decent men. Shortly before nine, Luke received a text on his mobile, and the two men became instantly anxious and agitated.

"Right, follow us but not too closely, and don't speak to us in front of anyone," said Josh. "When the car arrives, keep your distance and stay out of sight, okay?"

She nodded her agreement. "Whatever you say."

Following the two men at a suitable distance, Gloria was led out of the underpass and into a multi-storey car park. Luke and Josh went up two flights of stairs to the second floor. Following, she hoped unobtrusively, Gloria began to notice what she assumed were several other users heading in the same direction.

Having stepped out from the stairwell onto level two, Gloria stayed between two cars and close to the stairs. She watched as the drug users, including Luke and Josh, converged on the far end of the level. She could hear excited chattering and counted around fifteen people in the crowd. Most looked like they lived on the streets, but one or two looked like office workers, dressed smartly in suits.

Cars came and went, with normal members of the public parking and driving out their vehicles as usual. Gloria noticed that they seemed to ignore the crowd of drug users, as though this was nothing out of the ordinary.

Twenty minutes later, she spotted a car climbing the up ramp which was almost exactly opposite where she was hiding. Ducking down, she saw the very same BMW, with the same driver and passenger that she'd confronted at Christmas. The car moved speedily down to the far end where, as soon as it stopped, it was swiftly engulfed by people. Gloria noticed the personalised number-plate; it was RE4DY. *We'll see just how ready you are.*

Within just a few minutes, the car sped off and the crowd dispersed. Gloria waited until all was quiet, before heading back down the stairs to the underpass, where she saw Luke and Josh back on their cardboard.

They didn't seem anxious or agitated anymore, so Gloria assumed they'd already taken their drugs.

"Hello again." Trying to ensure she stayed in their good books, Gloria handed a ten-pound-note to each of them, "There you go lads, get yourselves a meal on me."

Josh looked at her with unfocused eyes, his pupils dilated.

"That's really kind of you, Holly, you're a lovely person," he slurred.

She could see he was gently shaking.

"Well, you've been really helpful. I need to head back now; perhaps I'll see you again over the next few days. Nice to have met you lads."

With that, Gloria walked away and headed for the Premier Inn. She was tired after the day's travelling, and the events of the evening, but what a successful evening it had been. Tomorrow, Gloria would be searching for an empty office block near Barrack Road.

FORTY-NINE
Tuesday 16th February 1999

FOLLOWING AN EXCELLENT night's sleep, Gloria felt refreshed. She opened the top clasp of her black handbag and removed the Glock. Releasing the magazine, she checked that the bullets were raised correctly in position, checked the trigger mechanism while the magazine was out, and made sure everywhere was clean of dust. Satisfied that all was in order, she replaced the handgun in her bag, checked herself in the mirror, then left her room.

She was planning a full day and decided she couldn't face it on an empty stomach; the Premier Inn's full English breakfast was the perfect preparation, washed down with three cups of strong tea. Gloria shared pleasant conversation with a family of South African tourists at her table, talking mainly about the Royal Family. Eventually the time came for her to depart, so she made her apologies and left the hotel.

The weather was forecast to be cloudy but dry, and Gloria was fully aware that she was likely to be out in the cold for long periods, so she'd purchased her change of clothes with that in mind. On her back, she carried a black rucksack which she knew would be invaluable later. It was now nearly ten, and she was ready to start her reconnaissance.

Before breakfast, Gloria had sussed out the route to Barrack Road, which was about three quarters of a mile away. She had no idea which block of offices she was looking for, or the name of the company, or even where around Barrack Road the block might be. She only knew that finding that building was her priority.

The mid-morning traffic was stationary in places, belching exhaust fumes that made Gloria cough. She walked quickly through morning shoppers, men in suits and groups of tourists taking photos of the sights. Reaching the beginning of Barrack Road, at the junction with Gallowgate,

Gloria was surprised how much greenery there was, how wide the road was, with two lanes in each direction, and how few pedestrians there were.

She walked slowly north-west, past Newcastle United's football stadium to her right. Her eyes carefully scanned each building on both sides of the road, hoping to find the empty office block. More importantly, one with an underground car park. She quickly realised that the combination would be quite rare.

After passing Leazes Park on her right, Gloria was feeling less confident, and was beginning to think her informants might have been mistaken, but she carried on searching. A few minutes later, she noticed a small unmade road on her right, leading down to a side road, running parallel with Barrack Road. She could just make out the edge of a tall, brick building, which looked like it could be an office block.

Walking down the track, between pleasant looking grey stone buildings, she reached an office block, with the name 'Style Curtains' proudly displayed above the third-floor windows. It was clearly deserted and dilapidated, with two broken windows on the ground floor that had been boarded up, and a fading 'Offices to Let' sign in a separate ground-floor window. Gloria's hopes began to rise.

There was a car park sign to the right of the building, so she walked towards it. This led her down a drive to the right-hand side of the building and round to the rear, where she saw seven outdoor parking spaces. Weeds were sprouting up through the tarmac in places, giving the car park an abandoned and forlorn appearance.

On her left she saw a low brick wall, about a metre high, that appeared to section off a separate parking space. *Probably for the boss.* She decided to check it out anyway. Gloria walked to the wall, looked over the top, and there in front of her was a down-ramp leading to a shuttered underground car park. *Yes! This must be it.* She was almost certain she'd found the place she'd been looking for.

Returning to Barrack Road, Gloria turned right, away from the city centre. After a short distance she turned right again, into the next road along where she spotted a Londis supermarket. She would be glad of some food and drink to sustain herself later, so she went in and bought supplies of sandwiches, snacks and water.

With this in her rucksack, she was walking back towards Barrack Road when she noticed a small alleyway on her left leading down between rear yards. It appeared to lead in the direction of the disused office block, so she decided to check it out.

No wider than a metre and a half, the alleyway appeared to be used more as a dumping ground than a walkway. However, despite all the debris and overflowing rubbish bags, it was just about passable, so she decided to give it a try, and carefully picked her way along it.

Less than five minutes later, Gloria stood in the small car park at the rear of the offices; the alleyway had taken her almost directly there. Not only that, but from behind a large evergreen bush near the end of the alleyway, Gloria realised she would have a clear view into the car park from a safe distance, including the down-ramp into the underground parking. This, she decided, would be an ideal spot for an observation point later in the evening.

Checking her watch, Gloria noted it was almost half-eleven. She knew enough about street drug dealers, to know that they probably wouldn't start dealing until late afternoon at the earliest, but more likely early evening. This left her with plenty of time to kill, time she would use finding out all she could about the underground car park.

Walking carefully along the slippery down-ramp, looking regularly over her shoulder to check that she wasn't being observed, she reached the metal shutter door into the underground car park. She tried lifting it, but it was securely closed. The only method of opening the door appeared to be the card swipe entry system, a card she didn't have. Gloria stopped to think. She needed to get into the car park, however it was underground, so the only method of entry and exit was the closed shutter door. She simply had to learn the layout inside, as it may be vital later in the evening.

As a young office worker, Gloria remembered that she had once been employed in a block of offices with a similar gated car park. She also remembered how the staff had a system of leaving a couple of entry cards tucked into gaps in the brickwork around the frame of the shutter, thereby allowing every member of staff entry, even when someone had forgotten their own card. They were very well hidden, so anyone trying to gain entry who didn't work there would be unlikely to find them.

Searching high and low, Gloria worked her fingers into every crevice around the sides of the door, particularly where the brickwork met the metal frame of the shutter housing, but found nothing. She tried reaching above the door, but wasn't quite tall enough, so she decided to walk back up the ramp and search around the edge of the outside car park, hoping to find something suitable to stand on.

After only a couple of minutes, she found two loose house bricks under a hedge, bordering the parking spaces. Back at the shutter door, Gloria found that by standing on them on tiptoe, she could just reach into the gap over the housing above the door. After a brief search, at the extreme left-hand edge of the shutter, she came across a small flat object. Pulling it out, she was thrilled to see it was indeed a swipe card. Thank you, Josh and Luke!

Gloria stepped off the bricks, then moved towards the card device. Sure enough, when she swiped the card, the shutter door started to rise, and within seconds it was fully open. Things had been going her way so far, but she knew that, by going into the area in front of her, she would be taking a huge risk, not knowing what—or who—she might encounter. It was a risk worth taking, though.

Stepping inside, she registered the faint smell of petrol, then she noticed what a small space it was: there were only two parking spaces to the left of the door and three opposite. She also noticed a clearly marked 'door open' button just inside the door. There was a locked cupboard, with a very narrow door recessed into the left-hand wall, which opened outwards, and was secured with both latch and mortise locks.

Gloria congratulated herself on a great morning's work. She had identified the premises, obtained a method of entry, seen the inside of the car park, and discovered a reasonably good observation point. The day had gone remarkably well. So well, in fact, that after walking back outside and watching the underground car park door closing, she realised it was only just approaching mid-day. The dealers were unlikely to be active during daylight hours at this time of year, meaning she had plenty of time to walk back into town and treat herself to a proper lunch.

By the time Gloria had walked back towards the city centre she was ravenous, despite the generous breakfast she'd devoured earlier. A passerby directed her to a local pub where, he assured her, the food was excellent. He was right.

The pub was wonderfully old-fashioned, and she indulged herself in traditional fish and chips, two glasses of white wine, and a sticky toffee pudding with custard.

By the time she'd finished, it was still only half one, so Gloria decided to stay inside the pub and call Sandra. She had a burning desire to speak with her, to know how things were going, but more importantly, she needed to persuade her daughter that she was still in London. She tapped in her number and waited.

"Hi mum, great to hear from you. What time do you want collecting from the station tomorrow?"

"I'll be catching the seven forty-six from Euston, which arrives in Newcastle just before eleven."

"Okay, Steve will be there about fifteen minutes before that, just in case the train arrives early. He'll wait for you at the barrier."

"Great. I'm so looking forward to seeing you all."

"Same here."

"How's Katie?"

"She's fine thanks. Guess what? This morning an officer called round to inform us that Katie no longer needed to attend the police station; she served her with a form releasing her from bail. Isn't that great?"

Gloria beamed with delight.

"That's wonderful news, darling, and what about Ryan and Jason?"

"Ryan's been released too, but Jason has to answer bail. I think he's going to receive a juvenile caution."

"Well, that's good news all round. Under the circumstances, I think the police have been very fair. What's the situation like on your estate? Are those ghastly dealers still about?"

"Unfortunately, yes. Katie and James never go out to the green in the evening any more. Most of the parents around here drive their kids everywhere now. No-one wants them hanging around the estate."

"So, the dealing's as bad as ever, then? Is it still that black BMW with the two large, um, 'gentlemen'?" Her voice was heavy with sarcasm.

"If anything it's worse than when you visited mum. And I'm not sure that 'gentlemen' is the right term for those shitbags either! Where are you now? I can hear voices, and glasses chinking."

"I'm treating myself to a pub lunch, then I'll have a wander through Covent Garden market. I rarely visit these days, and I do love it down there."

"Good for you. Anyway, I need to get going; lots of shopping to do before you descend on us. You enjoy your day, and I'll say goodbye until tomorrow. Don't forget, Steve will meet you at the barrier."

"Okay, give Katie and James a kiss from me. Love you."

"Bye mum, see you tomorrow."

Ending the call, she left the pub, and treated herself to three hours in Newcastle's Life Science Centre, which was sure to take her mind off the evening ahead.

FIFTY

HER VISIT TO the Life Science Centre had been every bit as therapeutic as Gloria hoped; she now felt calm and relaxed. It was early evening, and she was back at the end of the alleyway, with an excellent view of the underground car park ramp; she could even see the top third of the shutter door. It felt very different from the morning; the twilight was unnerving, darkness was falling fast. Apart from glimmers of light from houses or offices, it would be completely dark soon. On the plus side, Gloria was sure she wouldn't be bothered by anyone coming down the alleyway, which appeared to have not been used as a thoroughfare for a while.

The unmade road in front of her that ran across the end of the alley also appeared to be rarely used. Gloria was extremely satisfied with the suitability of her hiding place. The ground was dry, so she removed the food and drink from the rucksack, placed it on a low wall behind the bush, and sat down to wait.

An hour-and-a-half passed, and the temperature had dropped markedly; Gloria was grateful that she'd dressed so warmly and tugged her scarf more tightly round her neck. Even so, her body was still shivering involuntarily from time to time; she was unsure whether this was from the cold or nerves.

Suddenly, she heard voices approaching from her left. She peered through the deepening gloom, but the few lights from house windows overlooking the unmade road did little to improve her vision. She strained her eyes and looked harder, but still couldn't see anyone. Getting to her feet as quietly as possible, she placed her food back into the rucksack, lifted it from the wall, and stepped into the alleyway, stumbling through the almost total darkness. Once she'd reached about ten metres into the alley—where she knew she'd be invisible—she crouched down and waited.

Two voices approached—one male, one female—discussing something about the woman's brother. The couple briefly crossed her vision at the end of the alleyway, then they were gone. Gloria remained frozen where she was for a couple of minutes, to make absolutely certain they'd gone, then stood, relieving the cramp in her legs, and walked back to the track to resume her vigil behind the bush.

Another hour-and-a-half passed and Gloria was getting peckish. She peeled open the wrapping on her tuna sandwich and tucked in, then picked up one of her bottles of water, intending to take a long drink. Just as she lifted the bottle to her lips, she saw headlights coming down the unmade road leading off Barrack Road, heading straight towards the empty office block.

The headlights turned right in front of the office block, and within a few seconds they illuminated part of the rear car park. "Here they come," she whispered to herself.

The car moved into the rear car park, with the headlights briefly shining straight at her, but Gloria wasn't concerned; she knew she was concealed behind the bush. Exactly as she'd anticipated, the car turned left and onto the down-ramp, and for the first time, Gloria saw for certain that it was the Black BMW with the registration number RE4DY; Chunks and Boon—as she now knew them to be—were in their usual seats, with Chunks driving.

She held her position as the underground car park shutter slowly opened. Once again, she found herself smiling; she didn't really understand why, she only knew that for some reason she felt good. *Maybe this is why Higgins wants me working for him. Perhaps I am a psychopath like him and his kids.*

The BMW disappeared into the car park, and shortly afterwards the shutter began to close.

Standing up, Gloria quickly put the uneaten food and drink into her rucksack, tidied up any mess she'd made, and lifted her handbag onto her shoulder. The rucksack would remain where it was, behind the bush on the wall. Sucking in a deep breath, she fully exhaled then stretched before walking silently towards the underground car park.

As Gloria edged down the ramp, taking care not to slip on the now partially frozen surface, she could hear deep voices, which grew in volume as she neared the shutter; she could also hear that apart from the voices, there was no noise coming from behind the shutter—the car engine had been switched off. However, bright slivers of light showed around the shutter, so they'd left the headlights on. Listening carefully, she recognised Chunks' voice.

"I thought that fucking police van was following us for a while there."

"So did I," replied Boon. "Would've been a great time for them to search the ride though, wouldn't it?"

"What's that supposed to mean?"

"Chunks, chill, what I mean is we've had a great evening so far; that last group totally cleaned us out! This is the earliest we've had to restock for months." They both laughed.

The sound of a key being put into a lock and a door being pulled open was followed by Boon saying, "We're getting low Chunks, when's the next meet?"

"I'm waiting for a call back. Don't worry, there's enough here for tonight and tomorrow. Grab that bag of white, that's a hundred, and that bag of brown, should be fifty in there, and those two bags of crack, that should be enough."

"You sure Chunks? Only a hundred crack?"

"Trust me, it's enough."

"Okay, if you say so."

Silently sliding the card from her pocket, Gloria crept up to the shutter and swiped. Instantly the shutter mechanism whirred and started to rise. She took the gun from her handbag and felt herself practically collapsing with fear. She knew they must be standing over by the cupboard somewhere. Her legs were so wobbly she was having trouble remaining upright.

Chunks suddenly realised what was happening.

"Hey! Who the fuck is there?"

When the shutter was only two-thirds open, Gloria ducked underneath, gun raised and pointing at the men, who were both standing by the open cupboard illuminated perfectly in the full glare of the headlights. She saw that Boon had pulled out a large knife which he held high, trembling slightly, she noticed.

"Good evening Chunks, Boon," she said calmly. "Boon, if that knife's not on the floor in two seconds, I'll blow your fucking balls off."

They were both shocked into silence, but Boon didn't move. Gloria pointed the gun straight at his groin, which had the desired effect, and he immediately dropped the knife to the floor. The shutter door was closing again on the automatic timer, which suited Gloria just fine.

"How the fuck do you know us, bitch?" asked Chunks.

Gloria raised the gun to head level again. She walked two steps towards them and said, "No need for name calling. Politeness costs nothing. I know who you are because you two have been ruining my family's life for months now, so I've made it my business to find out everything about you."

Chunks suddenly smirked and said, "Hang on a minute, I know you. You're the old bag who badmouthed me at Christmas!" A broad smile spread across his face. "You don't have a clue who you're talking to, do you?"

Gloria smiled back. "Oh, I do! A scumbag. Basic pondlife."

Chunks' expression changed instantly to one of fury. He took a step towards Gloria, his fists clenched.

"I'm the main man in this fucking town! No one disrespects me like that! And you don't fool me, that's a replica."

"Is it?" said Gloria, then pulled the trigger and saw the impact hole appear between his nose and his mouth. His head seemed to sink into his shoulders, and blood sprayed against the cupboard and onto the wall. Chunks' body collapsed like a house of cards. He'd fallen with his knees forward, his bottom sitting on his heels, his torso lying backwards, and his head on the bottom shelf of the cupboard.

A second after the bullet impacted, Gloria's gun was trained at Boon's head. She almost felt sorry for him, seeing the state he was in: total meltdown, tears in his eyes, quaking and whimpering in fear.

"You... you're that fucking vigilante, aren't you?" he managed to stammer; he was almost sobbing. Dropping to his knees, hands raised in surrender, he said, "Please, please, I beg you, don't shoot me! He was the real dealer. I'll stop all this shit, I promise. I'll get out of Newcastle, whatever you want..."

Taking another two steps towards him, Gloria said in a calm voice, "That's very moving Boon. You see, if you try really hard, you *can* be nice. However, too little, too late."

This time the bullet entered the middle of his forehead. He slowly fell back to his left, his arms falling limp at his sides, as blood and brain sprayed the wall behind him. He lay motionless on the floor on his left-hand side, quite dead. The bangs had echoed loudly in the small space and Gloria's ears were ringing.

She looked into the cupboard and was amazed at how many bags of drugs were there: only four or five larger bags, but each one contained dozens of smaller wraps, ready for sale on the street. *Each tiny little parcel carrying a world of misery.*

She turned and started to make her way out. She was about to press the door open button, when she heard a faint sound behind her. Walking back to the bodies she realised that Chunks was still alive, albeit only just. His right eye was open and the left eye half open; barely audible but ghastly, gurgling sounds were coming from his throat. Bubbles of blood oozed and popped out of the hole made by the bullet's impact. Gloria stood over him and leaned forward, looking straight into his eyes.

"Oh dear, Chunks. Still with us?" She watched his open eye move to stare straight at her. "Don't worry, I'm a decent human being, and a decent human being will always put an injured dog out of its misery."

As she said this, she noticed his right eye open wider with terror. Stepping back slightly to avoid blood spatters, she aimed carefully and placed a bullet into the centre of his forehead too. His eyes remained as they were, but all expression had left them; she was content that he was now quite dead. Gloria noticed that, to the sweet petrol smell in the confined space, was added the metallic tang of blood and she gagged. Time to leave.

She placed the Glock back in her handbag and pressed the button to open the door. Taking one final look at the carnage she'd left behind, Gloria stepped out into the cold night, breathing the air in deeply.

As she returned to her rucksack, she looked back towards the underground car park and saw that the shutter door had now firmly closed again.

Gloria walked slowly through the darkness of the alleyway, to prevent herself from stumbling over, and reached the side road in about two minutes. Turning right, she was pleased to see that the street was clear of pedestrians.

At the end of the street, she passed through a short alley into another residential road. A taxi was dropping off a young couple at their house, so Gloria approached the driver's window before he could drive off.

"Are you heading back into town? Could I hire you please?"

The middle-aged Asian driver shook his head. "Sorry, love, I can only accept pre-booked fares."

"I know that's the rule, but can't you make an exception, just this once, please?"

The driver didn't reply; he simply sat shaking his head.

Gloria persisted. "Please, I'll pay double the usual fare, I'll miss my last train home otherwise."

The taxi driver looked at her, shrugged his shoulders, then nodded his agreement and said, "All right then, just this once, get in."

Relieved, she climbed into the rear seat, and within five minutes was handing over a generous fare at the train station. After thanking the taxi driver profusely, she waited until he'd driven out of sight. She then turned and walked smartly back to the Premier Inn.

She was back in her room shortly before ten, still shaking from the adrenaline, and with the stench of the underground car park lingering in her nostrils. She stripped off her clothes and fell backwards onto the bed, totally naked, staring at the ceiling.

Images of the crude violence she'd just inflicted replayed again and again in her mind; then the concerns she'd felt so many times before re-surfaced. *Did anybody see me? Was there CCTV anywhere? Had someone heard the shots?*

Ten long minutes of fretting were followed by a period of calm as Gloria reassured herself that she had done the right thing. She was safe and, more importantly, so was her family.

Right, that's one problem dealt with. Now I just need to deal with Higgins without putting my family at risk.

Under a steaming hot shower, Gloria washed away the day's sweat and grime from her body. Lying on the bed, she turned on the television and watched news programmes until the early hours. There was still no mention of any killings in Newcastle.

Finally, with her eyes drooping, she turned the TV off and settled down into the warmth and comfort of the bed. Tomorrow, she would be with her precious family, where she would be reminded exactly why she'd killed two men that evening. Seeing her family happy, contented, and free from drug dealing on their estate, would reassure her that her actions were justified.

FIFTY-ONE
Wednesday 17th February 1999

GLORIA WAS UP, washed, breakfasted and checked out by nine thirty. Once again, she'd searched all the news programmes, and once again, to her immense satisfaction, there were no reports of any killings in Newcastle. On the whole, it would be better if the storm broke once she was safely back in London.

She asked the receptionist whether she could leave her suitcase at the Premier Inn for an hour, and it was placed into a securely locked cupboard behind the reception desk. Gloria thanked her and tried to give her a five-pound tip, which she politely declined.

Her charity shop purchases had been stuffed into a plain white plastic carrier bag, and Gloria knew that she needed to ensure they were safely disposed of. During her previous walks around the town centre, she'd spotted two dead-end streets, each with several large wheelie bins. One of these would be ideal for her purposes.

By half-past-ten, Gloria had disposed of her disguise, retrieved her suitcase, and walked to the train station. She waited by the barrier as arranged, and within ten minutes Steve arrived.

"Glo, great to see you! I thought you weren't arriving until eleven?" He gave her a hug and kissed her on both cheeks.

"I didn't sleep very well, so I caught an earlier train," she lied.

"Blimey, you must have started early!"

"Tell me about it; I'm so tired already! Right Steve, I want to see my family; where are you parked?"

"I'm in the multi-storey. This way." He took her suitcase and wheeled it across the concourse, Gloria walking alongside him. "The traffic was light on the way in, so we should be home in around fifteen minutes."

Sandra, James, and Katie ran outside to greet Gloria as the car pulled up. She hugged and kissed each in turn, saving an especially hard squeeze for Katie.

"It's wonderful to see you all," said Gloria. "Come on, let's get inside; it's cold out here and I'm dying for a cuppa."

Family lunch was followed by an afternoon walk through light drizzle around Gosforth Park. The black BMW, its drug dealing occupants, and the drug users on their estate were all frequent topics of conversation. Gloria joined in, as though she knew nothing more than everyone else. Unsurprisingly, considering the direct link to her family, Gloria felt a deeper sense of satisfaction than she had after any of the previous killings. As darkness fell, Sandra looked out of the window.

"Won't be long now mum, they're gathering. Look, there's about a dozen there already."

Gloria joined her daughter and looked outside. On the green among the small trees and bushes, but clearly illuminated by the street lighting, she saw people coming together in small groups, some on their phones, others chatting. She noticed that some had sleeping bags wrapped around their shoulders.

"What time do the dealers normally arrive?"

"You can never tell. They tend to gather over there to the right just before the car appears. But they haven't moved there yet, so they're obviously not close."

Nothing happened while they were looking, so they rejoined the others in the lounge.

"Right, I want you all to sit down and relax, because tonight I'm going to prepare the evening meal for my family," said Gloria.

Steve shook his head.

"No you won't, I've booked a window table at a riverside restaurant in the city. We're treating you tonight!"

Gloria was delighted. Although she would have loved cooking for her family, the idea of being spoiled at a posh restaurant sounded even better.

"Well, I won't refuse an offer like that. Thank you, Steve."

"Speaking of which, we'd better start getting ready," Sandra said as she walked to the kitchen and looked out again.

"That's unusual."

"What is?" asked Steve.

"The users are all still waiting for the car, but they're not gathering in the normal place yet. Some of them look a bit pissed off. There's nowhere near as many out there as usual. I wonder what's going on."

"Come on love," said Steve, guiding her from the window. "We need to get changed or we'll be late."

As they left the house, everyone noticed that a handful of drug users were still hanging around, obviously agitated, and raised voices could be heard.

"That's odd," said Sandra. "The dealers haven't turned up."

"Maybe they've been arrested mum," said James.

Sandra smiled broadly. "Oh, my God, no more dealers! How wonderful would that be?"

Gloria was thrilled to see the happy smiles. She allowed herself a discrete grin and climbed into the car.

The evening passed with great food and conversation, and Gloria felt truly happy for the first time in three days. They arrived home late, and everyone noticed there was a distinct absence of people hanging around the estate. Making the excuse of being tired, Gloria thanked James for sleeping on the settee, and retired to his bedroom.

Lying on his bed, under huge posters of Newcastle United, she turned on his TV and searched all through the channels for thirty minutes. Yet again, there were no reports of any murders. She undressed, snuggled between the sheets and after a fitful couple of hours, fell fast asleep.

Thursday passed with pleasant family activities, including a trip to Alnwick Castle and a little shopping. Returning home, it was noticeable that only a couple of users were hanging around the area. A neighbour was out emptying her bins, so Sandra called over to her.

"Hello Sue, it's really quiet isn't it? Have there been any problems today?"

Sue knew exactly what Sandra was referring to.

"No, it's been lovely. George at number four has been told by one of those druggies that the dealers just disappeared two nights ago. Nobody's heard from them, and they're not answering their phones. Looks like they've been arrested at long last, or just done a bunk."

Sandra clapped her hands together. "That's wonderful news, Sue! Thanks for telling me."

No-one felt like cooking, so Gloria ordered pizzas for everyone. In between mouthfuls she said, "Sounds like good news about those dealers, Sandra."

"It's fantastic; hopefully life will return to normal now. I wonder when they got arrested, if that's what's happened."

"They must have been arrested; what else could have happened?" asked Katie.

"They might have just moved on to a new patch," said Gloria. "But they live a dangerous life, Katie. Upset the wrong people in their line of business and you could end up in hospital, or worse."

"What, you mean they might be dead?"

"Possibly, who knows?"

Steve stood up, "Whatever the reason, I'm breaking open a lovely bottle of red to celebrate. Katie, James, in the circumstances, you can have a glass each too."

"I don't really like wine," said James. "Any chance of a beer instead?"

"Cheeky!"

Sandra turned on the news at ten, Gloria listened intently, but there was still no mention of the murders. She wondered how long their bodies would lie there undiscovered.

The weekend passed and still no mention anywhere of any killings, but Gloria knew that it would be huge news once the bodies were discovered. Although she was concerned about the likely furore, it didn't stop her enjoying her time with her family. It was lovely to see them visibly relaxing more and more with each passing day. They'd finally got their peaceful estate back, and they were absolutely loving it.

Her mission, it seemed, had been a complete success. If she wasn't caught, she would not be carrying out any further vigilante killings. Finding a way of removing herself and her friend Sean from the clutches of Higgins would now be the sole focus of her attention.

Following emotional goodbyes at Newcastle station on Sunday morning, Gloria boarded her train for London. Four hours later, she was sipping a cup of tea in her lounge. The Glock was once again wrapped in kitchen roll, placed inside a cellophane bag, and back inside the Cornflakes box. She'd done it!

Once again, she scoured the news programmes over a two-hour period. Five days had passed since she'd wiped out Chunks and Boon, yet there were still no news reports about it. Presumably the bodies were still undiscovered. If so, when would they be found and was this a good thing, or a bad thing? Could it be that the police, or maybe even a government department had placed a restriction on reporting, trying to starve the vigilante of the oxygen of publicity, hoping to draw them into the open?

Gloria had no idea. *No news is good news. Hopefully.*

FIFTY-TWO
Monday 22nd February 1999

GLORIA ROSE EARLY, listened to Radio 2 while enjoying a breakfast of muesli—she hadn't been able to bring herself to touch Cornflakes for months. She walked along Shaftesbury Avenue to her local newsagents, where she collected both the Daily Mail and Daily Express. Six days had passed, and still no bodies had been found in Newcastle.

By lunchtime, Gloria had unpacked her suitcase, loaded the washing machine, and brought home a few bits of food shopping from the supermarket. She'd also called Jules, who didn't pick up, so she left a very brief message saying she'd returned.

Now that the Newcastle issue had been dealt with, the situation with the Higgins family once more dominated her thoughts. How could she, a sixty-five-year-old pensioner, be part of an organised crime gang? And what was more disturbing, how on earth, when Higgins required her services, could she hurt, let alone kill, someone to order? Yet, if she didn't co-operate, the consequences would be dire.

She understood Sean's worries about anyone else learning that they were being coerced into working for the Higgins family, but she was unable to shoulder her fears alone, hence her decision to tell Jules.

HEINZ TOMATO SOUP had been Gloria's favourite since she was a little girl, and a pan of it was now simmering on the hotplate; she was in need of some comfort food. The kettle had boiled, and for a change she'd made herself a hot chocolate. Two slices of wholemeal bread with a thick layer of butter completed her late lunch.

After pouring her soup into a bowl, Gloria put everything onto a tray and moved into the lounge. *Only Fools and Horses* was being repeated for the umpteenth time on the TV, and when it was over, there was a brief news round-up, ahead of the main news programme.

"Good afternoon. The bodies of two males have been discovered in an underground garage in Newcastle-Upon-Tyne. Over now to our reporter at the scene, Christine Payne."

Gloria sat bolt upright in her chair, picked up the remote control and turned up the sound.

"Thank you, Steve. I'm standing just outside the police cordon, thirty metres from a disused office block on Smith's Close in Newcastle. The bodies of two black males were discovered in an underground car park, after police broke in this morning. Police have not yet informed us how they knew the bodies were there. Both men had been shot in the head. These murders carry all the hallmarks of similar attacks carried out by the so-called vigilante, who is still being hunted by police. It is now over three months since the first killings in London, and there is much speculation that these latest murders are the work of the same person. But detectives here say that at the moment they are keeping an open mind. Northumbria Police will be making a statement about the murders later this afternoon. Back to you in the studio."

"Thank you, Christine. Now, in other news—"

Sitting in her chair, with the tray on her lap, Gloria picked up the TV remote control and turned the sound off. She realised that she didn't feel too bad. Seeing the news report while she was sitting in her lounge eating a bowl of soup made the killings seem remote. Once again, it felt impossible that she'd actually had anything to do with them; they seemed totally removed from her. The first mouthful of soup tasted so much better than usual, and Gloria had finished the lot within ten minutes.

Putting the tray onto the coffee table, she sat back in her chair drinking hot chocolate, thinking. *There can't have been any witnesses, then. Not if it's taken them six days to find the bodies. I just might get away with it again.*

After lunch, she stood at her kitchen window looking across to St Giles High street. Compared to three months before, there were far fewer druggies, probably because dealers everywhere were being ultra-careful. Gloria knew the change was at least in part due to her actions. Her blank expression concealed the wonderfully smug feeling she had inside. Then her narcissistic revelry was interrupted by her home phone ringing. Picking up the receiver, Gloria was pleased to hear a friendly voice.

"Hello Glo, or should I say hello Mrs Vigilante? My God, you were taking a fucking chance, weren't you? Gloria Jones just happens to be visiting her family in Newcastle, when two men are shot dead in an underground garage!"

"I'm sure I don't know what you're talking about Juliet."

"Really? Have you forgotten everything you told me before you left?"

"Of course, I haven't," said Gloria, laughing. "Okay, what do you want to know?"

"Well, for a start, will you be available to make me a coffee at yours after I finish work, sometime after five?"

"Certainly."

"Great. See you in a bit."

Gloria loved hearing from her friend again, and was greatly reassured by how matter-of-fact she'd sounded. However, she couldn't imagine how she would react to news about her and Sean being forced into working for the Higgins family?

As it turned out, Juliet managed to sneak off early from work, and was in Gloria's lounge just before five. Having shrugged her jacket off, Jules turned to her friend, arms spread wide in greeting, and they exchanged a hug.

"I still can't believe what's going on. My whole career I'd always hoped that one day I'd be in the right place at the right time to nick a collar like yours, yet here I am, about to sit down and have coffee with you, while you tell me all about your latest exploits!"

"Juliet, we both know the reason you're here is because you can't resist my scintillating company and you enjoy the excitement!"

"You're taking the piss now," replied Jules. "Anyway, I want to hear all the gruesome details. I already know the why, now I would like you to please explain the how: how did you ever manage it?"

Gloria looked at the clock on the mantelpiece.

"You're going to have to wait, Jules. There's a police statement live at five and it should be an interesting one."

Gloria turned on the TV, and the two women settled down with their hot drinks to watch.

"Good evening, this is Andrew Beech with the five o'clock news. We are going straight to Newcastle Police Station for a statement on the shooting of two males, whose bodies were found this morning. Over to our northern affairs correspondent, Rahul Patel."

"Thank you, Andrew. You join me in Newcastle-Upon-Tyne, a city coming to terms with the possibility that the so-called vigilante may well have struck here." He looked over his shoulder and said, "I believe a Northumbria Police spokesperson is about to make a statement."

"Good afternoon ladies and gentlemen, thank you for coming. This morning, police forced entry to an underground car park in an unused office block in Smith's Close, Newcastle-upon-Tyne. They were acting on information received from a member of the public. Inside the car park, officers discovered the bodies of two black males, both of whom had been shot through the head at close range. Also inside the car park was a large quantity of drugs and a black BMW 525, registration number RE4DY. The keys were still in the ignition and the battery was flat because the car's headlights had been left switched on.

"One male has been identified as Winston George Leigh, thirty-seven years of age, from Gateshead. Leigh was shot twice through the head. The second male has been identified as William Steven Weald, thirty-four years of age, also from Gateshead. Weald was shot once through the head. Both males were killed at the location. It is almost certain that they were killed on Tuesday, the sixteenth of February, six days ago. Anyone with information should contact Northumbria Police. An incident room has been set up, and the direct line number will be released to the public later this evening.

"In the past hour, we have received ballistic results carried out on bullets recovered from the scene. These show that the bullets were fired from the same gun used in killings in London, Bristol, Birmingham and Norwich. This means that we are undoubtedly dealing with a serial killer who has now committed ten murders, in five cities across the length and breadth of England. A further statement will be made in due course, as more details come to light. At this stage, I will not be taking questions. However, there will be a further press briefing at ten p.m. Thank you."

The reporter spoke again. "Well, there you have it, the serial killer, murderer, vigilante—whatever you want to call them—has struck again. This brings their killing spree to ten in just over three months. The whole country will be asking when will the killings end, when will the vigilante be caught, and the main question of course, who are they? Now, back to Andrew in the studio."

Gloria picked up the remote control and turned the sound off.

"Oh dear Jules, I appear to have created a bit of a to-do! That's it though; I promise you I'm finished killing people by choice."

At this point she stopped, put down her cup, then looked steadily up at her friend.

"However, that's not quite the end of it. You see, there's something else I need to tell you—I've got a serious problem."

Juliet could see that her friend was genuinely agitated. "It's all right, you know you can tell me anything."

Their discussion was cut short when the phone started ringing. Gloria thought about leaving it to ring, but stood up and answered. It was Sandra, and she sounded almost hysterical.

"Mum, have you seen the news? Those two dealers in the black BMW, you know, the ones ruining our estate, the ones you argued with when we were out shopping, they've been shot and killed! It was the vigilante, they're dead!"

"Calm down, Sandra. Yes, I've just seen the news. Thank God we weren't around the city centre, or we might have been caught up in it."

"Unlikely. Whoever this vigilante is, they're an expert; they make sure there are no witnesses. Oh, and they were killed the day before you arrived. Anyway, it explains why it's been so quiet around here lately."

"That would explain it, yes. Look darling, I'd love to talk more, but I've got a police officer around here at the moment. We're discussing police and community matters." She winked at Jules, who smiled. "I'll call tomorrow and we'll talk properly then."

"Okay mum, sorry to interrupt. Love you, and thanks for a great few days, bye."

"Bye love, take care." Gloria ended the call. "Sorry about that, Jules."

"Don't apologise. It's incredible how casual you sounded talking to Sandra."

Juliet moved to sit on the arm of Gloria's chair.

"Now then, I know you want to tell me about your problem, but how about you give me all the gruesome details from Newcastle first?"

So, Gloria found herself explaining exactly how events had unfolded: from leaving home on Monday, choosing her disguise, her research among the drug users, the reconnaissance at the car park and finally the gory details of her night's exploits.

Jules sat back into the settee, an astonished look on her face. She gave a low whistle.

"That's incredible! It's like listening to the memoirs of an experienced assassin, or a professional contract killer! The amazing thing is that the Northumbria Police appear to have no witnesses, no sightings, and no leads. If they did, they would have given out a description, or made appeals for witnesses to come forward."

Gloria suddenly grinned widely at her friend.

"Come with me, I'd like to show you something." Gloria led Jules into the kitchen, and gestured for her to sit at the table. She reached up into one of the cupboards, lifted down a Cornflakes box, reached inside, and pulled out the Glock handgun, wrapped inside a tissue and small cellophane bag. Removing the gun from the bag, she placed it onto the table in front of Jules.

"There you go Jules, that's what everyone's looking for. Don't be frightened, pick it up and hold it if you want to."

Juliet stared down at the handgun, her expression one of fascination and horror.

"Fuck off! I don't want my DNA or fingerprints all over it!" She started smiling. "For fuck's sake Gloria, inside a Cornflakes box? Actually, not a bad hiding place; I'd never have guessed it was there. No wonder they didn't find it when you were arrested."

She looked down at the Glock again and said, "It's almost unbelievable. I can't believe I'm sitting here, at a kitchen table, looking at the weapon that's killed ten people."

"Well you are. So, how does it make you feel?"

"Honestly? Well, amongst other things, I suppose I'm a little humbled by the fact that you trusted me enough to show it."

"I trust you completely Jules, you'd have shopped me before now if you were intending to."

Juliet smiled and shrugged, "I've told you a thousand times, your secret's safe with me. Now, put the gun away. Thanks for having the courage to show me, and thanks for trusting me, but please put it away!"

"Sorry, Jules, that's its last outing. I'll need to think of somewhere to dispose of it safely soon. Perhaps you could give me some professional advice?" Gloria laughed, then wrapped the tissue around the Glock, placed it into the cellophane bag, and returned it to the Cornflakes box.

Juliet smiled at her friend. "Now, what's this problem that's causing you so much concern?"

FIFTY-THREE

"I DON'T REALLY know where to start, Jules."

"Try the beginning, that's usually the best place."

"Okay, I'll try." Gloria drew a deep breath and handed the first letter to Juliet. "Shortly after I killed those two in Barter Street, this arrived through my front door. I nearly died of shock! I didn't think anyone had seen me. Then, after the Bristol killings, I received another. The same happened after the Birmingham and Norwich killings, plus other letters in between. In fact, the letter after I wiped out those three in Norwich arrived at my hotel reception!" She handed Juliet the remaining letters.

"Last weekend Sean came round; he was in a real state. Look Jules, I'll cut a very long story short. The reason Sean's been so distracted and worried lately, is that he is being forced by the Higgins family to work for them. Not only that, but Paula, the cleaner at your station, has been recruited by them too. She was the person who witnessed the first murders and reported what she'd seen to Michael Higgins."

"Sean and Paula are working for Higgins?" said Juliet, "You're fucking with me!"

"I'm not Jules, I promise. The girl Sean had fallen for at the photography club, Gail, turns out she's the daughter of Michael Higgins, the head of the family. Apparently, they're a major crime organisation, but you probably know that already. They're threatening to hurt his family if he refuses to work for them, keep them supplied with information."

"Oh my God, the bastards!" Juliet looked horrified.

"While Sean was telling me all this, Higgins and his sons arrived at my door. Jules, he wants to recruit me too! He arranged for the letters to be sent because he likes my work. His hit-man is inside for life, and he needs a replacement. At first, I told him to poke his offer, but he then produced photos of Sandra and her family; he's got a man following them wherever they go. He got really angry and threatened horrible things if I didn't agree to join his organisation, just like Sean. At one point I lost my rag and went for him and got whacked over the head for my troubles."

"Christ Glo, what the fuck did you do?"

"I had no choice. I discussed it with Sean, and for the time being I've had to agree to work for them. We're going to try to work out an escape plan once we've convinced them that we're on board. Sean made me promise not to mention our involvement with Higgins to anyone, but I know I can trust you, and I really need your advice."

Juliet moved slightly away from Gloria. She was looking down at the letters in her lap and appeared to be completely lost in her own thoughts. For several seconds she said nothing.

Gloria was alarmed by Juliet's reaction.

"Jules. Say something. Please!"

Slowly raising her head, Juliet met Gloria's gaze.

"Gloria, listen to me. I've worked on operations targeting the Higgins family many times over the years and believe me they are not people to fuck with. Once you join their organisation, they won't let you leave, and they'll pursue you to the ends of the earth if you try. If they failed to find you, they'd hurt or kill someone you love." Jules studied her friend's face as her words sunk in.

Gloria started crying as the stark reality of her position hit home.

"There must be some way out; surely it's not completely hopeless!"

Juliet shook her head; her face was stony.

"When you fired that gun for the first time, Gloria, you crossed a line that made you vulnerable to people like Higgins. The only way out would be by bringing down the entire family from within. Everyone with power in the organisation would need to be arrested simultaneously. That means taking out four people all at once, Michael and his three children. Can you imagine a scenario where that could happen? Because I can't, it would be practically impossible. They rarely work together. They deliberately work on different operations, on completely different sections of their empire. Each of them is responsible for their own section, and they rarely have any overlap, so it's difficult, if not impossible, for the police to gather the evidence to completely dismantle their organisation in one fell swoop."

Gloria said, desperately, "So, it's practically impossible, but not totally?"

Juliet's voice rose. "You haven't been listening. The level of planning required to extricate the pair of you from this is mind boggling. Just think about the problem for a minute. The Met, whose resources are enormous, have been trying to dismantle the Higgins' operations for about twenty years. How the two of you can possibly carry out a successful strike to remove the main players on your own, I'm struggling to comprehend."

"But you're prepared to help us? You're prepared to at least think about it?"

Juliet stood and walked over to the window, looking down into the street and for the first time, Gloria saw her as a policewoman, rather than just a friend. There was an uncomfortable silence, then Juliet spoke slowly, deliberately.

"Look, by confiding in me, you've implicated me in this whole mess. You're my friend and I will do what I can to support you, but you've got to understand that my family comes first and I will do nothing to place them in jeopardy."

Gloria looked at her friend, the gravity of the situation fully sinking in. She nodded.

"I understand."

"Promise me one thing. You won't tell anyone else about this. Your life, Sean's life, both your families, and now me, are completely dependent on none of the Higgins family having any suspicion that we're planning something. They can't even know that we are friends. That is, if they don't already."

"I promise," said Gloria, gulping back the tears. "I'm so sorry for getting you involved."

"Yes, but I'm sure you promised Sean the very same thing, then almost immediately confided in me. That simply can't happen again."

Gloria looked down at her hands, turning a ring on her little finger round and round.

"No-one else will ever hear anything about it from my lips."

She looked up at Juliet's face, and could see the doubts she was still harbouring.

"You really can trust me on this, Jules."

Juliet's expression softened slightly. "Okay, I believe you." She bit her bottom lip, as though considering her options before continuing.

"Right, the first thing to remember is that complying with their wishes is the safest way to proceed for the next few weeks. Once that period is over with, we'll be in a better position to reassess the situation."

"What do you mean a better position?"

"Well, for a start you'll need to keep a record of the following things: how many times they've called on your services; how many times they've required Sean's services; what exactly have they instructed you to do; whether either of you have been taken to any of their properties; how often Michael and his children get together for meetings and whether there are any tensions within the hierarchy that we can exploit. There needs to be thorough research, before any kind of plan for extricating the two of you can be made."

Gloria looked disappointed.

"So, for now we simply carry on with our lives, and do the bidding of those bastards when required? Is that what you're telling me?"

"That's exactly what I'm telling you. Firstly though, you need to tell Sean that you've confided in me, and that I know everything. Don't expect him to be happy; he'll almost certainly be fucking furious. That's something you'll have to cope with and you'll need to calm him down. From what you've told me, he's on the verge of breaking down, so he will require very careful handling. Then you'll need to arrange for the three of us to get together. I would suggest somewhere busy, and not too close to here, and we'll need to arrive there separately. I cannot afford to be seen with you both by any of the Higgins mob."

Despite Juliet's misgivings, and her own feelings of guilt for having dragged her into the situation, Gloria couldn't help feeling relieved.

"Thank you, Jules. I am truly sorry for putting you in this position, and if you just want to walk out of that door I would understand."

"Glo, I will do all I can to help you out of this, and it would give me immense pleasure to help you take those bastards down, but if it comes to it, I would have to put my own family first—just as you would." She looked at her watch. "Look, I'm expected at home for dinner. Will you be okay on your own?"

Gloria nodded. "Of course, I'm fine. Will this coming Saturday be okay for our meeting?"

Juliet shrugged. "Fine for me. I'll tell David that we're having a day out together. You need to speak to Sean about the arrangements, then let me know when and where."

"Thanks for everything Jules. You get going and I'll call you with the details."

Juliet walked to the front door.

"Try to keep calm, that's really important at the moment. I'll do everything within my power to help, but we're dealing with a seriously dangerous adversary, so I can't promise anything."

After giving Gloria one final smile, she left.

FIFTY-FOUR

AFTER POURING HERSELF a glass of white wine, Gloria sank softly into a bubble-bath. She usually enjoyed luxuriating in a wonderfully hot bath, where she could feel her physical aches and strains evaporating, like the steam rising from the water, but tonight, her mental strain was not so easily soothed.

The conversation with Juliet earlier that evening had left her profoundly upset. To her other worries—what the Higgins family might require her to do, and whether the police were any closer to identifying her—was added a deeper awareness of the wider implications of her actions on those around her, the people she loved.

She climbed out of the bath and, wrapping herself in a massive bath towel, Gloria walked into the lounge and turned the television on. Hearing what the police had to say at the press briefing was a must.

"Good evening, this is Sky News at ten, with Siobhan O'Rourke. Northumbria Police have confirmed that two men found in an underground car park in Newcastle upon Tyne were shot and murdered by the so-called vigilante, whose killing spree now numbers ten victims. Both men were shot at close range in what police describe as execution style killings. We're going over to Rahul Patel at Newcastle Police Station."

Rahul was amongst a scrum of news crews and reporters, jostling for position.

"Thank you, Siobhan. Police have now released further details about the killings. The two men, identified as Winston George Leigh, thirty-seven, and William Steven Weald, thirty-four, both from Gateshead, are known to have been dealing controlled drugs in the Newcastle area. They believe the killer had somehow obtained a swipe card, allowing them swift access to the car park, and enabling them to take the victims by surprise.

They are searching all CCTV in surrounding areas, but nothing has come to light as yet." Rahul glanced over his shoulder as someone walked out from the police station's main door. "It looks like there is about to be a further statement."

A senior police officer appeared on screen, holding a piece of paper.

"Good evening. I can confirm that CCTV footage has been obtained from a private house in Carver Street, near to the scene of the murders. At nine thirty-five p.m. on the evening of Tuesday the seventeeth of February, a female was seen to exit an alleyway onto this street, turn right and walk north-east for twenty metres, before walking out of view of the camera. This alleyway leads almost directly from the office block where the murders occurred, and it is very rarely used by locals due to it being largely overgrown. Navigating this alleyway in darkness would have been very difficult, so why did she take this route? We would like to identify this woman as a priority. She is described as follows: female, aged between sixty and seventy-five years, slim, 5'4" to 5'6" tall, wearing a light-coloured mac and belt, cream or white woollen hat with a small peak, blue jeans, dark trainers, a black rucksack and carrying a black handbag over her left shoulder.

"The CCTV imaging has been passed to experts at Operation Chiddingstone, who are overseeing the nationwide search for the serial killer. They have tonight informed me that they believe this woman to be the same woman seen boarding a train in Birmingham following the murder of Alan Bramhall in Balsall Heath. Her description is also very similar to that given by a member of the public, following the murders of three males in Lyne Heath, Norwich. Assistant Commissioner Skelton, the officer in overall charge of this investigation, has asked me to inform you that police are now working on the assumption that this woman is the killer.

"I would like to appeal to this woman to please give yourself up now; we will eventually arrest you. I would also like to ask anyone who knows the identity of this woman, or who is suspicious of a friend, work colleague, or family member, to please contact either the Operation Chiddingstone Incident Room, or Northumbria Police. We have teams of detectives waiting for your calls. I am happy to take any questions."

Despite the warmth of her bathrobe, Gloria felt herself shivering. A forest of arms were raised from the press contingent, and the officer selected a female reporter.

"Sam Murphy, The Times. Do police have any idea where this woman comes from?"

"No, but from statements supplied by witnesses in a café before the Balsall Heath incident, she appears to have a London accent." He selected another reporter.

"Sarah Crabtree, BBC News. When will we receive copies of the CCTV?"

"Within the hour."

"Ben Jeffrey, Daily Telegraph. Are police attempting to secure extra funding from the government to speed up the investigation?

"I understand from AC Skelton that an application has been submitted to the Home Secretary for extra funding and resources."

The questions were coming thick and fast, but Gloria was not really taking in the answers.

"Fuck, fuck, fuck!" she shouted, almost loudly enough for her neighbours to hear. Her whole body was shaking and she couldn't think straight. The pressure on her was now almost unbearable: the investigations into the killings, the Higgins family coercing her into joining them, people knowing she was the killer, and now yet another CCTV image of her on national TV. Somebody was sure to recognise her. She curled up into a foetus-like ball on her chair, and stayed like that for ten minutes, until the panic began to subside.

The following hour passed slowly, as she waited for the images to be released. Then, on a later Sky News bulletin, a live interview with a female politician was interrupted for breaking news. Siobhan O'Rourke was still presenting.

"We have just received these CCTV images from Northumbria Police. They clearly show a white female leaving an alleyway, turning right on a side street, walking past the camera, and out of view."

Gloria watched transfixed as she saw herself walking out of the alleyway. The camera was obviously attached to a house on the opposite side of the road and appeared to have been set up to show people approaching the front porch and front door. However, it also showed a section of the roadway and both pavements. Unfortunately for Gloria, on the far right-hand side of the image, it also showed the end of the alleyway. Without breaking step after leaving the alleyway, Gloria walked quite quickly across the screen from right to left and disappeared from view.

At least she was pleasantly surprised at the poor quality of the imaging, the dim orange street lighting doing nothing to help the clarity; it looked like the camera had been about twenty metres from her. Her distinctive gait, as observed by both Sean Aylen and Jules, wasn't really visible from sideways on. Perhaps she would be okay? Nevertheless, things were closing in on all sides. She was still a free woman, but for how much longer she wondered.

FIFTY-FIVE
Friday 26th February 1999

FOUR DAYS HAD passed since Gloria had told Juliet about the approach from the Higgins family. Four days in which she'd broken the news to Sean about bringing Juliet into the equation, and as expected he'd been livid. It had taken a great deal of reassurance to calm him down, but eventually he managed to control his anger. In fact, he had to admit that Juliet could be an asset, providing information which might assist their plan.

Just as Juliet suggested, Gloria made arrangements for the three of them to meet the following Saturday, in Selfridges Restaurant, about a mile away at the far end of Oxford Street. Juliet and Sean would be walking there separately, with Gloria taking the bus.

LATER THAT FRIDAY afternoon, Gloria felt she absolutely had to get out of her flat, so she decided to take some exercise with a brisk walk to Russell Square. On reaching the square, she was slightly out of breath so she chose a seat on a metal bench underneath a tree, closed her eyes and reclined her head backwards, enjoying a moment of relaxation.

A woman's voice broke into her daydream.

"Fancy meeting you here."

Blinking through the dappled sunlight, which was flickering through the branches into her eyes, Gloria looked up, and was astonished to be looking into the face of Paula.

"You've got some fucking nerve speaking to me! I assume you'd like to explain yourself?"

"Glo, I know you must really hate me, and I can understand, but I'm begging you, please forgive me. I had no choice but to agree to whatever they asked. They forced me into joining them, the same as they have with you."

"Bollocks! Just because they'd recruited you, you didn't need to tell them what you saw! If you hadn't gone grassing to them about Barter Street in the first place, I wouldn't be in this fucking situation now!"

Paula pointed at the bench alongside Gloria with her right hand and raised her eyebrows. Gloria reluctantly nodded, and Paula sat down.

"They still follow me sometimes. Four years I've worked for them now, and they're still unsure about me! I never know when I'm being watched and when I'm not. I was terrified that if I didn't report it to them, they'd know and there could be repercussions. I'm truly sorry."

"How can you be certain they're not watching us now?" asked Gloria, looking around at the faces in the square.

"I can't, but they know we're friends and they know we're bound to meet up sooner or later, so they won't be bothered about us being together." She put a hand on Gloria's left knee. "I've honestly regretted telling them about you for three months now. Please try to forgive me."

Gloria could see that Paula's apology was sincere, but she wasn't ready to forgive and forget just yet. She realised, however, that this was an opportunity to probe her for information about how the Higgins family operated.

"How exactly did they get you working for them?"

"Same as you, Glo. You know the process by now; they threatened my family, that's how they always recruit people. I either went along with it, or my family suffered."

"What exactly do they expect from you?"

"Well, my cleaning at the station and at the NCS offices mainly takes place during the very early morning or during the night; either way, it's when there's hardly anyone about, sometimes there's no-one about. When that happens, I find files relating to investigations against Michael Higgins' interests, and pass on details of observation points, planned operations, details of witnesses, that kind of thing."

"How often do you have to do that?"

"It varies."

"What kind of reward do you get for providing them with this information?"

"If they're happy with what I've given them, somebody appears from nowhere and hands me an envelope full of cash. It's always at least five hundred pounds, but it can be anything up to a couple of thousand. I honestly hate working for them, and I'm living in constant fear of getting caught, but I've never been so well off in my life!"

Rubbing her hands on both thighs, Gloria looked blankly at the grass.

"I'm not sure I'm ready to forgive you yet, but maybe I will in time." She turned to look at Paula. "So, is this meeting by chance? Or are you following me on their instructions?"

Paula pursed her lips, then blew out hard.

"No, this isn't by chance; I followed you here today. As far as I'm aware, they aren't following me. I know all their surveillance staff by sight and haven't seen any of them, so I'm pretty certain they have no idea I'm speaking to you. I'm here completely on my own behalf. Glo, I'm scared."

Those words came as a complete surprise to Gloria; after all, Paula had worked with them for four years, so why would she be scared now?

"What do you mean you're scared? About what?"

Paula shifted uneasily on the bench.

"As you know, Sean has been working for them for a few weeks, and he knows that I'm working for them too. We've spoken about our situation occasionally since they recruited him. He was working late turn in the Incident Room last night, and he was still there when I started my night duty. When I started cleaning, he took me into a DI's office and told me he was being used quite frequently since they recruited him. I asked what he meant, and he explained that he was being told to pass on information about investigations into the family's activities, just like they used to ask me to do. The past few days he seems to have started relaxing into his new role. He almost seems back to his old self."

"So, what's your problem?"

"Well, since Sean's been around, they've stopped using me. In fact, they seem to have forgotten me, I haven't heard from them in ages." Paula looked visibly upset.

Gloria looked puzzled.

"But that's good, isn't it? Why would you be upset? They're leaving you alone for a while. Perhaps they won't bother you again."

Paula shook her head.

"Glo, you don't understand; when they have no further need of someone as a snout, they don't simply let them leave, they can't take that risk because of what they know. They get rid of them! They now have a police sergeant to pass on information from the station, making me surplus to requirements. I always worried the day would come when they might not need me anymore, but I didn't expect it so soon."

Gloria realised in that moment exactly what kind of pressure Paula had been living with for the past four years. Putting an arm around Paula's shoulders, she said, "Paula, it'll be okay. You've clearly been suffering at their hands for years now. I've got no idea what misery you've gone through, but I think I'm about to find out. Tell you what, it's getting cold sitting on this bench. Do you fancy a drink in that café over there? My treat."

The two women leaned towards each other and kissed cheeks, before making their way together across the grass. For the following hour they chatted in the comfort of the Garden Café. They discussed every aspect of Paula's plight, with Gloria desperately trying to reassure her that she was probably still a valuable asset to Michael Higgins, and that he would surely rather have two moles inside the police station than one.

Exchanging a quick hug as they walked back outside, they said goodbye in front of the café, and went their separate ways. Gloria urgently needed to speak with Juliet. The goalposts had just changed.

JUST BEFORE FOUR, Juliet received a text from Gloria, 'We need to talk - urgently!' Making an excuse, Juliet moved outside into the rear yard of Holborn Police Station, where she found a quiet area to make the call.

"Glo, what's up? Your text sounded a bit panicky."

Gloria explained about meeting Paula in Russell Square, telling Jules everything that she'd said, including the worrying news about her possibly being surplus to requirements.

"Sorry Glo," Juliet replied firmly, "but there's nothing you or I can do about that."

"How about if I approach Michael Higgins and tell him I won't work for him unless Paula remains part of the organisation?"

Juliet laughed sarcastically. "Are you kidding? Don't be an idiot! That would just be signing your own death warrant. You can't negotiate with the likes of Higgins; he does whatever is best for himself and the organisation, end of."

"So, we just carry on, and hope Paula's okay?"

"Sorry, but that's exactly what we do. Like I said, Michael Higgins will do whatever is best for him. We'll just have to hope that Paula's overreacting."

"Okay. If that's what you think is best."

"It is. I'll see you tomorrow. Take care, Glo."

"You too, Jules. See you tomorrow."

FIFTY-SIX
Saturday 28th February 1999

THE SHARP RING of Gloria's house phone roused her from a deep sleep. Putting on her dressing gown, she walked sleepily to the lounge. It was still practically dark outside, but she could just make out the phone clearly enough by the yellow glow of the streetlight coming through the window. Picking it up, she said groggily, "Hello?".

A bout of coughing greeted her, before she heard the unmistakable voice of Michael Higgins.

"Good morning, Mrs Jones. I want you to go to the Rose Garden Restaurant in Kilburn High Road as soon as possible; can you do that?"

This was the moment Gloria had been dreading. *My first assignment. What crap timing!*

"Yes, of course. It will take me about an hour though, I'm not even dressed yet. Is that okay?"

"That's grand, I'll be waiting for you. It will just be you, me and my three children." With that, Michael Higgins abruptly hung up.

Gloria's heart sank. Whatever he wanted from her, it was unlikely to be good news if he needed to phone her this early on a Saturday morning. She looked out at a frost-covered St Giles Churchyard with tears in her eyes.

Just over an hour later, Gloria knocked on the front door of the Rose Garden restaurant, a dingy, neglected looking place, with faded red and emerald green paint on the window frames and doors. She had dressed warmly against the cold, wearing her navy-blue coat, a bobble hat, and a pair of blue leather gloves.

The door was opened by Declan Higgins, who stepped aside and ushered Gloria inside. Resting his hand in the small of her back, he gently guided Gloria into the restaurant, which had the unmistakable smell of stale food and dusty upholstery. Her heart was hammering in her ribcage.

At the rear of the restaurant, Declan showed her into a side room where, seated around a small table, were Michael, Seamus, and a very attractive woman, about thirty-years-old, with jet black straight hair, a slim figure, wearing tight blue jeans and a thick red coat. The woman said to Declan in a strong Irish accent, "Have you searched her?"

Michael coughed, looked up at Gloria and said, "Sorry Mrs Jones, she's very cautious."

Gloria smiled and said, "Go ahead, I've got nothing to hide." She flung her arms out like a scarecrow and passed her handbag to Declan, who opened the top clasp.

Michael Higgins laughed.

"Don't waste your time, Dec, she's not that stupid." Turning to Gloria, he said, "Mrs Jones, this is my daughter Gail. I know what you're thinking— not a very Irish name. It was my wife's choice. She's English! As you can see, Gail likes to be thorough."

"Pleased to meet you," said Gloria coldly; although she could see why Sean had fallen for her.

Gail smiled back; she didn't reply, but nodded. Declan handed Gloria her handbag back and closed the door. Michael coughed again, wiping his mouth with a large handkerchief.

"Thank you for coming Mrs Jones. I've decided that you should see one of our properties. Down in Essex." He fixed Gloria with a sharp look before continuing. "You're being honoured here, Mrs Jones; other than the people in this room, the only person who has ever been invited to the house is Connor, and he's now serving a life sentence."

"Connor?"

"Your predecessor. He was excellent at his job, but I'm sure you'll be just as effective, possibly even better." He shifted uncomfortably in his chair and coughed again.

"Mostly, your duties will involve the elimination of targets as directed by me, maybe once or twice a year, exactly as you've been doing so effectively for the past three months. Occasionally, you'll be taken to the house to witness punishments." He smiled.

"Why on earth do I need to witness punishments?"

"Partly because you should be in no doubt what happens to people who cross us and also because, sometimes, I might want you to assist."

Gloria was horrified. "I never agreed to that. What kind of punishments?"

Michael Higgins leaned forward and stared at her.

"A bullet in the kneecap, the ankle, the wrist, the shoulder, or maybe the hip, something which will create a life-changing injury but not kill. Maybe giving someone a telephone scar, or breaking a bone or two with a pick-axe handle, depends on how much they've pissed us off." He laughed again. "Don't worry, the pick-axe jobs will be down to Declan and Seamus; you won't be required to do anything too physical." He smiled fondly at his boys.

Gloria was feeling increasingly queasy.

"What's a telephone scar?"

"It's what we give to people who've blabbed. We give them a razor cut from their ear to the corner of their mouth. It deters people from opening their mouths again and lets others know what they've done."

Gloria was beginning to understand just what she had committed herself to. She looked down at the floor, fighting back the tears.

Gail laughed and said, "Don't worry love, you'll be as hard as nails in a few months. Remember, what you'll be doing to those bastards isn't personal, it's just business."

"Right," said Michael. "That's enough chat, let's get moving."

Gloria was taken through a rear door, and out to a blue Bentley. She was surprised to see the whole family following her. Declan got into the driver's seat, with Michael in the front passenger seat. She noticed how weak he looked, slowly lowering himself into the car; he was clearly a sick man, and in a lot of pain.

Gail sat behind the driver's seat, and Gloria was pushed gently into the centre of the rear seat by Seamus, who climbed in beside her. Surrounded on all sides by the Higgins clan, Gloria fought to keep calm and stared ahead through the windscreen, trying to work out their route.

An hour and twenty minutes later, Gloria saw from the road signs that they were in the middle of Essex, somewhere between Brentwood and

Billericay. On the journey, they'd asked her endless questions about how and why she'd carried out the killings, how she'd felt after each one, whether she had begun to enjoy killing people. The two sons simply couldn't get enough of hearing about the aftermath of each shooting, wanting to know all the gory details.

Michael Higgins kept reminding his family what a great addition he thought Gloria would be to them; he seemed to be proudly parading her, while at the same time seeking their approval. He was still very much the head of the family, the man in charge, but with the state of his health, she wondered how much longer he could continue. And if he should suddenly drop dead and the younger generation take over, would they see her as such an asset?

After leaving the A12, they headed down a fairly busy road, before turning right down a narrow country lane, and finally, down a rough track. At the end of the track they came to an attractive detached house ironically bearing the name Paradise Lodge.

The Bentley pulled up on a wide gravel drive in front of a large, 1950s red-brick property, with a tile-hung upper floor. The windows looked like original wood, but were in good condition; everything looked neat and tidy from the outside, and the gardens were well tended. Once they had all climbed out of the car, Gloria noticed that there wasn't another house in sight.

FIFTY-SEVEN

MICHAEL HIGGINS DIDN'T say a word, just gestured for Gloria to follow him. He opened the front door by unlocking firstly two mortice locks, then a Yale lock; security obviously a priority.

The large hallway had stone slabs on the floor, covered in the centre by a patterned rug. There was a teak table on one side, with a large mirror hanging above it. Four doors led off the hallway, and Michael passed through the door at the far end which took them into a beautifully furnished lounge, with views out through patio doors over the garden.

A white leather three-piece-suite, luxurious cream carpet and glass topped mahogany coffee table were matched by a large, ultra-modern, flat-screen TV mounted on the wall. Gloria had previously only seen one of these on TV adverts; the whole place gave an impression of comfort and expensive taste.

Next to a large bookcase at the far end of the lounge, Higgins unlocked another door. Before opening it he turned to Gloria and said, "Have you heard of the singer Genna?"

"Of course," said Gloria. "Everyone's heard of her."

"Well, she owned this house before I bought it, and she had a soundproof studio built in the basement. It was so well made that she could record her music down there—full band and all—and you couldn't hear it if you were sitting up here in the lounge. Now that's impressive, don't you think?"

Gloria nodded. "Very."

"Aren't you getting a little warm Mrs Jones? You've still got your hat and gloves on."

"Actually, these days I suffer badly with poor circulation, so I like to keep well wrapped up."

Michael shrugged and said, "Okay, as long as you're happy." He led the way through the door and down a flight of stairs. He was followed by Gail, then Gloria, Seamus and Declan. At the bottom of the stairs was a solid metal door, which opened with a sucking sound as Michael Higgins pushed it. She realised that the door was an airtight fit.

The group filed into the room, stepping over polythene, and Gloria suddenly felt very scared. *Are they about to give me a taste of what could happen if I don't do as I'm told?*

The room was bare, with sound absorbing grey cladding on the walls, and a large sheet of polythene on the floor which extended a little way up each wall of the room. She'd seen this type of room before on films and TV dramas; she was horrified and fighting hard to control her shaking.

"This is where the fun happens," laughed Michael. "I'm too old for that sort of thing these days. I'm sixty-eight now, and not as strong as I once was, so I leave all that to Seamus and Declan. Sometimes Gail likes to get stuck in too. They take pride in their work, don't you kids?"

"We certainly do," said Seamus.

"Always," said Declan.

Gail said nothing, just continued to stare at Gloria, observing her reactions.

"Why the polythene?" asked Gloria, although secretly she knew the answer.

Michael suddenly looked serious. "It collects blood and bodily fluids. It saves damage to the floor and walls and ensures that no evidence is left behind by accident. Afterwards, the polythene can be wrapped up, and disposed of in an incinerator out the back. Then, the room is prepared and made ready for the next time. I do love efficiency."

He gestured to his sons, who took an arm each and gently lowered Michael down into a seated position on the floor at one end of the room.

Gloria was allowed to walk around unhindered. She couldn't help imagining the terror that victims must have felt when they were taken into such a room. *Jesus Christ. They're just like the Krays, only worse!*

Declan and Seamus had joined their father. All three were sitting down on the polythene and leaning back on the wall. They seemed to be sharing a joke, presumably enjoying Gloria's discomfort, leaving the two women standing together at the other end. Gloria felt nauseous, terrified, and short of breath. She summoned up the courage to speak again.

"How often is this room used?"

Gail said, "About three or four times a year. Sometimes it's not used for six or seven months, but then it might be needed twice in a month. Don't worry love, with your track record, you'll probably start to enjoy it after a while."

She stood sideways on to Gloria and placed her right hand on Gloria's left shoulder, in a mocking show of reassurance. *Now or never.*

With surprising agility, Gloria pulled a carving knife from her left coat pocket and, swinging her left arm upwards, plunged the blade deep into Gail's neck. She just had time to register the astonished look on Gail's face, before drawing the Glock from her handbag with her right hand, and shooting Seamus in the chest. He remained slumped where he'd been seated, his head lolling uselessly to one side.

Declan reacted quickly; he leapt to his feet and had taken a couple of steps towards Gloria when he was felled by a bullet to the centre of his chest. He was in the process of drawing a gun from his pocket when Gloria had fired, and he collapsed to his right, the gun dropping from his hand as he fell. Blood had sprayed over his father, who had managed to struggle onto his knees. Looking down, she saw that Declan's gun was identical to hers, a Glock 17.

Gail was writhing in agony, with the knife still sticking in her neck. Blood poured from the wound and she clawed desperately to free the blade, but it was lodged firm. Seamus appeared to be dead, lying contorted on the floor in a growing pool of blood, and Declan was groaning quietly, still making the occasional tiny movement. Michael was on his hands and knees, screaming, coughing and crying for his children.

"You fucking bitch!" he screamed at her. "They're my babies!"

Gloria bent down and with a gloved hand picked up the gun that Declan had dropped.

"Oh, Michael, you should have searched me, shouldn't you? I knew if I offered myself up for a search, there was always a chance you wouldn't bother. I'd made my mind up that by the end of today, I'd either be free, or dead."

"You vicious old whore!" he screamed before doubling over in a violent coughing fit.

She stared dispassionately down at him.

"I brought the knife with me especially for you and Gail. I only had two bullets left in my gun, one for Declan, and one for Seamus. You seemed so pathetic that I was prepared to take my chances with you with the knife; I didn't realise it would stick so hard in your bitch daughter's neck."

Michael's face was turning purple with exertion. "Help her, please help her, have some fucking pity."

Gloria moved a couple of paces towards him.

"Pity! You don't know the meaning of the word. I knew I'd only get one opportunity. I just needed to wait for that one chance, and you cocky Irish bastards gave it to me."

She looked around at the carnage and smiled.

"Thank heavens Declan brought along another gun for me. Just goes to show, Michael, you should never trust a serial killer!"

Michael said nothing. Struggling now to support himself, he stayed on his hands and knees, tears pouring from his eyes.

"By the way," said Gloria, "I wanted you to witness this; it's what you've done to so many fathers, mothers, brothers and sisters before. It'll be interesting to see whether you enjoy it or not."

She aimed the gun at the side of Gail's head and fired into her temple. Gail stopped writhing instantly, lying quite still, her blood oozing onto the floor.

An inhuman howl came from Michael; he seemed to be struggling to catch his breath.

Gloria then trained the barrel on Declan, who was lying face down on the polythene, twitching gently. She fired into the back of his head and all movement stopped. Blood trickled out from under his body and meandered through creases in the polythene.

Michael painfully hauled himself to his feet.

"I'll kill you, you fucking evil bitch!"

"How do you propose to do that, Michael? How about another taste of your own medicine?"

Over the next thirty seconds, Gloria inflicted on Michael some of the injuries he had so graphically and gleefully described to her earlier. Shooting him in his extremities with his son's gun. By the time she had finished, blood was pumping from his left leg and right shoulder and Michael was shrieking in pain.

"Now that you know exactly what you've been doing to others for years, I'll be merciful enough to put you out of your misery, you disgusting piece of shit!"

And with that, Gloria fired into his forehead; his body slumped and the blood pooled around his head, soaking into his sparse hair, his lifeless eyes staring up at her.

Looking around at all the bloodshed, Gloria suddenly felt sick and started to gag. Her breathing had become erratic and the room began to spin. She knew that she had to get control of herself and make sure she left no traces of her presence, so she leaned against a clean patch of wall, shut her eyes for a few seconds and took several deep, steady breaths.

Feeling somewhat better, she removed the knife from Gail's neck, which took some considerable effort; the tip must have lodged in her bone. Taking a carrier bag out of her handbag, she wiped the blood from the blade onto Gail's coat, and placed it into the carrier bag, before tucking it into her handbag. The knife was a small carving knife from her own kitchen, so she couldn't risk leaving it there.

She then placed her own gun back into her handbag and threw Declan's on the floor. She walked over to Michael's corpse, and felt for the house keys in his pockets. Finding them, she moved over to Declan's body, where she found the car keys in his pocket. She walked out of the room, the heavy metal door closing behind her with the same sucking sound.

At the top of the basement stairs, she re-entered the lounge, and closed the door leading to the basement, locking it behind her. Once in the hallway, she searched on the bunch for the front door key, and while doing so, noticed that one key was labelled 'Key Cupboard'. She tried it on the small cupboard just inside the front door; it fitted, and seconds later she had located a key for the garage.

After closing and locking the key cupboard, then securely locking the front door, she made her way to the garage, and opened the door. The garage was large and roomy, probably just wide enough for two cars. It was cluttered along both side walls with tools, boxes and other household junk, leaving an empty space in the middle which she assumed was reserved for the Bentley.

Gloria walked back out onto the drive, where she unlocked the Bentley and climbed into the driver's seat. Starting the car, she guided it carefully into the garage, applied the handbrake, removed the keys from the ignition, and locked the car.

Just as she was about to leave the garage, Gloria spotted something against the rear wall: a lilac coloured ladies' bike, possibly left by the previous owner. She was delighted; she knew from the journey in the Bentley that she was at least two miles from the nearest village and this would cut her time down considerably. She carefully manoeuvred it past the car and out of the garage.

Closing and locking the garage door, Gloria took one last look around to make sure she hadn't left any clues. She had worn gloves, a coat and a bobble hat throughout, so there was very little risk of her fingerprints or DNA being transferred anywhere. Satisfied that everything was okay, she checked the bicycle's tyres, climbed on, and pedalled off along the track.

Fifteen minutes later and almost two miles from the house, Gloria spotted a large stagnant pond just off a quiet country lane inside woodland. There was no traffic about, so she pulled over. The pond looked dirty and muddy; it was an almost perfect circle, around 20 metres wide. She checked quickly around her before removing her Glock from the front pouch. She took one last look at it, kissed the cold black metal, and launched it into the centre of the pond. She then took out both sets of keys and hurled those into the pond as well. For a moment Gloria stood watching the ripples diminish and finally disappear, then she sighed deeply and returned to the bike.

Fairly sure the gun would never be found, she cycled into the village of Hutton. After enquiring where she could catch a bus to Brentwood, she abandoned the bicycle against railings.

The number 81 bus arrived twenty minutes later, and took her into town, where she caught a train to London Liverpool Street Station, then the underground back to Tottenham Court Road, leaving her just a five-minute walk home.

FIFTY-EIGHT
Saturday 28th February 3.10pm

SEAN AND JULIET had been sitting in Selfridges Restaurant since ten to two. They were finishing their drinks, and wondering what could have happened to Gloria, when she suddenly appeared and hurriedly made her way between the tables to join them.

"Thought you weren't coming," said Juliet, the worry etched on her face. "You're normally early."

Gloria looked a little flustered. "Sorry," she panted, "I've had rather a busy morning."

She shrugged out of her coat and placed it carefully over the back of the spare chair before sinking down on it with a deep exhale of breath.

"That's all very well, Glo," said Sean, a little icily, "but how can anything be more important than what we need to discuss?"

Juliet glanced over at him; he was clearly on edge and looked as if he hadn't slept for a week.

"Anyway, you're here now, and that's the most important thing," Juliet said, pointedly.

Sean nodded his agreement, then stood up. "Who wants what? Drinks and cakes are on me."

"Thanks Sean," said Juliet. "Another coffee for me, and a pain-au-chocolat if they've got one.

Looking up at Sean, Gloria said, "I'd like a cappuccino, please, and a chocolate éclair."

Five minutes later, Sean returned with a tray of drinks and cakes.

"Here you go," he said. "Tuck in."

"Right. Let's get down to business," said Juliet. "When the time comes, we need to find the best way to extricate the two of you from the Higgins family. Now, I've been thinking that perhaps we should...."

At first Gloria thankfully sipped her hot cappuccino and let Juliet talk, but after a few minutes, she put her cup down firmly and interrupted.

"I have to say something."

Juliet looked surprised. "What's up?"

"I've come up with a plan, and I guarantee it will work."

Sean leaned back, his face unreadable. "Go on."

Gloria sat up straight.

"How about I get them to phone me really early on a Saturday morning, to arrange a meet at a restaurant in Kilburn High Road? Then I get them to drive me to a secluded house in Essex, and take me down into a soundproof basement where I manage to stab one of them in the neck, and shoot the other three. Not only that, but the house's location is only known by the four of them and their former hitman, who is in prison. So they're unlikely to be discovered for weeks, possibly months!"

She picked up her éclair and took a large bite.

"Mmm, I'm ravenous!"

Sean looked at Gloria, incredulously; Juliet was looking just as shocked, and it was she who broke the silence.

"Are you fucking with us, Glo, because if you are, it's not very funny."

Gloria returned Juliet's gaze and slowly shook her head. Taking Sean's right hand, she said, "Let's just say that Sean and I have nothing to worry about, at least as far as the Higgins family is concerned." She turned to Juliet, "And Jules, thanks for offering to help us, but we'll no longer be requiring your assistance."

A smile slowly spread across Sean's face.

"This is incredible. I mean really incredible!" he said out loud, pulling Gloria towards him and planting a kiss on her forehead. "Tell us all about it; how the fuck did you manage it?"

Gloria however looked serious.

"I'd really rather not say. I honestly think that the less you two know, the better."

Juliet looked at her in frustration.

"Fucking hell, you can't leave us hanging like that! At least tell us whereabouts in Essex."

Gloria was hunched forward; she gazed into the froth on top of her cappuccino, which she was gently moving with the tip of her teaspoon, and slowly, but determinedly, shook her head.

"Please don't ask me anymore about what happened, either of you." She raised her head, looking at both of them for several seconds. "It's over, that's all you need to know."

Juliet looked at Sean, shrugged, and raised her eyebrows a fraction, conceding defeat. Sean was still clearly in shock and shook his head as if he couldn't quite accept the truth. He then looked at Gloria, concerned.

"Are you okay?"

Continuing to play with the froth on the top of her cappuccino, Gloria said quietly, "Well, if I'm honest, I'm still coming down from the buzz, it's all been a bit much. One minute my nerves are shredded, the next I feel huge relief that we have one less, massive, problem on our hands. It still hurts though, killing someone, even total scumbags like them. It still hurts. Just about."

She started tapping the cup with her spoon, clearly deep in thought. Images of the basement room in Paradise Lodge flashed into her mind; she almost spat out her next words.

"But those fucking bastards will never hurt anyone again."

The three friends sat in a dazed silence for a few moments, while normal life continued around them. Then Juliet broke the spell.

"So, you're free of them. What are you going to do with yourself now?"

Gloria thought for a few moments, then without looking up said, "I just want to live a normal life. I know there's still the police investigation, and I know life will never be completely straightforward again, but things will be markedly better. I've had enough of dealing with other people's problems. I just want to be Gloria again, a retired lady who enjoys spending time with her friends and family."

Sean grunted and nodded his head.

"Me too. I just want to go back to being an ordinary copper, catching the bad guys. Paula shouldn't be too much of a problem, she'll be so happy that the Higgins threat has been removed. And I'll be very wary

when suspiciously good-looking women make a play for me in future."
He looked sheepish.

Juliet grinned and raised her coffee mug into the air. "Here's to a peaceful future."

They clinked their mugs together and tucked into their pastries.

That's that, then, thought Gloria. *I can finally enjoy my retirement.*

ACKNOWLEDGEMENTS

Writing a book is something that can't be achieved without help from so many others. I've had moments of being so engrossed in writing that I have unwittingly forgotten to pay more attention to the people who matter most. Getting a book published and for people to hand over their hard-earned money to purchase a copy is a dream for so many people, and I genuinely understand how very lucky I am. On this page I'll attempt to pass on my eternal gratitude to those who helped me along the way, as I stumbled haplessly through the process.

To friends who listened to me reading, or read through the early drafts, Melissa (Millie) Maxwell-Payne, Susan and Tony Corbett, and Sue Bamford. Your comments, ideas and advice helped me develop the plotline into something that made sense, the first stage in making the book a success.

To my sons Luke and Josh, and their wonderful families, for giving me encouragement to keep going when I started writing again after an 18-year break. Looking after the grandchildren is a perfect antidote when you can think of nothing but your book.

To Red Dog Press for believing in me, especially Sean Coleman, who has helped and guided me through every stage of the process, and who always seemed to find the time for me, even when he was snowed under with work. Thank you for your kindness, and for taking a huge chance on the bumbling writing of an ex-cop approaching his dotage.

I'd like to thank Neil Lancaster, author of Going Dark and Going Rogue. Neil, you've given me more help, advice and encouragement than I could have hoped for, you're one of the reasons I'm writing this now.

The biggest thank you goes to my amazing editor Gail Williams. I told her once I thought her critique was brutal, she said it wasn't brutal, it was robust! Well, thanks to your incredible robustness, you have turned my ramblings into a book that publishers wanted to invest time and effort in, and for that I'm eternally grateful.

A special thank you goes to my wife Virginia, aka Ginny, aka Jumps (don't ask). You have supported me and stuck by my dream throughout this process, including many evenings when you were watching TV, while

I was still hammering away at the keyboard, how you put up with it I'll never know. You're the best and I love you so much.

Then there's you, the reader, you are the icing on the cake, you're what every author needs to be a success, without someone to read our books, all our efforts are for nothing. Thank you for choosing to read Bang Bang, You're Dead, it means so much.

ABOUT THE AUTHOR

Evan was born in Pembury, Kent in 1956 and attended grammar school in Tunbridge Wells.

He left the Metropolitan Police after 30 years of service in 2011, serving as one of the country's first Football Intelligence Officers until 1996, then transferring to West End Central, where for 15 years he worked in Soho.

For several years Evan helped run the Soho Unit, specialising in combating drug dealing in the West End. During his career he frequently ran test purchase and buy-bust operations against drug dealers, resulting in the seizure of large amounts of drugs, and the successful prosecution of over 200 dealers, many of whom received lengthy prison sentences.

After retiring from the Metropolitan police, Evan opened 'Sweet Expectations' in Rochester, Kent, the UK's first vegetarian sweet shop.

In 2016 he sold the shop business and retired, before taking up writing in January 2019.